AMERICAN LITERATURE

美国文学

张　颖/主编

东北师范大学出版社　长春
Northeast Normal University Press

图书在版编目（CIP）数据

美国文学/张颖主编. —2 版. —长春：东北师范大学出版社，2015.3（2025.7 重印）
ISBN 978-7-5681-0369-5

I. 美… II. 张… III. 文学研究—美国 IV. I712.06

中国版本图书馆 CIP 数据核字（2015）第 280861 号

□责任编辑：张小磊 □封面设计：宋 超
□责任校对：刘小军 □责任印制：刘兆辉

东北师范大学出版社出版发行
长春净月经济开发区金宝街 118 号（邮政编码：130117）
网址：http：//www.nenup.com
东北师范大学出版社激光照排中心制版
河北省廊坊市永清县晔盛亚胶印有限公司
河北省廊坊市永清县燃气工业园榕花路 3 号（065600）
2015 年 3 月第 2 版 2025 年 7 月第 3 次印刷
幅面尺寸：170 mm×227 mm 印张：21.75 字数：397 千

定价：63.00 元

目　录

第一章 早期及浪漫主义时期文学

第一节　早期文学

每节导读

本节简要介绍美国的早期文学及其发展的脉络。

美国文学的历史不长，它几乎和美国自由资本主义同时出现，较少受到封建贵族文化的束缚。美国早期人口稀少，有大片未开发的土地，为个人理想的实现提供了很大的可能性。美国人民富于民主自由精神，个人主义、个性解放的观念较为强烈，这在文学中有突出的反映。美国又是一个多民族的国家，移民不断涌入，各自带来了本民族的文化，这决定了美国文学风格的多样性和庞杂性。美国早期文学的发展过程受欧洲文学影响较深。美国早期文学的题材多以歌颂新兴国家和边疆开拓精神为主。

At the beginning of the 17th century, the vast continental area that was to become the United States had been probed only slightly by English and European explorers. At last early in the 17th century, the English settlements in Virginia and Massachusetts began the main stream of what we recognize as the American national history.

The forms of early American literature:

1) Early American literature begins with the orally transmitted myths, legends, tales, and lyrics of Indian cultures.

2) There was no written literature among the more than 500 different Indian languages and tribal cultures that existed in North America before the first Europeans arrived. However, American literature was not based on native Indian culture. It was a descendant of European literature.

Ⅰ. The Literature of Exploration

In the 17th century, pirates, adventurers, and explorers opened the way of permanent colonists, bringing their wives, children, farm implements, and craftsmen's tools. The early literature of exploration, made up of diaries, letters, travel journals, ships' logs, and reports to the explorers' financial backers—European rulers or, in England and Holland, joint stock companies—gradually was supplanted by records of the settled colonies. Because England eventually took possession of the North American colonies, the best-known and most-anthologized colonial literature is English. As American minority literature continues to flower in the 20th century and American life becomes increasingly multicultural, scholars are rediscovering the importance of the continent's mixed ethnic heritage. Although the story of literature now turns to the English accounts, it is important to recognize its richly cosmopolitan beginnings.

Ⅱ. New England Literature

1. An Introduction of New England Literature

It is likely that no other colonists in the history of the world were as intellectual as the Puritans. Between 1630 and 1690, there were as many university graduates in the northeastern section of the United States, known as New England, as in the mother country—an astounding fact when one considers that most educated people of the time were aristocrats who were unwilling to risk their lives in wilderness conditions. The self-made and often self-educated Puritans were notable exceptions. They wanted education to understand and execute God's will as they established their colonies throughout New England.

The Puritan definition of good writing was that which brought home a full awareness of the importance of worshipping God and of the spiritual dangers that the soul faced on Earth. American Puritanism was a dominant factor in American life. It was one of the most enduring shaping influences in American thought and American literature. It has become so much a state of mind and a part of the national cultural atmosphere that the American breathes, that we may state with a degree of safety that, without some understanding of Puritanism, there can be no real understanding of America and its literature.

The American Puritans believed that the Church should be restored to the "purity" of the first-century Church as established by Jesus Christ. To them religion was a matter of primary importance. They made it their chief business to see that man lived and thought and acted in a way which tended to the glory of God. They accepted the doctrine of predestination, original sin and total depravity, and the salvation of a selected few through a special infusion of grace from God.

To sum up, American Puritanism could be defined as following:

1) It is originally used to refer to the theology advocated by a party within the Church of England.

2) It is also used in a broader sense to refer to attitudes and values held by Puritans.

3) As a cultural heritage, American Puritanism exerted great influences over American moral values and literature.

4) Puritans holds three concepts: original sin; predestination and the salvation of selected few.

American Puritanism influences early American literature on the following aspects:

1) idealism: American literature is in good measure a literary expression of the pious idealism of the American Puritan bequest.

2) symbolism: American Puritan's metaphorical mode of perception was chiefly instrumental in calling into being a literary symbolism which is distinctly American. Puritan doctrine and literary practice contributed to no small extent to the development of an indigenous symbolism. To the pious Puritan the physical, phenomenal world is nothing but a symbol of God. It is impossible to overlook the very symbolizing process that was constantly at work in Puritan minds. This process became, in time, part of the intellectual tradition in which American authors were brought up along with their people.

3) plain style: With regard to technique one naturally thinks of the simplicity, which characterizes the Puritan style of writing. With regard to their writing, the style is fresh, simple and direct; the rhetoric is plain and honest, not without a touch of nobility often traceable to the direct influence of the Bible. All this has left an indelible imprint on American writing.

Thus American Puritanism has been, by and large, a healthy legacy to the Americans.

American literature grew out of humble origins. As previously we discussed, diaries, histories, journals, letters, common books, travel books, sermons, poems and personal literature in its various forms, occupy a major position in the literature of the early colonial period. Among them, sermon and poetry were two major genres. In content these early writings served either God or colonial expansion or both. In form, English traditions were faithfully imitated and transplanted.

2. Some New England Writers

1) Anne Bradstreet (1612—1672)

The first published book of poems by an American was also the first American book to be published by a woman—Anne Bradstreet. It is not surprising that the book was published in England, given the lack of printing presses in the early years of the first American colonies. Born and educated in England, Anne Bradstreet was the daughter of an earl's estate manager. She emigrated with her family when she was 18. Her husband eventually became governor of the Massachusetts Bay Colony, which later grew into the great city of Boston. She preferred her long, religious poems on conventional subjects such as the seasons, but contemporary readers mostly enjoy the witty poems on subjects from daily life and her warm and loving poems to her husband and children. She was inspired by English metaphysical poetry, and her book *The Tenth Muse Lately Sprung Up in America* (1650) shows the influence of Edmund Spenser, Philip Sidney, and other English poets as well.

2) Edward Taylor (1644—1729)

Like Anne Bradstreet, and, in fact, all of New England's first writers, the intense, brilliant poet and minister, Edward Taylor was born in England. The son of a yeoman farmer—an independent farmer who owned his own land—Taylor was a teacher who sailed to New England in 1668 rather than took an oath of loyalty to the Church of England. He studied at Harvard College, and, like most Harvard-trained ministers, he knew Greek, Latin, and Hebrew. A selfless and pious man, Taylor acted as a missionary to the settlers when he accepted his lifelong job as a minister in the frontier town of Westfield, Massachusetts, 160 kilometers into the thickly forested, wild interior. Taylor was the best-educated man in the area, and he put his knowledge to use, working as the town minister, doctor, and civic leader.

Modest, pious, and hard working, Taylor never published his poetry, which was discovered only in the 1930s. He would, no doubt, have seen his work's discovery as divine providence; today's readers should be grateful to have his poems—the finest examples of 17th century poetry in North America.

Taylor wrote a variety of verse: funeral elegies, lyrics, a medieval "debate", and a 500-page *Metrical History of Christianity* (mainly a history of martyrs). His best works, according to modern critics, are the series of short *Preparatory Meditations*.

3) Jonathan Edwards (1703—1758)

Jonathan Edwards was born on October 5, 1703, in East Windsor, Connecticut, into a Puritan household. From 1726 to 1750 Edwards served as the pastor of Northampton, Massachusetts, the largest and most influential church outside of Boston, succeeding his grandfather, the famous revivalist Solomon Stoddard. Turning his attention from theoretical to practical divinity, Edwards himself gained international fame as a revivalist.

The widespread revivals of the early 1740s, known to historians as the "Great Awakening", stimulated one of the two most fruitful periods for Edwards' writings. Edwards furthered his renown as a revivalist preacher who subscribed to an experiential interpretation of Reformed Theology that emphasized the sovereignty of God, the depravity of humankind, the reality of hell, and the necessity of a "New Birth" conversion. While critics assailed the convictions of many supposed converts as illusory and even the work of the devil, Edwards became a brilliant apologist for the revivals. *In the Distinguishing Marks of a Work of the Spirit of God* (1741), *Some Thoughts Concerning the Present Revival* (1742), *A Treatise Concerning Religious Affections* (1746), and *The Life of David Brainerd* (1749), he sought to isolate the signs of true sainthood from false belief. The intellectual framework for revivalism he constructed in these works pioneered a new psychology and philosophy of affections, later invoked by William James in his classic *Varieties of Religious Experience* (1902).

Edward's published writings at Northampton also reflect strong millenarian and prophetic interests. In "A History of the Work of Redemption", originally preached as a sermon series in 1739 but not published until after his death, Edwards cast theology into "a method entirely new" by showing God's work as a history structured around God's scriptural promises and periods of the outpouring of the Spirit. "*An Humble Attempt to Promote...Extraordinary Prayer*" (1747) was part of a larger movement towards Anglo-American "concerts of prayer" and was an important contribution to millennial thought. Scholars such as Alan Heimert have recognized the signal importance of these works in American history, particularly their contribution to revolutionary ideology. Both of these works have already been published in the *Yale Edition* (1989).

In late 1757, he accepted the presidency of the College of New Jersey (later Princeton University). However, he did not live to leave a permanent mark on the college. After only a few months there he died on March 22, 1758, following complications from a smallpox inoculation. He is buried in the Princeton Cemetery (The Grave of Jonathan Edwards in the Princeton Cemetery, Princeton, New Jersey).

Edward's reputation grew rapidly after his death. At the end of the twentieth century, as both the American scholarly community and the nation at large are rediscovering religion's role in the formation of the country and are grappling with the issues of religion and society, the name of Jonathan Edwards continues to be invoked.

As Edwards has been studied over the generations, he has come to emerge as a quintessential "representative man", not in the usual sense but because in some profound sense he marked the culmination of one era and prefigured a subsequent one. While other colonial figures exerted comparable influence on their own age, none, with the possible exception of William Penn and Benjamin Franklin, so completely anticipated the subsequent shape of an American culture, at once material and spiritual, piously secular and pragmatically sacred, as did Edwards. It is due to the intersection of Edwards' colonial times with an ever-changing American "present" that he enjoys a uniquely representative status in American thought and letters.

Ⅲ. The Literature of Reason and Revolution

1. An Introduction to the Literature of Reason and Revolution

In 1770s the English colonies in North America rose in arms against their mother country. The War for Independence lasted for eight years (1776—1783) and ended in the formation of a Federative bourgeois democratic republic—the United States of America.

This event of epoch-making significance had been predetermined by the whole course of historical development of the colonial America ever since the beginning of the 18th century. The spiritual life in the colonies during that period was to a great degree mould by the bourgeois Enlightenment—a movement supported by all progressive forces of the country which opposed themselves to the old colonial order and religious obscurantism. The representatives of the Enlightenment set themselves the task of disseminating knowledge among the people and advocating revolutionary ideas. They also actively participated in the War for Independence.

In 1783, the year the United States achieved its independence, Noah Webster declared, "America must be as independent in literature as she is in politics, as famous for the arts as for arms." The beginnings of literary independence were evident in such celebrations of the American scene as Jefferson's *Notes on the State of Virginia* (1785), and *Bartram's Travels* (1791). Yet American literature throughout the century was largely patterned on the writing of eighteenth century Englishmen. Philip Freneau, the most important poet of the period, derived his power and style, his sentiments and regular couplets from English models. Franklin shaped his writing after *The Spectator Papers* (1711—1712) of the English essayists Addison and Steele.

However, while imaginative literature in America remained derivative and dependent, the heroic and revolutionary ambitions of the age had created great political pamphleteering and state papers. Essayists and journalists had shaped the nation's beliefs with reason dressed in clear and forceful prose. Out of the tumult of the age came the inspired writing of Jefferson in the Declaration of

Independence, of T. Paine in *Common Sense* (1776), which stirred the world and helped form the American republic.

The best writings of the age were done by the founding fathers of the country and the popular literary forms then were as follows:

1) Speech: Patrick Henry (1736—1799) was the representative of the genre. His revolutionary speeches were marked by force and sincerity as in his famous phrases "I know not what course others may take, but as for me, give me liberty or give me death!"

2) Pamphlet: Thomas Paine (1737—1809) is considered the best writer of the genre. His pamphlets are characterized with clear thinking and exciting language. His best-known work is *Common Sense*, the most historically important pamphlet in American history.

3) Essay: Thomas Jefferson's (1743—1826) Declaration of Independence was regarded the best example. The characteristics of Jefferson's essays are logical statement and freedom from emotional appeal.

4) Poetry: Philip Freneau (1752—1832) was nicknamed the poet of revolution. The characteristics of his poetry are lyric quality, sensuous images and fresh perception of nature and "noble savagery".

2. Some Important Writers

1) Thomas Paine (1737—1809)

The life of Thomas Paine was one of the revolutionary fighters for the rights of man. He wrote a number of works of such a revolutionary and inflammatory character, with which he helped to spur and inspire the greatest revolutions that his age had witnessed. His *Common Sense*, declaring as it did that "government, even in its best state, is but a necessary evil; in its worst state an intolerable one", not only attacked British monarchy, but also helped in uniting the feelings of the colonial people in fighting against the British ruler in order to gain their independence. Paine declared that the crisis with which the North American colonies were then faced could only be solved by an appeal to man's instincts and common sense and to "the clear, uniform and irresistibly obeyed" impulses of conscience. The booklet was warmly received in the colonies both as a justification for their cause of independence and as an encouragement to the painfully fighting people. Paine became a major influence in the American Revolution. Another important work of his to mention here is his *American Crisis* series of pamphlets, the first of which came out at one of the darkest moments of the revolution when Washington's troops had just suffered one of the worst defeats in the war and were in the process of retreating. "These are the times that try men's souls," it declared. "The harder the conflict, the more glorious the triumph." The words turned out to be the inspiration to the soldiers and encouraged them with hope and confidence. Paine was highly praised by the Congress of the United States for his distinguished service to the country. Later he participated in the French Revolution, and wrote *The Rights of Man* and *The Age of Reason*, spreading the ideals of the French Revolution among the people. He was imprisoned during the "Reign of Terror" and escaped the guillotine only narrowly. He returned to America and died in poverty.

2) Philip Freneau (1752—1832)

Philip Freneau was important in American literary history in a number of ways. First of all, he used his poetic talents in the service of a nation struggling for independence, writing verses for the righteous cause of his people and exposing British colonial savageries, and for this he was called the poet of revolution in American literature. Secondly, he was also a notable representative of dawning nationalism in American literature. While still an undergraduate, he wrote, with one of his friends, a poem entitled "The Rising Glory of America", the national spirit of which pointed forward to the intellectual and literary independence which achieved its maturity first in the writings of men like Emerson and Whitman and other pre-eminent writers of the nineteenth century. Almost alone of his generation, he managed to peer through the pervasive atmosphere of imitativeness, to see life around directly, to appreciate the natural scenes on the new continent and the native Indian civilization. Some of his most famous works are distinctly American with unique features. Poems such as "The Wild Honey Suckle", "The Indian Burying Ground" are among the best-known.

In 18th century America, Freneau was certainly the most significant poet whose themes and images anticipated the works of such 19th century American Romantic writers as Cooper, Emerson, Poe and Melville.

The period of some two centuries from the arrival of the Mayflower through the end of the 18th century was, from a literary point of view, one in which the national experience of the American settlers building the wilderness into a habitable place searched and struggled for literary expression. It represents a process in which colonial literature strove for a higher degree of excellence and evolved slowly but steadily toward the native literature. If the 18th century literary scene looked still barren and bleak, there appeared at least certain figures who had more or less influenced the later development of American literature. Benjamin Franklin is one of these.

3) Benjamin Franklin (1706—1790)

America has never forgotten Benjamin Franklin because of his greatness in American history. He lived these words of wisdom by writing as much as he possibly could and by doing even more. He became famous as a printer and publisher, a scientist and inventor, a diplomat and statesman, last but not least, a writer.

Franklin was born in Boston, Massachusetts on January 6 from a very large family. He was the tenth son in the family. Franklin did have a bit more education than his brothers, but it was impossible for him to continue because they were not a rich family. His father was a soap boiler and candle maker. At the age of 12, Franklin was apprenticed to his half-brother, James Franklin, who was a newspaper printer in Boston. In 1722, when Franklin was only 16, he ran the paper on his own for a short time. One year later, he went to Philadelphia almost penniless. There he worked as a newspaper printer. He attracted the notice of the governor of Pennsylvania and then Franklin went to London through his influence. He stayed in London for two years. In 1726, he began to work industriously to set up his own press. In 1729, he already owned his own printing shop and published the newspaper *Pennsylvania Gazette*. In 1732 he offered his *Poor Richard's Almanac* for sale. By 1748, at the age of 42, Franklin had earned enough money so that he retired. Then he became so active in civic and scientific activities.

Franklin was a rare genius in human history. He became almost everything: a printer, postmaster, almanac maker, essayist, scientist, orator, statesman, philosopher, political economist, ambassador and parlor man—Jack of all trades.

Franklin's claim to a place in literature rests chiefly on his *Autobiography*. *The Autobiography of Benjamin Franklin* was probably the first of its kind in literature. It is the simple yet immensely fascinating record of a man rising to wealth and fame from a state of poverty and obscurity into which he was born, the faithful account of the colorful career of America's first self-made man. The book is in four parts, written at different times.

The Autobiography is important in several aspects. First of all, it is a Puritan document. It is Puritan because it is a record of self-examination and self-improvement. *The Autobiography* is also a reflection of his age because of the fact that Franklin was spokesman for the new order of 18th-century enlightenment, and that he represented in America all its ideas, that man is basically good and free, by nature endowed by God with certain inalienable rights of liberty and the pursuit of happiness. Thirdly, it is an illustration of American dream of which Franklin himself is an embodiment since he rose to success from a very humble beginning. Fourthly, the book has the features of plainness of its style, the homeliness of imagery, the simplicity of diction and the syntax and expression are salient, therefore, it is a good example of Puritan plain style.

第二节 浪漫主义文学简介

每节导读

本节简要介绍美国浪漫主义文学的背景及主要特点。

1781 年美国独立战争结束。1783 年，英美签订凡尔赛合约，英国承认美国独立。随着美利坚合众国的成立，美国从政治上摆脱了英国的统治，但同时也迫切需要在文化上摆脱对英国的依附。从取得国家独立到内战不到一百年的时间里，美国社会面貌发生了根本的变化，也出现了美国历史上第一次文学艺术的繁荣，形成了在世界文学史占有一席之地的美国 19 世纪浪漫主义文学运动，也被称为美国文学第一次文艺复兴。美国浪漫主义的产生，一方面是谋求民族文化独立的结果，另一方面是受英国浪漫主义文学影响的结果。

美国早期浪漫主义文学以欧文、库柏等作家为代表。他们写出了具有民族风格的作品，可以说是美国民族文学的先驱。从 30 年代开始形成后期浪漫主义文学，以超验主义为基础，以爱默生、梭罗等作家为代表。19 世纪 50 年代惠特曼《草叶集》发表，美国浪漫主义进入高峰时期。1892 年，随着惠特曼的去世，美国浪漫主义走向衰落，随之而来的是现实主义的繁荣。

Ⅰ. American Romanticism (the New England Renaissance)

The Romantic Movement, which originated in Germany but quickly spread to England, France, and beyond, reached America around the year 1820, some 20 years after William Wordsworth and Samuel Taylor Coleridge had revolutionized English poetry by publishing *Lyrical Ballads*. In America as in Europe, fresh new vision inspired artistic and intellectual circles. Yet there was an important difference: Romanticism in America coincided with the period of national expansion and the discovery of a distinctive American voice. The consolidation of a national identity and the surging idealism and passion of Romanticism nurtured the masterpieces of "the American Renaissance" which is also known as the "New England Renaissance".

Romantic ideas centered on art as inspiration, the spiritual and aesthetic dimension of nature, and metaphors of organic growth. Art, rather than science, Romantics argued, could best express universal truth. The Romantics underscored the importance of expressive art for the individual and society. In his essay "The Poet" (1844), Ralph Waldo Emerson, perhaps the most influential writer of the Romantic era, asserts:

"For all men live by truth, and stand in need of expression. In love, in art, in avarice, in politics, in labor, in games, we study to utter our painful secret. The man is only half himself, the other half is his expression."

The development of the self became a major theme; self-awareness a primary method. If, according to Romantic theory, self and nature were one, self-awareness was not a selfish dead end but a mode of knowledge opening up the universe. If one's self were one with all humanity, then the individual had a moral duty to reform social inequalities and relieve human suffering. The idea of "self", which suggested selfishness to earlier generations was redefined. New compound words with positive meanings emerged: "self-realization", "self-expression", "self-reliance".

As the unique, subjective self became important, so did the realm of psychology. Exceptional artistic effects and techniques were developed to evoke heightened psychological states. The "sublime"—an effect of beauty in grandeur (for example, a view from a mountaintop)—produced feelings of awe, reverence, vastness, and a power beyond human comprehension.

Romanticism was affirmative and appropriate for most American poets and creative essayists. America's vast mountains, deserts, and tropics embodied the sublime. The Romantic spirit seemed particularly suited to American democracy: It stressed individualism, affirmed the value of the common person, and looked to the inspired imagination for its aesthetic and ethical values. Certainly the New England Transcendentalists—Ralph Waldo Emerson, Henry David Thoreau, and their associates—were inspired to a new optimistic affirmation by the Romantic Movement. In New England, Romanticism fell upon fertile soil.

1. Historical Background

1) Politically, America established bourgeoisie democracy, which became the basis of American Romanticism.

After the Independence, there was one fierce struggle between Hamilton, who represented the interests of bankers and businessmen and Jefferson, who spoke for agricultures and commonplaces. Subsequently, Jefferson's election to Presidency showed the first victory of American democracy. In 1928, Jackson, the 7th president who believed in equality and wanted a fair chance for every man to rise, pushed American democracy to a new era.

2) Economically, it was a period of booming and prosperity, which made the Americans optimistic towards their futures and optimism became the essential spirit of American Romanticism. The economic boom was related to the following factors.

①Industry

During the period from 1820s to 1860s, America's gross value of industrial output was 11 times what it was before and American economy came to take the 4th place in the world.

In fact, the whole nation was experiencing an industrial transformation, which affected the rural as well as the urban life. The use of steam power in industry and agriculture, the erection of factories and textile mills, the demand of a large employment, and the technological inventions and innovations all helped restructure the economical life. In addition, the sudden influx of immigration gave a high push to the already booming industry.

②Westward Movement

Pioneers pushed the frontier further. In 1803, Jefferson bought Louisiana from France, which increased the physical dimensions of the nation greatly. All of these contributed to the economic boom.

At that time, the government called the citizens to go to the west, advocating "Exploit, open up" or "Develop the west". The western movement enlarged American territory and created optimism. The western boundary had reached the Pacific by 1860. The number of its states had increased from the original thirteen at the time of its independence to twenty-one by the middle of the 19th century. Its total population increased from four million people in 1790 to 30 million in 1860.

③Diplomatic Relations

Monroe Message claimed, "America is American people's America". It established a peaceful environment, which was vital for America's economic development. In the Monroe doctrine, it was first expressed in 1823 against a background of continued involvement and threat expansion from European colonial powers in South America. The Monroe doctrine created a peaceful international environment.

3) Culturally, Noah Webster's *An American dictionary of the English language* was published in 1828, which symbolizes the achievement and independence in culture.

It was epoch striking, marking that America was going to be independent in every aspect.

Ⅱ. Romanticism

1. Reasons for the Rise of Romanticism

1) It owes to the development and experiences in the nick time of history;

American bourgeois democracy laid the basis for American Romanticism and economic boom produced the spirit of optimism.

2) It is indebted to foreign influences, especially the European's and English Romanticism. William Wordsworth, Byron, Robert Burns, Walter Scott and many other romantic masters made a stimulating, powerful and enduring impact.

2. Peculiarities of American Romanticism

1) It has its own new experiences, geography, races and its Westward Expansion.

American romanticism presented an entirely new experience alien to European culture—the exotic landscape, the frontier life, the westward expansion. The most important thing is that the spirit of the place was radically new and alien.

2) It is largely influenced by Puritanism, therefore, it has strong sense of moral preaching.

American's ideals of individualism and political equality, and their dream that America is to be a new Garden of Eden for man is distinctly American. To sum up, deriving from both foreign influences and newness of its own, American Romanticism seems to be both imitative and independent.

3. Common Themes and Subject Matters in American Romanticism

1) Celebration of natural beauty and simple life as in Thoreau's *Walden*.

2) Idealization of the common people, for example, in Whitman's *Leaves of Grass*.

3) Interests in the past and remote places and this can be seen especially in some of Melville's novels.

4) The writers eulogized individualism especially in some transcendental works.

5) Some writers, for instance, Cooper, were interested in historical romance.

Ⅲ. Transcendentalism (1829—1860s)—the Peak of American Romanticism

1. Emergence

Some rich New Englanders were unhappy with their material-oriented life and formed an informal club to discuss matters concerning spiritual things. In 1836 *Nature* by Emerson was published and pushed American Transcendentalism into its peak. Their journal was *The Dial* the publication of which made Transcendentalism nationally known. This was the first American intellectual movement which exerted a tremendous impact on the consciousness of American people.

2. Major Features of Transcendentalism

"What is popularly called Transcendentalism among us," Emerson declares, "is idealism."

1) It stresses the Oversoul or Spirit as the most important thing in the universe.

"Spirit is presented everywhere." In fact, it is God, which exists in nature and man, and makes up the chief elements in the universe.

2) It emphasizes the importance of individualism.

To them, individual is the most important element of society. The ideal type of man is the self-reliant individual.

3) It offers a fresh perception of nature as symbolic of the Spirit or God.

Nature is, to them, not purely matter. It is alive, filled with God's overwhelming presence. It is the garment of the Oversoul and physical world is the symbol of spiritual world.

3. Its Significance

1) It inspires a whole generation of writers such as Thoreau and Whitman.

2) It stresses man's subjective initiative as opposed to materialism. The industrialization of New England was turning men into nonhumans. People were losing their individuality. Transcendentalism asserted the importance of the individual and emphasized the significance of men regaining their lost personality.

3) It believed in the basic goodness of man, thus liberating people from Calvin's original sin.

4. Its Limitation

Even though Transcendentalism was an important intellectual movement, we can still find its limitation in some aspects.

1) It was somewhat cut off from the real life or reality. It was initiated by the well-off people, who are limited in a certain circle. They can't completely understand the sufferings of the common people. In Mednick's words, "Their shallow optimism made it impossible to understand human suffering."

2) It is idealistic in that it emphasizes that knowledge is gained by intuition, and ignores the importance of experience.

5. Two Important Transcendental Writers

1) Ralph Waldo Emerson (1803—1882)

Emerson is the chief spokesman of Transcendentalism. He was born in Boston, the son of an Unitarian minister. While a student at Harvard, he began keeping journals—records of his thoughts—which later became the source of his literary works. In 1832, he went on a tour of Europe during which he met some important Romantic writers in England and was greatly influenced by their ideas. After he was back from the trip, he formed a club, the Transcendental club, at Concord. In 1836, he published *Nature* which became the unofficial manifesto of Transcendentalism. In this book and other essays, Emerson put forward his philosophy of the Over soul, the importance of the individual and nature. The next year appeared an essay entitled "The American Scholar" which is regarded as America's declaration of intellectual independence. In this essay, Emerson called on American scholars to create real national literature. Emerson is the most representative of the philosophical and literary school of Transcendentalism and inspired a whole generation of famous writers like Whitman.

2) Henry David Thoreau (1817—1962)

Considered a disciple of Emerson, Thoreau was one of the three important Transcendental figures, the other two being Emerson and Whitman. He was born in 1817 in Concord and graduated from Harvard in 1837. In 1845, he built a cabin by Walden Pond and lived there in a very simple manner for a little over two years. This experience gave birth to his masterpiece, a great transcendental work, *Walden* (1854). The book not only demonstrates Emersonian ideas of self-reliance but also develops Transcendental philosophy. In 1949, after a short experience in prison, he wrote an essay "Civil Disobedience" in which he advocated non-violent resistance which later influenced Mahatma Gandhi in India and Martin Luther King, the African-American leader in the 1960s.

第三节　早期浪漫主义重要作家及作品

每节导读

本节主要讲解欧文、库柏和爱伦·坡的生平、主要作品、创作风格、写作技巧、作品的意义以及局限性等。

欧文（Washington Irving，1783—1859）是美国建国后第一位获得国际声誉的作家，有"美国文学之父"之称。欧文是散文大师，是美国文学奠基人之一。他的文笔优雅自然，清新精致，时常流露出温和的幽默。

欧文代表作《见闻札记》（*The Sketch Book*，1820）使欧文获得国际声誉。其中，在《睡谷传说》（*The Legend of Sleepy Hollow*）这个故事里，欧文很注意环境和气氛的描写，突出表现了"睡谷"与社会隔绝的特点及由此造成的人们思想上的停滞与迷信。欧文的用意是美化早期殖民地宗法社会，试图形象地展现这种社会较熙熙攘攘的现代化城市的优越性。

库珀（James Fenimore Cooper，1789—1851），小说家。在美国文学史上开创了三种不同类型的小说，即革命历史小说《间谍》、边疆冒险小说《拓荒者》和海上冒险小说《舵手》。

库珀在30年创作生涯中写了50多部小说和其他著作。他最有成就的作品，如《皮袜子故事集》（*Leatherstocking Tales*）五部曲，对美国的西部小说产生很大影响，至今仍拥有不少读者。

爱伦·坡（Edgar Allen Poe，1809—1849），诗人，小说家，批评家。

爱伦·坡的诗中大多是古怪、奇特、病态的形象。他强调写忧郁的情绪，著名的《乌鸦》（*The Raven*，1845）一诗就是这方面的代表作。爱伦·坡的短篇小说也颇有影响。他的小说大致可分为恐怖小说和推理小说。前者包括《厄舍古厦的倒塌》（*The Fall of the House of Usher*）、《红色死亡假面舞》（*The Masque of the Red Death*）等，后者如《莫格街谋杀案》

(*The Murder in the Rue Morgue*)、《被窃的信件》(*The Purloined Letter*) 等。爱伦·坡在西方还被认为是侦探小说的鼻祖。

Ⅰ. Washington Irving (1783—1859)

1. Life and Works

The youngest of 11 children born to a well-to-do New York merchant family, Washington Irving became a cultural and diplomatic ambassador to Europe, like Benjamin Franklin and Nathaniel Hawthorne. Through friends, he was able to publish his *The Sketch Book* (1819—1820) simultaneously in England and America, obtaining copyrights and payment in both countries.

The Sketch Book of Geoffrye Crayon (Irving's penname) contains his two best-remembered stories, "Rip Van Winkle" and "The Legend of Sleepy Hollow". This book aptly describes Irving's delicate, elegant, yet seemingly casual style. In *The Sketch Book*, Irving transforms the Catskill Mountains along the Hudson River north of New York City into a fabulous, magical region.

American readers gratefully accepted Irving's imagined "history" of the Catskills, despite the fact (unknown to them) that he had adapted his stories from a German source. Irving gave America something it badly needed in the brash, materialistic early years: an imaginative way of relating to the new land.

No writer was as successful as Irving at humanizing the land, endowing it with a name and a face and a set of legends. The story of "Rip Van Winkle", who slept for 20 years, waking to find that the colonies had become independent, eventually became folklore. It was adapted for the stage, went into the oral tradition, and was gradually accepted as authentic American legend by generations of Americans.

Irving discovered and helped satisfy the raw new nation's sense of history. His numerous works may be seen as his devoted attempts to build the new nation's soul by recreating history and giving it living, breathing, imaginative life. For subjects, he chose the most dramatic aspects of American history: the discovery of the New World, the first president and national hero, and the westward exploration. His earliest work was a sparkling, satirical *History of New York* (1809) under the Dutch, written by Diedrich Knickerbocker (hence the name of Irving's friends and New York writers of the day, the "Knickerbocker School"). His later writings include biographies of Christopher Columbus and George Washington, travel books, and—especially—a series of wonderful tales, modeled on folklore but containing a humorous, typically American (and typically Romantic) fascination with the exotic, the ancient, and the odd.

In 1832 Irving returned from Europe to New York where he established his home Sunnyside in Tarrytown. On November 28, 1859, on the eve of the Civil War, Washington Irving died at Sunnyside surrounded by his family. He was buried in the Sleepy Hollow Cemetery at the Old Dutch Church in Sleepy Hollow, N. Y.

2. Contributions

1) He was the first American writer to gain international fame, which is a sign to show that American literature became independent. He was therefore called "Father of American Literature". *The Sketch Book* is set on a fictional ground of New England in which reality and imagination converge. The stories achieve a distinct American tone and theme. With the book, he proved that an American writer could win a British and continental audience.

2) He started the writing of short story as a literary genre. The short story as a genre in American Literature probably began with Irving's *The Sketch Book*. Later, Nathaniel Hawthorne, Herman Melville and Edgar Allan Poe made the short story perfect as a literary tradition.

3) His writing marked the beginning of Romanticism in American literature. The Gothic, the supernatural, the longing for the good days which some of his pieces clearly exhibit, are romantic enough in subject if not exactly in style, for Irving wrote in the neoclassical tradition of Joseph Addison and Oliver Goldsmith.

3. Writing Characteristics

1) His writing is humorous. He intended to amuse readers instead of teaching and instructing them. He tried to avoid moralizing because he believed that the purpose of literature was to entertain readers.

2) The characters in his works are both vivid and true so that they tend to linger in the mind of the reader because he was good at enveloping his stories in an atmosphere, the richness of which is often more than compensation for the slimness of plot.

3) He is apt at finished, refined and musical language. It is said that he modeled his language on that of Goldsmith.

4. Introduction to the Story of "The Legend of Sleepy Hollow"

The story of "The Legend of Sleepy Hollow" takes place in Tarrytown. It tells the story of schoolmaster, Ichabod Crane, a Connecticut native, who comes to teach in a one-room schoolhouse. Subsequently, he becomes the neighborhood song master, reads Cotton Mather and makes himself in local folklore. Foremost of all, he competes with Brom Bones for the love of Katrina. One afternoon, after being refused by Katrina, he briskly rides off on his landlord's horse. On his way, he sees a specter of a headless horseman, and is never seen again in Sleepy Hollow. The townspeople have a lot of guesses about his disappearance.

5. Selected Reading of "The Legend of Sleepy Hollow"

In the bosom of one of those spacious coves which indent the eastern shore of the Hudson, at that broad expansion of the river denominated by the ancient Dutch navigators the Tappan Zee, and where they always prudently shortened sail, and implored the protection of St. Nicholas when they crossed, there lies a small market town or rural port, which by some is called Greensburgh, but which is more generally and properly known by the name of Tarry Town. This name was given, we are told, in former days, by the good housewives of the adjacent country, from the inveterate① propensity of their husbands to linger about the village tavern on market days. Be that as it may, I do not vouch for the fact, but merely advert to it, for the sake of being precise and authentic. Not far from this village, perhaps about two miles, there is a little valley, or rather lap of land, among high hills, which is one of the quietest places in the whole world. A small brook glides through it, with just murmur enough to lull one to repose; and the occasional whistle of a quail, or tapping of a woodpecker, is almost the only sound that ever breaks in upon the uniform tranquillity.

I recollect that, when a stripling, my first exploit in squirrel-shooting was in a grove of tall walnut-trees that shades one side of the valley. I had wandered into it at noon time, when all nature is peculiarly quiet, and was startled by the roar of my own gun, as it broke the Sabbath[②] stillness around, and was prolonged and reverberated by the angry echoes. If ever I should wish for a retreat, whither I might steal from the world and its distractions, and dream quietly away the remnant of a troubled life, I know of none more promising than this little valley.

From the listless repose of the place, and the peculiar character of its inhabitants, who are descendants from the original Dutch settlers, this sequestered[③] glen has long been known by the name of SLEEPY HOLLOW, and its rustic lads are called the Sleepy Hollow Boys throughout all the neighboring country. A drowsy, dreamy influence seems to hang over the land, and to pervade the very atmosphere. Some say that the place was bewitched by a high German doctor, during the early days of the settlement; others, that an old Indian chief, the prophet or wizard of his tribe, held his pow wows there before the country was discovered by Master Hendrick Hudson. Certain it is, the place still continues under the sway of some witching power, that holds a spell over the minds of the good people, causing them to walk in a continual reverie. They are given to all kinds of marvelous beliefs; are subject to trances and visions; and frequently see strange sights, and hear music and voices in the air. The whole neighborhood abounds with local tales, haunted spots, and twilight superstitions; stars shoot and meteors glare oftener across the valley than in any other part of the country, and the nightmare, with her whole nine fold, seems to make it the favorite scene of her gambols.

The dominant spirit, however, that haunts this enchanted region, and seems to be commander-in-chief of all the powers of the air, is the apparition of a figure on horseback without a head. It is said by some to be the ghost of a Hessian trooper, whose head had been carried away by a cannon-ball, in some nameless battle during the revolutionary war; and who is ever and anon seen by the country folk hurrying along in the gloom of night, as if on the wings of the wind. His haunts are not confined to the valley, but extend at times to the adjacent roads, and especially to the vicinity of a church at no great distance. Indeed, certain of the most authentic historians of those parts, who have been careful in collecting and collating the floating facts concerning this spectre, allege that the body of the trooper, having been buried in the church-yard, the ghost rides forth to the scene of battle in nightly quest of his head; and that the rushing speed with which he sometimes passes along the Hollow, like a midnight blast, is owing to his being belated, and in a hurry to get back to the church-yard before daybreak.

Such is the general purport of this legendary superstition, which has furnished materials for many a wild story in that region of shadows; and the spectre is known, at all the country firesides, by the name of the Headless Horseman of Sleepy Hollow.

It is remarkable that the visionary propensity I have mentioned is not confined to the native inhabitants of the valley, but is unconsciously imbibed by every one who resides there for a time. However wide awake they may have been before they entered that sleepy region, they are sure, in a little time, to inhale the witching influence of the air, and begin to grow imaginative—to dream dreams, and see apparitions.

I mention this peaceful spot with all possible laud; for it is in such little retired Dutch valleys, found here and there embosomed in the great State of New-York, that population, manners, and customs, remain fixed; while the great torrent of migration and improvement, which is making such incessant changes in other parts of this restless country, sweeps by them unobserved. They are like those little nooks of still water which border a rapid stream; where we may see the straw and bubble riding quietly at anchor, or slowly revolving in their mimic harbor, undisturbed by the rush of the passing current. Though many years have elapsed since I trod the drowsy shades of Sleepy Hollow, yet I question whether I should not still find the same trees and the same families vegetating in its sheltered bosom.

In this by-place of nature, there abode, in a remote period of American history, that is to say, some thirty years since, a worthy wight of the name of Ichabod Crane; who sojourned, or, as he expressed it, "tarried," in Sleepy Hollow, for the purpose of instructing the children of the vicinity. He was a native of Connecticut; a State which supplies the Union with pioneers for the mind as well as for the forest, and sends forth yearly its legions of frontier woodsmen and country schoolmasters. The cognomen of Crane was not inapplicable to his person. He was tall, but exceedingly lank, with narrow shoulders, long arms and legs, hands that dangled a mile out of his sleeves, feet that might have served for shovels, and his whole frame most loosely hung together. His head was small, and flat at top, with huge ears, large green glassy eyes, and a long snipe nose, so that it looked like a weather-cock, perched upon his spindle neck, to tell which way the wind blew. To see him striding along the profile of a hill on a windy day, with his clothes bagging and fluttering about him, one might have mistaken him for the genius of famine descending upon the earth, or some scarecrow eloped from a cornfield.

His school-house was a low building of one large room, rudely constructed of logs; the windows partly glazed, and partly patched with leaves of old copy-books. It was most ingeniously secured at vacant hours, by a withe twisted in the handle of the door, and stakes set against the window shutters; so that, though a thief might get in with perfect ease, he would find some embarrassment in getting out; an idea most probably borrowed by the architect, Yost Van Houten, from the mystery of an eel-pot. The school-house stood in a rather lonely but pleasant situation just at the foot of a woody hill, with a brook running close by, and a formidable birch tree growing at one end of it. From hence the low murmur of his pupils' voices, conning over their lessons, might be heard in a drowsy summer's day, like the hum of a bee-hive; interrupted now and then by the authoritative voice of the master, in the tone of menace or command; or, peradventure, by the appalling sound of the birch, as he urged some tardy loiterer along the flowery path of knowledge. Truth to say, he was a conscientious man, and ever bore in mind the golden maxim, "Spare the rod and spoil the child." Ichabod Crane's scholars certainly were not spoiled.

I would not have it imagined, however, that he was one of those cruel potentates of the school, who joy in the smart of their subjects; on the contrary, he administered justice with discrimination rather than severity; taking the burthen off the backs of the weak, and laying it on those of the strong. Your mere puny stripling, that winced at the least flourish of the rod, was passed by with indulgence; but the claims of justice were satisfied by inflicting a double portion on some little, tough, wrong-headed, broad-skirted Dutch urchin, who sulked and swelled and grew dogged and sullen beneath the birch. All this he called "doing his duty by their parents"; and he never inflicted a chastisement without following it by the assurance, so consolatory to the smarting urchin, that "he would remember it, and thank him for it the longest day he had to live."

When school hours were over, he was even the companion and playmate of the larger boys; and on holiday afternoons would convoy some of the smaller ones home, who happened to have pretty sisters, or good housewives for mothers, noted for the comforts of the cupboard. Indeed it behooved him to keep on good terms with his pupils. The revenue arising from his school was small, and would have been scarcely sufficient to furnish him with daily bread, for he was a huge feeder, and though lank, had the dilating powers of an anaconda; but to help out his maintenance, he was, according to country custom in those parts, boarded and lodged at the houses of the farmers, whose children he instructed. With these he lived successively a week at a time; thus going the rounds of the neighborhood, with all his worldly effects tied up in a cotton handkerchief.

That all this might not be too onerous on the purses of his rustic patrons, who are apt to consider the costs of schooling a grievous burden, and schoolmasters as mere drones, he had various ways of rendering himself both useful and agreeable. He assisted the farmers occasionally in the lighter labors of their farms; helped to make hay; mended the fences; took the horses to water; drove the cows from pasture; and cut wood for the winter fire. He laid aside, too, all the dominant dignity and absolute sway with which he lorded it in his little empire, the school, and became wonderfully gentle and ingratiating. He found favor in the eyes of the mothers, by petting the children, particularly the youngest; and like the lion bold, which whilom so magnanimously the lamb did hold, he would sit with a child on one knee, and rock a cradle with his foot for whole hours together.

In addition to his other vocations, he was the singing-master of the neighborhood, and picked up many bright shillings by instructing the young folks in psalmody. It was a matter of no little vanity to him, on Sundays, to take his station in front of the church gallery, with a band of chosen singers; where, in his own mind, he completely carried away the palm from the parson. Certain it is, his voice resounded far above all the rest of the congregation; and there are peculiar quavers still to be heard in that church, and which may even be heard half a mile off, quite to the opposite side of the mill-pond, on a still Sunday morning, which are said to be legitimately descended from the nose of Ichabod Crane. Thus, by divers little make-shifts in that ingenious way which is commonly denominated "by hook and by crook," the worthy pedagogue got on tolerably enough, and was thought, by all who understood nothing of the labor of headwork, to have a wonderfully easy life of it.

The schoolmaster is generally a man of some importance in the female circle of a rural neighborhood; being considered a kind of idle gentlemanlike personage, of vastly superior taste and accomplishments to the rough country swains, and, indeed, inferior in learning only to the parson. His appearance, therefore, is apt to occasion some little stir at the tea-table of a farmhouse, and the addition of a supernumerary dish of cakes or sweetmeats, or, peradventure, the parade of a silver tea-pot. Our man of letters, therefore, was peculiarly happy in the smiles of all the country damsels. How he would figure among them in the churchyard, between services on Sundays, gathering grapes for them from the wild vines that overrun the surrounding trees; reciting for their amusement all the epitaphs on the tombstones; or sauntering, with a whole bevy of them, along the banks of the adjacent mill-pond; while the more bashful country bumpkins hung sheepishly back, envying his superior elegance and address.

From his half itinerant life, also, he was a kind of traveling gazette, carrying the whole budget of local gossip from house to house; so that his appearance was always greeted with satisfaction. He was, moreover, esteemed by the women as a man of great erudition, for he had read several books quite through, and was a perfect master of Cotton Mather's History of New England Witchcraft, in which, by the way, he most firmly and potently believed....

NOTES

①inveterate：(of people) habitually doing the specified bad thing，addicted 成癖的。

②the Sabbath：day of the week intended for rest and worship of God (Saturday for Jews and Sunday for Christians) 安息日。

③sequestered：quiet and secluded 偏僻的。

Topic Discussion

1. How would you like to comment on Ichabod Crane in the story?
2. What are the artistic features of Irving's writing?

Ⅱ. James Fenimore Cooper (1789—1851)

1. Life and works

James Fenimore Cooper was America's first successful popular novelist. Son of the prominent federalist William Cooper，founder of the Cooperstown settlement，James was educated at Yale in preparation for a genteel life as a federalist gentleman. He was expelled in his junior year because of improper behavior. He went and spent five years at sea；then，while still in his early twenties，he inherited his father's vast fortune and settled down to a life of comfort and even luxury. Cooper quickly squandered his inheritance，and at thirty was on the verge of bankruptcy. His career as an author began quite by accident. One day while reading an English novel，he was so disgusted with it that he threw it down and said he could do better. His wife challenged him and he decided to try his hand at writing as a career，carefully modeling his work after Sir Walter Scott's successful Waverley Novels. His first novel，*Precaution* (1820)，a domestic comedy set in England，lost money，but Cooper had discovered his vocation.

Cooper established his reputation after his second novel, *The Spy*, and in his third book, the autobiographical *Pioneers* (1823), Cooper introduced the character of Natty Bumppo, a unique American personification of rugged individualism and the pioneer spirit. Emerson called *Pioneers* "our first national novel." A second book featuring Bumppo, *The Last of the Mohicans* (1826), quickly became the most widely read work of the day, consolidating Cooper's popularity in the U. S. and in Europe.

Cooper was a prolific writer, publishing 32 novels, 12 works of nonfiction, a play and numerous pamphlets and articles. His most lasting contributions to American literature were his five books about Natty Bumppo, varying in genre from romantic adventure to realistic narrative. Later anthologized as the *Leatherstocking Tales*, they are best read in the order written: *The Pioneers* (1823), *The Last of the Mohicans* (1826), *The Prairie* (1827), *The Pathfinder* (1840), and *The Deerslayer* (1841). Cooper's popularity declined in his later years as he entered into the nationalistic and partisan disputes of the Jacksonian era, becoming increasingly contentious toward reviewers and the public. His Leatherstocking series, however, continue to maintain a cultural significance in the American literary canon.

2. Cooper's significance

1) Cooper is the first real national writer who tried to work American scenes, events and people in his works and who realized that a new literature must be created from inside out, from feeling to form. Irving's writing is based on European legend; however, Cooper's writing is based on the real American settings, scenes and characters.

2) Cooper is considered the first American writer in the writing of three types of novels, namely, historical romance—*The Spy* (1821), sea adventure tale—*The Pilot* (1824) and frontier novel—*Leatherstocking Tales* (1823—1841).

3) Cooper wrote about Indians who are among the first Indians to appear in American fiction.

He is called the American Scott.

3. Writing features

Cooper's writing has its strong points: there is a variety of incidents and tension, complicated plot and structure, and a beautiful description of nature.

But Cooper's style is dreadful. His characterization is weak and his language, especially his use of dialect, is not authentic. He was not free from syntactical awkwardness.

4. Introduction of the story of the *Leatherstocking Tales*

1) *The Pioneers* (1823): The story takes place in a raw frontier-village on Lake Champlain, at the end of the eighteenth century. Natty Bumppo, who insists on man's old forest freedom conflicts with Judge Temple, standing at the head of the squire-archy on the frontier, for whom man remains savage without law and order. Judge Temple makes some deer-laws forbidding shooting out of season, but Leatherstocking (Natty Bumppo's another name) breaks it somehow. He is arrested, tried and found guilty. He finally escapes with his young friend, Oliver Effingham's help, who tells the truth about his own identity as the grandson of Major Effingham, with whom Leatherstocking has served in the frontier wars, before Oliver and Elizabeth, Judge Temple's daughter, are duly married.

2) *The Last of the Mohicans* (1826): Natty Bumppo, a matured and seasoned scout, is known as Hawkeye. The central event is the capture of the British Fort William Henry by the French and their Huron allies in 1757. The English commander's daughters, Cora and Alice Munro, have been guided through the forest by Nagua, an Indian secret agent of the French, who hopes to gain possession of Cora by betraying the party to the French. Hawkeye has foiled this plot, assisted by his faithful friends, the Delaware chieftain Chingachgook and his warrior son Uncas, and by David Gamut, a wandering music master.

3) *The Prairie* (1827): Natty Bumpo, or Leatherstocking is nearly ninety at the time of his death in 1804. He has abandoned the dwindling forests of the East where, as he thinks, the new settlements have brought a kind of sophisticated softness; and he has followed the frontier to the Indian country of

the great western plains. There in his old age his skill and bravery have won him the reverence due a "white sachem" from the Pawness, among whom he has settled down to meet his death, still "the trapper" with is hound Hector and the famous rifle, ill-deer.

4) *The Pathfinder* (1840): The story takes place at The Great Lakes. Natty, a man of about thirty-five makes an abortive proposal to a beautiful girl, daughter of the Sergeant at the Fort. It is also set during the war, and mainly talks about betrayal and love. Jasper Western, a sailor is suspected of being disloyal to the English and is arrested to the despair of Mabel, who is in love with him. The real traitor is Muir-the lieutenant who had accused Jasper. He is killed by Arrowhead, a Tuscarora Indian.

5) *The Deerslayer* (1841): Young Natty is involved in the French and Indian Wars against the hostile Huron Indians (allies of the French) near Lake Otsego, New York. Early in the novel, he had been trained as a hunter by the friendly Delawares and had won the name Deerslayer. Now, however, the Hurons have captured him. They have released him to accomplish a mission for them, but he is on his word of honor to return at an appointed hour. The mission has been unsuccessful.

5. Importance of the *Leatherstocking Tales*

1) It is a creation of American myth in its formative period.

D. H. Lawrence comments: "The Leatherstocking novels...go backward, from old age to golden youth. That is the true myth of America." It is about the creation of American nation: it started "old" with an old "skin" of European culture; then the colony died and a new nation was born.

2) It creates a typical American hero.

The central figure in the novel, Natty Bumppo, always with a pair of leatherstocking, goes by the various names of Leatherstocking, Deerslayer, Pathfinder and Hawkeye. He is a master of all skills and has deep love for nature and sympathy for people. He embodies the idea of brotherhood of man and of nature and freedom.

Ⅲ. Edgar Allan Poe (1809—1849)

1. His life and works

Edgar Allan Poe was a famous American poet, short story writer, journalist, and literary critic who lived from 1809—1849. He was born in Boston on January 19th, 1809 and was orphaned at an early age, after which he was sent to live with a foster family (The Allans) in Richmond. He was never officially adopted by the Allans and he was eventually disowned by the family.

Poe won a short story contest in 1833, and two years later became a literary critic for the magazine (*The Southern Literary Messenger*). Shortly after, he then married his 13-year-old cousin, Virginia in 1836. He became nationally famous upon the publication of his poem *The Raven* in 1845.

His life was marred by infrequent but intense drinking, which gave him a bad reputation. However, he continued to produce excellent short stories (*Murders in the Rue Morgue*, *The Gold Bug*), which brought him acclaim in America, England, and especially in France.

Unfortunately, after the death of Poe's wife (1847), he fell apart and died two years later on October 7, 1849. Poe's controversial life and reputation have earned him the following comments:

With the aid of his psychological stories, critics have proclaimed him necrophilic, dipsomanic, paranoid, impotent, neurotic, oversexed, a habitual taker of drugs, until all that is left in the public eye is an unstable creature sitting gloomily in a dim room, the raven.

Poe is a great writer. In his whole life, he created about 50 short stories, 70 poems and several critical essays and plays. His popularity has been on the increase in the last half of 20th century.

2. Poe's significance

1) Poe is famous for his various practices in literature forms. Poe wrote short stories, poems, and criticism. He is credited with "Father of detective story".

2) Poe is also noted for his criticism, which influenced French symbolists

and devotees of "art for art's sake".

3) Poe anticipates 20th century literature in his treatment of the disintegration of the self and is regarded as the father of psychoanalytic criticism.

3. Poe's critical ideas

1) Single effect

According to Poe, every piece of literary work must produce the single effect. The very first sentence ought to help bring out the single effect. In *The Fall of the House of Usher*, the feeling of the building gives the visitor and the description of the wall of the building all intend to create a kind of atmosphere-the terror of the soul, which Poe calls the single effect.

2) Beauty

For poetry, in Poe's opinion, its chief aim is beauty to produce a feeling of beauty in the reader. He stresses rhythm, defines true poetry as "the rhythmical creation of beauty," and declares that "music is the perfection of the soul, or idea, of poetry."

3) Brevity

As for short story, Poe thinks that the short story must be of such length as to be readable at one sitting, otherwise, the single effect might be damaged.

4) Originality both in form and content

Poe tries to be peculiar and unique in form, and he experimented with different types of short story. He is also original in content, for example, his description of disintegration of the self. Prior to Freud's theory, Poe is the first writer in America to make the neurotic as protagonist in writing.

4. Introduction to *The Fall of the House of Usher*

1) Plot Overview

It is narrated by a friend of Roderick Usher, whose family used to be rich. Roderick has a twin sister called Madeline, both of whom lived in a decaying and disintegrating house. The sister is so ill that the brother buries her alive and puts the coffin away in one secluded part of the house. Having buried his sister alive, Roderick asked his friend to his house. Then on a stormy night, the sister breaks out of her coffin and dies in embrace of her brother, who then also dies. The house collapses into the lake on the shore of which it has stood. The friend flees in panic and then recalls the story.

2) Features of the Story

①Brevity

There are 15 pages in all.

②Single effect：

Gloomy and horrible atmosphere is the center of the writing. There are many words used to strength the horrible atmosphere，such as winter evening，dry land，broken house and half-cut-tree likewise.

③Originality in the theme—a man going mad

The house in the story is the symbol of Roderick，therefore when Roderick dies，the house falls down. Further Madeline is the emblem of Roderick's reason，in fact，his double. From his death，we know when one's reason is buried，one is mad. This is also in agreement with Poe's idea that the death of a beautiful woman gives a sense of beauty.

5. Selected Reading of *The Fall of the House of Usher*

During the whole of a dull，dark，and soundless day in the autumn of the year，when the clouds hung oppressively low in the heavens，I had been passing alone，on horseback，through a singularly dreary tract of country; and at length found myself，as the shades of the evening drew on，within view of the melancholy House of Usher. I know not how it was—but，with the first glimpse of the building，a sense of insufferable gloom pervaded my spirit. I say insufferable; for the feeling was unrelieved by any of that half-pleasurable，because poetic，sentiment，with which the mind usually receives even the sternest natural images of the desolate or terrible. I looked upon the scene before me upon the mere house，and the simple landscape features of the domain upon the bleak walls upon the vacant eye-like windows upon a few rank sedges and upon a few white trunks of decayed trees with an utter depression of soul which I can compare to no earthly sensation more properly than to the after-dream of the reveler upon opium—the bitter lapse into everyday life—the hideous dropping off of the veil. There was an iciness，a sinking，a sickening of the heart—an unredeemed dreariness of thought which no goading of the imagination could torture into aught of the sublime. What was it—I paused to think—what was it that so unnerved me in the contemplation of the House of Usher? It was a mystery all insoluble; nor could I grapple with the shadowy fancies that crowded upon me as I pondered. I was forced to fall back upon the unsatisfactory conclusion, that while, beyond doubt, there are combinations of very simple natural objects which have the power of thus affecting us, still the analysis of this power lies among considerations beyond our depth. It was possible, I reflected, that a mere different arrangement of the particulars of the scene, of the details of the picture, would be sufficient to modify, or perhaps to annihilate its capacity for sorrowful impression; and, acting upon this idea, I reined my horse to the precipitous brink of a black and lurid tarn ① that lay in unruffled lustre by the dwelling, and gazed down, but with a shudder even more thrilling than before-upon the re-modelled and inverted images of the gray sedge, and the ghastly tree-stems, and the vacant and eye-like windows.

Nevertheless, in this mansion of gloom I now proposed to myself a sojourn of some weeks. Its proprietor, Roderick Usher, had been one of my boon companions in boyhood; but many years had elapsed since our last meeting. A letter, however, had lately reached me in a distant part of the country—a letter from him—which, in its wildly importunate nature, had admitted of no other than a personal reply. The MS. gave evidence of nervous agitation. The writer spoke of acute bodily illness of a pitiable mental idiosyncrasy which oppressed him-and of an earnest desire to see me, as his best, and indeed his only personal friend, with a view of attempting, by the cheerfulness of my society, some alleviation of his malady. It was the manner in which all this, and much more, was said—it was the apparent heart that went with his request—which allowed me no room for hesitation; and I accordingly obeyed forthwith what I still considered a very singular summons.

Although, as boys, we had been even intimate associates, yet I really knew little of my friend. His reserve had been always excessive and habitual. I was aware, however, that his very ancient family had been noted, time out of mind, for a peculiar sensibility of temperament, displaying itself, through long ages, in many works of exalted art, and manifested, of late, in repeated deeds of munificent yet unobtrusive charity, as well as in a passionate devotion to the intricacies, perhaps even more than to the orthodox and easily recognizable beauties, of musical science. I had learned, too, the very remarkable fact, that the stem of the Usher race, all time-honored as it was, had put forth, at no period, any enduring branch; in other words, that the entire family lay in the direct line of descent, and had always, with very trifling and very temporary variation, so lain. It was this deficiency, I considered, while running over in thought the perfect keeping of the character of the premises with the accredited character of the people, and while speculating upon the possible influence which the one, in the long lapse of centuries, might have exercised upon the other—it was this deficiency, perhaps, of collateral issue, and the consequent undeviating transmission, from sire to son, of the patrimony with the name, which had, at length, so identified the two as to merge the original title of the estate in the quaint and equivocal appellation of the "House of Usher" —an appellation which seemed to include, in the minds of the peasantry who used it, both the family and the family mansion.

I have said that the sole effect of my somewhat childish experiment-that of looking down within the tarn—had been to deepen the first singular impression. There can be no doubt that the consciousness of the rapid increase of my superstition—for why should I not so term it—served mainly to accelerate the increase itself. Such, I have long known, is the paradoxical law of all sentiments having terror as a basis. And it might have been for this reason only, that, when I again uplifted my eyes to the house itself, from its image in the pool, there grew in my mind a strange fancy—a fancy so ridiculous, indeed, that I but mention it to show the vivid force of the sensations which oppressed me. I had so worked upon my imagination as really to believe that about the whole mansion and domain there hung an atmosphere peculiar to themselves and their immediate vicinity—an atmosphere which had no affinity with the air of heaven, but which had reeked up from the decayed trees, and the gray wall, and the silent tarn—a pestilent and mystic vapor, dull, sluggish, faintly discernible, and leaden-hued. Shaking off from my spirit what must have been a dream, I scanned more narrowly the real aspect of the building. Its principal feature seemed to be that of an excessive antiquity. The discoloration of ages had been great. Minute fungi overspread the whole exterior, hanging in a fine tangled web-work from the eaves. Yet all this was apart from any extraordinary dilapidation. No portion of the masonry had fallen; and there appeared to be a wild inconsistency between its still perfect adaptation of parts, and the crumbling condition of the individual stones. In this there was much that reminded me of the specious totality of old wood-work which has rotted for long years in some neglected vault, with no disturbance from the breath of the external air. Beyond this indication of extensive decay, however, the fabric gave little token of instability. Perhaps the eye of a scrutinizing observer might have discovered a barely perceptible fissure, which, extending from the roof of the building in front, made its way down the wall in a zigzag direction, until it became lost in the sullen waters of the tarn.

Noticing these things, I rode over a short causeway to the house. A servant in waiting took my horse, and I entered the Gothic archway of the hall. A valet, of stealthy step, thence conducted me, in silence, through many dark and intricate passages in my progress to the studio of his master. Much that I encountered on the way contributed, I know not how, to heighten the vague sentiments of which I have already spoken. While the objects around me—while the carvings of the ceilings, the sombre tapestries of the walls, the ebon blackness of the floors, and the phantasmagoric armorial trophies which rattled as I strode, were but matters to which, or to such as which, I had been accustomed from my infancy—while I hesitated not to acknowledge how familiar was all this—I still wondered to find how unfamiliar were the fancies which ordinary images were stirring up. On one of the staircases, I met the physician of the family. His countenance, I thought, wore a mingled expression of low cunning and perplexity. He accosted me with trepidation and passed on. The valet now threw open a door and ushered me into the presence of his master.

The room in which I found myself was very large and lofty. The windows were long, narrow, and pointed, and at so vast a distance from the black oaken floor as to be altogether inaccessible from within. Feeble gleams of encrimsoned light made their way through the trellised panes, and served to render sufficiently distinct the more prominent objects around; the eye, however, struggled in vain to reach the remoter angles of the chamber, or the recesses of the vaulted and fretted ceiling. Dark draperies hung upon the walls. The general furniture was profuse, comfortless, antique, and tattered. Many books and musical instruments lay scattered about, but failed to give any vitality to the scene. I felt that I breathed an atmosphere of sorrow. An air of stern, deep, and irredeemable gloom hung over and pervaded all.

Upon my entrance, Usher arose from a sofa on which he had been lying at full length, and greeted me with a vivacious warmth which had much in it, I at first thought, of an overdone cordiality—of the constrained effort of the ennuye[②]; man of the world. A glance, however, at his countenance, convinced me of his perfect sincerity. We sat down; and for some moments, while he spoke not, I gazed upon him with a feeling half of pity, half of awe. Surely, man had never before so terribly altered, in so brief a period, as had Roderick Usher! It was with difficulty that I could bring myself to admit the identity of the wan being before me with the companion of my early boyhood. Yet the character of his face had been at all times remarkable. A cadaverousness of complexion; an eye large, liquid, and luminous beyond comparison; lips somewhat thin and very pallid, but of a surpassingly beautiful curve; a nose of a delicate Hebrew model, but with a breadth of nostril unusual in similar formations; a finely moulded chin, speaking, in its want of prominence, of a want of moral energy; hair of a more than web-like softness and tenuity; these features, with an inordinate expansion above the regions of the temple, made up altogether a countenance not easily to be forgotten. And now in the mere exaggeration of the prevailing character of these features, and of the expression they were wont to convey, lay so much of change that I doubted to whom I spoke. The now ghastly pallor of the skin, and the now miraculous lustre of the eye, above all things startled and even awed me. The silken hair, too, had been suffered to grow all unheeded, and as, in its wild gossamer texture, it floated rather than fell about the face, I could not, even with effort, connect its Arabesque expression with any idea of simple humanity.

In the manner of my friend I was at once struck with an incoherence—an inconsistency; and I soon found this to arise from a series of feeble and futile struggles to overcome an habitual trepidancy—an excessive nervous agitation. For something of this nature I had indeed been prepared, no less by his letter, than by reminiscences of certain boyish traits, and by conclusions deduced from his peculiar physical conformation and temperament. His action was alternately vivacious and sullen. His voice varied rapidly from a tremulous indecision (when the animal spirits seemed utterly in abeyance) to that species of energetic concision—that abrupt, weighty, unhurried, and hollow-sounding enunciation—that leaden, self-balanced and perfectly modulated guttural utterance, which may be observed in the lost drunkard, or the irreclaimable eater of opium, during the periods of his most intense excitement.

It was thus that he spoke of the object of my visit, of his earnest desire to see me, and of the solace he expected me to afford him. He entered, at some length, into what he conceived to be the nature of his malady. It was, he said, a constitutional and a family evil, and one for which he despaired to find a remedy—a mere nervous affection, he immediately added, which would undoubtedly soon pass off. It displayed itself in a host of unnatural sensations. Some of these, as he detailed them, interested and bewildered me; although, perhaps, the terms, and the general manner of the narration had their weight. He suffered much from a morbid acuteness of the senses; the most insipid food was alone endurable; he could wear only garments of certain texture; the odors of all flowers were oppressive; his eyes were tortured by even a faint light; and there were but peculiar sounds, and these from stringed instruments, which did not inspire him with horror.

To an anomalous species of terror I found him a bounden slave. "I shall perish," said he, "I must perish in this deplorable folly. Thus, thus, and not otherwise, shall I be lost. I dread the events of the future, not in themselves, but in their results. I shudder at the thought of any, even the most trivial, incident, which may operate upon this intolerable agitation of soul. I have, indeed, no abhorrence of danger, except in its absolute effect-in terror. In this unnerved—in this pitiable condition—I feel that the period will sooner or later arrive when I must abandon life and reason together, in some struggle with the grim phantasm, FEAR."

I learned, moreover, at intervals, and through broken and equivocal hints, another singular feature of his mental condition. He was enchained by certain superstitious impressions in regard to the dwelling which he tenanted, and whence, for many years, he had never ventured forth—in regard to an influence whose supposititious force was conveyed in terms too shadowy here to be re-stated—an influence which some peculiarities in the mere form and substance of his family mansion, had, by dint of long sufferance, he said, obtained over his spirit—an effect which the physique of the gray walls and turrets, and of the dim tarn into which they all looked down, had, at length, brought about upon the morale of his existence.

He admitted, however, although with hesitation, that much of the peculiar gloom which thus afflicted him could be traced to a more natural and far more palpable origin—to the severe and long-continued illness—indeed to the evidently approaching dissolution—of a tenderly beloved sister—his sole companion for long years-his last and only relative on earth. "Her decease," he said, with a bitterness which I can never forget, "Would leave him (him the hopeless and the frail) the last of the ancient race of the Ushers." While he spoke, the lady Madeline (for so was she called) passed slowly through a remote portion of the apartment, and, without having noticed my presence, disappeared. I regarded her with an utter astonishment not unmingled with dread-and yet I found it impossible to account for such feelings. A sensation of stupor oppressed me, as my eyes followed her retreating steps. When a door, at length, closed upon her, my glance sought instinctively and eagerly the countenance of the brother—but he had buried his face in his hands, and I could only perceive that a far more than ordinary wanness had overspread the emaciated fingers through which trickled many passionate tears.

The disease of the lady Madeline had long baffled the skill of her physicians. A settled apathy, a gradual wasting away of the person, and frequent although transient affections of a partially cataleptical character, were the unusual diagnosis. Hitherto she had steadily borne up against the pressure of her malady, and had not betaken herself finally to bed; but, on the closing in of the evening of my arrival at the house, she succumbed (as her brother told me at night with inexpressible agitation) to the prostrating power of the destroyer; and I learned that the glimpse I had obtained of her person would thus probably be the last I should obtain—that the lady, at least while living, would be seen by me no more.

For several days ensuing, her name was unmentioned by either Usher or myself: and during this period I was busied in earnest endeavors to alleviate the melancholy of my friend. We painted and read together; or I listened, as if in a dream, to the wild improvisations of his speaking guitar. And thus, as a closer and still closer intimacy admitted me more unreservedly into the recesses of his spirit, the more bitterly did I perceive the futility of all attempt at cheering a mind from which darkness, as if an inherent positive quality, poured forth upon all objects of the moral and physical universe, in one unceasing radiation of gloom.

I shall ever bear about me a memory of the many solemn hours I thus spent alone with the master of the House of Usher. Yet I should fail in any attempt to convey an idea of the exact character of the studies, or of the occupations, in which he involved me, or led me the way. An excited and highly distempered ideality threw a sulphurous lustre over all. His long improvised dirges will ring forever in my ears. Among other things, I hold painfully in mind a certain singular perversion and amplification of the wild air of the last waltz of Von Weber[③]. From the paintings over which his elaborate fancy brooded, and which grew, touch by touch, into vaguenesses at which I shuddered the more thrillingly, because I shuddered knowing not, why from these paintings (vivid as their images now are before me) I would in vain endeavor to educe more than a small portion which should lie within the compass of merely written words. By the utter simplicity, by the nakedness of his designs, he arrested and overawed attention. If ever mortal painted an idea, that mortal was Roderick Usher. For me at least—in the circumstances then surrounding me—there arose out of the pure abstractions which the hypochondriac contrived to throw upon his canvass, an intensity of intolerable awe, no shadow of which felt I ever yet in the contemplation of the certainly glowing yet too concrete reveries of Fuseli[④].

One of the phantasmagoric conceptions of my friend, partaking not so rigidly of the spirit of abstraction, may be shadowed forth, although feebly, in words. A small picture presented the interior of an immensely long and rectangular vault or tunnel, with low walls, smooth, white, and without interruption or device. Certain accessory points of the design served well to convey the idea that this excavation lay at an exceeding depth below the surface of the earth. No outlet was observed in any portion of its vast extent, and no torch, or other artificial source of light was discernible; yet a flood of intense rays rolled throughout, and bathed the whole in a ghastly and inappropriate splendor.

I have just spoken of that morbid condition of the auditory nerve which rendered all music intolerable to the sufferer, with the exception of certain effects of stringed instruments. It was, perhaps, the narrow limits to which he thus confined himself upon the guitar, which gave birth, in great measure, to the fantastic character of his performances. But the fervid facility of his impromptus could not be so accounted for. They must have been, and were, in the notes, as well as in the words of his wild fantasias (for he not unfrequently accompanied himself with rhymed verbal improvisations), the result of that intense mental collectedness and concentration to which I have previously alluded as observable only in particular moments of the highest artificial excitement. The words of one of these rhapsodies I have easily remembered. I was, perhaps, the more forcibly impressed with it, as he gave it, because, in the under or mystic current of its meaning, I fancied that I perceived, and for the first time, a full consciousness on the part of Usher, of the tottering of his lofty reason upon her throne. The verses, which were entitled "The Haunted Palace," ran very nearly, if not accurately, thus: ...

NOTES

①tarn: a small lake, normally in the mountains 小湖，一般在山中。

②ennuye: bored 厌倦的。

③Von Weber: Karl Maria Von Weber(1786—1826) established Romanticism in German opera; *The Last Waltz of Von Weber* was composed by Karl Gottlieb Reissiger (1798—1859).

④Fuseli: Henry Fuseli (1741—1825), Swiss painter who made his reputation in London; noted for his interest in the supernatural. 瑞士画家。

Topic Discussion

1. D. H. Lawrence saw Poe's stories as the disintegrating process of the soul. What do you think of this comment according to our selected reading?

2. What, do you perceive, are the features of Poe's short stories after reading the selected pieces?

第四节　浪漫主义后期重要作家与作品

每节导读

本节分别讲解霍桑、麦尔维尔、惠特曼和迪金森的生平、主要作品、创作风格、写作技巧、作品的意义以及局限性等。

霍桑（Nathaniel Hawthorne 1804—1864），小说家。艺术上，他擅长揭示人物内心冲突和心理描写，充满丰富想象，惯用象征手法，且潜心挖掘隐藏在事物后的深层意义，但往往带浓厚的宗教气氛和神秘色彩。其代表作是以殖民时期新英格兰生活为背景的长篇小说《红字》（*The Scarlet Letter*，1850）。小说通过叙述一个受不合理婚姻束缚的少妇海丝特·白兰因犯“通奸”罪被监禁、示众和长期隔离的故事，揭露了政教合一体制统治下殖民地社会的冷酷虚伪，探讨了有关罪恶和人性的道德、哲理问题。

麦尔维尔（Herman Melville，1819—1891），小说家、诗人。学习这一作家的重点在于了解其代表作品《白鲸》（*Moby Dick*，1851）。《白鲸》是作者对社会和人生认识的全面总结，它描写了捕鲸工人的辛勤劳动和智慧，揭露了资本主义的残酷剥削。麦尔维尔还对一些重大问题进行了探讨，这些问题包括民主与贵族政治、真假基督教徒的区别、名誉声望与崇高的博爱精神的意义等。

惠特曼（Walt Whitman，1819—1892）是美国浪漫主义时期杰出的诗人和美国资本主义上升阶段民主、自由崇高理想的伟大歌手。1855 年春，他精选 12 首诗，自费出版了《草叶集》（*Leaves of Grass*）。诗集取名《草叶集》有深刻寓意。“草叶”象征惠特曼的诗。草叶也是包括诗人在内的千千万万具有强大生命力的美国“新人”形象。它象征独特的美国的精神。

学习惠特曼这一部分，重点在于了解其自由体诗及诗歌主题中所表现出来的美国特性。

迪金森（Emily Dickinson，1830—1886），美国著名女诗人。她的诗歌的显著特征是感情真挚，绝无造作的痕迹。迪金森认为死亡和永生相连，死亡导向永生。读《因为我不能停下等待死神》（*Because I could not Stop for Death*），人们会感到诗人似相信死亡和永生的不可分割性。迪金森的意象总能发人深思，有她的杰作中，每一个字都是一幅图画。她的词语以其简短、直接和普通而著称。其诗歌的特点及主题应为这一部分重点掌握的内容。

Ⅰ. Nathaniel Hawthorne (1804—1864)

1. Life and Works

Descended from a prominent Puritan family, Hawthorne was the son of a sea captain who died when Nathaniel was 4 years old. When he was 14 he and his mother moved to a lonely farm in Maine. After attending Bowdoin College (1821—1825), he devoted himself to writing. His first novel, *Fansawe* (1829), published anonymously, was unsuccessful. His short stories won notice and were collected in *Twice-Told Tales* (1837; second series, 1842). Unable to support himself by writing and editing, he took a job at the Boston Custom House.

Later, Hawthorne lived at the experimental community Brook Farm for about six months, but he did not share the optimism and idealism of the transcendentalist participants, and he did not feel himself suited to communal life. In 1842 he married Sophia Peabody, a friend and follower of Emerson, Thoreau, and Margaret Fuller, and they settled in Concord. There he wrote the tales and sketches in the collection *Mosses from an Old Manse* (1846).

In order to earn a livelihood Hawthorne served as surveyor of the port at Salem (1846—49), where he began writing his masterpiece, *The Scarlet Letter* (1850). Set in 17th century Puritan New England, the novel tells of the passionate, forbidden love affair linking a sensitive, religious young man, the Reverend Arthur Dimondale, and the sensuous, beautiful townsperson, Hester Prynne. Set in Boston around 1650 during early Puritan colonization, the novel highlights the Calvinistic obsession with morality, sexual repression, guilt and confession, and spiritual salvation. The novel explores deeply the human heart, presenting the problems of moral evil and guilt through allegory and symbolism. It is often considered the first American psychological novel. Hawthorne's next novel, *The House of the Seven Gables* (1851), takes place in the New England of his own period but nevertheless also deals with the effects of Puritanism.

For a time Hawthorne lived at "Tanglewood", near Lenox, Massachusetts, where he wrote *A Wonder Book* (1852), based on Greek mythology, which became a juvenile classic, and *Tanglewood Tales* (1853), also for children. At this time he befriended his neighbor Herman Melville, who was one of the first to appreciate Hawthorne's genius. Returning to Concord, Hawthorne completed *The Blithedale Romance* (1852), a novel based on his Brook Farm experience.

A campaign biography of his college friend Franklin Pierce earned Hawthorne the post of consul at Liverpool (1853—1857) after Pierce became President. Hawthorne's stay in England is reflected in the travel sketches of *Our Old Home* (1863), and a visit to Italy resulted in the novel *The Marble Faun* (1860). After returning to the United States, he worked on several novels that were never finished. He died during a trip with Franklin Pierce.

2. Hawthorne's Short Stories

Aside from his importance as a novelist, Hawthorne is also justly celebrated as a short story writer. He helped to establish the American short story as a significant art form with his haunting tales of human loneliness, frustration, hypocrisy, eccentricity, and frailty. Among his most brilliant stories are "The Minister's Black Veil", "Roger Malvin's Burial", "Young Goodman Brown", "Rappaccini's Daughter", "The Great Stone Face", and "My Kinsman, Major Molineux". Hawthorne's recurring themes, and characteristic settings in Puritan colonial New England, are trademarks of those of his best-known short stories.

3. Hawthorne's Dominating Ideas

1) The influence of Puritanism had a strong impact on him. Hawthorne was from a Puritan family, therefore, he seemed to be haunted by the sense of evil or sin all his life. He believed that evil is at the core of human heart. This idea is quite different from the pervading Transcendentalism, especially Thoreau's ideas. So he was a romantic writer standing aloof from Transcendentalism.

2) Hawthorne held a negative or conservative attitude towards science. To him, science was one source that caused evil. One theme, therefore, often occurs in his writing, that is the tension between head (wisdom and intellect) and heart (feelings and emotions). Accordingly, scientists represent head,

while ordinary people represent heart.

4. Introduction to *The Scarlet Letter*

1) Plot Overview

An aging English scholar sends his beautiful young wife, Hester, to make their new home in New England. When he comes over two years later he is bewildered to see his wife wearing a scarlet letter A on her breast, holding her illicit child in her arms. Determined to find out who her lover is, the old scholar disguises himself as a physician and changes his name to Chillingworth. Gradually he discovers that the villain is no other than the much admired brilliant clergyman, Dimmmesdale. Tormenting himself ruthlessly for his sin, Dimmesdale cuts himself off from community and withers spiritually as well as physically. Hester's response to the scarlet letter A is a positive one. Though living on the fringe of the community, she does her best to reestablish her fellowship with her neighbors on a new, honest basis and finally wins their love and admiration. At one time she plans to leave America with Dimmesdale, but he refuses her help. He dies in her arms while confessing his sin at a public gathering. Chillingworth withers. Pearl, Hester' daughter, grows up to be married into a noble family of Europe.

2) Interpretation of the Story

①Hawthorne drew heavily from the past. The story is set in 17th century New England, which shows his interest in connecting a bygone time with the very present.

②Hawthorne is strongly influenced by humanistic view of the 19th century. We can see his positive attitude toward Hester through the creation of this character. Here he criticizes Puritan morals, especially those concerning sex and marriage. At the same time, he also criticizes the Puritan way of punishment, which brings psychological hurt to the victim.

③He is concerned with moral, psychological and emotional effect of sin on man.

The effect on Hester brings her moral growth. We can see this from the fact that the meaning of scarlet letter A shifts from Adultery at the beginning to Able and then Angel at last. Opposite to Hester is Dimmesdale who conceals his sin but suffers a physical and spiritual disintegration. From these, we know Hawthorne intended to teach the readers that man should show his worst to the world and to be true and honest.

5. Selected Readings

The Scarlet Letter

Chapter 5

Lonely as was Hester's situation, and without a friend on earth who dared to show himself, she, however, incurred no risk of want. She possessed an art that sufficed, even in a land that afforded comparatively little scope for its exercise, to supply food for her thriving infant and herself. It was the art—then, as now, almost the only one within a woman's grasp—of needle-work. She bore on her breast, in the curiously embroidered letter, a specimen of her delicate and imaginative skill, of which the dames of a court might gladly have availed themselves, to add the richer and more spiritual adornment of human ingenuity to their fabrics of silk and gold. Here, indeed, in the sable simplicity that generally characterized the Puritanic modes of dress, there might be an infrequent call for the finer productions of her handiwork. Yet the taste of the age, demanding whatever was elaborate in compositions of this kind, did not fail to extend its influence over our stern progenitors, who had cast behind them so many fashions which it might seem harder to dispense with. Public ceremonies, such as ordinations, the installation of magistrates, and all that could give majesty to the forms in which a new government manifested itself to the people, were, as a matter of policy, marked by a stately and well-conducted ceremonial, and a sombre, but yet a studied magnificence. Deep ruffs, painfully wrought bands, and gorgeously embroidered gloves, were all deemed necessary to the official state of men assuming the reins of power; and were readily allowed to individuals dignified by rank or wealth, even while sumptuary laws[①] forbade these and similar extravagances to the plebeian order. In the array of funerals, too, —whether for the apparel of the dead body, or to typify, by manifold emblematic devices of sable cloth and snowy lawn[②], the sorrow of the survivors, —there was a frequent and characteristic demand for such labor as

Hester Prynne could supply. Baby-linen—for babies then wore robes of state—afforded still another possibility of toil and emolument.

By degrees, nor very slowly, her handiwork became what would now be termed the fashion. Whether from commiseration for a woman of so miserable a destiny; or from the morbid curiosity that gives a fictitious value even to common or worthless things; or by whatever other intangible circumstance was then, as now, sufficient to bestow, on some persons, what others might seek in vain; or because Hester really filled a gap which must otherwise have remained vacant; it is certain that she had ready and fairly requited employment for as many hours as she saw fit to occupy with her needle. Vanity, it may be, chose to mortify itself, by putting on, for ceremonials of pomp and state, the garments that had been wrought by her sinful hands. Her needle-work was seen on the ruff of the Governor; military men wore it on their scarfs, and the minister on his band; it decked the baby's little cap; it was shut up, to be mildewed and moulder away, in the coffins of the dead. But it is not recorded that, in a single instance, her skill was called in aid to embroider the white veil which was to cover the pure blushes of a bride. The exception indicated the ever relentless vigor with which society frowned upon her sin.

Hester sought not to acquire any thing beyond a subsistence, of the plainest and most ascetic description, for herself, and a simple abundance for her child. Her own dress was of the coarsest materials and the most sombre hue; with only that one ornament, —the scarlet letter, —which it was her doom to wear. The child's attire, on the other hand, was distinguished by a fanciful, or, we may rather say, a fantastic ingenuity, which served, indeed, to heighten the airy charm that early began to develop itself in the little girl, but which appeared to have also a deeper meaning. We may speak further of it hereafter. Except for that small expenditure in the decoration of her infant, Hester bestowed all her superfluous means in charity, on wretches less miserable than herself, and who not unfrequently insulted the hand that fed them. Much of the time, which she might readily have applied to the better efforts of her art, she employed in making coarse garments for the poor. It is probable that there was an idea of penance in this mode of occupation, and that she offered up a real sacrifice of enjoyment, in devoting so many hours to such rude handiwork. She had in her nature a rich, voluptuous, Oriental characteristic, —a taste for the gorgeously beautiful, which, save in the exquisite productions of her needle, found nothing else, in all the possibilities of her life, to exercise itself upon. Women derive a pleasure, incomprehensible to the other sex, from the delicate toil of the needle. To Hester Prynne it might have been a mode of expressing, and therefore soothing, the passion of her life. Like all other joys, she rejected it as sin. This morbid meddling of conscience with an immaterial matter betokened, it is to be feared, no genuine and steadfast penitence, but something doubtful, something that might be deeply wrong beneath.

In this manner, Hester Prynne came to have a part to perform in the world. With her native energy of character, and rare capacity, it could not entirely cast her off, although it had set a mark upon her, more intolerable to a woman's heart than that which branded the brow of Cain③. In all her intercourse with society, however, there was nothing that made her feel as if she belonged to it. Every gesture, every word, and even the silence of those with whom she came in contact, implied, and often expressed, that she was banished, and as much alone as if she inhabited another sphere, or communicated with the common nature by other organs and senses than the rest of human kind. She stood apart from mortal interests, yet close beside them, like a ghost that revisits the familiar fireside, and can no longer make itself seen or felt; no more smile with the household joy, nor mourn with the kindred sorrow; or, should it succeed in manifesting its forbidden sympathy, awakening only terror and horrible repugnance. These emotions, in fact, and its bitterest scorn besides, seemed to be the sole portion that she retained in the universal heart. It was not an age of delicacy; and her position, although she understood it well, and was in little danger of forgetting it, was often brought before her vivid self-perception, like a new anguish, by the rudest touch upon the tenderest spot. The poor, as we have already said, whom she sought out to be the objects of her bounty, often reviled the hand that was stretched forth to succor them. Dames of elevated rank, likewise, whose doors she entered in the way of her occupation, were accustomed to distil drops of bitterness into her heart; sometimes through that alchemy of quiet malice, by which women can concoct a subtle poison from ordinary trifles; and sometimes, also, by a coarser expression, that fell upon the sufferer's defenseless breast like a rough blow upon an ulcerated wound. Hester had schooled herself long and well; she never responded to these attacks, save by a flush of crimson that rose irrepressibly over her pale cheek, and again subsided into the depths of her bosom. She was patient, —a martyr, indeed, —but she forbore to pray for enemies; lest, in spite of her forgiving aspirations, the words of the blessing should stubbornly twist themselves into a curse.

Continually, and in a thousand other ways, did she feel the innumerable throbs of anguish that had been so cunningly contrived for her by the undying, the ever-active sentence of the Puritan tribunal. Clergymen paused in the street to address words of exhortation, that brought a crowd, with its mingled grin and frown, around the poor, sinful woman. If she entered a church, trusting to share the Sabbath smile of the Universal Father, it was often her mishap to find herself the text of the discourse. She grew to have a dread of children; for they had imbibed from their parents a vague idea of something horrible in this dreary woman, gliding silently through the town, with never any companion but one only child. Therefore, first allowing her to pass, they pursued her at a distance with shrill cries, and the utterance of a word that had no distinct purport to their own minds, but was none the less terrible to her, as proceeding from lips that babbled it unconsciously. It seemed to argue so wide a diffusion of her shame, that all nature knew of it; it could have caused her no deeper pang, had the leaves of the trees whispered the dark story among themselves, —had the summer breeze murmured about it, —had the wintry blast shrieked it aloud! Another peculiar torture was felt in the gaze of a new eye. When strangers looked curiously at the scarlet letter, —and none ever failed to do so, —they branded it afresh into Hester's soul; so that, oftentimes, she could scarcely refrain, yet always did refrain, from covering the symbol with her hand. But then, again, an accustomed eye had likewise its own anguish to inflict. Its cool stare of familiarity was intolerable. From first to last, in short, Hester Prynne had always this dreadful agony in feeling a human eye upon the token; the spot never grew callous; it seemed, on the contrary, to grow more sensitive with daily torture.

But sometimes, once in many days, or perchance in many months, she felt an eye—a human eye—upon the ignominious brand, that seemed to give a momentary relief, as if half of her agony were shared. The next instant, back it all rushed again, with still a deeper throb of pain; for, in that brief interval, she had sinned anew. Had Hester sinned alone?

Her imagination was somewhat affected, and, had she been of a softer moral and intellectual fibre, would have been still more so, by the strange and solitary anguish of her life. Walking to and fro, with those lonely footsteps, in the little world with which she was outwardly connected, it now and then appeared to Hester, —if altogether fancy, it was nevertheless too potent to be resisted, —she felt or fancied, then, that the scarlet letter had endowed her with a new sense. She shuddered to believe, yet could not help believing, that it gave her a sympathetic knowledge of the hidden sin in other hearts. She was terror-stricken by the revelations that were thus made. What were they? Could they be other than the insidious whispers of the bad angel④, who would fain have persuaded the struggling woman, as yet only half his victim, that the outward guise of purity was but a lie, and that, if truth were everywhere to be shown, a scarlet letter would blaze forth on many a bosom besides Hester Prynne's? Or, must she receive those intimations—so obscure, yet so distinct—as truth? In all her miserable experience, there was nothing else so awful and so loathsome as this sense. It perplexed, as well as shocked her, by the irreverent inopportuneness of the occasions that brought it into vivid action. Sometimes, the red infamy upon her breast would give a sympathetic throb, as she passed near a venerable minister or magistrate, the model of piety and justice, to whom that age of antique reverence looked up, as to a mortal man in fellowship with angels. "What evil thing is at hand?" would Hester say to herself. Lifting her reluctant eyes, there would be nothing human within the scope of view, save the form of this earthly saint! Again, a mystic sisterhood would contumaciously assert itself, as she met the sanctified frown of some matron, who, according to the rumor of all tongues, had kept cold snow within her bosom throughout life. That unsunned snow in the matron's bosom, and the burning shame on Hester Prynne's, —what had the two in common? Or, once more, the electric thrill would give her warning, — "Behold, Hester, here is a companion!" — and, looking up, she would detect the eyes of a young maiden glancing at the scarlet letter, shyly and aside, and quickly averted, with a faint, chill crimson in her cheeks; as if her purity were somewhat sullied by that momentary glance. O Fiend, whose talisman was that fatal symbol, wouldst thou leave nothing, whether in youth or age, for this poor sinner to revere? —Such loss of faith is ever one of the saddest results of sin. Be it accepted as a proof that all was not corrupt in this poor victim of her own frailty, and man's hard law, that Hester Prynne yet struggled to believe that no fellow-mortal was guilty like herself ⑤.

The vulgar, who, in those dreary old times, were always contributing a grotesque horror to what interested their imaginations, had a story about the scarlet letter which we might readily work up into a terrific legend. They averred, that the symbol was not mere scarlet cloth, tinged in an earthly dye-pot, but was red-hot with infernal fire, and could be seen glowing all alight, whenever Hester Prynne walked abroad in the night-time. And we must needs say, it seared Hester's bosom so deeply, that perhaps there was more truth in the rumor than our modern incredulity may be inclined to admit....

NOTES

①sumptuary laws: laws governing elaborateness of apparel allowed to various social ranks. 限定个人费用的节约法令。

②sable cloth and snowy lawn: black cloth (of whatever kind) and white lawn (fine, light cotton or linen fabric). 黑布和白色棉布。

③Cain: a story from the Bible: "And the Lord set a mark upon Cain, lest any finding him should kill him". 圣经中该隐的故事。

④bad angel: Satan 撒旦。

⑤no fellow-mortal was guilty like herself: Hawthorne indicates that loss of faith in others is a result of one's own sins. 这里反映了作者的观点，个人的罪过导致对他人信任的消失。

Topic Discussion

1. What is Hawthorn's opinion on evil? How can we overcome it?

2. What are artistic features of The Scarlet Letter?

Ⅱ. Herman Melville (1819—1891)

1. Melville's Life and Works

Herman Melville was born on the first of August in 1819 in New York City, the third of eight children of Allan and Maria Gansevoort Melville. His ancestors included several Scottish and Dutch settlers of New York as well as prominent leaders in the American Revolution. His paternal grandfather, Major Thomas Melville, was a member of the Boston Tea Party and his maternal grandfather, General Peter Gansevoort, was famous for leading the defense of Ft. Stanwix against the British during the revolution.

Melville's father was involved in the felt and fur import business, yet in 1830 his business collapsed and the Melville family moved from New York City to Albany, where Allan Melville died two years later. As a child, Herman suffered from extremely poor eyesight caused by a bout of scarlet fever, but he was able to attend Male High School despite his difficulties. Herman Melville worked as a bank clerk before attending the Albany Classical School, and then worked for a short time as a teacher in Pittsfield, Massachusetts.

Although he studied surveying at Landingsburgh Academy in order to take part in the Erie Canal Project, he did not gain a post with the project and instead shipped out of America as a cabin boy on the St. Lawrence bound for Liverpool. By this time, Melville had already started writing. In January of 1841 Melville undertook a second voyage on the whaler Acushnet from New Bedford to the South Seas. By June of the following year the Acushnet landed in the Polynesian Islands, and Melville's adventures in this area became the basis for his first novel, *Typee* (1846). This novel is the reputed story of his life among the cannibalistic Typee people for several months in 1842, but is likely a highly fictionalized dramatization of the actual events. Melville's second novel, *Omoo* (1847) detailed the adventures of another whaling journey in which Melville took part in a mutiny and landed in a Tahitian jail from which he later easily escaped.

In the summer of 1850, spurred by the influence of Nathaniel Hawthorne's

The Scarlet Letter, Melville bought the Arrowhead farm near Pittsfield so that he could live near Hawthorne, and the two men, who shared similar philosophies, became close. This relationship with Hawthorne reawakened Melville's creative energies, and in 1851 Melville published his most renowned novel, *Moby Dick*. Although now heralded as a landmark work in American literature, the novel received little acclaim upon its release. Melville completed *Billy Budd*, the story of a sailor who accidentally kills his master after being provoked by a false charge. Melville finished the novel in April of 1891, and five months later he died on September 28 in New York City.

2. Moby Dick

1) Introduction of *Moby Dick*:

Critics have agreed that *Moby Dick* is one of the world's greatest masterpieces. To get to know the nineteenth-century American mind and America itself, one has to read this book. It is an encyclopedia of everything, history, philosophy, religion, etc. in addition to a detailed account of the operations of the whaling industry.

The novel *Moby Dick* was the sixth novel published by Herman Melville, a landmark of American literature that mixed a number of literary styles including a fictional adventure story, historical detail and even scientific discussion. As the story of the voyage of the whaling ship Pequod, the novel draws at least partially from the experiences of its author while a sailor and a harpooner on whaling ships before settling in New England as a writer.

The title character of *Moby Dick* was inspired by an article in *Knickerbocker* magazine in May 1839 entitled "Mocha Dick: or the White Whale of the Pacific". The author of this article, Jeremiah Reynolds, detailed the capture of a giant sperm whale legendary among whalers for its vicious attacks on ships. The whale was named as such after the Mocha Islands, the area where the whale was commonly sighted ("Dick" was used simply because it was a common male name). The origin of the "Moby" of the novel's title has never been conclusively determined.

Melville intended *Moby Dick* as a return to the type of adventure stories such as Typee and Omoo that made his reputation, but the novel instead took a different turn. In his letters he described the novel as a romantic and fanciful adventure, yet the final novel took a far different turn. During this time Melville had become deeply influenced by Nathaniel Hawthorne, whose cynical and imposing works bear some resemblance to the tragic epic that Melville produced.

The first publication of *Moby Dick* was in London in October of 1851. Entitled *The Whale*, the novel was published in three volumes and was censored for some of its political and moral content. The British publisher of the novel, Richard Bentley, inadvertently left out the Epilogue to the novel, leading many critics to wonder how the tale could be told in the first person by Ishmael, when the final chapter witnesses the sinking of the Pequod with presumably no survivors.

The first American publication of the novel came the following month. The American version of the novel, published by Harper & Brothers, although fixing the narrative error of the British version through the inclusion of the epilogue, was poorly received by critics and readers who expected a romantic high seas adventure akin to Melville's first successes. The reputation of the novel floundered for many years, and it was only after Melville's death that it became considered one of the major novels in American literature.

2) Summary of *Moby Dick*

The outcast youth Ishmael, feeling depressed, signs for a voyage on the whaler Pequod and meets Queenqueg, a Polynesian prince who later becomes his intimate friend. They board the Pequod and leave Nantucket on Christmas Day.

The captain, Ahab, is a monomaniac whose single purpose is to capture the fierce, cunning white whale, Moby Dick, which has torn away his leg during their last encounter. Ahab posts a doubloon on the mast as a reward for the man who first sights the white whale. People on board the ship react to the announcement differently.

Omens arise to indicate the disastrous end of Ahab: storms, lightening, loss of the compass, the drowning of a man, and the insanity of Ahab's favorite, Pip.

The white whale is finally sighted, and in the first day's chase he smashes a whaleboat. The second day, another boat is swamped, and the captain's ivory leg is snapped off. On the third day the whale is harpooned, but the rope from Ahab coils around his neck and snatches him from his boat. The Pequod is sunk and the whole crew perish in the sea except Ishmael, who is rescued by Queequeeg's canoe-coffin.

3) Major Characters

Captain Ahab: Ahab is the Captain of the Pequod, a grave older man reaching his sixties who has spent nearly forty years as a sailor, only three of which he has spent on dry land (Melville alludes to Ahab as having a wife and son, but their existence seems of little significance to Ahab). The novel is essentially the story of Ahab and his quest to defeat the legendary Sperm Whale Moby Dick, for this whale took Ahab's leg, causing him to use an ivory leg to walk and stand. In many respects Melville portrays Ahab as barely human, barely governed by human mores and conventions and nearly entirely subject to his own obsession with Moby Dick. Melville describes him in mostly alien terms, he is in some ways a machine, unaffected by human appetites and without recognizable emotion.

Ishmael: Ishmael is the narrator of the novel, a simple sailor on the Pequod who undertakes the journey. As the narrator Ishmael establishes himself as somewhat of an everyman. His primary task is to observe the conflicts around him. Nevertheless, Melville does give his narrator several significant character traits, the most important of which is his idealization of the Sperm Whale and his belief in its majesty. Also, it is Ishmael who has the only significant personal relationship in the novel; he becomes a close friend with the pagan harpooner Queequeg and comes to cherish and adore Queequeg to a somewhat improbable level open to great interpretation; Melville even describes their relationship in terms of a marriage. Ishmael is the only survivor of the Pequod's voyage, living to tell the tale of Moby Dick only because he is by chance on a whaling boat when Moby Dick sinks the Pequod and is rescued by a nearby ship.

4) Main Themes

①Blasphemous Ahab as a Blasphemous Figure: A major assumption that runs through Moby Dick is that Ahab's quest against the great whale is a blasphemous activity, even apart from the consequences that it has upon its crew. This blasphemy takes two major forms: the first type of blasphemy to prevail within Ahab is the idea that Ahab thinks himself the equal of God. The second type of blasphemy is a rejection of God altogether for an alliance with the devil. The idea that Ahab's quest for Moby Dick is an act of defiance toward God assuming that Ahab is omnipotent first occurs before Ahab is even introduced during Father Mapple's sermon.

②The Whale as a Symbol of Unparalleled Greatness: When Melville, through Ishmael, describes the Sperm Whale during the many non-narrative chapters of Moby Dick, the idea that the whale has no parallel in excellence recurs as a nearly labored point. Melville approaches this theme from a variety of standpoints, whether biological or historical, in order to prove the superiority of the whale over all other creatures. The theme of the excellence of the whale serves to place Ahab's quest against Moby Dick as, at best, a virtually insurmountable task in which he is doomed to failure. Melville constructs the whale as a figure that cannot be easily vanquished, if it can be defeated at all.

③Foreshadowing and Superstition: A recurring theme throughout Moby Dick is the appearance of foreshadowing, superstitious that foreshadow a tragic end to the story. Even before Ishmael boards the Pequod, the Nantucket strangers Elijah warns Ishmael and Queequeg against traveling with Captain Ahab. The Parsee Fedallah also has a prophetic dream concerning Ahab's quest against Moby Dick, dreaming of hearses (although he misinterprets the dream to mean that Ahab will certainly kill Moby Dick). Indeed, the characters are bound by superstition and myth: the only reason that the Pequod kills a Right Whale is the legend that a ship will have good luck if it has the head of a Right Whale and the head of a Sperm Whale on its opposing sides.

④It is a tragedy of man fighting against overwhelming odds in an indifferent and even hostile universe. Moby Dick represents the sum total of Melville's bleak view of the world in which he lived. Man in this universe lives a meaningless and futile life, meaningless because futile. The loss of faith and the sense of futility and meaninglessness which characterize modern life of the West was expressed in Melville's work so well that the twentieth century has found it both fascinating and great.

⑤The important thing that Melville intended to reveal is alienation, which he sensed existing in the life of his time on different levels, between man and man, man and society, and man and nature. Moby Dick reveals the basic pattern of nineteenth-century American life: loneliness and suicidal individualism in a self-styled democracy.

⑥ Ahab may have been Melville's portrait of an Emersonian self-reliant individual. Melville lost no opportunity in his criticism of New England Transcendentalism. Constantly under his attack is his emphasis on individualism and Oversoul. To say that the whole of Moby Dick is a negative reflection upon Transcendentalism is not in fact an exaggeration.

Ⅲ. Walt Whitman (1819—1892)

1. Whitman's Life and Works

Whitman was brought up in a working-class background on Long Island, New York. He had five years of schooling and a good deal of "loafing" and reading. Whitman liked experience, so he tried at a variety of jobs. At the same time, he got a first hand knowledge of life and people in the new world. He worked as an office boy, a printer's apprentice, schoolmaster, printer, editor and journalist. He wrote some frightened tales and some traditional verse. In 1848 he traveled to New Orleans and saw very much of the Mississippi heartlands. The first edition of *Leaves of Grass* came out in 1855. It contained twelve poems and did not sell well, but it made a stir on the American literary scene. Whitman's poems broke with the poetic convention, and its sexuality and exotic and vulgar language brought harsh criticisms on it. Some critics regarded Whitman's *Leaves of Grass* as "poetry of barbarism," and a mass of stupid filth, one of the New England poets, John Greeleaf Whittier even threw his gift-copy into the fire. However, the *Leaves of Grass* received a warm welcome from Emerson. The first edition is important to American literature for the following reasons. One of them is the fact that it revealed some strengths of Whitman's art. Just like Malcolm Cowley said, it is a "buried masterpiece of American writing." Whitman showed his freshest and boldest in language, that is the great shock to the traditional American poetic form and language.

During the Civil War, Whitman worked as a volunteer nurse in military hospitals. The experience further enriched his knowledge of life and the world.

In the meantime he continued to revise and expand his *Leaves of Grass*. It went through nine editions altogether: 1855, 1856, 1860, 1867, 1871, 1876, 1881, 1889, 1891—1892. Whitman began to receive recognition in England and America when his fifth edition appeared. Whitman suffered a paralytic stroke in 1873, but he continued to work at his *Leaves of Grass* until his death. In his last time he prepared the "Deathbed Edition" which containing all of his 400-odd poems.

2. Whitman's Importance

1) Whitman was a catalog of American and European thought. As "the great acceptor", he was susceptible to many influences. The enlightenment and its ideals of the rights and dignity of the individual, idealism and in the Transcendentalism of Carlyle, Coleridge, Wordsworth and Emerson, German philosophy, especially Hegel's "doctrine of a cosmic consciousness that unfolds through conflict to divine ends", with Newtonian and evolutionary, the idea of progress, and current American life with its western frontier spirit, individualism and Civil War Unionism. All these can be found in his system and his poetry.

2) Whitman broke the poetic convention by creating the Free Verse.

Free Verse:

①It is a form of poetry without fixed beat nor regular rhyme scheme.

②The lines and stanzas can be different in length.

③The purpose is to deliver poetry from the restrictions of formal metrical patterns and to recreate the free rhythms of natural speech.

3) Emerson influenced Whitman so much. Whitman was considered one of the representative writers of Transcendentalism.

3. Themes

1) Whitman extols the ideals of equality and democracy and celebrates the dignity, the self-reliant spirit and the joy of the common man. *Song of Myself* reveals a world of equality, without rank and hierarchy. The prostitute draggling her shawl, the President holding a cabinet council, the stately and friendly matrons on the piazza walk, the Missourian crossing the plains and an

infinite number of other things and people find their way into his poem and juxtapose with one another, illustrating the principle of democracy and equality.

2) Whitman's poetry is an inclusion of the commonplace. The poet hears America singing. The mother is singing while setting food on the table. The carpenter is singing, planning his boards. And the day is singing "What belongs to the day." Long catalogues of different people and different occupations indicate that here the new children of Adam are being restored to the Garden of Eden, developing their potentiality to the fullest extent possible. In a general sense *Leaves of Grass* is an Adamic song, and its author an Adamic singer.

3) In his poems, Whitman responds enthusiastically to the expansion of America. The new bustling and progressive republic, with its dynamic creative fertility and its indomitable energy, finds a willing and refreshing voice in Whitman. Read again *Song of Myself* and poems like *There Was a Child Went Forth* and we see the spirit of an emerging America at its most aggressive and daring.

4) In later years Whitman came to see the failure of democracy and social and moral corruption in America, but he thought these curable by the self-reform of the individual. Material gains are fruitless without personal morality; individualism without brotherhood is suicide. Thus *Passage to India* extols "the marriage of continents" and different races, and *Proud Music of the Storm* envisages unity of "all the tongues of nations." The emphasis is clearly on brotherhood and social solidarity. This shows that Whitman was a transitional figure from Romanticism and Transcendentalism to realism.

5) In Whitman's poetry, people could see the unity of all men and of men with universe.

6) Whitman concentrated some of his poems on the cycle of life and death, for example, in *Out of the Cradle, Endlessly Rocking*, the death of the she-bird gives life to the poem.

7) One of the themes of Whitman's poetry is anti-slavery which is clearly demonstrated in poems like *Song of Myself*.

8) Whitman praises American individualism as one of the themes.

4. Whitman's Writing Style

Whitman was a daring experimentalist who, in the words of Ezra Pound, "broke the new wood". His early poems are in conventional rime and meter, but obviously he found the restrictions disappointing.

1) One of the major principles of Whitman's technique is parallelism.

2) Another main principle of Whitman's versification is phonetic recurrence, for example, the systematic repetition of words and phrases at the beginning of the line, in the middle or at the end.

The two principles coordinate with and reinforce each other.

3) Whitman broke free from the traditional iambic pentameter and wrote "free verse". It is a poetic form without fixed beat nor regular rhymes scheme.

4) Whitman is the first person who is the master of the technique. His snapshot and long "catalogs" of lines gave free rein to his imagination in his life.

5. Whitman's Influence

Whitman's influence on modern poetry is great in the world as well as in America.

1) His best work has become part of the common property of Western culture. Many poets in England, France, Italy and Latin America are in his debt. Even in China, people can find Whitman's influence in Guo Moruo's works.

2) In America, it is true that his optimism seems to have become a liability to his reputation in the present century, but modern American poets like T. S. Eliot and Ezra Pound would not have been what they were without Whitman. Ezra Pond, who called him a "pigheaded father", recognized him nonetheless as a father figure who led the break from the past. Carl Sandburg was probably the only great poet who carried, in his Chicago poems, the Whitman's tradition into the twentieth century in a whole-hearted way. Whitman has been compared to a mountain in American literary history. You may go around him if you like, but you cannot pretend that he is not there. His excessive optimism led to a decline of his reputation, but the last few decades have seen an immense change in critical attitude toward him and his poetry. Contemporary American poetry, whatever school or form, bears witness to his great influence.

6. Introduction to the Poem *I Hear America Singing*

I Hear America Singing presents an image of America that America would like to believe true—an image of proud and healthy individualists engaged in productive and happy labor. Mechanic, carpenter, mason, boatman, deckhand, shoemaker, hatter, wood-cutter, plowboy—from city to country, from sea to land, the "varied carols" reflect a genuine joy in the day's creative labor that makes up the essence of the American dream or myth. America singing emerges as a happy, individualistic, proudly procreative, and robustly comradely America. It is surprising that in such a brief poem so much of Whitman's total concept of modern man could be implied.

In *I Hear America Singing*, Whitman imagined the dynamic power of the nation not as a geographical entity spreading westward but as an activity—and one of his favorite ones, at that: singing. The poem consists of a vision of the various units of the country—the mechanic, the carpenter, the mason, the young wife, the boatman—each person separately "singing" his or her individual song. But where in the poem each person acts his or her role separately, this poem blends the individual acts of singing into a harmonious participial ensemble of America singing.

7. Selected Reading

I Hear America Singing

I hear America singing, the varied carols I hear,
Those of mechanics, each one singing his as it should be blithe and strong,
The carpenter singing his as he measures his plank or beam,
The mason singing his as he makes ready for work, or leaves off work,
The boatman singing what belongs to him in his boat, the deck hand singing on the steamboat deck,
The shoemaker singing as he sits on his bench, the hatter singing as he stands,
The woodcutter's song, the ploughboy's on his way in the morning, or at

noon intermission or at sundown,

The delicious singing of the mother, or of the young wife at work, or of the girl sewing or washing,

Each singing what belongs to him or her and to none else,

The day what belongs to the day-at night the party of young fellows, robust, friendly,

Singing with open mouths their strong melodious songs.

Topic Discussion

1. Comment on Whitman's style and language.
2. What is America in the poet's mind?

Ⅳ. Emily Dickinson (1830—1886)

1. Life

Emily Dickinson was born in 1830 into a Calvinist family of Amherst, Mssachusetts. Dickinson spent almost all her life in her birthplace. Her father was a prominent lawyer who was active in civic affairs. His three children (Emily; a son, Austin; and another daughter, Lavinia) thus had the opportunity to meet many distinguished visitors. Emily Dickinson attended Amherst Academy irregularly for six years and Mount Holyoke Seminary for one, and in those years lived a normal life filled with friendships, parties, church, and housekeeping. Before she was 30, however, she began to withdraw from village activities and gradually ceased to leave home at all. While she corresponded with many friends, she eventually stopped seeing them. She often fled from visitors and eventually lived as a virtual recluse in her father's house. As a mature woman, she was intense and sensitive and was exhausted by emotional contact with others.

Even before her withdrawal from the world Dickinson had been writing poetry, and her creative peak seems to have been reached in the period from 1858 to 1862. Although she was encouraged by the critic Thomas Wentworth Higginson, who never truly comprehended her genius, and Helen Hunt Jackson, who believed she was a great poet, Dickinson published only seven poems during her lifetime. Dickinson's mode of existence, although circumscribed, was evidently satisfying, even essential, to her. After her death in 1886, Lavinia Dickinson discovered over 1 000 poems in her sister's bureau. For too long Dickinson was treated less as a serious artist than as a romantic figure who had renounced the world after a disappointment in love. This legend, based on conjecture, distortion, and even fabrication, has been known to plague even some of her modern biographers.

Dickinson was considered one of the greatest poets in the 19th century.

1) Both being unconventional in poetic form, Dickinson and Whitman worked together to create American national poetry.

2) Dickinson and Crane were considered the great forerunners of American Imagism in literature.

3) Unlike Whitman who was interested more in social matters, Dickinson was a kind of personal poet concerned with topics of universal significance.

2. Works

During her lifetime, Dickinson wrote, altogether, 1775 poems. While Dickinson wrote love poetry that indicates a strong attachment, it has proved impossible to know the object of her feelings, or even how much was fed by her poetic imagination. The chief tension in her work comes from a different source: her inability to accept the orthodox religious faith of her day and her longing for its spiritual comfort. Immortality she called "the flood subject", and she alternated confident statements of belief with lyrics of despairing uncertainty that were both reverent and rebellious. Her verse, noted for its epigrammatic style, its wit, its delicate metrical variation and irregular rhymes, its directness of statement, and its bold and startling imagery, has won enormous acclaim and had a great influence on 20th-century poetry.

Dickinson's posthumous fame began when Mabel Loomis Todd and

Higginson edited and published two volumes of poems (1890, 1891) and some of her correspondence (2 vol., 1894). Other editions of verse followed, many of which were marred by unskillful and unnecessary editing. A definitive edition of her works did not appear until the 1950s, when T. H. Johnson published her poems (3 vol., 1955) and letters (3 vol., 1958); only then was serious study of her work possible. Dickinson scholarship was further advanced by R. W. Franklin's variorum edition of her poetry (3 vol., 1998).

3. Writing Style

1) Dickinson is good at catching the charm of something but dropping the thing itself. *A narrow Fellow in the Grass* talks about the snake all the while, but the word "snake" never occurs. This may have, in a way, made Dickinson obscure and inscrutable sometimes.

2) Like Whitman she was a courageous experimentalist. "I have no monarch in my life," she confessed. Indeed, little that she wrote seemed conventional: her choice of words, her verbal constructions, even her spelling and her images. To her poetry is "a bodying forth by means of concrete images" of an inspired thought.

3) She did not use punctuation marks and capital letters regularly.

4) Her poetry abounds in telling images. In the best of her poems every word is a picture seen.

5) A salient feature of her technique was a severe economy of expression. Her poetic idiom is noted for its laconic brevity, directness and plainest words.

4. Themes

Emily Dickinson's poetry comes out in bursts. The poems are short, many of them being based on a single image or symbol. But within her little lyrics Miss Dickinson writes about some of the most important things in life.

1) love and a lover, whom she either never really found or else gave up.

2) Nature, which she considers attractive but unknowable.

3) mortality and immortality, which puzzled her quite often.

4) life and death and the relations between them.

5) success, which she considered her constant companion.

She writes of these things so brilliantly that she is now ranked as one of America's great poets.

Her poetry is read today throughout much of the world and yet its exact wording has not been completely determined, nor has its arrangement and punctuation. Since Emily never prepared her poems for publication, one of the bitterest battles in American literary history has been fought over who should publish and edit what she wrote. However, regardless of details or conflicts, there is no doubt that the solitary Miss Dickinson of Amherst, Massachusetts, is a writer of great power and beauty.

5. Selected Reading

1) Introduction to the poem *Because I could not stop for Death*

Emily Dickinson's poem *Because I could not stop for Death* is a remarkable masterpiece that exercises thought between the known and the unknown. In this poem, there is much impression in the tone, in symbols, and in the use of imagery that exudes creativity.

In this poem, Dickinson uses controlling adjectives "slowly" and "passed" to create a tone that seems rather calm.

"We slowly drove, he knew no haste/...We passed the School.../We passed the Setting Sun" sets a slow, quiet, calm, and dreamy atmosphere. The tone in Dickinson's poem will put its readers the ideas on a track heading towards a confusing atmosphere.

Dickinson's masterpiece lives on complex ideas that appear through symbols, which carry her readers through her poem. Dickinson brought to light the mysteriousness of life cycle. Ungraspable to many, the cycle of one's life, as symbolized by Dickinson, has three stages and then a final stage of eternity. In addition to these three stages, the final stage of eternity was symbolized in the last two lines of the poem, the Horses Heads, leading towards Eternity.

Emily Dickinson dresses the scene such that mental pictures of sight, feeling, and sound come to life. The imagery begins the moment Dickinson invites her reader into the Carriage. Death slowly takes the readers on a sight seeing trip where they see the stages of life. In example, often times, when one experiences a joyous time, time seems to fly. This poem exercises both the thoughts and emotions of its reader and can effectively change one's viewpoint of an eternal future.

Eternity and Death are two important characters in Emily Dickinson's *Because I could not stop for Death*. One can say that Emily Dickinson's sole purpose in this poem is to show no fear of death. Emily Dickinson's poem, *Because I could not stop for Death*, will leave many readers talking for years to come. This poem then, puts on immortality through an act of mere creativity. You can say that creativity was captured at all angles in this outstanding piece of literature.

2) Because I could not stop for Death

Because I could not stop for Death—
He kindly stopped for me—
The Carriage held but just Ourselves—
And Immortality.

We slowly drove—He knew no haste
And I had put away
My labor, and my leisure too,
For his Civility—

We passed the School, where Children strove
At Recess-in the Ring—
We passed the Fields of Gazing Grain—
We passed the Setting Sun—

Or rather—He passed Us—

The dews grew quivering and chill—
For only Gossamer, my Gown—
My tippet-only Tulle—

We paused before House that seemed
A Swelling of the Ground—
The Roof was scarcely visible—
The Cornice-in the Ground—

Since then-'tis centuries-and yet
Feels shorter than the Day
I first surmised the Horses' Heads
Were toward Eternity—

Topic Discussion

1. Dickinson used a lot of symbols in this poem. Could you please pick up and explain some of them?

2. Could you find some examples to show Dickinson's writing style?

第二章 现实主义时期文学

第一节　现实主义文学简介

每节导读

本节介绍现实主义文学背景、主要作家作品及主要特点。

现实主义文学产生的历史背景：美国内战结束后到第一次世界大战爆发前，变化冲击着美国社会的政治、经济、文化、宗教等各个方面。

1）其思想和价值体系也发生根本的变化；

2）美国从农业国过渡到工业国、商业国；

3）科技快速发展；

4）城市化进程加快；

5）伴随工业化和城市化而来的是无数劳动人民的苦难，贫富差距越来越大；

6）人们开始怀疑人的本质和上帝仁爱。

新一代的作家对社会现实表现出了极大的兴趣。

现实主义时期文学受资产阶级民主思想影响很大，特点为如实地反映人类现实，表现为对典型环境下的典型性格的刻画，其描写的主要对象是各行各业的芸芸众生。

现实主义时期的三位代表作家：威廉·豪威尔斯，马克·吐温，亨利·詹姆斯。豪威尔斯侧重的是处于上升阶段的中产阶级；马克·吐温是乡土文学的重要代表，主要描写的是他所成长的地方和熟悉的人民；亨利·詹姆斯的创作则表现为心理现实主义，人物多为上层社会人士。

Ⅰ. Historical background

1. Effect of the Civil War

Political and social events influence writers in both theme and technique and this is true with the period called American realism. The most important single influence on American Literature in this period is the American Civil War during which the industrialized Hamiltonian North fought the agrarian Jeffersonian South like two separate countries for supremacy. With the factory defeating the farm, the United States headed toward capitalism. The war, however, led many to question the assumptions shared by the Transcendentalists—natural goodness, the optimistic view of nature and man, benevolent God. Men realized after the war that life was not so good, man was not and God was not. The war actually marked a change in the quality of American life, a downfall of American moral values.

2. Development of Industry and Trade

In the first decades after the Civil War, Americans ceased to be isolated from the world and from each other. Telegraph lines spanned the nation, and in 1866 a trans-Atlantic cable joined America and Europe. The first transcontinental railroad was completed in 1869, linking the Atlantic and the Pacific. Soon the United States had the most extensive railroad system in the world, which in turn generated enormous commercial expansion. The cost of transporting raw materials and finished goods dropped. Inexpensive goods replaced products once made locally by costly handwork. Commerce, too, took the lead in national economy and by 1894 the whole value of industrial output held the first place in the world.

As the population doubled, the national income quadrupled, and by the mid-1890s the United States could boast 4 000 millionaires. The rich prospered mightily, and immense power came to such industrial and banking magnates as John D. Rockefeller, Andrew Carnegie, and J. Pierpont Morgan. Yet the growth of business and industry also widened the gulf between the rich and the poor, giving rise to reform movements and labor unions that voiced the complaints of debt-ridden farmers and of immigrant workers living in city slums and laboring in giant, impersonal factories. It was a time of radiant prospects, when ministers preached (and congregations believed) a belief of wealth, suggesting that riches were at last in league with virtue and the age of unlimited progress had finally dawned. But facts showed that what had been expected to be a "Golden Age" turned out to be a "Gilded Age".

3. Closing of Frontier

The frontier had been a factor of great importance in American life. As long as the frontier was there, people could always hope to escape troubles over the next hill and have a better life ahead. But now the Westward Expansion had pushed the frontier nearer the Pacific coast and settlers found themselves under the manipulation of different forces. As a result, the frontier was about to close and the safety value was ceasing to operate, a reexamination of life began. The worth of the American dream, the idealized, romantic view of man and his life in the new world, began to lose its hold on the imagination of the people.

Ⅱ. Literary Scene of the Age

Although Americans continued to read the works of Irving Cooper, Hawthorne, and Poe, the great age of American romanticism had ended. A new generation of young writers started to write and publish their works different from those in romantic period.

Some new writers appeared, among them Bret Harte, William Dean Howells, Hamlin Garland, and Mark Twain. Their background and training were middle-class and journalistic rather than academic. Influenced by such Europeans as Flaubert, Balzac, Dostoyevsky, and Tolstoy, America's most notable new authors established a literature of realism. They sought to portray American life as it really was, insisting that the ordinary and the local were as suitable for artistic portrayal as the magnificent and the remote.

As in most literary rebellions, the new literature rose out of a desire to renovate the literary theories of the previous age. Realists had grown scornful of artistic ideals that had been trivialized, worn thin by derivative writers eager to supply the "great popular want" for sentiment, adventure, and "tingling excitement". In contrast, the realists had what Henry James called "a powerful impulse to mirror the unmitigated realities of life". Earlier in the nineteenth century, James Fenimore Cooper had insisted on the author's right to present an idealized and poetic portrait of life, to avoid representations of "squalid misery". But by the last of the nineteenth century the realists, and the literary naturalists who followed them, rejected the portrayal of idealized characters and events. Instead, they sought to describe the wide range of American experience and to present the subtleties of human personality, to portray characters who were not simply all good or all bad.

Realism had originated in France as realism, a literary doctrine that called for "reality and truth" in the depiction of ordinary life. "Realism" first appeared in the United States in the literature of local color, a combination of romantic plots and realistic descriptions of things immediately observable: the dialects, customs, sighs, and sounds of regional America, Bret Harte in the 1860s was the first American writer of local color to achieve wide popularity, presenting stories of western mining towns with colorful gamblers, outlaws, and scandalous women. Thereafter editors, ever sensitive to public taste, demanded, and such writers as Harte, Harriet Beecher Stowe, Kate Chopin, Hamlin Garland, and Mark Twain provided, regional stories and tales of the life of America's Westerners, Southerners and Easterners' local color. Local Colorism is defined as one having such a quality texture and background that it could not have been written in any other place or by anyone else than a native.

The champion and one of the representatives of 19th century literary realism in America was William Dean Howells. He defined realism as "nothing more and nothing less than the truthful treatment of material," and he best exemplified his theories in such novels as *A Modern Instance* (1882), *The Rise of Silas Lapham* (1885), and A Hazard of New Fortunes (1890). Howells spoke for a generation of writers who attempted to sustain an objective point of view and who found their subject matter in the experiences of the American middle class, describing their houses, families, and jobs, their social customs, achievements, and failures. The bulk of America's literary realism was limited to optimistic treatment of the surface of life. Yet the greatest of America's realists, Henry James and Mark Twain, moved well beyond a superficial portrayal of 19th-century America. James probed deeply at the individual psychology of his characters, writing in a rich and intricate style that supported his intense scrutiny of complex human experience. Mark Twain, breaking out of the narrow limits of local color fiction, described the breadth of American experience as no one had ever done before or since, and he created, in *The Adventures of Huckleberry Finn* (1884), a masterpiece of American realism that is one of the great books of world literature.

In the 1880s, Howells spoke out against the writing of a bleak fiction of failure and despair. He called for the treatment of the smiling aspects of life as being the more "American", insisted that America was truly a land of hope and of possibility that should be reflected in its literature. But at the end of the century, a generation of writers arose whose ideas of the workings of the universe and whose perception of society's disorders led them to naturalism, which is a theory applied scientific concept and methods to such problem as plot development and characterization. America's literary naturalists dismissed the validity of comforting moral truths. They attempted to achieve extreme objectivity and frankness, presenting characters of low social and economic classes who were dominated by their environment and heredity. In presenting the extremes of life, the naturalists sometimes displayed an affinity to the sensationalism of early romanticism, but unlike their romantic predecessors, the naturalists emphasized that the world was amoral, that men and women had no free will, that their lives were controlled by heredity and the environment, that religious "truths" were illusory, that the destiny of humanity was misery in life and oblivion in death.

Important features of American realism are as follows:

1) Objective description of reality life and concern for the commonplace. Realist writers objectively described reality and truthfully depicted life around them.

2) Exposure of dark side in human life and human nature. Realist writers wrote to express their dissatisfaction with the ruling class and described human cruelty and greed.

3) Creation of typical character in typical surroundings and pursuit for verisimilitude of detail derived from observation.

4) They were more or less influenced by American Bourgeois democracy. They sought to reform the society; some like Howells even tended to beautify the society.

Another literary phenomenon that is worth mentioning is the Muckraking Movement which started in the 1900s with the aim to expose corruption and evil existing in American social, economic and political life.

第二节　现实主义重要作家与作品

每节导读

本节主要介绍美国现实主义代表作家马克·吐温及其代表作《哈克贝利·费恩历险记》，亨利·詹姆斯及其代表作《贵妇人的画像》。

马克·吐温是美国现实主义文学的奠基人之一。1869 年他出版了《傻子国外旅行记》，真正开始了他的文学生涯。他早期的作品充满了乐观幽默的基调，但后期的作品由于生意上的挫折和个人的灾难而充斥了一种悲观绝望的情绪，颇有宿命论的倾向。他的代表作是《哈克贝利·费恩历险记》。在书中，他成功地塑造了主人公哈克的形象并开创了美国小说口语化的先河，对后世的作家产生了巨大的影响。

亨利·詹姆斯既是小说家、剧作家、散文家，又是评论家，开创了“国际小说”和“国际题材”，并被誉为心理分析小说的先驱。他的创作分三个阶段：

①“国际题材”：描写美国和欧洲新老世界的不同素质，并加以对比，赞颂美国人的天真和纯洁；

②尝试了不同的题材和形式，如戏剧创作；

③又回到“国际题材”。

其主要作品有：早期的《黛西·米勒》、《贵妇人的画像》等，晚期则有《鸽翼》及《金碗》等。

Ⅰ. Mark Twain (1835—1910)

1. Life and Works

Samuel Langhorne Clemens was born in Florida, Missouri, on November 30, 1835; When he was four, his family moved to Hannibal, Missouri, a small township on the Mississippi, where he continued to live until the age of eighteen. His formal education ended soon after his father's death in 1847, when he became a printer's apprentice, working for a time on the Missouri Courier, under the editorship of his elder brother, Orion.

From 1853, Mark Twain traveled widely, as a journeyman printer, in the Eastern States and in the west. As a result of a steamboat journey down the Mississippi, he met Horace Bixby, the captain of the boat, and turned to a career on the river. After an apprenticeship of one and a half years, he became a licensed pilot in 1859. He left the Mississippi at the outbreak of the Civil War, and became, in swift succession, an army volunteer, a gold prospector in Nevada, a timber speculator and a journalist. He met Artemus Ward and Bret Harte during this time and turned increasingly towards a professional literary career. While working for the Virginia City Enterprise, he adopted the pseudonym "Mark Twain", the cry of a boatman taking soundings, and meaning two fathoms, i. e. twelve feet. The choice of name may have been characteristically ironic, since two fathoms was presumably an uncomfortable depth for a large steamboat.

Mark Twain's first book, *Jumping Frog*, appeared in 1865. Assignments as a travelling reporter to the Sandwich Islands and then to the Mediterranean and Middle East brought him success as a public lecturer and also material for his first major literary success, *Innocents Abroad* (1869). He married Olivia Landon the following year, and in 1871 established himself as a successful writer, in a large mansion in Hartford, Connecticut. He continued to live there for the next seventeen years. It was during this period that his most famous works were written, *Roughing It* (1872), *The Gilded Age* (1873), *The Adventures of Tom Sawyer* (1876), *Life on the Mississippi* (1883), *and The Adventures of Huckleberry Finn* (1884). He combined his writing with public lecturing and foreign traveling, becoming American ambassador at large, and acquiring an international reputation as humorist-cum-frontier-philosopher. He indulged in frequent financial speculation, particularly in typesetting machinery and the Charles L. Webster publishing house.

Although Mark Twain literary reputation became increasingly secure (received an M. A. of Yale in 1888), his intellectual pessimism and despair of human nature increased with his success. *The Gilded Age*, written in collaboration with his Dudley Warner, had already pointed towards his uneasy acceptance of the values of 19th-century American society. In the year of *Pudd'nhead Wilson's* publication (1894), he was bankrupted by the failure of both the type-setting and publishing companies, and was compelled to restart his travels to raise the money to discharge his debts. It was during his absence on this voyage that his daughter Susy died. In 1898, the year that he cleared his debts, he wrote three works expressing his acute pessimism, *The Man that Corrupted Hadleyburg* (published 1900), the philosophizing treatise *What is Man?* (published 1906) and *The Mysterious Stranger* (published posthumously in 1916). From this time until his death, he maintained a bitter skepticism, relieved at times by outraged commentary on world affairs, notably on Belgian cruel acts in the Congo and American behavior in the Philippines. His last years were saddened by losing his relations; his wife dying in 1904 and his daughter Jean in 1909. In 1906 he started preparing material for his Autobiography and in 1907 received an honorary doctorate of Oxford University. He died at Redding, Connecticut, on 21 April 1910, at the age of seventy-five.

2. Technique in writing

1) Humor: Mark Twain is considered to be a master of humor. He was skillful at capturing things that Americans thought funny. His humor is of different kinds, for example, tall-tale and dead-pan. Tall-tale is a type of frontier anecdote characterized by exaggeration or understatement with realistic details of characters or local customs that work toward a humors effect. Dead-pan is originally a type of oral humor in telling which the teller has a straight face

with the listener laughing.

2) Language: Mark Twain used dialects as form of art. He was not the first to use dialect in the works but it was he who made dialect an accepted form of art. His *The Adventures of Huckleberry Finn* is written in the colloquial style with different versions of dialects, in the speech of uneducated Americans.

3) Satire: Mark Twain's social criticism is made sharp with the use of satire. In all his life, Mark Twain loved life and people and freedom and justice. In his books, he criticized tyranny and iniquity, despised meanness and cruelty in a humorous way.

3. Introduction to *The Adventure of Huckleberry Finn*:

1) Plot overview: The story takes place along the Mississippi River, on both sides of which there was unpopulated wilderness and a dense forest. Along this river floats a small raft, with two people on it: one is ignorant, uneducated Black slave named Jim and the other is a little white boy of about the age of thirteen, called Huckleberry Finn, or Huck Finn. Huck Finn comes from the very lowest level of society. His father is the poor town drunkard who would willingly commit any crime just for the pure pleasure of it. Huck Finn is an outcast, with no mother, no home, sleeping in barrels, eating scraps and leavings and dressed in rags. The book relates the story of the escape of Jim from slavery and, more important, how Huck Finn, floating along with him and helping him as best he could, changed his mind, his prejudice, about Black people, and came to accept Jim as a man and as a close friend as well.

2) Themes:

① The book shows the author's view on civilization. Life on the river represents the ideal life while shore symbolizes corrupting civilization.

②It is a book containing sharp social criticism. Through Huck Finn's eyes, he observed many brutal and corrupting things in the society.

③This novel reflects the moral growth of Huck Finn. At the beginning, Huck Finn believes that blacks are lower than whites as inferior animals. However, Through their travel down the river, Huck Finn gets to know Jim better and becomes more and more convinced that he is not only a man, but also a good man. He reaches his moral maturity when he decides to help Jim against the law.

4. Selected reading:

The Adventures of Huckleberry Finn

CHAPTER XXXI

We dasn't stop① again at any town, for days and days; kept right along down the river. We was down south in the warm weather, now, and a mighty long ways from home. We begun to come to trees with Spanish moss on them, hanging down from the limbs like long gray beards. It was the first I ever see it growing, and it made the woods look solemn and dismal. So now the frauds② reckoned they was out of danger, and they begun to work the villages again.

First they done a lecture on temperance; but they didn't make enough for them both to get drunk on. Then in another village they started a dancing school; but they didn't know no more how to dance than kangaroo does; so the first prance they made, the general public jumped in and danced them out of town. Another time they tried a go at yellocution; but they didn't yellocute long till the audience got up and give them a solid good cussing and made them skip out. They tackled missionarying, and mesmerizering, and doctoring, and telling fortunes, and a little of everything; but they couldn't seem to have no luck. So at last they got just about dead broke, and laid around the raft, as she floated along, thinking and thinking, and never saying nothing, by the half a day at a time, and dreadful blue③ and desperate.

And at last they took a change, and begun to lay their heads together in the wigwam and talk low and confidential two or three hours at a time. Jim and me got uneasy. We didn't like the look of it. We judged they was studying up some kind of worse deviltry than ever. We turned it over and over, and at last we made up our minds they was going to break into somebody's house or store, or was going into the counterfeit—money business, or something. So then we was pretty scared, and made up an agreement that we wouldn't have nothing in the world to do with such actions, and if we ever got the least show we would give them the cold shake, and clear out and leave them behind. Well, early one morning we hid the raft in a good safe place about two mile below a little bit of a shabby village, named Pikesville, and the king he went ashore, and told us all to stay hid whilst he went up to town and smelt around to see if anybody had got any wind of the Royal Nonesuch there yet. ("House to rob, you mean," says I to myself, "And when you get through robbing it you'll come back here and wonder what's become of me and Jim and the raft—and you'll have to take it out in wondering.") And he said if he warn't back by midday, the duke and me would know it was all right, and we was to come along.

So we staid where we was. The duke he fretted arid sweated around, and was in a mighty sour way. He scolded us for everything, and we couldn't seem to do nothing right; he found fault with every little thing. Something was a-brewing, sure. I was good and glad when midday come and no king; we could have a change, anyway? and maybe a chance for the change, on top of it. So me and the duke went up to the village, and hunted around there for the king, and by-and-by we found him in the back-room of a little low doggery, very tight, and a lot of loafers bullyragging him for sport, and he a cussing and threatening[4] with all his might, and so tight he couldn't walk, and couldn't do nothing to them. The duke he begun to abuse him for an old fool, and the king begun to sass back; and the minute they was fairly at it, I lit out, and shook the reefs out of my hind legs, and spun down the river road like a deer—for I see our chance; and I made up my mind that it would be a long day before they ever see me and Jim again. I got down there all out of breath but loaded up with joy, and sung out—Set her loose, Jim, we're all right, now! But there warn't no answer, and nobody come out of the wigwam. Jim was gone! I set up a shout—and then another—and then another one; and run this way and that in the woods, whooping and screeching; but it warn't no use—old Jim was gone. Then I set down and cried; I couldn't help it. But I couldn't set still long. Pretty soon I went out on; the road, trying to think what I better do, and I run across a boy walking, and asked him if he'd seen a stranger nigger, dressed so and so, and he says:

"Yes."

"Whereabouts?" says I.

Down to Silas Phelps's[5] place, two mile below here. He's a run-away nigger, and they've got him. Was you looking for him?

"You bet I ain't! I run across him in the woods about an hour or two ago, and he said if I hollered he'd cut my livers out-and told me to lay down and stay where I was; and I done it. Been there ever since; afeard[6] to come out."

"Well," he says, "You needn't be afeard no more, becuz they've got him. He run off f'm down South, som'ers.[7]"

"It's a good job they got him."

"Well, I reckon! There's two hundred dollars reward on him. It's like picking up money out'n the road."

"Yes, it is—and I could'a' had it if I'd been big enough; I see him first. Who nailed him?"

"It was an old fellow—a stranger—and he sold out his chance in him for forty dollars, becuz he's got to go up the river and can't wait. Think o' that, now! You bet I'd wait, if it was seven year."

"That's me, every time," says I. "But maybe his chance ain't worth no more than that, if he'll sell it so cheap. Maybe there's something ain't straight about it."

"But it is, though—straight as a string. I see the handbill myself. It tells all about him, to a dot—paints him like a picture, and tellls the plantation he's frum, below Newr leans. No—sirreebob, they ain't no trouble'bout that speculation, you bet you. Say, gimme a chaw tobacker, won't ye?[8]"

I didn't have none, so he left. I went to the raft, and set down in, wigwam to think. But I couldn't come to nothing. I thought till I wore my head sore, but I couldn't see no way out of the trouble. After all this long journey, and after all we'd done for them scoundrels, here was it all come to nothing, everything all busted up and ruined, because they could have the heart to serve Jim such a trick as that, and make him a slave again all his life, and amongst strangers, too, for forty dirty dollars.

Once I said to myself it would be a thousand times better for Jim to be a slave at home where his family was, as long as he'd got to be a slave, and so I'd better write a letter to Tom Sawyer and tell him to tell Miss Watson where he was. But I soon give up that notion, for two things: she'd be mad and disgusted at his rascality and ungratefulness for leaving her, and so she'd sell him straight down the river again; and if she didn't, everybody naturally despises an ungrateful nigger, and they'd make Jim feel it all the time, and so he'd feel ornery and disgraced. And then think of me! It would get all around, that Huck Finn helped a nigger to get his freedom; and if I was to ever see anybody from that town again, I'd be ready to get down and lick his boots for shame. That's just the way: a person does a low—down thing, and then he don't want to take no consequences of it. Thinks as 1ong as he can hide it, it ain't no disgrace. That was my fix exactly. The more I studied about this, the more my conscience went to grinding me, and the more wicked and low—down and ornery I got to feeling. And at last, when it hit me all of a sudden that here was the plain hand of Providence slap-ping me in the face and letting me know my wickedness was being watched all time from up there⑨ in heaven, whilst I was stealing a poor old woman's nigger that hadn't ever done me no harm, and now was showing me theie's One that's alway on the lookout, and ain't agoing to allow no such miserable doings to go only just so fur and no further. I most dropped in my tracks I was so scared. Well, I tried the best I could to kinedrsoften it up somehow for myself, by saying I was brung up wicked, and so I warn't so much to blame; but something inside of me kept saying "There was the Sunday school, you could'a'gone to it; and if you'd'a' done it they'd'a' learnt you there that people that acts as I'd been acting about that nigger goes to everlasting fire."

It made me shiver. And I about made up my mind to pray; and see if I couldn't try to quit being the kind of a boy I was, and be better. So I kneeled down. But the words wouldn't come. Why wouldn't they? It warn't no use to try and hide it from Him. Nor from me, neither. I knowed very well why they wou1dn't come. It was because my heart warn't right; it was because I warn't square; it was because I was playing double. I was letting on to give up sin, but away inside of me I was ho1ding on to the biggest one of all. I was trying to make my mouth say I would do the right thing and the clean thing, and go and write to that nigger's owner and tell where he was; but deep down in me I knowed it was a lie—and he knowed it. You can't pray a lie—I found that out.

So I Was full of trouble, full as I could be; and didn't know what to do. At last I had an idea; and I says, I'll go and write the letter and then see if I can pray. Why, it was astonishing, the way I felt a slight as a feather, right straight off, and my troubles all gone. So I got a piece of paper and a pencil, all glad and excited, and set down and wrote,

> Miss Watson your runaway nigger Jim is down here two mile be-low Pikesville and Mr. Phelps has got him and he will give him up for the reward if you send.
>
> HUCK FINN

I felt good and all washed clean of sin for the first time I had ever felt so in my life, and I knowed I could pray now. But I didn't do it straight off, but laid the paper down and set there thinking, thinking how good it was all this happened so, and how near I come to being lost and going to hell. And went on thinking and got to thinking over our trip down the river; and I see Jim before me, all the time, in the day, and in the nighttime, sometimes moonlight, sometimes storms, and we a floating along, talking and singing, and laughing. But somehow I couldn't seem to strike no places to harden me against him, but only the other kind. I'd see him standing my watch on top of his'n, 'stead of calling me, so I could go on sleeping; and see him how glad he was when I come back out of the fog; and when I come to him again in the swamp, up there where the feud was; and such-like times; and would always call me honey, and pet me, and do everything he could think of for me, and how good he always was; and at last I struck the time saved him by telling the men we had smallpox aboard, and he was so grateful, and said I was the best friend old Jim ever had in the world, and the only one he's got now; and then I happendec to look around, and see that paper.

It was a close place. I took it up, and held it in my hand. I was a-trembling, because I'd got to decide, forever, betwixt two things, and I knowed it. I studied a minute, sort of holding my breath, and then says to myself:

"All right, then, I'll go to hell" —and tore it up.

It was awful thoughts, and awful words, but they was said. And I let them stay said; and never thought no more about reforming. I shoved the whole thing out of my head; and said I would take up wickedness again, which was in my line, being brung up to it, and the other warn't. And for a starter, I would go to work and steal Jim out of slavery again; and if I could think up anything worse, I would do that, too; because as long as I was in, and in for good, I might as well go the whole hog.

Then I set to thinking over how to get at it, and turned over considerable many ways in my mind; and at last fixed up a plan that suited me. So then I took the bearings of a woody island that was down the river a piece, and as soon as it was fairly dark I crept out with my raft and went for it, and hid it there, and then turned in. I slept the night through, and got up before it was light, and had my breakfast, and put on my store clothes, and tied up some others and one thing or another in a bundle, and took the canoe and cleared for shore. I landed below where I judged was Phelp's place, hid my bundle in the woods, and then filled up the canoe with water, and loaded rocks into her and sunk her where I could find her again when I wanted her, about a quarter of a mile below a little steam sawmill that was on the bank.

Then I Struck up the road, and when I passed the mill I see a sign on it, "Phelps's Sawmill," and when I come to the farm—houses, two or three hundred yards further along, I kept my eyes peeled, but didn't see nobody around, though it was good daylight, now. But l didn't mind, because I didn't want to see nobody just yet—I only wanted to get the lay of the land. According to my plan, I was going to turn up there from the village, not from below. So I just took a look, and shoved along, straight for town. Well, the very first man I see, when I got there, was the duke. He was sticking up a bill for the Royal Nonesuch—three-night performance—like that other time. They had the cheek, them frauds! I was right on him, before I could shirk. He looked astonished, and says:

"Hel—lo! Where'd you come from?" Then he says, kind of glad and eager,"Where's the raft? —got her in a good place?"

I says:

"Why, that's just what I was agoing to ask your grace.

Then he didn't look so joyful—and says:

"What was your idea for asking me?" he says.

"Well," I says, "When I see the king in that doggery yesterday, I says to myself, we can't get him home for hours, till he's soberer; so I went a loafing around town to put in the time, and wait. A man up and offered me ten cents to help him pull a skiff over the river and back to fetch a sheep, and so I went along; but when we was dragging him to the boat, and the man left me a—holt of the rope and went behind him to shove him along, he was too strong for me, and jerked loose and run, and we after him. We didn't have no dog, and so we had to chase him all over the country till we tired him out. We never got him till dark, then, we fetched him over, and I started down for the raft. When I got there and see it was gone, I says to myself, 'they've got into trouble—leand had to leave; and they've took my nigger, which is the only nigger I've got in the world, and now I'm in a strange country, and ain't got no property no more, nor nothing, and no way to make my living'; so I set down and cried. I slept in the woods all night. But what did become of the raft then? —and Jim, poor Jim!"

"Blamed if I know—that is, what's become of the raft. That old fool had made a trade and got forty dollars, and when we found him in the doggery the loafers had matched half dollars with him and got every cent but what he'd spent for whisky; and when I got him home late last night and found the raft gone, we said, That little rascal has stole our raft and shook us, and run off down the river."

"I wouldn't shake my nigger, would I? —the only nigger I had in the world, and the only property."

"We never thought of that. Fact is, I reckon we'd come to consider him our nigger; yes, we did consider him so—goodness knows we had trouble enough for him. So when we see the raft was gone, and we flat broke,[10] there warn't anything for it but to try the Royal Nonesuch' another shake. And I've pegged along ever since, dry as a powder-horn. Where's that ten cents? Give it here."

I had considerable money, so I give him ten cents, but begged him to spend it for something to eat, and give me some I because it was all the money I had, and I hadn't had nothing to eat since yesterday. He never said nothing. The next minute he whirls on me and says:

"Do you reckon that nigger would blow on us? We'd skin him if he done that!"

"How can he blow? Hain't he run off?"

"No! That old fool sold him, and never divided with me, and the money's gone."

"Sold him?" I says, and begun to cry; "why, he was my nigger, and that was my money. Where is he? —I want my nigger."

"Well, you can't get your nigger, that's all—so dry up your blub-bering. Looky here—do you think you'd venture to blow on us? Blamed if I think I'd trust you. Why, if you was to blow on us?"

He stopped, but I never see the duke look so ugly out of his eyes before. I went on a whimpering [11], and says:

"I don't want to blow on nobody; and I ain't got no time to blow, nohow; I got to turn out and find my nigger."

He looked kinder bothered, and stood there with his bills fluttering on his arm, thinking, and wrinkling up his forehead. At last he says:

"I'll tell you something. We got to be here three days. If you'll promise you won't blow, and won't let the nigger blow, I'll tell you where to find him."

So I promised, and he says:

"A farmer by the name of Silas Ph—" and then he stopped. You see he started to tell me the truth; but when he stopped, that way, and begun to study and think again, I reconed he was changing his mind. And so he was. He wouldn't trust me, he wanted to make sure of having me out of the way the whole three days. So pretty soon he says: "The man that bought him is named Abram Foster—Abram G. Foster and he lives forty mile back here in the country, on the road to Lafayette."

"All right," I says, "I can walk it in three days. And I'll start this very afternoon." "No you won't, you'll start now'; and don't you lose any time about it, neither, nor do any gabbing by the way. Just keep a tight tongue in your head and move right along, and then you won't get into trouble with us, d'ye hear?" That was the order I wanted, and that was the one I played for. I wanted to be left free to work my plans.

"So clear out," he says; "and you can tell Mr. Foster whatever you want to. Maybe you can get him to believe that Jim is your nigger—some idiots don't require documents—leastways I've heard there's such down South here. And when you tell him the handbill and the reward's bogus, maybe he'll believe you when you explain to him what the idea was for getting'em out. Go'long, now, and tell him anything you want to; but mind you don't work your jaw any between here and there."

So I left, and struck for the back country. I did't look around, but I kinder felt like he was watching me. But I knowed I could tire him out at that. I went straigth out in the country as much as a mile, before I stopped; then I doubled back through the woods towards Phelps's. I reckoned I better start in on my plan straight off, without fooling around, because I wanted to stop Jim's mouth till these fellows could getaway. I didn't want no trouble with their kind. I'd seen all I wanted to of them, and wanted to get entirely shut of them.

NOTES

①We dasn't stop=we didn't dare stop. 本章出现的不规范英语，如主语和谓语动词的数不一致或动词的时态和形式的误用等，是作者刻意突出的语言风格。

②the frauds: person of thing that decieves 指书中冒充公爵和国王的两个骗子。

③dreadful blue: Dreadful=dreadfully, blue means depressed 愁眉苦脸。

④and he a cussing and threatening=and he was cursing and threatening 他咒骂恐吓。

⑤Silas Phelps: the name of Tom's uncle to whom the frauds sold Jim 塞拉斯·菲尔普斯，汤姆的姨父，骗子把吉姆卖给了他。

⑥afread（古）=afraid 恐怕

⑦He run off f'm down South som'ers=He ran off from down South, somewhere. 他从南部什么地方逃跑出来的

⑧Say, gimme a chaw tabacker, won't ye? =Say, give me a chew of tobacco, won't you? 嘿，给我一口烟行吗?

⑨up there:（Am. Slang）heaven（美俚）天堂

⑩We flat broke=We were flat broke 我们一个子儿也没有了

⑪whimpering=crying 哭泣

Topic Discussion

1. Analyze Mark Twain's writing style.
2. Discuss the character of Huck in the chapter.

Ⅱ. Henry James (1843—1916)

1. Life and works

Henry James was born in New York City, the second child of wealthy, somewhat, aristocratic parents. His father, Henry James, Sr., was a philosopher and a friend of Emerson's; his brother William became a prominent philosopher and psychologist. Henry James, Sr. disapproved of most schools in America and consequently, sent his sons to a variety of tutors and European schools in search of the best education for them. The children received the major part of their education at home. The James family's travels in Europe were another source of education for Henry.

When he was growing up in New York, Henry was given a great deal of independence, so much in fact, that he felt isolated from other people. A quiet child among exuberant brothers and cousins, Henry was more often an observer than a participant in their activities. Henry's family lived for a time in Boston, where he became acquainted with New England authors and friends of his father, began his friendship with William Dean Howells, and attended Harvard Law School.

After 1866, James lived in Europe much of the time and in 1875 decided to make it his permanent home. He lived in Paris for a year, where he met Turgenev (屠格涅夫), Flaubert (福楼拜), and Zola (左拉). The next year he settled in London and lived there and in the English countryside for the rest of his life. In 1915, a year before his death, to show his support to England in World War I, James became a British citizen.

In 1871 *the Atlantic Monthly* (大西洋月刊) serialized James's first novel, *Watch and Ward*, with which he hoped, but failed, to achieve fame. Years later, looking back and finding such early works *Hideous*, James preferred to declare that his first real novel was *Roderick Hudson* (1875). The next decade saw the appearance of novels that brought him popular success: *The American* (1877), with its "international theme" of the traditionless American confronting the complexity of European life; *Daisy Miller* (1878), which one American critic described as "an outrage to American girl-hood" but which brought James his first international fame; and *The Portrait of a Lady* (1881), the finest example of James's early work.

The most ambitious novels of James's second period, *The Bostonians* (1886), *The Princess Casamassima* (1886), and *The Tragic Muse* (1890), were public failures as were his attempts, in the 1890s, to write for the stage. But he continued to write short stories and novels, and while James never recovered his early popularity, his last, full-length novels, *The Wings of the Dove* (1902), *The Ambassadors* (1903), and *The Golden Bowl* (1904) exemplify the mature and formidable style of a third literary period, which critics have come to praise as "the Major Phase".

2. Position in Literature

Unlike Howells, James's greatest influence was exerted not on his own age but on the one that followed. When he was alive, he was not welcomed by readers chiefly because of the following reasons. First, readers of his homeland were not really familiar with him since he mostly lived in Europe. Second, he was good basically at "international theme" which is thought to be too narrow in subject matter. Third, his language was considered too difficult and complex. At the time of his death, James's audience was small, his impact slight. He had been attacked for criticizing his native land and for the narrow emotional and social range of his characters. And he had been ridiculed for the obscure and costive style of his final period, a style that was able to express the subtlest meanings but was based on the assumption that the reader was as well educated as exquisitely attuned, and in as little hurry as the author. James's latest were derided as "cathedrals of frosted glass", and at the end of his life he acknowledged that his writing had become "insurmountably unsaleable".

Yet his influence has come to be immense. In twenty-two novels and over a hundred short stories, and in his critical commentaries, he made major contributions to the art of fiction itself, helping to transform the novel from its alliances with journalism and romantic storytelling into an art form of penetrating analysis of individuals confronting society, chronicles of the psychological perceptions that James himself defined as the highest form of experience. Now literary history has restored James' position in American literature as one of the great realist writers. People have recognized his unique contribution to American literature in aspects of international theme, psychological realism and refined language.

3. Introduction to *The Portrait of a Lady*

1) Plot overview:

It tells about the fate of an American girl, Isabel Archer, whose father died and who had been visited by her aunt, Mrs. Touchett. She proved so attractive to the older woman that Mrs. Touchertt decided to give her the advantage of more cosmopolitan experience, and Isabel was quickly carried off to Europe so she was full of hope, and with a will to live a free and noble life. When she was in Europe, she had three suitors. One was a young nobleman, Lord Warburton who was kind and thoughtful. However, when he proposed to her, he was refused. Another suitor was her American friend Caspar Goodwood, who followed her abroad. Isabel showed her indifference to him. Eventually, after receiving a fortune given to her by her uncle, Isabel married Gilbert Osmond who was an American artist. However, after marriage, her life was not happy because Osmond was interested only in Isabel's money. She also realized that she had been the victim of a fortune-hunting plot. So her dreams and expectations evaporated.

2) Theme:

During his lifetime, Henry James's fame rested largely on his handling of his major fictional theme, "the International theme": American innocence in face of European sophistication and the conflicts arising from the confrontations. For the American it was a process of progression from inexperience to experience, from innocence to knowledge and maturity. In *The Portrait of a Lady*, Isabel is full of hope while arriving in Europe. She has a will to live a free and noble life, but she falls prey to the sinister designs of two vulgar and unscrupulous expatriates, Madam Merle and Gilbert Osmond. Isabel's unawareness of evil around her and her money combined to work her undoing.

3) Technique:

①Absence of narrator: The novel is narrated through the eyes of the center character or a kind of invisible narrator. Henry James believes that to correspond to life the author should avoid artificial omniscience as much as possible. James makes his characters reveal themselves with minimal intervention of the author. In *The Portrait of a Lady* James placed the center of the subject in the consciousness of the heroine, Isabel Archer. Isabel's vigil and meditation is presented as a very elaborate internal monologue, so that the reader is within her mind and has her inner vision.

②Psychological realism: Henry James concentrates and records the inner conflicts of the characters in the novel. Thus because James emphasizes the inner awareness and inward movements of his characters in face of outside occurrence rather than merely delineating their environment in any detail, he became probably the first of the modern psychological analysts in the novel.

4. Selected Reading:

The Portrait of a Lady

Chapter Ⅶ

The two amused themselves, time and again, with talking of the attitude of the British public as if the young lady had been in a position to appeal to it; but in fact the British public remained for the present profoundly indifferent to Miss Isabel Archer, whose fortune had dropped her, as her cousin said, into the dullest house in England. Her gouty uncle received very little company, and Mrs Touchett, not having cultivated relations with her husband's neighbours, was not warranted in expecting visits from them. She had, however, a peculiar taste; she liked to receive cards. For what is usually called social intercourse ① she had very little relish; but nothing pleased her more than to find her hall table whitened with oblong morsels of symbolic pasteboard. She flattered herself that she was a very just woman, and had mastered the sovereign truth that nothing in this world is got for nothing. She had played no social part as mistress of Gardencourt, and it was not to be supposed that, in the surrounding country, a minute account should be kept of her comings. But it is by no means certain that she die not feel it to be wrong that so little notice was taken of them and that her failure (really very gratuitous) to make herself important in the neighbourhood had not much to do with the acrimony ② of her allusions to her husband's adopted country. Isabel presently found herself in the singular situation of defening the British constitution against her aunt; Mrs Touchett having formed the habit of sticking pins into this venerable instrument. Isabel always felt an impulse to pull out the pins; not that she imagined they inflicted any damage on the tough old parchment, but because it seemed to her aunt might make better use of her sharpness. She was very critical herself—it was incidental to her sex, and her antionalit but she was very sentimental as well, and there was something in Mrs Touchett's dryness that set her own moral fountains flowing.

'Now what's your point of view?' she asked of her aunt. 'When you criticize everything here you should have a point of view. Yours doesn't seem to be American you thought everything over there so disagreeable. When I have mine, it's thoroughly American!'

'My dear young lady,' said Mrs Touchett, 'there are as many points of view in the world as there are people of sense to take them. You may say that doesn't make them very numerous American? Never in the world; that's shockingly narrow. My point of view, thank God, is personal!'

Isabel thought this a better answer than she admitted; it was a tolerable description of her own manner of judging, but it would not have sounded well for her to say so. On the lips of a person less advanced in life and less enlightened by experience than Mrs Touchett such a declaration would savour of immodesty, even of arrogance. She risked it nevertheless in talking with Ralph, with whom she talked a great deal and with whom her conversation was of a sort that gave a large licence to extravagance. Her cousin used, as the phrase is, to chaff her; he very soon established with her a reputation for treating everything as a joke, and he was not a man to neglect the privileges such a reputation conferred. She accused him of an odious want of seriousness, of laughing at all things, beginning with himself. Such slender faculty of reverence as he possessed centred wholly upon his father; for the rest, he exercised his wit indifferently upon his father's son, this gentleman's weak lungs, his useless life, his fantastic mother, his friends (Lord Warburton in especial), his adopted, and his native country, his charming new-found cousin, "I keep a band of music in my ante-room" ③, he said once to her. "It has orders to play without stopping; it renders me two excellent services. It keeps the sounds of the world from reaching the private apartments, and it makes the world think that dancing's going on within. ' It was dance-music indeed that you usually heard when you came within ear-shot of Ralph's band; the liveliest waltzes seemed to float upon the air." Isabel often found herself irritated by this perpetual ④ fiddling; she would have liked to pass through the ante-room, as her cousin called it, and enter the private apartments. It mattered little that he had assured her they were a very dismal place; she would have been glad to undertake to sweep them and set them in order. It was but half-hospitality to let her remain outside; to punish him for which Isabel administered innumerable taps with the ferule of her straight young wit. It must be said that her wit was exercised to a large extent in self-defence, for her cousin amused himself with calling her "Columbia" and accusing her of a patriotism so heated that it scorched. He drew a caricature ⑤ of her in which she was represented as a very pretty young woman dressed, on the lines of the prevailing fashion, in the folds of the national banner. Isabel's chief dread in life at this period of her development was that she should appear narrowminded; what she feared next afterwards was that she should really be so. But she nevertheless made no scruple of abounding in her cousin's sense and pretending to sigh for the charms of her native land. She would be as American as it pleased him to regard her, and if he chose to laugh at her she would give him plenty of occupation. She defended England against his mother, but when Ralph sang its praises on purpose, as she said, to work her up, she found herself able to differ from him on a variety of points. In fact, the quality of this small ripe country seemed as sweet to her as the taste of an October pear; and her satisfaction was at the root of the good spirits which enabled her to take her cousin's chaff and return it in kind. If her good humour flagged at moments it was not because she thought herself ill-used, but because suddenly felt sorry for Ralph. It seemed to her he was talking as a blind and had little heart in what he said.

"I don't know what's the matter with you," she observed to him once; "but I suspect you're a great humbug."

"That's you privilege," Ralph answered, who had not been used to being so crudely addressed.

I don't know what you care for; I don't think you care for anything. You don't really care for England when you praise it; you don't care for America even when you pretend to abuse it.

"I care for nothing but you, dear cousin," said Ralph.

"If I could believe even that, I should be very glad."

"Ah well, I should hope so!" the young man exclaimed.

Isabel might have believed it and not have been far from the truth. He thought a great deal about her: she was constantly present to his mind. At a time when his thoughts had been a good deal of a burden to him her sudden arrival, which promised nothing and was an open-handed gift of fate, had refreshed and quickened them, given them wings and something to fly for. Poor Ralph had been for many weeks steeped in melancholy; his outlook, habitually somber, lay under the shadow of a deeper cloud. He had grown anxious about his father, whose gout, hitherto confined to his legs, had begun to ascend into regions more vital. The old man had been gravely ill in the spring, and the doctors had whispered to Ralph that another attack would be less easy to deal with. Just now he appeared disburdened of pain, but Ralph could not rid himself of a suspicion that this was a subterfuge of the enemy, who was waiting to take him off his guard. If the manoeuvre should succeed there would be little hope of any great resistance. Ralph had always taken for granted that his father would survive him—that his own name would be the first grimly called. The father and son had been close companions, and the idea of being left alone with the remnant of a tasteless life on his hands was not gratifying to the young man, who had always and tacitly counted upon his elder's help in making the best of a poor business. At the prospect of losing his great motive Ralph lost indeed his one inspiration. If they might die at the same time it would be all very well; but without the encouragement of his father's society he should barely have patience to await his own turn. He had not the incentive of feeling that he was indispensable to his mother; it was a rule with his mother to have no regrets. He bethought himself of course that it had been a small kindness to his father wish that, of the two, the active rather than the passive party should know the felt wound; he remembered that the old man had always treated his own forecast of an early end as a clever fall cay, which he should be delighted to discredit so far as he might by dying first. But of the two triumphs, that of refuting a sophistical son and that of holding on a while longer to a state of being which, with all abatements, he enjoyed, Ralph deemed it no sin to hope the latter might be vouchsafed to Mr. Touchett.

These were nice questions, but Isabel's arrival put a stop to his puzzling over them. It even suggested there might be compensation for the intolerable ennui of surviving his genial sire. He wondered whether he was harbouring "love" for this spontaneous young woman from Albany; but he judged that on the whole he was not. After he had known her for a week he quite made up his mind to this, and every day he felt a little more sure. Lord Warburton had been right about her; she was a really interesting little figure. Ralph wondered how their neighbour had found it out so soon; and then he said it was only another proof of his friend's high abilities, which he had always greatly admired. If his cousin were to be nothing more than an entertainment to him, Ralph was conscious she was an entertainment of a high order. "A character like that", he said to himself— "a real little passionate force to see at play is the finest thing in nature: It's finer than the finest work of art—than a Greek bas-relief, than a great Titian, than a Gothic cathedral. It's very pleasant to be so well treated where one had least looked for it. I had never been more blue, more bored, than for a week before she came; I had never expected less that anything pleasant would happen. Suddenly I receive a Titian, by the post, to hand on my wall—a Greek bas-relief to stick over my chimney-piece. The key of a beautiful edifice is thrust into my hand, and I'm told to walk in and admire. My poor boy, you've been sadly ungrateful, and now you had better keep very quiet and never grumble again." The sentiment of these reflections was very just; but it was not exactly true that Ralph Touchett had had a key into his hand. His cousin was a very brilliant girl, who would take, as he said, a good deal of knowing; but she needed the knowing, and his attitude with regard to her, though it was contemplative and critical, was not judicial. He surveyed the edifice from the outside and admired it greatly; he looked in at the windows and received an impression of proportions equally fair. But he felt that he saw it only by glimpses and that he had not yet; stood under the roof. The door was fastened, and though he had keys in his pocket he had a conviction that none of them would fit. She was intelligent and generous; it was a fine free nature; but what was she going to do with herself? This question was irregular, for with most women one had no occasion to ask it. Most women did with themselves nothing at all; they waited, in attitudes more or less gracefully passive, for a man to come that way and furnish them with a destiny. Isabel's originality was that she gave one an impression of having intentions of her own. "Whenever she executes them," said Ralph, "may I be there to see!"

NOTES

①social intercourse: social dealings between indeviduals 社会交际

②acrimony: bitterness of temper, manner, language 尖酸刻薄

③ante-room: waiting room 客厅

④perpetual: never ending 永久的，不断的

⑤ caricature: picture of sb. or sth., imitation of a person's voice, behavior, etc., stressing certain features in order to cause amusement or ridicule 漫画

Topic Discussion

Analyze the point of view after reading the chapter.

第三节 自然主义文学简介

每节导读

本节要重点掌握的内容为自然主义文学背景、主要作家及作品、主要特点及其对文学的影响。

自然主义是从现实主义中演化而来的，是现实主义的一种极端形式。达尔文的进化论和法国自然主义作家的作品推动了美国自然主义文学的发展。美国自然主义作家接受了达尔文《物种起源》中自然选择论的消极一面，并用它来解释文学作品中的人物行为。此外他们还受法国小说家和理论家左拉的影响。左拉认为，“文学家对待文学人物及其感情，还有人物和社会生活的描写要像化学家和物理学家对待惰性体以及生理学家对待活体一样。”美国自然主义作家从社会下层中选题，描写社会和自然的受害者形象。人类的“兽性”在社会生活中的反映是他们的主题之一。他们的创作基调比现实主义更悲观，更具有讽刺性。

Ⅰ. Brief Explanation of Naturalism

As a literary movement, naturalism grew out of 19th century realism, and it is an extreme form of realism. It wanted to tell the whole truth about life and to show the reality of that time faithfully. The naturalist writers used scientific method to test the mental and social world of man. They saw the everyday life of the common people against the background of constant historical movement. This greatly affected the traditions of novel, drama, and to some degree, lyric poetry.

Naturalism developed best in America. At first it was a response to a darkening social situation. Jack London (1876—1916) wrote on the bitter futility of life in nature as in *The Call of the Wild*; Hamilin Garland (1860—1900) told about the hard life on the farm; Stephan Crane (1871—1900) wrote about the useless struggle of life in the city. In the second period, naturalists put a sociological emphasis on heredity and environment. Dreiser's *Sister Carrie* (1901) set the interrelationship of sexual and economic desires as controlling factors in the lives of human beings in his fictions.

The American naturalists also recognized the political implications of economic forces. Frank Norris (1870—1902) wrote the two volumes of his projected trilogy *The Epic of Wheat* (1901, 1903), and Upton Sinclair wrote *The Jungle* (1906), *King Coal* (1917), and Oil (1927). Their works influenced the works of the next generation—Dos Passos wrote a trilogy: *U. S. A.* (1930—1936), and Erskine Caldwell wrote *Tobacco Road* (1932) in more or less this manner.

Though we as readers see a bitter and wretched world in the works of American naturalism, yet we cannot deny that we also find humanistic values which are shown through the desire to assert human dignity and the struggle against the social and natural forces one confronts. In American naturalism, three names deserve special mention: Stephen Crane (1871—1900) whose *Maggie: A Girl of the Street* is the first American naturalistic work, Frank Norris (1870—1902) whose *McTeague* is regarded as the manifesto of American naturalism and Theodore Dreiser (1871—1945) in whose *Sister Carrie* American naturalism attained maturity.

Ⅱ. Historical, Social and Theoretical Background

The term of naturalism was introduced to the United States by Frank Norris at the end of the 1880s. The United States were changing into "Modern America" in the economic, social and cultural aspects at that time. Industrialism, science and the new philosophy of life based upon science influenced the change of the country. Industrialism made some people rich, but at the same time created an industrial working class. These workers' life was decided by the external forces beyond their control. There appeared a lot of slums. The conditions in the slums became worse and worse. The city poor lived a life of insecurity, suffering and violence. Westward expansion continued to push the frontier nearer the Pacific coast. But the settlers found themselves controlled by the cruel forces as railroad companies. These forces charged heavy rates and drove farmers to bankruptcy.

The deterministic philosophical theories of the 19th century dominated both natural and social sciences. Charles Darwin (1890—1882), T. H. Huxley

(1825—1895), and Herbert Spencer (1820—1903) made a revolution in the field of science through their writings. In *The Origin of Species* (1859) and *Descent of Man* (1871), Darwin wrote that man had evolved from lower forms of life over a long period of time. Humans were special, not because God had created them in His image. It was because humans had successfully fitted to the changing environmental conditions and had passed on their survival-making characteristics by gene to their next generations. The American naturalists accepted the more negative meaning of this theory. They used it to explain the acts of those characters in literary works. The characters were described as more or less complex combinations of inherited features. Their habits were decided by social and economic forces.

The American naturalists followed the French novelist and theorist Emile Zola's call. Zola held that the literary artist "must operate with characters, passions, human and social data as the chemist and the physicist work on inert bodies, as the physiologist works on living bodies". The American naturalists chose their subjects from the lower ranks of society, and wrote about hard and poor life of the victims of society and nature. One of the most familiar themes in American naturalism is the theme of human "bestiality", especially as an explanation of sexual desire.

Ⅲ. Major features of naturalism

Naturalism has the following major features in thought and technique:

1. Human is controlled by laws of heredity and environment. And since they are controlled, they lack freedom of their own will. The force of nature is greater than that of man. Any human desire to create greatness will be crushed. Therefore, naturalistic fiction has no evidence of effective choice, or free will, or autonomous action.

2. The universe is indifferent and hostile to human desires. Life is meaningless and is only a struggle for survival. Therefore, naturalistic novels reflect the struggle of man to adapt to environment. The Darwinian idea of the survival of the fittest becomes the natural concerns of naturalistic fiction and drama.

3. The naturalists are different from the realists. Though the naturalists write about real life, they do not look at the average. They look at the violent, unpleasant and ugly sides of life. Instead of reflecting the middle-class life, they write about the life of failure, poverty and even crime. They think that the true reality is not found in the smiling aspects of middle-class life. The reality is found when the forces of Nature are most powerful in checking human desires, in keeping humans from realizing their dreams.

4. There are fewer happy endings in the naturalistic fictions than in the realistic ones. Unlike the realist writers, the naturalist writers try to avoid creating the typical character in the typical circumstances. The tone of Naturalistic writings is more ironic and pessimistic and less sympathetic and serious than realistic writings.

5. The naturalist writers report the life of the helpless people truthfully and objectively. They write their novels with a passion for scientific accuracy. There are a lot of factual details in their works. They paint life as it is lived in the slums, and are blamed of telling just the ugly side of it.

Ⅳ. Contributions and limitations of naturalism

Naturalism helps modern literature come to maturity. Naturalists made a lot of new themes and materials easy to get. They encouraged writers to choose and treat subjects in a wider field. They made a continual favor toward biological evolution. Naturalism has bravely battled romance by writing about the daily life actually and by replacing facile idealizing with "a slice of life". Their works are unsophisticated in language.

But naturalism has defects. Naturalist writers rely too often on literal fact and precisely documented circumstance. Their material is often so flat and external as to hold back the search for value and meaning. This greatly limits the variety of creative means at the disposal of the artist.

Now the concept of reality with which 19th century science operated is no longer in use. Human personality and experience which was seen in terms of the broadly typical can not answer the perplexity of postmodern man. Like many other styles before and after it, naturalism can only be viewed as one of several powerful conventions which have left their mark on contemporary literature.

第四节 自然主义重要作家与作品

每节导读

本节主要介绍美国自然主义代表作家斯蒂芬·克兰及其代表作《红色英勇勋章》，西奥多·德莱塞及其代表作《嘉莉妹妹》，要求熟悉作家生平、重要作品、写作特点，了解《红色英勇勋章》和《嘉莉妹妹》的情节、主题等。

斯蒂芬·克兰（Stephan Crane，1871—1900）是美国自然主义小说家、诗人，其作品多反映社会的黑暗面，基调是悲观的。他侧重描写自然、环境及遗传对人的影响，自然主义色彩浓厚。他擅长冷嘲，语言简洁明快，通俗流畅，富有诗意和象征性。

《红色英勇勋章》（*The Red Badge of Courage*，1895）是一部战争小说，描写一名毫无作战经验的年轻士兵弗莱明在战争中从狂热到恐惧，从恐惧到狂怒，勇敢战斗后再回顾战争的成长过程。克兰以他那丰富的想象力、独具匠心的语言和形象生动的意象在读者面前展示了一幅宏大的战争画卷。值得注意的是，克兰使用众多动物意象来表现战争使人丧失理智、失去人性这一主题。

美国另一自然主义代表作家是德莱塞（Theodore Dreiser，1871—1945）。美国自然主义文学创作在德莱塞的作品中趋于成熟。

《嘉莉妹妹》发表于1900年，是德莱塞第一部长篇小说。小说真实地展示了美国下层人民的生活，以及人与人之间冷酷的金钱关系，表现了生命没有目的、人在社会环境和遗传力的控制之下不能操纵自己的命运的思想。嘉莉的悲剧在于她生活在冷酷的世界里，只好受外界力量的摆布。小说中体现的这些自然主义命题标志着美国自然主义文学已日臻成熟。

Ⅰ. Stephen Crane（1871—1900）

1. Life

Stephen Crane was born on November 1, 1871 in a New Jersey Methodist clergyman's family. He was the fourteenth and last child of Mary Peck Crane and Reverend Jonathan Crane. By the time his father died in 1880, Crane had lived in several places in New York and New Jersey and had been thoroughly educated in the faith he was soon to reject. Also around this time, he wrote his poem, "I'd Rather Have". His first short story was Uncle in Pennington

Seminary, where he stayed until 1887. He attended Claverack College, Hudson River Institute, Lafayette College, and Syracuse University between 1888 and 1891. He never graduated from any of these. Then Crane moved into New York. He earned his living as a free-lance journalist. In 1892, *the New York Tribune* published many of his New York City sketches and some Sullivan county tales. He gave a sympathetic report of a worker's strike that criticized middle-class values. That same year, the mechanics union took exception to Crane's article on their annual fete. This resulted in Crane's brother, Townley being fired from the Tribune. After that, Crane lived the down-and-out life of a penniless writer in the slums. During this period, he developed his power as an observer of psychological and social reality. Then he met Hamlin Garland and William Dean Howells who helped him in his work, and also the painters whose impressionism influenced him in his writing.

In 1893, Crane published at his own expense an early version of *Maggie: A Girl of the Street*. The book was taken as the first important naturalist novel in America. In 1894, the Philadelphia Press published an abbreviated version of *The Red Badge of Courage*. During the first half of 1895, Crane traveled in the West. He met Willa Cather there. His first book of poems, *The Black Riders and Other Lines* was published in May. *The Red Badge of Courage* appeared in October. In the novel, Crane talked about war in alarming honesty against the romantic view of war as a symbol of courage and heroism. The book won the praise of writers such as W. D. Howells, Henry James and Joseph Conrad. By December, he was famous when he just had turned twenty-four. In 1896, he published *George's Mother*, *The Little Regiment and Other Stories*, and fell in love with Cora Stewart. They never got married but Crane lived with her for the rest of his life.

In January, 1897, on the way to report the insurgency in Cuba, Crane was shipwrecked off the Florida Coast. After the ship sunk, he struggled 50 hours with the waves before he was saved. This experience became the theme of his best-known short story, "The Open Boat". Four months later, he was in Greece, reporting on the Greco-Turkish War. Moving back to England, he became friends with Conrad, Henry James, Harold Frederic, H. G. Wells, and others. During that year, he wrote most of his great short stories: "The

Open Boat", and "The Blue Hotel".

Crane was never healthy. He began to weaken in 1898 as a result of malaria contracted in Cuba while he was reporting on the Spanish American War. By 1899, Crane was back in England and was living well above his income. Although he published *War Is Kind*, *Active Service and The Monster and Other Stories*, he continued to fall more deeply in debt. By 1900, he suffered from illness and heavy debts. He went to Germany in the hope of recovery, but he died of tuberculosis in Badenweiler, Germany on June 5, 1900. His body was brought back to America and buried at Elizabeth, New Jersey. Crane died at the age of twenty-eight, leaving works that fill ten sizable volumes.

2. Major Works and Influence

Crane was a pioneer writing in the naturalistic tradition. Some critics noted that Crane's writings gave the whole aesthetic movement of the nineties "a sudden direction and a fresh impulse". Crane's writing has been called realistic, naturalistic and impressionistic. He presented incomplete characters and a broken world. It is Crane's power with words and his ability to live with paradox that made him interesting.

In *Maggie: A Girl of the Streets*, Crane describes the slum life vividly and nakedly. It tells the story of a good woman's downfall and destruction in a slum environment. Maggie is a factory girl. She is seduced by a bartender, a friend of her truck-driver brother. When she becomes pregnant, she is thrown out of her home by her mother. She is rejected by her lover and forced into prostitution. She soon drowns herself. In all her short life Maggie has been struggling to escape from the hopeless slum. But she failed. As Crane says, environment is a "tremendous" thing for an insignificant human being to fight against.

The basic theme of the animal man in a cold world runs through his novel *The Red Badge of Courage*. Crane looked into man's primitive emotions and tried to tell the basic truth about human life. In this war novel, there is nothing like heroism on the battlefield. There is only fear of death, cowardice, the natural instinct of man to run from danger.

Crane's best short stories include "Open Boat", "The Blue Hotel", and

"An Experiment in Misery". They all stress the basic Crane motif of environment and heredity overwhelming man.

In his novels, Crane started the modern tradition of telling the truth at all costs about the elemental human situation, and writing about war as a real human experience. This was a revolutionary event both in theme and technique. It produced a far-reaching influence on later writers: Hemingway, Dos Passos, and in recent history, Kurt Vonnegut and other writers. It is no exaggeration to say that Crane anticipated the chief phenomena of American literature in the first few decades of the twentieth century. He was a also a pioneer in the field of modern poetry. His early poems were brief, quotable, and had unrhymed, unorthodox conciseness and impressionistic imagery. These put a significant influence on modern poetry. He and Emily Dickinson are now recognized as the two precursors of Imagist poetry.

3. Introduction to *The Red Badge of Courage*

1) Plot Overview

Stephen Crane's war novel, *The Red Badge of Courage*, is not an ordinary Civil War novel. It is about a young farm boy Henry Fleming's experience in the war.

Henry dreams of becoming a hero in the battlefield. He joins the army, regardless of his mother's warning. But his dreams disappear when he comes to the real battlefield. In the first attack, Henry is boxed in by his fellow soldiers, realizes that he could not run even if he wants to. He fires mechanically, feeling like a cog in a machine.

A second attack causes his sudden panic and flight. He is driven by shame and wanders on the fringe of the battle field. He seems to be helplessly wandering in a nightmarish atmosphere. He meets a "tattered soldier" whose wounds seems "a red badge of courage" to Henry. He repeatedly asks Henry where he is wounded. This embarrassing question increases Henry's sense of guilt. The two men are caught up in the procession of wounded soldiers who make their way to the rear. Among them they see Henry's friend, Jim Conklin. This severely wounded "tall soldier" dies under their frightened gaze after horrible sufferings. After his shocking experience Henry abandons the "tattered man" whose very presence seems to him an accusation. Retreating Union soldiers run past him and one of them knocks him down with the butt of his rifle, ironically giving him the "red badge of courage" he has been longing for.

After regaining consciousness Henry meets a man with "a cheery voice" who takes him back to the regiment. His friend Wilson, believing that Henry has been shot, cares for him tenderly. From then on, Henry's attitude is altogether changed. He feels full of aggressive but specious self-confidence and, because he does not tell others the real cause of his wound, he gets much respect from his fellow soldiers for his brave conduct.

The last chapter shows him fighting like a lion at the head of his unit during a victorious charge. As he and the others march back to their position, Henry reflects on his experiences in the war. Though he revels in his recent success in battle, he feels deeply ashamed of his behavior the previous day, especially his abandonment of the tattered man. But after a moment, he puts his guilt behind him and realizes that he has come through "the red sickness" of battle. He is now able to look forward to peace, feeling a quiet, steady manhood within himself. But at the end of the story, Henry's regiment finds itself crossing the same river that it crossed a few days ago and thus going back to its previous position as if nothing happened. Henry's first impression is right after all: "It was all a trap."

2) Character Analysis

Throughout the novel, Crane refers to Henry Fleming as "the young soldier" and "the youth". He believes in traditional models of courage and honor, and romanticizes the image of dying in battle by invoking the Greek tradition of a dead soldier being laid upon his shield. On the other hand, because he is young, Henry has to experience enough to test these ideas. So his most passionate beliefs are based on fantasies. This makes him seem vain and self-centered.

Henry desires a reputation. He hopes that an impressive deed on the battlefield will make him remembered as a hero among men. Ironically, after fleeing from battle, Henry feels little guilt. He condemns the soldiers who stayed to fight as fools who were not "wise enough to save themselves from the flurry of death". This is how he restores his fragile self-pride. When Henry returns to camp and lies about the nature of his wound, he doubts neither his manhood nor his right to behave as pompously as an experienced soldier. Henry's lack of a true moral sense shows the emptiness of the honor and glory that he seeks. He feels no responsibility to earn these praises. If others call him a hero, he believes he is one.

When Henry finally faces battle, however, he feels a "temporary but sublime absence of selfishness". A great change occurs within him: as he fights, he loses his sense of self. He is no longer interested in winning the praise and attention of other men. He allows himself to disappear into the action and become one component of a great fighting machine. As Henry finds himself deeply involved in battle, the importance of winning a name for himself disappears with the gun smoke. "It was difficult to think of reputation when others were thinking of skins." It is ironic, then, that Henry establishes his reputation at these very moments. Officers who witness his fierce fighting regard him as one of the regiment's best. Henry does not cheat his way to the honor that he so desperately wants when the novel opens; instead, he earns it. This marks a tremendous growth in Henry's character. He learns to reflect on his mistakes, such as his earlier retreat, without defensiveness. He abandons the hope of false heroism and understands more of what it means to be a man.

3) Themes

The novel has several themes. Here we will discuss courage, manhood, the universe's disregard for human life and the dehumanizing effect of war.

①Courage

Henry Fleming defines it, desires it, and finally achieves it. As the novel opens, Henry's understanding of courage is traditional and romantic. At the end of the novel, as the mature Henry marches victoriously from battle, he has a more subtle and complex understanding of courage: it is not simply a function of other people's opinions, but it does include self concerns such as a soldier's regard for his reputation.

②Manhood

Throughout the novel, Henry struggles to preserve his manhood. As he is in the battlefield, he believes he will be a hero. These early conceptions of manhood are simplistic, romantic, adolescent fantasies. By the novel's end,

Henry learns that the measure of one's manhood doesn't lie in one's conduct on the battlefield, but in the complex ways in which one settles one's mistakes and responsibilities.

③The universe's disregard for human life

Crane stresses the universe's disregard for human life in the novel. Henry realizes that the natural world goes on regardless of the manner in which men live and die. In the woods, Henry saw a dead soldier, whose rotting body is a powerful reminder of the universe's indifference to human life. Death is nothing more than a necessary and unremarkable part of nature. As he reflects at the end of the novel: "He had been to touch the great death, and found that, after all, it was but the great death." Here Crane establishes the hard opposing forces in Henry's mind: the belief that human life deserves such distinctions as courage and honor is fruitless, and all human life meets the same end.

④The dehumanizing effect of war

War is seen as a force moving men ruthlessly and blindly as if they were pawns on a chess-board. The young soldier is moved about as if in a box with no free will, serving as an instrument of blind fate. And men fighting are like helpless animals. Crane uses animal images to show this theme. Henry runs away from the battlefield "like a rabbit". Later he fights like "a mad horse". The soldiers in the war "showed their teeth; their eyes shone all white". The battle is "an encounter of strange beaks and claws, as of eagles".

4. Selected Reading

The Red Badge of Courage

CHAPTER 24

The roarings that had stretched in a long line of sound across the face of the forest began to grow intermittent and weaker. The stentorian speeches of the artillery continued in some distant encounter, but the crashes of the musketry had almost ceased. The youth [①] and his friend [②] of a sudden looked up, feeling a deadened form of distress at the waning of these noises, which had become a part of life. They could see changes going on among the troops. There were marchings this way and that way. A battery [③] wheeled leisurely. On the crest of a small hill was the thick gleam of many departing muskets.

The youth arose. "Well, what now, I wonder?" he said. By his tone he seemed to be preparing to resent some new monstrosity in the way of dins and smashes. He shaded his eyes with his grimy hand and gazed over the field.

His friend also arose and stared. "I bet we're goin' t' git along out of this an' back over th' river,[4]" said he.

"Well, I swan!" said the youth.

They waited, watching. Within a little while the regiment received orders to retrace its way. The men got up grunting from the grass, regretting the soft repose. They jerked their stiffened legs, and stretched their arms over their heads. One man swore as he rubbed his eyes. They all groaned "O Lord!" They had as many objections to this change as they would have had to a proposal for a new battle.

They trampled slowly back over the field across which they had run in a mad scamper.

The regiment marched until it had joined its fellows. The reformed brigade, in column, aimed through a wood at the road. Directly they were in a mass of dust-covered troops, and were trudging along in a way parallel to the enemy's lines as these had been defined by the previous turmoil.

They passed within view of a stolid white house, and saw in front of it groups of their comrades lying in wait behind a neat breastwork. A row of guns were booming at a distant enemy. Shells thrown in reply were raising clouds of dust and splinters. Horsemen dashed along the line of entrenchments.[5]

At this point of its march the division curved away from the field and went winding off in the direction of the river. When the significance of this movement had impressed itself upon the youth he turned his head and looked over his shoulder toward the trampled and debris-strewed[6] ground. He breathed a breath of new satisfaction. He finally nudged his friend. "Well, it's all over," he said to him.

His friend gazed backward. "B'Gawd, it is," he assented. They mused.

For a time the youth was obliged to reflect in a puzzled and uncertain way. His mind was undergoing a subtle change. It took moments for it to cast off its battleful ways and resume its accustomed course of thought. Gradually his brain emerged from the clogged clouds, and at last he was enabled to more closely comprehend himself and circumstance.

He understood then that the existence of shot and countershot was in the past. He had dwelt in a land of strange, squalling upheavals and had come forth. He had been where there was red of blood and black of passion, and he was escaped. His first thoughts were given to rejoicings at this fact.

Later he began to study his deeds, his failures, and his achievements. Thus, fresh from scenes where many of his usual machines of reflection had been idle, from where he had proceeded sheeplike, he struggled to marshal all his acts.

At last they marched before him clearly. From this present view point he was enabled to look upon them in spectator fashion and criticise them with some correctness, for his new condition had already defeated certain sympathies.

Regarding his procession of memory he felt gleeful and unregretting, for in it his public deeds were paraded in great and shining prominence. Those performances which had been witnessed by his fellows marched now in wide purple and gold, having various deflections. They went gaily with music. It was pleasure to watch these things. He spent delightful minutes viewing the gilded images of memory.

He saw that he was good. He recalled with a thrill of joy the respectful comments of his fellows upon his conduct.

Nevertheless, the ghost of his flight from the first engagement appeared to him and danced. There were small shoutings in his brain about these matters. For a moment he blushed, and the light of his soul flickered with shame.

A specter of reproach [7] came to him. There loomed the dogging memory of the tattered soldier—he who, gored by bullets and faint of blood, had fretted concerning an imagined wound in another; he who had loaned his last of strength and intellect for the tall soldier; he who, blind with weariness and pain, had been deserted in the field.

For an instant a wretched chill of sweat was upon him at the thought that he might be detected in the thing. As he stood persistently before his vision, he gave vent to a cry of sharp irritation and agony.

His friend turned. "What's the matter, Henry?" he demanded. The youth's reply was an outburst of crimson oaths.

As he marched along the little branch-hung roadway among his prattling companions this vision of cruelty brooded over him. It clung near him always and darkened his view of these deeds in purple and gold. Whichever way his thoughts turned they were followed by the somber phantom of the desertion in the fields. He looked stealthily at his companions, feeling sure that they must discern [8] in his face evidences of this pursuit. But they were plodding in ragged array, discussing with quick tongues the accomplishments of the late battle.

"Oh, if a man should come up an' ask me, I'd say we got a dum good lickin'. [9]"

"Lickin'—in yer [10] eye! We ain't licked, sonny. We're goin' down here aways, swing aroun', an' come in behint'em."

"Oh, hush, with your comin' in behint'em. I've seen all'a that I wanta [11]. Don't tell me about comin' in behint—"

"Bill Smithers, he ses [12] he'd rather been in ten hundred battles than been in that heluva [13] hospital. He ses they got shootin' in th' nighttime, an' shells dropped plum [14] among'em in th' hospital. He ses sech hollerin' [15] he never see."

"Hasbrouck? He's th' best off'cer in this here reg'ment. He's a whale."

"Didn't I tell yeh [16] we'd come aroun' in behint'em? Didn't I tell yeh so? We—"

"Oh, shet yeh mouth! [17]"

For a time this pursuing recollection of the tattered man took all elation from the youth's veins. He saw his vivid error, and he was afraid that it would stand before him all his life. He took no share in the chatter of his comrades, nor did he look at them or know them, save when he felt sudden suspicion that they were seeing his thoughts and scrutinizing each detail of the scene with the tattered soldier.

Yet gradually he mustered force to put the sin at a distance. And at last his eyes seemed to open to some new ways. He found that he could look back upon the brass and bombast [18] of his earlier gospels and see them truly. He was gleeful when he discovered that he now despised them.

With this conviction came a store of assurance. He felt a quiet manhood, nonassertive but of sturdy and strong blood. He knew that he would no more quail before his guides wherever they should point. He had been to touch the great death, and found that, after all, it was but the great death. He was a man.

So it came to pass that as he trudged from the place of blood and wrath his soul changed. He came from hot plowshares to prospects of clover tranquilly, and it was as if hot plowshares were not. Scars faded as flowers.

It rained. The procession of weary soldiers became a bedraggled ⑲ train, despondent and muttering, marching with churning effort in a trough of liquid brown mud under a low, wretched sky. Yet the youth smiled, for he saw that the world was a world for him, though many discovered it to be made of oaths and walking sticks ⑳. He had rid himself of the red sickness of battle. The sultry nightmare was in the past. He had been an animal blistered and sweating in the heat and pain of war. He turned now with a lover's thirst to images of tranquil skies, fresh meadows, cool brooks—an existence of soft and eternal peace.

Over the river a golden ray of sun came through the hosts of leaden rain clouds.

NOTES

①the youth: Henry Fleming, a private in the American Civil War. He is serving in a Union regiment fighting the Confederates 指主人公亨利·弗莱明

②his friend: Wilson 弗莱明的朋友威尔逊

③battery: army unit of big guns, with men and vehicles 炮兵连

④I bet we're goin' t' git along out of this an' back over th' river: I bet we're going to get along out of this and back over the river 我打赌我们将离开这里，过河去。

⑤entrenchment: defense; fortification 堡垒，阵地

⑥debris-strewed: covered by bits and pieces of stone 布满石头的

⑦reproach: a disgrace; a cause of shame or blame 责备，责骂

⑧discern: to perceive; to make out clearly 辨别，分清

⑨a dum good lickin': (*colloq.*) a damned good licking; a thorough defeat 惨败

⑩yer: (*colloq.*) your 你的

⑪wanta: (*colloq.*) want to 想要

⑫ses：(*colloq.*) says 说道

⑬heluva：(*colloq.*) hell of a 用以加强语气或咒骂

⑭plum：plumb；straight down 垂直的

⑮sech hollerin'：such hollering；such yelling 这样的嚎叫

⑯yeh：(*colloq.*) you 你

⑰shet yeh mouth：(*colloq.*) shut your mouth 闭嘴

⑱bombast：high sounding but unimportant or silly language 夸大其词的话

⑲bedraggled：soiled and wet 又湿又脏

⑳walking stick：The Lieutenant's sword is mentioned as his "walking-stick" by Stephen Crane in the novel. This allusion was obscured. The world of war fever is epitomized by the Lieutenant of Henry's company 中尉的刀被作者称为"他的手杖"，突显战争的狂热

Topic Discussion

1. In this novel, the images of animals and their features are frequently used, which add up to 80 times in the plot, in the dialogues or in the illusions of Henry. Does it show that man is a beast with illusions?

2. What are the distinctive features of Crane's writing style that is regarded as one of the achievements of the novel?

Ⅱ. Theodore Dreiser (1871—1945)

1. Life

Theodore Dreiser is generally known as one of American naturalists. He possessed none of the usual aids to a writer's career: no money, no friend in power, no formal education worthy of mention, no family tradition in letters. With every disadvantage piled upon him, Dreiser, by his strong will and his dogged persistence, eventually burst out and became one of the important American writers.

Theodore Herman Albert Dreiser was born in Terre Hante, Indiana, on August 27, 1871, into a German immigrant family. Living in a poor and intensely religious family, Dreiser had a very unhappy childhood. He was the ninth of ten children. His father, John Paul, had previously been a cotton mill manager, but a series of unfortunate accidents caused his fortunes to dwindle. In 1864 the cotton mill burned down, and during the reconstruction John Paul was hit in the head with a beam. He never fully recovered and as a result become deeply religious. He was further cheated by his business partners. The family was forced to move from one Indiana town to another in order to survive. Theodore Dreiser later blamed his father for the family's poverty.

At the age of fifteen Dreiser moved to Chicago and held jobs washing dishes, clerking a hardware store, and tracing freight cars. Dreiser had some education at a Catholic school in Terre Hante, and later went to a public school of Warsaw, Indiana. He met a teacher there who appreciated his school work and made it possible for him to spend a year at Indiana University. Apart from school education, Dreiser read widely by himself. He immersed himself in Dickens and Thackeray, read widely Shakespeare, and tasted Bunyan, Fielding, Pope, Thoreau, Emerson, and Twain, but his true literary influences were from Balzac, Charles Darwin and Herbert Spencer. Dreiser had longed to become a writer, so he went up to Chicago afterwards and made a beginning by placing himself with one of Chicago's newspapers, where he learned by experience. Later on, he slowly groped his way to authorship.

Dreiser first entered the newspaper world by dispensing toys for the needy at Christmas for the Chicago Herald. He subsequently got hired as a cub reporter with the *Chicago Globe* and later went to St. Louis as a feature writer for *the Globe-Democrat*. He left St. Louis and moved to Pittsburgh, working with the Dispatch. With a secure job again, Dreiser married Sara Jug White after meeting her at the Chicago World's Fair. The couple moved to New York where he received a job as a magazine editor. At the suggestion of his editor friend Arthur Henry, Dreiser began writing his first novel, the result of which was *Sister Carrie*.

Dreiser is a prolific writer and many of his works are familiar to us Chinese readers. Among them, *Sister Carrie* (1900) is the best known. In his early period some of his best short fictions were written, among which are *Nigger Jeff* and *Old Rogaun and His Theresa*. In 1911, *Jennie Gerhardt* came out, followed by two volumes of his "Trilogy of Desire", *The Financier* (1912) and *The Titan* (1914), the third, *The Stoic*, being published in 1947. *The Genius*

(1915), a classic story of a "misunderstood artist", was once condemned for "obscenity and blasphemy". Although a score of American men of letters lent their support, the novel remained unpublished until 1923. In 1925 Dreiser's greatest work *An American Tragedy* appeared. But it was banned in Boston in 1927. During the last twenty years of his life, Dreiser turned away from fiction and involved himself in political activities and debating writing. In 1927 he accepted an invitation to visit Russia and wrote *Dreiser Looks at Russia* the following year. He joined the Communist Party shortly before his death in 1945. Unable to write well towards the end of his life, he moved to Hollywood in 1939 and supported himself by the sale of film rights of his earlier works. He died there in 1945 at the age of seventy-four.

2. Works and Themes

With the publication of *Sister Carrie*, Dreiser started his long literary career that finally made him one of the most important American writers of the school of literary naturalism. Naturalism emphasized heredity and environment as important deterministic forces which shaped individualized characters presented in special and detailed circumstances. At bottom, life was shown to be ironic, even tragic. Once Dreiser described earthly existence as "a welter of inscrutable forces", in which was trapped each individual human being. In his words, man is a "victim of forces over which he has no control". To him, life is "so sad, so strange, so mysterious and so inexplicable". That's why the characters in his books are often subject to the control of the natural forces—especially those of environment and heredity.

The effect of Darwinist idea of "survival of the fittest" was very strong. It is not surprising to find in Dreiser's fiction a world of jungle, where "kill or to be killed" was the law and where only the fittest could survive. In almost every book he wrote Dreiser was expressing his naturalistic ideas in one aspect or another. In *Sister Carrie* Dreiser expressed his naturalistic view by presenting the purposelessness of life and attacking the conventional moral standards. After a series of incidents and coincidents, Carrie rises to fame and comfort while Hurstwood falls by losing his wealth, social position, pride and eventually his life. In his "Trilogy of Desire", Dreiser's focus shifted from the suffereings of the helpless characters at the bottom of the society to the power of the American financial giants in the late 19th century. An American Tragedy proves to be his greatest work. In a book with such a title, Dreiser intended to tell us that it is the social pressure that makes Clyde's downfall inevitable. Clyde's tragedy is a tragedy caused by the American social system which encouraged people to pursue selfishly the "dream of success" at all costs.

From the first novel *Sister Carrie* on, Dreiser set himself to project the American values for what he had found them to be—materialistic to the core. Living in such a society with such a value system, the human individual is obsessed with a endless, yet meaningless search for satisfaction of his desires. One of the desires is for money which was a motivation purpose of life and measurement of success in the United States in the late 19th century. For example, in *Sister Carrie*, the social status of all the characters is determined economically. Sex is another human desire that Dreiser explored to considerable lengths in his novels to reveal the dark side of human nature. In *Sister Carrie*, Carrie climbs up the social ladder by means of her sexual appeal; and Drouet's and Hurstwood's possession of Carrie might be seen as a sign of success. Also in the "Trilogy of Desire", the possession of sexual beauty symbolizes the acquisition of some social status of great magnitude. However, Dreiser never forgot to imply that these human desires in life are there like a powerful "magnetism" governing human existence and reducing human beings to nothing. So like all naturalists he was restrained from finding a solution to the social problems that appeared in his novels and accordingly almost all his works have pessimistic, even tragic endings.

3. Style and Influence

Dreiser's style has been a controversial aspect of his work from the beginning. It is said that artistically his works are seriously flawed. For lack of concision, his writings appear more inclusive and less selective, and the readers are sometimes burdened with massive detailed descriptions of characters and events. Though the time sequence is clear and the plot straightforward, he has been always accused of being awkward in sentence structure, inept and occasionally flatly wrong in word selection and meaning, and mixed and disorganized in voice and tone. Language is a means of communication rather than an art form for Dreiser.

However, Dreiser's contribution to the American literary history cannot be ignored. He broke away from the genteel tradition of literature and dramatized the life in a very realistic way. There is no comment, no judgment but facts of life in the stories. His style is not polished but very serious and well calculated to achieve the thematic ends he sought. Dreiser's stories are always solid and intensely interesting with their simple but highly moving characters. Dreiser is good at employing the journalistic method of reiteration to burn a central impression into the reader's mind. His interest in painting is reflected in his taste for word-pictures, sharp contrast, truth in color, and movement in outline. His very energy and enthusiasm carry his stories across the artistic faults and here lies the power and permanence that have made Dreiser one of America's foremost novelists.

4. Introduction to Sister Carrie

1) Plot Overview

Caroline Meeber, known as Carrie, leaves her home at the age of eighteen and takes the train to Chicago. The man sitting behind her on the train, named Drouet, starts talking to her. Carrie soon becomes interested in him due to his fine clothing and manners.

Carrie begins to live with her sister Minnie Hanson. Carrie soon realizes that the Hansons expect her to find a job and pay them rent. After several days of searching she finds employment in a shoe factory.

Carrie works hard at her job, but the salary is too low for her to pay rent and purchase clothes for the winter. Winter is coming and she is seriously ill. She loses her job. Carrie accidentally meets Drouet on the street. He kindly offers her a meal and takes her to a fine restaurant. He convinces her to meet him again the next day and presses twenty dollars into her hand. The next day he takes her out shopping, buying her an entire wardrobe.

Carrie is so delighted by the way he treats her that she agrees to allow him to rent an apartment for her. Drouet then introduces Carrie to his friend Hurstwood, the manager of one of the top bars in the city. Hurstwood is far more refined and elegant than Drouet. He falls madly in love with Carrie and starts to think of getting her to run away with him.

Hurstwood's family life falls apart rapidly as he has been neglecting his wife in order to see Carrie. Meanwhile, Drouet has also discovered that Carrie has been spending far more time with Hurstwood then he ever thought. Drouet is angry with Carrie. Hurstwood foolishly fights with his wife, not realizing that his wife has the entire property in her name. She then files for divorce, locks him out of the house.

Hurstwood goes to his workplace and spends his nights at a local hotel. One evening he pulls out over ten thousand dollars in cash from his workplace and rushes to Carrie's apartment. He tells her that Drouet has had an accident and that they need to go to the hospital. With that lie he gets her onto a train heading to Detroit and from there to Montreal. Carrie is upset and furious with him, but passively does nothing to resist.

From Montreal they go to New York City where Hurstwood rents an apartment for them. He has sent back most of the money he stole while in Montreal in order to avoid being put into the prison. Hurstwood keeps only thirteen hundred in order to set up his own business. He and Carrie are soon forced to move into a smaller apartment. Failing to find work, Hurstwood slowly gets used to idleness. He takes up some gambling and loses over a hundred dollars in one night. Carrie loses interest in him.

When Hurstwood is almost out of money, Carrie decides that she will have to get a job to support them. After a few days she is given a spot in the chorus line of a Broadway show. Her salary is barely enough for them to live on. She is soon promoted to lead the chorus line and later to an even better paying dancing position. Carrie refuses to tell Hurstwood about her success because she needs the extra money to purchase clothes for herself.

Hurstwood takes one last job as a cab driver when the trolley car workers go on strike. An angry mob soon manages to stop his car and beats Hurstwood. Hurstwood decides to give up and head home. Carrie luckily is given a speaking part one day and at that point decides to leave Hurstwood in order to live with an actress friend of hers. She moves out while he is taking a walk.

The rest of the novel traces Carrie's rise and Hurstwood's fall. Carrie becomes an overnight star and signs a contract paying her a hundred and fifty dollars a week. Drouet moves to New York and tries to reestablish his relationship with Carrie, but she refuses him. Hurstwood loses his apartment and becomes a homeless beggar. In despair, he commits suicide by gassing himself in his hotel room one night. Hurstwood's wife and daughter take a voyage to Rome with a wealthy young man that his daughter has married while Hurstwood's dead body is carried away on a ship. Carrie meanwhile has become unhappy with her state in the world, wishing that she could perform drama rather than comedy.

2) Major Characters and the Themes

①Major Characters

Carrie is a poor county girl who comes to the city to seek whatever she can find. Carrie does rise, but she does so by using men as ladder. She is not a simple gold digger; she is much more complex than that. Her goals are clothes, money, and fame, and the means by which she achieves them are relatively unimportant. More important, however, is that Carrie is a seeker and a lover. She cannot be satisfied. There must always be a new world to conquer, new goals to achieve. Carrie uses everything to reach her consuming ambition. She comes to understand the usefulness of sex, but she also understands the emotional commitment necessary to love, and she refuses to do that. In the pursuit of the fullest expression and fulfillment of life she can achieve, human attachments are only temporary, and Drouet and Hurstwood are only means to an end for Carrie. Drouet is an escape for Carrie. She does not love him, but his means are a source of amazement. She recognizes that the relative good things in his chambers and in the apartment he rents for her are the signs of that for which she wants. She knows early that Drouet is only a bridge in her movement from poverty to riches. Carrie's desertion of Hurstwood can be seen as cold and cruel, but she stays with him until it is clear that no one can save him. In New York, when she has finally gotten all that she has sought, Ames shows her that there is a world beyond the material, a world of literature and philosophy; it is an aesthetic world of which Carrie has not dreamed and which she takes as a new level to achieve. The promise of an aesthetic world beyond material affluence offers hope for Carrie, and that hope seems illusory. The rocking chair is the perfect symbol of Carrie. It is an instrument that forever moves but never goes anywhere and never truly achieves anything. Carrie's every success is at last unsatisfying and every new horizon offers only hollow promise.

Hurstwood is the bar manager of a famous Chicago bar. As he watches Carrie perform in a cheap theatrical performance, he is shocked by her youth and her energy. As a middle-aged married man whose wife is a bad-tempered woman, he is naturally attracted to Carrie. Carrie in turn recognizes the quality of Hurstwood's clothes, his style, and his bearing and makes it clear that she will accept his love. When Hurstwood and Carrie come to New York, he fails to open his own business or find a good job. The more he fails the further he withdraws from life and from Carrie, until he becomes completely dependent on her. When Carrie leaves him, he drifts deeper into New York's lower class world until he kills himself. Hurstwood is a weak man trapped by circumstance. He is unwilling or unable to cope with situations. His love with Carrie is based on mutual attraction, but he also enjoys his daily life and the prestige that his social position provides him. Only when his wife threatens him, he is forced to run away with Carrie and loses everything. Hurstwood dies because he is no longer the fittest and is tired of the struggle.

②The Themes

Dreiser's real theme in *Sister Carrie* is the purposelessness of life. While looking at individuals with warm, human sympathy, he also sees the disorder and cruelty of life in general. While Carrie gains fame and comfort, Hurstwood loses his wealth, social position and pride. His tragedy is just as accidental as Carrie's success. Dreiser does not try to explain why these things happen. In this form of naturalism, the working of fate can never be explained. As a character in Jennie Gerhardt, his next novel, says: "The individual doesn't count much in the situation...We are moved about like chessman...we have no control." It is a "most terrible truth" that "the purpose of nature have no relation to the purpose of men".

"Survival of the fittest" is another theme that we can clearly see in the rise of Carrie and the fall of Hurstwood.

Criticism of prevailing values such as money and sex is also demonstrated here in the novel. Carrie's sexual appeal has become a tool and money determines people's fate and position.

5. The selected reading

Sister Carrie

An excerpt from Chapter XLⅧ

…

Hurstwood put his hands, red from cold, down in his pockets. Tears came into his eyes.

"That's right," he said; "I'm no good now. I was all right. I had money. I'm going to quit this," and, with death in his heart, he started down toward the Bowery[①]. People had turned on the gas before and died; why shouldn't he? He remembered a lodginghouse where there were little, close rooms, with gas-jets in them, almost pre-arranged, he thought, for what he wanted to do, which rented for fifteen cents. Then he remembered that he had no fifteen cents.

On the way he met a comfortable-looking gentleman, coming, clean-shaven, out of a fine barber shop.

"Would you mind giving me a little something?" he asked this man boldly.

The gentleman looked him over and fished for a dime. Nothing but quarters were in his pocket.

"Here," he said, handing him one, to be rid of him. "Be off, now."

Hurstwood moved on, wondering. The sight of the large, bright coin pleased him a little. He remembered that he was hungry and that he could get a bed for ten cents. With this, the idea of death passed, for the time being, out of his mind. It was only when he could get nothing but insults that death seemed worth while.

One day, in the middle of the winter, the sharpest spell of the season set in. It broke grey and cold in the first day, and on the second snowed. Poor luck pursuing him, he had secured but ten cents by nightfall, and this he had spent for food. At evening he found himself at the Boulevard and Sixty-seventh Street, where he finally turned his face Bowery-ward. Especially fatigued because of the wandering propensity which had seized him in the morning, he now half dragged his wet feet, shuffling the soles upon the sidewalk. An old, thin coat was turned up about his red ears—his cracked derby hat was pulled down until it turned them outward. His hands were in his pockets.

"I'll just go down Broadway," he said to himself.

When he reached Forty-second Street, the fire signs were already blazing brightly. Crowds were hastening to dine. Through bright windows, at every corner, might be seen gay companies in luxuriant restaurants. There were coaches and crowded cable cars.

In his weary and hungry state, he should never have come here. The contrast was too sharp. Even he was recalled keenly to better things. "What's the use?" he thought. "It's all up with me. I'll quit this."

People turned to look after him, so uncouth was his shambling figure. Several officers followed him with their eyes, to see that he did not beg of anybody.

Once he paused in an aimless, incoherent sort of way and looked through the windows of an imposing restaurant, before which blazed a fire sign, and through the large, plate windows of which could be seen the red and gold decorations, the palms, the white napery, and shining glassware, and, above all, the comfortable crowd. Weak as his mind had become, his hunger was sharp enough to show the importance of this. He stopped stock still, his frayed trousers soaking in the slush, and peered foolishly in.

"Eat," he mumbled. "That's right, eat. Nobody else wants any."

Then his voice dropped even lower, and his mind half lost the fancy it had.

"It's mighty cold," he said. "Awful cold."

At Broadway and Thirty-ninth Street was blazing, in incandescent fire, Carrie's name. "Carrie Madenda," it read, "and the Casino Company." All the wet, snowy sidewalk was bright with this radiated fire. It was so bright that it attracted Hurstwood's gaze. He looked up, and then at a large, gilt-framed posterboard, on which was a fine lithograph of Carrie, lifesize.

Hurstwood gazed at it a moment, snuffling and hunching one shoulder, as if something were scratching him. He was so run down, however, that his mind was not exactly clear.

He approached that entrance and went in.

"Well?" said the attendant, staring at him. Seeing him pause, he went over and shoved him. "Get out of here," he said.

"I want to see Miss Madenda," he said.

"You do, eh?" the other said, almost tickled at the spectacle. "Get out of here," and he shoved him again. Hurstwood had no strength to resist.

"I want to see Miss Madenda," he tried to explain, even as he was being hustled away. "I'm all right. I—"

The man gave him a last push and closed the door. As he did so, Hurstwood slipped and fell in the snow. It hurt him, and some vague sense of shame returned. He began to cry and swear foolishly.

"God damned dog!" he said. "Damned old cur," wiping the slush from his worthless coat. "I—I hired such people as you once."

Now a fierce feeling against Carrie welled up—just one fierce, angry thought before the whole thing slipped out of his mind.

"She owes me something to eat," he said. "She owes it to me."

Hopelessly he turned back into Broadway again and slopped onward and away, begging, crying, losing track of his thoughts, one after another, as a mind decayed and disjointed is wont to do.

It was truly a wintry evening, a few days later, when his one distinct mental decision was reached. Already, at four o'clock, the sombre hue of night was thickening the air. A heavy snow was falling—a fine picking, whipping snow, borne forward by a swift wind in long, thin lines. The streets were bedded with it—six inches of cold, soft carpet, churned to a dirty brown by the crush of teams and the feet of men. Along Broadway men picked their way in ulsters and umbrellas. Along the Bowery, men slouched through it with collars and hats pulled over their ears. In the former thoroughfare businessmen and travellers were making for comfortable hotels. In the latter, crowds on cold errands ② shifted past dingy stores, in the deep recesses of which lights were already gleaming. There were early lights in the cable cars, whose usual clatter was reduced by the mantle about the wheels. The whole city was muffled by this fast-thickening mantle ③.

In her comfortable chambers at the Waldorf ④, Carrie was reading at this time "Pere Goriot," [5] which Ames had recommended to her. It was so strong, and Ames's mere recommendation had so aroused her interest, that she caught nearly the full sympathetic significance of it. For the first time, it was being borne in upon her how silly and worthless had been her earlier reading, as a whole. Becoming wearied, however, she yawned and came to the window, looking out upon the old winding procession of carriages rolling up Fifth Avenue.

"Isn't it bad?" she observed to Lola.

"Terrible!" said that little lady, joining her. "I hope it snows enough to go sleigh riding."

"Oh, dear," said Carrie, with whom the sufferings of Father Goriot were still keen. "That's all you think of. Aren't you sorry for the people who haven't anything to-night?"

"Of course I am," said Lola; "but what can I do? I haven't anything."

Carrie smiled.

"You wouldn't care, if you had," she returned.

"I would, too," said Lola. "But people never gave me anything when I was hard up."

"Isn't it just awful?" said Carrie, studying the winter's storm.

"Look at that man over there," laughed Lola, who had caught sight of some one falling down. "How sheepish men look when they fall, don't they?"

"We'll have to take a coach to-night," answered Carrie absently.

In the lobby of the Imperial [6], Mr. Charles Drouet was just arriving, shaking the snow from a very handsome ulster. Bad weather had driven him home early and stirred his desire for those pleasures which shut out the snow and gloom of life. A good dinner, the company of a young woman, and an evening at the theatre were the chief things for him.

"Why, hello, Harry!" he said, addressing a lounger in one of the comfortable lobby chairs. "How are you?"

"Oh, about six and six, [7]" said the other. "Rotten weather, isn't it?"

"Well, I should say," said the other. "I've been just sitting here thinking where I'd go to night."

"Come along with me," said Drouet. "I can introduce you to something dead swell. [8]"

"Who is it?" said the other.

"Oh, a couple of girls over here in Fortieth Street. We could have a dandy [9] time. I was just looking for you."

"Supposing you get'em and take'em out to dinner?"

"Sure," said Drouet. "Wait'll I go upstairs and change my clothes."

"Well, I'll be in the barber shop," said the other. "I want to get a shave."

"All right," said Drouet, creaking off in his good shoes toward the elevator. The old butterfly [10] was as light on the wing as ever.

On an incoming vestibuled Pullman [11], speeding at forty miles an hour through the snow of the evening, were three others, all related.

"First call for dinner in the dining-car," a Pullman servitor was announcing, as he hastened through the aisle in snow-white apron and jacket.

"I don't believe I want to play any more," said the youngest, a black-haired beauty, turned supercilious by fortune, as she pushed an euchre hand [12] away from her.

"Shall we go into dinner?" inquired her husband, who was all that fine raiment can make.

"Oh, not yet," she answered. "I don't want to play any more, though."

"Jessica," said her mother, who was also a study in what good clothing can do for age, "push that pin down in your tie—it's coming up."

Jessica obeyed, incidentally touching at her lovely hair and looking at a little jewel-faced watch. Her husband studied her, for beauty, even cold, is fascinating from one point of view.

"Well, we won't have much more of this weather," he said. "It only takes two weeks to get to Rome."

Mrs. Hurstwood nestled comfortably in her corner and smiled. It was so nice to be the mother-in-law of a rich young man—one whose financial state had borne her personal inspection. [13]

"Do you suppose the boat will sail promptly?" asked Jessica, "if it keeps up like this?"

"Oh, yes," answered her husband. "This won't make any difference."

Passing down the aisle came a very fair-haired banker's son, also of

Chicago, who had long eyed this supercilious beauty. Even now he did not hesitate to glance at her, and she was conscious of it. With a specially conjured show of indifference, she turned her pretty face wholly away. It was not wifely modesty at all. By so much was her pride satisfied.

At this moment Hurstwood stood before a dirty four story building in a side street quite near the Bowery, whose one-time coat of buff had been changed by soot and rain. He mingled with a crowd of men—a crowd which had been, and was still, gathering by degrees.

It began with the approach of two or three, who hung about the closed wooden doors and beat their feet to keep them warm. They had on faded derby hats with dents in them. Their misfit coats were heavy with melted snow and turned up at the collars. Their trousers were mere bags, frayed at the bottom and wobbling over big, soppy shoes, torn at the sides and worn almost to shreds. They made no effort to go in, but shifted ruefully about, digging their hands deep in their pockets and leering at the crowd and the increasing lamps. With the minutes increased the number. There were old men with grizzled beards and sunken eyes, men who were comparatively young but shrunken by diseases, men who were middle-aged. None were fat. There was a face in the thick of the collection which was as white as drained veal. There was another red as brick. Some came with thin, rounded shoulders, others with wooden legs, still others with frames so lean that clothes only flapped about them. There were great ears, swollen noses, thick lips, and, above all, red, blood-shot eyes. Not a normal, healthy face in the whole mass; not a straight figure; not a straightforward, steady glance.

In the drive of the wind and sleet they pushed in on one another. There were wrists, unprotected by coat or pocket, which were red with cold. There were ears, half covered by every conceivable semblance of a hat, which still looked stiff and bitten. In the snow they shifted, now one foot, now another, almost rocking in unison.

With the growth of the crowd about the door came a murmur. It was not conversation, but a running comment directed at any one in general. It contained oaths and slang phrases.

"By damn, I wish they'd hurry up."

"Look at the copper [14] watchin'."

"Maybe it ain't winter, nuther!"

"I wisht [15] I was in Sing Sing [16]."

Now a sharper lash of wind cut down and they huddled closer. It was an edging, shifting, pushing throng. There was no anger, no pleading, no threatening words. It was all sullen endurance, unlightened by either wit or good fellowship.

A carriage went jingling by with some reclining figure in it. One of the men nearest the door saw it.

"Look at the bloke ridin'."

"He ain't so cold."

"Eh, eh, eh!" yelled another, the carriage having long since passed out of hearing.

Little by little the night crept on. Along the walk a crowd turned out on its way home. Men and shop-girls went by with quick steps. The cross-town cars began to be crowded. The gas lamps were blazing, and every window bloomed ruddy with a steady flame. Still the crowd hung about the door, unwavering.

"Ain't they ever goin' to open up?" queried a hoarse voice, suggestively.

This seemed to renew the general interest in the closed door, and many gazed in that direction. They looked at it as dumb brutes look, as dogs paw and whine and study the knob. [17] They shifted and blinked and muttered, now a curse, now a comment. Still they waited and still the snow whirled and cut them with biting flakes. On the old hats and peaked shoulders it was piling. It gathered in little heaps and curves and no one brushed it off. In the centre of the crowd the warmth and steam melted it, and water trickled off hat rims and down noses, which the owners could not reach to scratch. On the outer rim the piles remained unmelted. Hurstwood, who could not get in the centre, stood with head lowered to the weather and bent his form.

A light appeared through the transom overhead. It sent a thrill of possibility through the watchers. There was a murmur of recognition. At last the bars grated inside and the crowd pricked up its ears. Footsteps shuffled within and it murmured again. Some one called: "Slow up there, now," and then the door opened. It was push and jam for a minute, with grim, beast silence to prove its quality, and then it melted inward, like logs floating, and disappeared. There were wet hats and wet shoulders, a cold, shrunken, disgruntled mass, pouring in between bleak walls. It was just six o'clock and there was supper in every hurrying pedestrian's face. And yet no supper was provided here—nothing but beds.

Hurstwood laid down his fifteen cents and crept off with weary steps to his allotted room. It was a dingy affair—wooden, dusty, hard. A small gas-jet furnished sufficient light for so rueful a corner.

"Hm!" he said, clearing his throat and locking the door.

Now he began leisurely to take off his clothes, but stopped first with his coat, and tucked it along the crack under the door. His vest he arranged in the same place. His old wet, cracked hat he laid softly upon the table. Then he pulled off his shoes and lay down.

It seemed as if he thought a while, for now he arose and turned the gas out, standing calmly in the blackness, hidden from view. After a few moments, in which he reviewed nothing, but merely hesitated, he turned the gas on again, but applied no match. Even then he stood there, hidden wholly in that kindness which is night, while the uprising fumes filled the room. When the odour reached his nostrils, he quit his attitude and fumbled for the bed.

"What's the use?" he said, weakly, as he stretched himself to rest.

And now Carrie had attained that which in the beginning seemed life's object, or, at least, such fraction of it as human beings ever attain of their original desires. She could look about on her gowns and carriage, her furniture and bank account. Friends there were, as the world takes it—those who would bow and smile in acknowledgment of her success. For these she had once craved. Applause there was, and publicity—once far off, essential things, but now grown trivial and indifferent. Beauty also—her type of loveliness—and yet she was lonely. In her rocking-chair she sat, when not otherwise engaged—singing and dreaming. [13]

Thus in life there is ever the intellectual and the emotional nature—the mind that reasons, and the mind that feels. Of one come the men of action—generals and statesmen; of the other, the poets and dreamers—artists all.

As harps in the wind, the latter responds to every breath of fancy, voicing in their moods all the ebb and flow of the ideal.

Man has not yet comprehended the dreamer any more than he has the ideal. For him the laws and morals of the world are unduly severe. Ever hearkening [19] to the sound of beauty, straining for the flash of its distant wings, he watches to follow, wearying his feet in travelling. So watched Carrie, so followed, rocking and singing.

And it must be remembered that reason had little part in this. Chicago dawning, she saw the city offering more of loveliness than she had ever known, and instinctively, by force of her moods alone, clung to it. In fine raiment and elegant surroundings, men seemed to be contented. Hence, she drew near these things. Chicago, New York; Drouet, Hurstwood; the world of fashion and the world of stage—these were but incidents. Not them, but that which they represented, she longed for. Time proved the representation false.

Oh, the tangle of human life! How dimly as yet we see. Here was Carrie, in the beginning poor, unsophisticated, emotional; responding with desire to everything most lovely in life, yet finding herself turned as by a wall. Laws to say: "Be allured, if you will, by everything lovely, but draw not nigh [20] unless by righteousness." Convention to say: "You shall not better your situation save by honest labour." If honest labour be unremunerative and difficult to endure; if it be the long, long road which never reaches beauty, but wearies the feet and the heart; if the drag to follow beauty be such that one abandons the admired way, taking rather the despised path leading to her dreams quickly, who shall cast the first stone? Not evil, but longing for that which is better, more often directs the steps of the erring. Not evil, but goodness more often allures the feeling mind unused to reason. [21]

Amid the tinsel and shine of her state walked Carrie, unhappy. As when Drouet took her, she had thought: "Now I am lifted into that which is best"; as when Hurstwood seemingly offered her the better way: "Now am I happy." But since the world goes its way past all who will not partake of its folly, she now found herself alone. [22] Her purse was open to him whose need was greatest. In her walks on Broadway, she no longer thought of the elegance of the creatures who passed her. Had they more of that peace and beauty which glimmered afar off, then were they to be envied.

Drouet abandoned his claim and was seen no more. Of Hurstwood's death she was not even aware. A slow, black boat setting out from the pier at Twenty-seventh Street upon its weekly errand bore, with many others, his nameless body to the Potter's Field.

Thus passed all that was of interest concerning these twain in their relation to her. Their influence upon her life is explicable alone by the nature of her longings. Time was when both represented for her all that was most potent in earthly success. They were the personal representatives of a state most blessed to attain—the titled ambassadors of comfort and peace, aglow with their credentials. It is but natural that when the world which they represented no longer allured her, its ambassadors should be discredited. Even had Hurstwood returned in his original beauty and glory, he could not now have allured her. She had learned that in his world, as in her own present state, was not happiness.

Sitting alone, she was now an illustration of the devious ways by which one who feels, rather than reasons, may be led in the pursuit of beauty. Though often disillusioned, she was still waiting for that halcyon day when she would be led forth among dreams become real. Ames had pointed out a farther step, but on and on beyond that, if accomplished, would lie others for her. It was forever to be the pursuit of that radiance of delight which tints the distant hilltops of the world.

Oh, Carrie, Carrie! Oh, blind strivings of the human heart! Onward onward, it saith, [23] and where beauty leads, there it follows. Whether it be the tinkle of a lone sheep bell o'er some quiet landscape, or the glimmer of beauty in sylvan places, or the show of soul in some passing eye, the heart knows and makes answer, following. It is when the feet weary and hope seems vain that the heartaches and the longings arise. Know, then, that for you is neither surfeit nor content. In your rocking-chair, by your window dreaming, shall you long, alone. In your rocking-chair, by your window, shall you dream such happiness as you may never feel.

NOTES

①the Bowery: a place or district in New York City where the poor or the homeless dwelt 纽约贫民窟

②crowds on cold errands: people who have something urgent to do in such cold weather 冬日里忙碌的人们

③mantle: covering, here it refers to snow 盖罩，指雪覆盖了城市

④the Waldorf: a luxuriant hotel in New York City at that time 当时纽约一家豪华旅馆

⑤ "Pere Goriot": Father Goriot, famous novel of Balzac, critical realist writer of France 法国作家巴尔扎克的《高老头》

⑥the Imperial: another top-quality hotel in the City where the businessmen liked to stay 当时纽约另一家高级宾馆

⑦about six and six: just so so 很一般

⑧something dead swell: some wonderful people or things 一些非常棒的人或事物

⑨dandy: (*sl.*) excellent 最好的，第一流的

⑩the old butterfly: refers to Drouet, since he is still very nimble 指德鲁特

⑪vestibuled Pullman: sleeping-car with an enclosed passage at each end of the carriage which connects it with the next carriage on a railway train 卧铺车厢

⑫an euchre hand: a hand of paper cards 一把牌

⑬one whose financial state had borne her personal inspection: she had the right to examine his financial state 她有权知道他的财政状况。

⑭copper: (sl.) policeman 警察

⑮I wisht: I wished 我希望

⑯Sing Sing: name of a prison in New York state 纽约州星星监狱

⑰They looked at it…and study the knob: A metaphor is used here to suggest that the beggars looked at the door greedily and they were so eager to go in 比喻乞丐们贪婪地看着那门，渴望进去。

⑱In her rocking-chair she sat, when not otherwise engaged—singing and dreaming: She was dreaming of the bright future. Although she was often disillusioned, she was not at all in despair 她在梦想美好的未来。尽管她有幻灭感，但并没完全绝望。

⑲hearken: (*liter.*) listen (to) 听

⑳nigh: near 附近

㉑who shall cast the first stone: who shall be the first to "throw the first stone" is from

The Bible. People bring a woman who commits adultery to Jesus, "Teacher," they said to Jesus, "this woman was caught in the very act of committing adultery. In our Law Moses commanded that such a woman must be stoned to death. Now, what do you say?" They said this to trap Jesus, so that they could accuse him. But he bent over and wrote on the ground with his finger. As they stood there asking him questions, he straightly ended up and said to them, "whichever one of you has committed no sin may throw the first stone at her." Then he bent over again and wrote on the ground. When they heard this, they all left, one by one, the older ones first 源于《圣经》中的一个故事，耶稣对要用石头砸死通奸妇人的人们说："你们中间谁是没有罪的，谁就可以先拿石头打她。"他们听见这话，就从老到少一个一个地都出去了。

㉒But since the world goes its way..., she now found herself alone: Because Carrie didn't want to go with the tide, she felt lonely 因为嘉莉不愿随波逐流，她感到孤独。

㉓it saith: it says 它说

Topic Discussion

1. What does Carrie's loneliness stand for?
2. Do you think Dreiser's prose style is awkward or appropriate? Explain.

第三章 两战时期文学

第一节 意象派诗歌

每节导读

学习本节需要掌握意象派诗歌特点及代表诗人。

意象派诗歌兴起于20世纪初。它的兴起给英美诗歌带来了一场革命，并从此翻开了英美现代派诗歌的新篇章。意象派诗歌经历了三个阶段：从理论准备到鼎盛时期，再到衰落。意象派诗歌创作遵循三个原则：①用直接的手法来处理“事物”；②不使用对于表现无益的语言；③在韵律方面用自然的乐句，而不是节拍的顺序写作。

埃兹拉·庞德是意象主义运动的主要代言人。他所倡导的意象派诗歌都比较短，富于乐感，避免抽象，用清楚的意象而不是象征的手法表达意义。意象派诗歌深受日本俳句的影响。大多数诗人采用自由诗强调题材和形式的自由性。他仅有两行之长的诗作《地铁车站》是意象派诗歌的代表作品。庞德研究中国文化，在其诗作中也可看出东方文化对他的影响。

Ⅰ. Background

During the first decades of the 20th century, modernism became an international tendency in art and literature, whose essence was a break with the past. Actually, modernism was the consequence of the transformation of society brought about by industrialism and technology in the course of the 19th century. It did not refer to a school but included a wide range of artistic expressions such as symbolism, impressionism, post-impressionism, futurism, imagism and surrealism etc.

Ⅱ. Imagism

1. Emergence

The movement is generally divided into three phases. It began with Thomas Ernest Hulme, an English philosopher and writer who founded the Poet's Club in London in 1908. In this period there was much talking, but not much writing. It can be seen as the theoretical preparation for Imagist poetry. Then the movement entered a new period from 1912 to 1914 when Ezra Pound became the leader of the new poetry. This is the period when Imagism reached its peak. It is in this period that something like an Imagist manifesto and three poetic principles came out. The three principles are: 1) direct treatment of the "thing"; 2) economy of expression; 3) musical phrasing. And the third phase was characterized by Amy Lowell, who pushed the movement into the period of "Amygism", called by Pound. It is also in this period that the Imagist poetry finally ceased to be a literary movement in 1917.

2. Major features

Imagism was only one of the new techniques writing poetry that was part of the modernist period and it was one of the most essential techniques. With a spirit of revolt against conventions, imagism was anti-romantic and anti-Victorian. Victorian poetry was characteristic of moralizing tendencies, over padding of extra-poetic matter, and traditional iambic pentameter. But Imagism stressed free choice of subject matters, concreteness of imagery, musical phrases, economy of expression and the use of a dominant image of a quick succession of related images.

Imagism produced free verse without imposing a rhythmical pattern.

This means that the poet created new rhymes in the sequence of the musical phrase as the expressions of a new mood.

In a sense, imagism was equivalent to naturalism in fiction.

Imagism in poetry came from the same basis as naturalism in fiction.

They emphasized scientific observation, a feeling of determinism that the reader should only look at the outside objects with no attempt to get inside of them. Imagists never stated the emotion in the poem. They just presented an image.

Imagism tried to record objective observations of an object or a situation without interpretation or comment by the poet.

Imagists merely wanted to give the reader an image. It may be a picture, a sound, a smell, a taste or a touch. All of those were concrete images that appealed to senses.

3. Comment

Imagism was a rebellion against traditional poetry which failed to reflect the new life and it offered a new way of writing poetry. The imagist theories call for brief language, pinpoint the precise picture in as few words as possible. This new way of poetry composition has a lasting influence on the 20th century poetry. Most of the 20th century top poets are somewhat related with it and benefit from it. In this sense, it was also a kind of training school for modern poets.

Significant as it is, Imagism also has its defects. First of all, a single dominant image is incapable of sustaining a longer poetic effort. In addition, Imagists were against didacticism in poetry and tended to pursue artistic techniques only, therefore, pure imagist poetry seldom has important social meanings.

The most outstanding figures of the movement were Ezra Pound, Amy Lowell (1974—1925), and Hilda Doolittle (1886—1961). Pound, leader of the movement from 1912 to 1914, set down the Imagist principles. Then Lowell led the movement into the period of "Amygism" from 1914 to 1917. Doolittle was the only poet who throughout her career remained an imagist.

Ⅲ. Ezra Loomis Pound (1885—1972)

1. Life

Pound was born in 1885 in Idaho and grew up in Pennsylvania. In 1908 he left for Europe and got involved in Imagist Movement. In 1920s he moved to Paris and became the center of American expatriates. In 1930s he became a supporter of Mussolini for which he was arrested and tried, but instead of going to prison, he was sent to a hospital in Washington because the court judged him insane. After he was released from the hospital he went to Italy and died there in 1972.

Often identified as the father of modern American poetry, he led the experiment in revolutionizing poetry. Pound was America's first self-conscious innovator in poetry and one of the most important imagist poets and critics of his time. He wrote 70 books of his own, and contributed as editor to 70 books of other writers. He also wrote more than 1500 articles. His major works of poetry is the *Cantos*, a long poem which he wrote from 1915 to 1949.

2. Literary Career

Pound's early work was extraordinarily varied. It included some unusual translation of Chinese poems. In 1915 he finished Cathay, a volume of Chinese translations. In London, he came into contact with T. E Hulme and the Poet's club. He also made friends with the great Irish poet W. B. Yeast (1865—1939). As the leader of the imagist movement, he helped some British and American writers to pursue their literary careers. He was tireless in seeking out new talents, securing first publication or recognition for gifted young writers such as Robert Frost and T. S. Eliot. In 1915, in London, he began working on *Cantos*, a modern epic, which he continued for over fifty years. In 1920 he moved to Paris. As part of Gertrude Stein's circles, he helped T. S. Eliot and Ernest Hemingway by editing their early writings. In 1925 he settled down in Italy. His critical essays are collected in *Make It New* (1934), *The ABC of Reading* (1934), *Polite Essays* (1937), *Guide to Kulchur* (1938) *and Literary Essays* (1954).

Pound later showed bitter hatred of American finance and moneyed interests which he blamed for the degeneration of American life. He turned to the worship of Mussolini. In 1939 he visited the United States and then he worked for Radio Rome, making pro-Fascist, anti-Jewish propaganda broadcasts to the United States. He was arrested for treason in 1945. But he was not tried because of a plea of insanity. He died in Venice on November 1, 1972. He was buried in the Protestant cemetery on the nearby island of San Michele.

第二节　重要诗人

每节导读

学习本节需要掌握T·S·艾略特、罗伯特·弗罗斯特的代表作品和艺术特色。

T·S·艾略特是美国现代派诗歌的奠基者之一。他和庞德两人共同建立了现代派诗学，后来又分为两条不同的诗歌创作路线，影响了20世纪整个美国诗坛。他的代表作《荒原》与庞德的《诗章》是现代派诗歌史上的两座丰碑。艾略特在文学理论上有独特的见解，他的诗歌就是他创作理论的很好实践。《杰·阿尔弗里德·普鲁弗洛克情歌》、《荒原》和《四首四重奏》代表了艾略特创作生涯早期、中期和后期的诗歌风貌。

罗伯特·弗罗斯特是20世纪美国最伟大的民族诗人，擅长田园诗及自然诗。他的自然诗以新英格兰为背景，以朴实无华的乡土白话作为诗的语言，在素描淡抹中隐含了深刻的喻义，探索了现实和人生。他的诗作脍炙人口，如《未选择的路》、《雪夜停马在林边》在美国家喻户晓，老少皆知，可见其语言之大众化，喻义之深刻。

Ⅰ. T. S. Eliot（1888—1965）

1. Life

Eliot was a poet, playwright, and literary critic. He became an acknowledged leader of the new poetry and criticism by 1925 and nearly dominated poetry and criticism in the period between two world wars and shaped the tastes and the critical vocabulary of a generation.

Eliot was born on September 26, 1888 in St. Louis, Missouri in the Midwest. He studied as an undergraduate at Harvard in 1906—1910, at the Sorbonne in Paris in 1910—1911, and again at Harvard in 1911—1914 for a Ph. D in philosophy. During his studies, he gained a good command of French, Italian, English literature, and Sanskrit. He began writing poems as a college student, and in traditional modes at first. Then he was greatly influenced by the French symbolist poets. In 1911 he drafted "The Love Song of J. Alfred

Prufrock", a poem that reveals the spiritual crisis of modern intellectual. In 1922 he published his masterpiece *The Waste Land*. Eliot finally settled in England and got married. He worked first as a teacher and later in the foreign department of Lloyds Bank. In 1927, he became a British citizen and in 1948 he was awarded the Nobel Prize.

He described himself as "a royalist in politics, a classicist in literature and an Anglo-Catholic in religion".

2. Literary Career

Eliot, as a modernist poet, composed poetry difficult to understand. He inherited literary traditions from the classics and the poets at the time of Shakespeare. He transformed the traditions and made them the foundations of his poetry and criticism. In 1915 he published "The Love Song of J. Alfred Prufrock" in *Poetry and Preludes* in Blast. His first book of poetry, *Prufrock and Other Observations*, came out in 1917; and in 1922, *The Waste Land*, which is generally regarded as one of his great works, was published. *The Waste Land* precisely describes the state of culture and society after World War I and illustrates the spiritual poverty of the West of the time.

The Waste Land consists of five segments, each of which contains many fragments of various voices and characters. It has not only literary and historical allusions but contemporary life as well. The organizing principle of the poem is the myth of death and rebirth. *The Waste Land*, characterized by its originality and severe attack on postwar Europe, reads like the manifesto of the "Lost Generation".

Eliot became the editor of the Criterion in 1922. Then he also wrote some plays, such as, *Murder in the Cathedral*, *The Cocktail Party*, *The Confidential Clerk*, all religious in theme. And in 1943, his best work, a group of four long poems entitled Four Quartets was first published together.

Collections of Eliot's critical essays include *The Sacred Wood*, *The Use of Poetry and the Use of Criticism*, *On Poetry and Poets*, *etc.*

3. Features

Eliot did not accept the validity of the American dream. He was not as optimistic as the other poets like Whitman. His audience was not the common people but elites who took a view of society different from mass culture. Therefore, his audience was small.

It is said that his poems are characterized with the following features: 1) learned quotations and allusions (广征博引); 2) objective correlative (客观投射); 3) juxtaposition (同时并存).

4. Introduction to "The Love Song of J. Alfred Prufrock"

"The Love Song of J. Alfred Prufrock" was published in 1917, which has been one of the American literary classics.

The poem depicts a typical western intellectual of 20th century, Prufrock. He was a gloomy, inefficient and radical character. He was caught between the two worlds—life and death—in that he had a strong desire but could never fulfill it. His idealism tortured him all the time because he was so timid that he never took action. Thus he fell in the state of depression. Such conflict went through the whole poem reflecting his embarrassment in love.

The form of the poem, a sort of inner monologue, well suits the content. Lots of seemingly unrelated scenes, events and images were put together in random. The poet turned from one scene to another, jumped from one thought to another readily and easily. Therefore, the poem seems rather fragmented and disordered. Yet, the mood, as a consistent clue runs through the whole poem and links the various images. Eliot was good at employing analogy and symbol to illustrate his ideas, and his poem was full of observation, memory, meditation and comment as well. In this poem, even punctuations are very unique, which contribute to the depiction of a hesitant intellectual.

5. Selected Reading

The Love Song of J. Alfred Prufrock ①

S'io credessi che mia risposta fosse
A persona che mai tornasse al mondo,
questa fiamma staria senza piu scosse.

Ma per cio che giammai di questo fondo
non torno uiuo alcun, s'i'odo il uero,
asenza tema d'infamia ti rispondo.[②]

Let us go then, you and I,
When the evening is spread out against the sky
Like a patient etherized upon a table;
Let us go, through certain half-deserted streets,
The muttering retreats
Of restless nights in one-night cheap hotels
And sawdust restaurants with oyster-shells:
Streets that follow like a tedious argument
Of insidious intent
To lead you to an overwhelming question...
Oh, do not ask, "What is it?"
Let us go and make our visit.

In the room the women come and go
Talking of Michelangelo.

The yellow fog that rubs its back upon the window-panes,
The yellow smoke that rubs its muzzle on the window-panes
Licked its tongue into the corners of the evening,
Lingered upon the pools that stand in drains,
Let fall upon its back the soot that falls from chimneys,
Slipped by the terrace, made a sudden leap,
And seeing that it was a soft October night,
Curled once about the house, and fell asleep.

And indeed there will be time[③]
For the yellow smoke that slides along the street

Rubbing its back upon the window-panes;
There will be time, there will be time
To prepare a face to meet the faces that you meet;
There will be time to murder and create,
And time for all the works and days of hands
That lift and drop a question on your plate;
Time for you and time for me,
And time yet for a hundred indecisions,
And for a hundred visions and revisions,
Before the taking of a toast and tea.

In the room the women come and go
Talking of Michelangelo.

And indeed there will be time
To wonder, "Do I dare?" and, "Do I dare?"
Time to turn back and descend the stair,
With a bald spot in the middle of my hair—
(They will say: "How his hair is growing thin!")
My morning coat, my collar mounting firmly to the chin,
My necktie rich and modest, but asserted by a simple pin—
(They will say: "But how his arms and legs are thin!")
Do I dare
Disturb the universe?
In a minute there is time
For decisions and revisions which a minute will reverse.

For I have known them all already, known them all—
Have known the evenings, mornings, afternoons,
I have measured out my life with coffee spoons;
I know the voices dying with a dying fall ④
Beneath the music from a farther room.
So how should I presume?

And I have known the eyes already, known them all—
The eyes that fix you in a formulated phrase,
And when I am formulated, sprawling on a pin,
When I am pinned and wriggling on the wall,
Then how should I begin
To spit out all the butt-ends of my days and ways?
And how should I presume?

And I have known the arms already, known them all—
Arms that are braceleted and white and bare
(But in the lamplight, downed with light brown hair!)
Is it perfume from a dress
That makes me so digress?
Arms that lie along a table, or wrap about a shawl.
And should I then presume?
And how should I begin?
...
Shall I say, I have gone at dusk through narrow streets
And watched the smoke that rises from the pipes
Of lonely min in shirt-sleeves, leaning out of windows? ...

I should have been a pair of ragged claws
Scuttling across the floors of silent seas. ⑤
...
And the afternoon, the evening, sleeps so peacefully!
Smoothed by long fingers.
Asleep...tired...or it malingers,
Stretched on the floor, here beside you and me.
Should I, after tea and cakes and ices,
Have the strength to force the moment to its crisis?
But though I have wept and fasted, wept and prayed
Though I have seen my head (grown slightly bald)

brought in upon a platter, [6]

I am no prophet-and here's no great matter;
I have seen the moment of my greatness flicker,
And I have seen the eternal Footman hold my coat, and snicker,
And in short, I was afraid.

And would it have been worth it, after all.
After the cups, the marmalade, the tea,
Among the porcelain, among some talk of you and me,
Would it have been worth while,
To have bitten off the matter with a smile.
To have squeezed the universe into a ball
To roll it towards some overwhelming question,
To say: "I am Lazarus, [7] come the dead,
Come back to tell you all, I shall tell you all" —
If one, settling a pillow by her head,
Should say: "That is not what I meant at all.
That is not it, at all."

And would it have been worth it, after all,
Would it have been worth while,
After the sunsets and the dooryards and the sprinkled streets,
After the novels, after the teacups, after the skirts that trail along the floor—
And this, and so much more? —
It is impossible to say just what I mean!
But as if a magic lantern threw the nerves in patterns on a screen:
Would it have been worth while
If one, settling a pillow or throwing off a shawl,
And turning toward the window, should say:
"That is not it at all,
That is not what I meant, at all."

...

No! I am not prince Hamlet, nor was meant to be;
Am an attendant lord, one that will do
To swell a progress, [8] start a scene or two,
Advise the prince: no doubt, an easy tool,
Deferential, glad to be of use,
Politic, cautious, and meticulous;
Full of high sentence, [9] but a bit obtuse;
At times, indeed, almost ridiculous—
Almost, at times, the Fool.

I grow old...I grow old...
I shall wear the bottoms of my trousers rolled.

Shall I part my hair behind? Do I dare to eat a peach?
I shall wear white flannel trousers, and walk upon the beach.
I have heard the mermaids singing, each to each,
I do not think that they will sing to me.
I have seen them riding seaward on the waves
Combing the white hair of the waves blown back
When the wind blows the water white and black.

We have lingered in the chambers of the sea
By sea-girls wreathed with seaweed red and brown
Till human voices wake us, and we drown.

NOTES

① Composed at Harvard, this dramatic monologue is a symbolist poem written in intermittently rhymed free verse. The title suggests an ironic contrast between a "love song" and a poem that proves to be about the absence of love, while the speaker's name suggests an ironic contrast between his ordinary surname (that of a St. Louis furniture dealer) and the elegant convention of using the first initial and middle name as a form of address, in a world which includes Prufrock but renders him profoundly alien in it. 题目为“情歌”，但诗是关于爱的缺失，形成讽刺性的对比。Prufrock一名取自密苏里州路易斯市的一个家具店主的名字，J. Alfred听上去给人一种门第高贵的感觉，也是一处讽刺对比。

② “If I thought that my reply would be to one who would ever return to the world, this flame would stay without further movement; but since none has ever returned alive from this depth, if what I hear is true, I answer you without fear of infamy” (Dante, inferno, XXVII, 61—66). The speaker, Guido do Montefeltro, consumed in his flame as punishment for giving false counsel, confesses his shame without fear of its being reported since he believes Dante cannot return to earth. 序诗取自但丁《地狱篇》第二十八章，是吉多·蒙特菲尔特罗同过访地狱的诗人但丁讲话。吉多因欺骗而在地狱受煎熬，全身被火焰包围。

③And indeed there will be time: An echo of Andrew Marvell's seductive plea in To His Coy Mistress (1681): “Had we but world enough, and time...” 仿自安德鲁·马维尔在《致腼腆的情人》(1681) 中求爱的话。

④the voices dying with a dying fall: Echo of Duke Orsino's self-indulgent invocation of music in Shakespeare's Twelfth Night, Act I, Scene Ⅰ, Ⅱ. 1—4:

“If music be the food of love, play on...That strain again! It had a dying fall.” 仿自莎士比亚《第十二夜》。

⑤ Scuttling across the floors of silent seas: Cf. Hamlet's mocking of Polonius in Shakespeare's Hamlet (1602), Ⅱ. 205—206: “you yourself, sir, should be old as I am, if like a crab you could go backward.” 引自莎士比亚《哈姆雷特》。

⑥seen my head (grown slightly bald) brought in upon a platter: As did John the Baptist, beheaded by the temptress Salome, who presented his head to Queen Herodia, in the story recounted in Mark. 6. 17—20, Matthew 14. 1—Ⅱ, and Oscar Wilde's play Salome (1894). 据《圣经·马太福音》记载，莎乐美把先知约翰的头砍下献给王后希罗底，后成为奥斯卡·王尔德的戏剧《莎乐美》的素材。

⑦I am Lazarus: The resurrection of Lazarus is recounted in Luke 16. 19—31 and John Ⅱ. 1—44. 拉撒路复活的故事记载于《圣经》的《路加福音》和《约翰福音》中。

⑧To swell a progress: A journey or procession made by royal courts and often portrayed on Elizabethan stages. 〔古语〕(特指王侯的) 视察，巡行，游历，在伊丽莎白时代剧作中多有描写。

⑨high sentence: Opinions, sententiousness 高见

Topic Discussion

1. What's the purpose of mentioning Hamlet?
2. Discuss the image of yellow smoke.

Ⅱ. Robert Lee Frost (1874—1963)

1. Life

Frost was born in San Francisco on March 26. His father was originally a New Englander and a graduate of Harvard. When his father died, his mother brought the family back to New England which later became the poetic background of his poetry. While studying at Lawrence High School, Frost wrote poems and finished his studies with honor. He attended Harvard College from 1899 and then fell ill with tuberculosis. So he had to take his family to the countryside in order to get recovered. He loved farm life and wrote many poems. All through his life, he got four Pulitzer Prizes and in 1961, he was invited by President Kennedy to read his poems at the inauguration, the first poet to be so honored. He is considered the most popular poet in the 20th century.

2. Literary Career

In 1912 he went to England, where he met Ezra Pound, who helped him publish his poems. In 1915 he returned to America and settled down in New Hampshire. Most of his major poetry was written before 1930. His major books include *Mountain Interval* (1916), *New Hampshire* (1923), *West-Running Brook* (1928), *Collected Poems* (1930), *A Further Range* (1936), *A Witness Tree* (1942) *and In the Clearing* (1962). He received the Ballinger Prize in 1963 and died on January of that year at the age of 88.

3. Features

Robert Frost was the most popular American poet from 1914 to his death. Different from the other modernist poets who were obscure and incomprehensible, Frost was not in the mainstream of modern poetry and therefore could be understood by the average person. His poetry is full of life, truth and wisdom. For his achievement in poetry, Frost won the Pulitzer Prize four times. His poems are characterized by the following:

The setting in his poems is New England. The subjects come from daily life of ordinary people. Frost wrote about farmers, shepherds, and rural events, isolated from urban society. Building fences and picking apples are not uncommon to appear in his poems. His theme includes landscape and people of New England, loneliness and poverty of farmers; beauty, terror and tragedy.

Frost was conservative politically. He stood aside from the literary movements of the 20th century since he showed little interest in experimentation in form. Under his pen the New England landscape reflects the fragmentation of modern society. The characters were confronted with the tension of modern life and alienation among modern people.

Frost took a simple style in his poetry. He used simple language, graceful style and traditional forms. He liked regular iambic meter and sometimes used blank verse. He was good at expressing profound ideas through symbols.

4. Introduction to *Mending Wall*

This poem was published in *North of Boston*, a collection of poems, in 1914. One of the subjects frequently occurring in Frost's poems is about mending and maintaining wall.

Mending Wall presents us such a scene in which people are mending wall in spring. In this poem, "I" (the narrator) bear some ideas unconventional and therefore speak differently, while the neighbor clings to the old thought passing from his father. At first, the narrator talks about how the wall works against nature; later, he turns to the talking of their mending wall once a year. People intend to separate themselves from others and keep privacy by building wall, but actually the wall is not very effective. The narrator mentions the absurdity of having a wall between him and his neighbor and thinks that the old saying "Good fences make good neighbors" is really old.

This poem seemingly describes daily reality, but in fact it is a fable in which the poet tries to explore the relation between tradition and nature. He tries to tell readers about the embarrassment of human being that people want to make good neighbors by having a wall, but the wall just keeps friendship away. Such is the situation of western civilization.

"Mending Wall" employs blank verse of iambic pentameter, and it is full of colloquial and direct expressions, which are easily understood.

5. Selected Reading

Mending Wall

Something there is that doesn't love a wall,
That sends the frozen-ground-swell under it
And spills the upper boulders in the sun,
And makes gaps even two can pass abreast.
The work of hunters is another thing:
I have come after them and made repair
Where they have left not one stone on a stone,
But they would have the rabbit out of hiding,
To please the yelping dogs. The gaps I mean,
No one has seen them made or heard them made,
But at spring mending-time we find them there.
I let my neighbor know beyond the hill;
And on a day we meet to walk the line
And set the wall between us once again.
We keep the wall between us as we go. ①
To each the boulders that have fallen to each. ②
And some are loaves and some so nearly balls
We have to use a spell to make them balance:
"Stay where you are until our backs are turned!"
We wear our fingers rough with handling them.
Oh, just another kind of outdoor game,
One on a side. It comes to little more:

There where it is we do not need the wall:
"Why do they make good neighbors? Isn't it
Where there are cows? But here there are no cows.
Before I built a wall I'd ask to know
What I was walling in or walling out,
And to whom I was like ③ to give offense.
Something there is that doesn't love a wall,
That wants it down. I could say "Elves" to him, ④
But it's not elves exactly, and I'd rather
He said it for himself. I see him there,
Bringing a stone grasped firmly by the top
In each hand, like an old-stone savage armed. ⑤
He moves in darkness ⑥ as it seems to me,
Not of wood s only and the shade of trees.
He will not go behind his father's saying,
And he likes having thought of it so well
He says again, "Good fences make good neighbors." ⑦

NOTES

①We keep the wall between us as we go: It explains the relationship among people in the reality. 我们走着，中间始终隔一堵墙。这句话表现了生活中人际关系的现实。

②To each the boulders that have fallen to each: 落到谁那边的石头，就由谁去料理。

③like=likely 很可能的

④I could say "Elves" to him: The narrator might tell his neighbor that maybe the elves had broken the wall. 叙事人本来可以告诉邻居，是妖精作怪推倒了墙。

⑤like an stone-age savage armed: The neighbor hold stones just like the armed savage in the old-stone time. 像旧石器时代的野人一样手持武器。

⑥darkness: ignorance 愚昧无知，尚未受到启蒙

⑦He says again, "Good fences make good neighbors": the neighbor follows his father's instruction. 他信守父辈教诲。

Topic Discussion

Discuss the theme of the poem.

第三节　迷惘的一代与海明威

每节导读

学习本节需要掌握迷惘的一代的特点和代表作家，海明威代表作品和艺术特色。

迷惘的一代指的是20世纪20年代出现的、具有相似倾向的一些年轻作家。他们有的参加了第一次世界大战并对帝国主义战争感到厌恶，如海明威；有的对战后社会大失所望，如菲次杰拉德。他们相似的倾向是迷惘、失望和悲观的情绪。该词源自斯泰因对海明威所说的一句话："你们都是迷惘的一代。"后来海明威将其用于小说《太阳照样升起》而流行起来。

欧内斯特·海明威为"迷惘的一代"最杰出代表，并以独树一帜的"海明威风格"创建了一种洗练、简捷的现代叙事文体。"硬汉"形象、"重压下的风度"、"冰山"原则等都是海明威小说的艺术特色。

Ⅰ. The Lost Generation

It is a term in frequent use after the First World War in reference to the young men who had survived physically but were afterwards spiritually and morally adrift. This term was coined by Gertrude Stein and was used as a preface to Hemingway's novel *The Sun Also Rises*. Major writers of the Lost Generation are Scott Fitzgerald, Ernest Hemingway, John Dos Passos and E. E. Cummings etc. They lived in a special period of American history—the 1920's. During the decade, people lived a luxurious life and enjoyed money-making and pleasure seeking. And they doubted what was going to happen in the U. S. A.

The group of American young writers moved to Paris of France. They were dissatisfied with American society for American society could not value their artistic works. They shared the belief that they would find personal and artistic fulfillment in an older civilization. The group of young people lost their American ideals and America lost their finest young writers. Though they were not satisfied with American society, they went back to their country later.

Ⅱ. Ernest Hemingway (1899—1961)

1. Life and Literary Career

Ernest Hemingway is generally regarded as the spokesman for the Lost Generation. He is famous for his novels and short stories written in intense prose with short sentences and very specific details. Almost all his stories deal with the theme of courage in face of tragedy. They reveal man's impotence and despairing courage to assert himself against overwhelming odds.

Hemingway was born on July 21, 1899 in Oak Park, Illinois, one of six children in the family. His father was a highly respected doctor who was fond of hunting and fishing. His mother was a singer and music teacher. Young Hemingway was an outstanding student at high school, and he already wrote some short stories at that age. After graduation from Oak Park High School in 1917, instead of attending university, Hemingway worked briefly as a journalist, for the star in Kansas City. And he really wanted to take part in the First World War. But when the U. S. Army rejected him because of one bad eye, he volunteered first as an ambulance driver in France, and then as a soldier in the Italian infantry. He was badly wounded at the age of 18. While he lay in an Italian hospital, he fell in love with a Red Cross nurse, but she refused his proposal of marriage.

In 1919 Hemingway returned to Chicago to complete his recovery and there he met and married his first wife. As soon as he was fully recovered, they left for Paris as a correspondent for a Canadian newspaper, and as an assistant for an

American literary magazine. But his main purpose was to write his own stories.

Hemingway met Gertrude Stein, Ezra Pound and Sherwood Anderson in Paris who encouraged him and helped him to develop his characteristic style. With their help he published his first collection of 15 short stories, *In Our Time* in 1925. In 1926, his full-length novel, *The Sun Also Rises*, met with great success. It was about the disillusionment of the lost generation. A second novel, *A Farewell to Arms*, firmly established his reputation in 1929. This novel shows that not only war threatens people, but the very texture of life itself involves violence and death. In Paris he divorced his first wife in 1927 and married the second one.

During the 1930s he wrote less because he had a strong desire for adventure. He spent a large part of his time in deep-sea fishing near Cuba, big game hunting in Africa, or following bullfights in Spain. Hemingway's own adventurous life provided much raw material for his strongly masculine stories.

In 1936 he took part in the Spanish Civil War as a journalist, strongly supporting the losing Republican side against the Fascist forces of Franco (1892—1975). He predicted that the Spanish Civil War would be a prelude to the Second World War. While he was in Spain, he met and fell in love with a writer and journalist whom he married, after divorcing his second wife. His experiences provided material for one of his best novels, *For Whom The Bell Tolls* (1940). This is a love story of great appeal, and this is also a war novel containing the message that all liberals must help each other, must act collectively, if good is to endure. Then Hemingway and his third wife traveled together to China, as journalists, to report on the Japanese invasion, and then returned to Cuba.

At first, Hemingway created an organization to report on German spies in Cuba and then he went to London as a Journalist. He flew on several missions with the Royal Air Force, into the heart of the battle. He crossed the English Channel with the American forces to report on the invasion of France, and he was present at the liberation of Paris. After the war, he returned to Cuba, divorced his third wife, and married a journalist whom he had met in London.

She stayed with him for the rest of his life. In 1952, Hemingway published his last successful novel, *The Old Man And the Sea*. This novel is a Parable of inner strength and courage about a Cuban Fisherman's struggle to bring home a great marlin he has caught. It highlights the theme that a man can be destroyed but not defeated. In 1954, he was awarded the Nobel Prize for literature.

After the Cuban Revolution, Hemingway had to leave Cuba. He settled down in Idaho, a wild part of the U. S. A. in the Rocky Mountains. But he became deeply depressed and so tormented by failing artistic and physical power that he had to receive electric shock treatment. That treatment, in fact, did not work. Two days after returning to Idaho, he committed suicide by shooting himself with his hunting gun.

2. His Point of View

Hemingway's point of view was shaped by his experience as a young man in the First World War, and his near death on the battlefield. Many of his stories dealt with war or injury and nearly all of them examined the nature of courage. By living through the impersonal violence of the war, by suffering the violent accident of his wound, he felt that he had been cut off from the security of his own past life, and from all his old beliefs and assumptions about life. In a parallel way, he felt that the First World War had broken America's culture and traditions, and separated them from their roots. He wrote about men and women who were isolated from tradition, frightened, sometimes ridiculous, trying to find their own way. He gave no literary explanations, and no conventional "happy endings" to his stories.

In trying to understand the nature of injury and violent death and the courage needed to face them, Hemingway became a knowledgeable spectator of Spanish bull fighting. Many of his stories contained episodes in the bullring. Risk, danger, grace, skill and death were always present in this traditional ritualistic sport of Spain. His own love of big game hunting undoubtedly stemmed from his curiosity about these things. In the African jungles, he could test his own courage and skill against an impersonal, violent enemy, the wild beast, while avoiding the random devastation of modern war.

He also wrote about courage with which people face the tragedies in life. To him, man's greatest achievement is to show "grace under pressure" Here, "grace" refers to the behavior of the heroes under Hemingway's situation; "pressure" refers to Hemingway's situation. Hemingway's situation is usually characterized by all kinds of unpleasant things, such as crime, death, chaos and violence.

One of the important things that make Hemingway popular is that in a time of general despair and pessimism he wrote stories with heroes that the readers could admire. This is one of the reasons that his stories sold very well. Hemingway's hero is usually isolated, and fights a good fight. There is a particular term, "the code hero", for his character. The code hero with stoic courage lives by a pattern which gives life meaning and value. Usually, the code hero should be a master of many skills, demonstrate in resolution and endurance and exhibit pride and humiliation combined.

In his fiction the nihilistic vision of sterility, failure and death is modified by his affirmative assertion of the possibility of living with style and courage. Therefore, he often dealt with war and its effects on people, with contests such as hunting and bullfighting which demand strength and courage and with the question of how to live with pain. Nihilism is Hemingway's attitude toward the world.

3. His Literary Style

Hemingway's iceberg principle of writing is famous. Hemingway once said: "The dignity of movement of an iceberg is due to only one-eighth of it being above water." Think of an iceberg: one eighth of an iceberg is above the water. All of the rest is underneath the water. The rest is implied. One must go very deep beneath the surface to understand the full meaning of his writing. Hemingway's vocabulary is easy and his sentence patterns are easy, but they are extremely difficult to be fully and completely understood. His lean, economical style of writing is striking: sentence short, uncomplicated, but active; words simple but filled with emotion; few adjectives, and great control of pause with action of the story continuing during the silences. There are times when the most powerful effect comes from restraint and understatement for he believed that the strongest effect comes with an economy of means.

In his novels, Hemingway's dialogue can introduce setting; can help development of plot; can be used to portray a character and can be used to show the theme.

Hemingway is often called a lyric writer for he was interested in conveying a deep emotional feeling. He did have some realistic techniques, but on the whole he was not like the realist writers because he was more interested in conveying his personal emotions.

4. His Major Works

Hemingway's first novel, *The Sun Also Rises*, appeared in 1926 and it was an immediate success. He described the life of aimless expatriates, in Europe as seen through the eyes of a young man who must face the bitter fact that a war wound left him unable to have children. In this story, Hemingway used a bullfight in Spain symbolically, as a criticism of the feckless atmosphere of postwar life. This novel paints a picture of the whole Lost Generation.

His second big success was *A Farewell to Arms* (1929). This novel describes an American lieutenant fighting in Italy in the First World War, just as Hemingway himself did. The hero suffers from three shocking events. First, he receives a serious wound in battle. Second, he takes part in a retreat which turns into undisciplined chaos and destruction. The hero loses all sense of responsibility to the army and escapes to Switzerland with the nurse whom he loves. He is determined to build a decent life, have a family, and contribute a grain of sanity to the madness of the world. When his baby is stillborn and his wife dies in childbirth, he has nothing left but his own courage to rely on.

In the next ten years, Hemingway wrote a short novel about bullfighting entitled *Death in the Afternoon* (1932), and one about big game bunting called *Green Hills of Africa* (1936). He also wrote many short stories. But his next important work was his novel about the Spanish Civil War, *For Whom The Bell Tolls* (1940). This novel concerns a volunteer American guerrilla in Spain, who blows up a strategic bridge as part of an attack which he knows is doomed to failure. In the end, he is left to die, yet he does his best for his comrades-in-arms and for the cause which he believes in.

In 1952, he wrote another masterpiece, *The Old Man and the Sea*. This short novel is a simple story, containing some of Hemingway's best writing. It tells about a Cuban fisherman who catches a giant marlin, only to see it devoured by sharks. This book capped his career, and led to his receipt of the Nobel Prize two years later.

Throughout his life, Hemingway wrote short stories, some of which are as famous as his novels, "The Snows of Kilimanjaro" and "The Killers" are probably among the best known.

5. Introduction to *A Farewell to Arms*

1) Plot Overview

During the First World War young lieutenant Frederic Hanry, an American served in an Italian ambulance unit. He meets Catherine Barkly, an English nurse, by chance and falls in love with her. They plan to get married after the close of the War and to have a happy family. During a bombardment Henry is wounded in the head and legs and is then moved to a hospital in Milan where Catherine comes to nurse him. They have a happy summer together while Henry recovers after a successful operation. That autumn Catherine tells Henry that she is pregnant. They are overjoyed for that. But Catherine refuses to marry Henry because she fears to resign her job and to be sent back to England until the end of the war.

Henry arrives back at the front only to find that the combatants have grown more pessimistic than ever, and even the priest talks to him about his desperate hopes that the war will come to an end. After Austrians attack for several days running, the Italian Army retreats miserably. Henry and his men are depressed by monotonous horrors of the war, and bear great tribulations during the disastrous retreat. When the battle police threatens him that he will be mistaken for a spy owing to his foreign accents, he deserts his post.

But when he gets to the hospital, he learns that Catherine has been transferred to Stresa. Borrowing some civilian clothes, he joins her there. Overjoyed, they lead a short happy life until one night Henry is warned off because the military police suspect him as a German spy and are on their way to arrest him.

Henry, therefore, is forced to flee with Catherine to Switzerland. They they move to Lausanne in the winter, awaiting the birth of their child in peace, but the baby is stillborn and Catherine dies in the childbirth, leaving Henry forlorn and alone in an alien land.

2) Brief Comment

①Importance of the Novel

A Farewell to Arms is one of the best novels about the World War I.

It established Hemingway's position in American literature and is said to be the book that explains the reason why the Lost Generation is lost. It can be called a sister book to *The Sun Also Rise* which paints a complete picture of the Lost Generation. It is one of the works which completely demonstrate his style.

②Hemingway Style

Hemingway was influenced by Mark Twain, Sherwood Anderson and Gertrude Stein. He used colloquialism; his language was plain and simple. He learned simplicity and economy of expression as a way to reach his goal. His use of short, uncomplicated active sentences with fundamental words such as nouns, verbs and very few adjectives and connectives such as and, but, so, then etc. became his recognizable style.

His dialogue can introduce setting, can help development of plot, can be used to portray a character and can be used to show the theme. For his Iceberg Principle, Hemingway thinks, a writer should write little... He should write in this way that readers can understand much more. So his sentences are seemingly simple, but deeper in meaning if read carefully.

He also used some modern writing techniques such as symbolism, stream of consciousness etc.

Ⅲ. Selected Reading

A Farewell to Arms

BOOK Ⅰ

1

In the late summer of that year we lived in a house in a village that looked across the river and the plain to the mountains. In the bed of the river there were pebbles and boulders, dry and white in the sun, and the water was clear and swiftly moving and blue in the channels. Troops went by the house and down the road and the dust they raised powdered the leaves of the trees. The trunks of the trees too were dusty and the leaves fell early that year and we saw the troops marching along the road and the dust rising and leaves, stirred by the breeze, falling and the soldiers marching and afterward the road bare and white except for the leaves.

The plain was rich with crops; there were many orchards of fruit trees and beyond the plain the mountains were brown and bare. There was fighting in the mountains and at night we could see the flashes from the artillery. In the dark it was like summer lightning, but the nights were cool and there was not the feeling of a storm coming.

Sometimes in the dark we heard the troops marching under the window and guns going past pulled by motor-tractors. There was much traffic at night and many mules on the roads with boxes of ammunition on each side of their pack-saddles and gray motor trucks that carried men, and other trucks with loads covered with canvas that moved slower in the traffic. There were big guns too that passed in the day drawn by tractors, the long barrels of the guns covered with green branches and green leafy branches and vines laid over the tractors. To the north we could look across a valley and see a forest of chestnut trees and behind it another mountain on this side of the river. There was fighting for that mountain too, but it was not successful, and in the fall when the rains came the leaves all fell from the chestnut trees and the branches were bare and the trunks black with rain. The vineyards were thin and bare-branched too and all the country wet and brown and dead with the autumn. There were mists over the river and clouds on the mountain and the trucks splashed mud on the road and the troops were muddy and wet in their capes; their rifles were wet and under their capes the two leather cartridge-boxes on the front of the belts, gray leather boxes heavy with the packs of clips of thin, long 6. 5mm. cartridges, bulged forward under the capes so that the men, passing on the road, marched as though they were six months gone with child.

There were small gray motor cars that passed going very fast; usually there was an officer on the seat with the driver and more officers in the back seat. They splashed more mud than the camions even and if one of the officers in the back was very small and sitting between two generals, he himself so small that you could not see his face but only the top of his cap and his narrow back, and if the car went especially fast it was probably the King ①. He lived in Udine and came out in this way nearly every day to see how things were going, and things went very badly.

At the start of the winter came the permanent rain and with the rain came the cholera. But it was checked and in the end only seven thousand died of it in the army. ②

NOTES

①the king of Italy：指意大利国王。

②...only seven thousand died of it in the army：海明威的含蓄笔法（understatement）。这是对战争的无情抨击，在平淡无奇的文字下面饱含激愤的情绪。

Topic Discussion

1. What techniques did the author use to set the tone?

2. It is the very beginning of the whole novel. Can you learn in which year the story took place here? Can you know the name of the village, the name of the river and even the name of the country? Why or why not? What kind of attitude of the author can you learn toward the war from this?

第四节　“爵士乐时代”与菲兹杰拉德

每节导读

学习本节需要掌握“爵士乐时代”特点和代表作家司各特·菲兹杰拉德代表作品和艺术特色。

“爵士乐时代”指美国的20世纪20年代，准确地说是从1919年至1929年间。该年代一大特点是经济的高度繁荣，因此该年代又称“金元年代”。这一时代的另一特点是人们同传统观念及道德的决裂，例如人们为了赚钱可以无视法律，人们还疯狂追求享乐，所以这一阶段还有“喧嚣的20年代”之称。

司各特·菲兹杰拉德是20世纪20年代“爵士乐时代”的代言人及命名人，其作品充分表现了“美国梦”的幻灭。他的代表作《了不起的盖茨比》描写了人们在“爵士乐时代”对“美国梦”不择手段的追求和理想的幻灭。

Ⅰ. The Jazz Age

The Jazz Age is the period in the U. S. history (starting in 1919 and ending in 1929). It has two characteristics. The first one is economic boom. During that period of time, heavy industry increased and cars became popular because of the Fords' contribution. There were high profit and full employment. People could make a lot of money. So it was also called "Dollar-Decade". The second one is that people broke away from traditions. The change of value appeared. In the past, people would work hard and be thrifty to be a good man. But now they were absorbed in money-making. Being successful means having a lot of money. Good men were the people with a lot of money. They enjoyed themselves greatly. They behaved strangely for all these shocked the older generation. It was also called "Roaring Twenties". The Jazz Age got its name from Fitzgerald's book entitled *Tales of the Jazz Age*.

Ⅱ. F. Scott Fitzgerald (1896—1940)

1. Life and Literary Career

Fitzgerald is generally regarded as the spokesman of the 1920s, the peculiar decade that combined the postwar economic boom and the sense of spiritual disorientation. He was born just before the turn of the century, and his life roughly coincided with the consolidation of monopoly capitalism in the United States. He was both a leading participant in the typically pleasure-seeking and money-making life of the 1920s, and at the same time, he was a cool self-conscious observer. During the 1920s, he enjoyed success, fame, and wealth, as a young lucky writer, but declined in spirit like his country when the New York stock market crashed in 1929, when the grim 1930s began to move into the Great Depression. During the 1930s, he tasted the bitterness in personal life and in literary career. So, he was the most representative novelist of the 1920s, the spokesman of the "Roaring 20s". His works not only reflected, but also helped to influence the prevailing mood of the time.

He was born in Saint Paul—in the Mid-west of America. He was the only son of an unsuccessful middle class father and an energetic mother of a common, Irish family. His family was socially prominent and genteelly poor. His grandfather on his mother's side had a small fortune in the business. This gave Scott some advantages in a money-oriented society, and eventually gave him his expensive education first in a fashionable Catholic preparatory school in New Jersey and then at Princeton University in 1913. He found American society vulgar yet full of bright opportunities. Although he wanted to be popular in this setting, he felt the snobbishness of his classmates because he came from the "wrong" part of the country and, on his mother's side, from the "wrong" social class. Furthermore, he was not rich and he felt inferior to his more brilliant classmates.

Fitzgerald tried to erase his background at Princeton. He was handsome and witty. He made a place for himself in the university's literary groups; he was invited to join the best clubs; and he wrote musical comedies which were well received. While he was still at the university, he fell in love with a rich girl who was known as a great beauty. After appearing to favor him, she then became engaged to another man. Fitzgerald fell ill, failed his exams, and left Princeton without graduating in 1917.

He decided to fight as a soldier in the First World War, but he was sent for training to Montgomery, Alabama in the South in 1918. There he met Zelda Sayre, the beautiful light-hearted daughter of a State Supreme Court judge. He fell violently in love again, but Zelda told him that if he could become rich enough to support her very well, she would marry him. As soon as he left the army in 1919, he went to New York to become rich, but the only job he could find paid him very little. When Zelda heard this, she broke their engagement. In despair, he went home to his parents in Saint Paul, to finish writing a novel which he had started at Princeton. He became a novelist for the sole purpose of earning enough money to marry Zelda.

In 1920, Fitzgerald's first novel *This Side of Paradise* was an instant success. It was the first American novel to portray the young, postwar, pleasure-seeking generation, and to reveal the new morality of the Twenties. Fitzgerald found himself rich and famous at the age of 23. At last he could afford the high style of life which Zelda demanded and which he himself longed for. They were married; throughout his life, Fitzgerald's greatest happiness and deepest sorrow were caused by Zelda.

For four years, this good-looking, dashing young couple plunged into the gaudy, wealthy society of their generation. They were treated like a prince and princess. They lived so extravagantly that they frequently spent more money than Fitzgerald earned for parties, liquor, entertaining their friends and traveling. It was this style of living which gave the decade of the 1920s such nicknames as "The Roaring Twenties". "The Jazz Age" and "The Dollar Decade".

In order to keep earning enough money, Fitzgerald wrote short stories for magazines and a second novel entitled *The Beautiful and Damned* (1922), all of which were immensely popular. People admired him for his spendthrift life and for his great literary production because this was the ideal the young Americans pursued in the 1920s. Yet *The Beautiful and the Damned* already betrayed the author's doubts and his fear that this way of life was destroying the people who pursued it.

In 1929, Fitzgerald and Zelda moved to France, where they joined the Lost Generation (Gertrude Stein's nickname for the young expatriates). There, in 1925, Fitzgerald wrote his best novel, *The Great Gatsby*. It is the story of an idealist who is destroyed by the influence of the wealthy, pleasure-seeking people around him, a portrait of moral decay. This book was not so well liked by the public as his earlier ones at first, but today it has been regarded as his masterpiece.

In the next few years, Zelda began to show signs of mental illness, and they returned to America. Zelda suffered a mental breakdown in 1930, and another one two years later, from which she never recovered. She had to be placed in a sanitorium. Throughout this time of anxiety, Fitzgerald wrote some fine short stories and a moving novel about the life they knew in France, entitled *Tender Is the Night*. The novel was not finished until 1934. Although it is now considered an excellent work, it was received very coldly then. Times had changed. America was deep in the Great Depression, and nobody wanted to read about expatriates in France. The failure of the book and despair over Zelda's illness caused Fitzgerald's health to break down, physically and spiritually. He drank to excess and became incurably alcoholic.

In 1937, he recovered enough to work again, but he no longer wrote stories. Instead he went to Hollywood as a script-writer for films. There he met a woman journalist who cared for him and acquainted him with the life of film makers and film stars. He began writing a novel about Hollywood, and many critics believe it would have been his masterpiece. It was only half finished when he died of a heart attack in 1940. A few years later, Zelda was killed in a fire which destroyed the sanatorium where she was confined.

2. His Point of View and Style

Fitzgerald's fiction reveals the hollowness of the American worship of wealth and the unending American dreams of love, splendor and gratified desires and shows what America meant in terms of the reckless 1920s: prohibition, speakeasies, new cars, victory abroad, popular fads and new wealth. *The Great Gatsby* represents the American scene during those riotous years.

American dream means that in America one might hope to satisfy every material desire and thereby achieve happiness. It is deceptive because it proposes the satisfaction of all desire as an attainable goal and identifies desire with material. Fitzgerald once said, "America's great promise is that something is going to happen, but it never does. America is the moon that never rose." This indictment of the American dream could well serve as an epigraph for the protagonist Gatsby.

Fitzgerald was the victim of his own success. Critics considered him so much a part of the rich, fashionable life of the 1920's that for many years they failed to understand the serious side of his books. There is no doubt that his early success damaged his life and spoiled his literary production.

In the long run, his understanding and moral interpretation of the era was far more important than his participation in its gaudy extravagances. His literature has outlasted his period he wrote about.

In his first books and stories, Fitzgerald saw life through "a haze of youth", where tragedy consisted only of growing older. He expressed what very young people believed in 1920s: that they could wipe out the past and rebuild the world into something much better, free from the ideas of the older generation. He wrote about himself and his friends. At first he presented the charm and glamour of the new generation, but within a few short years he turned from its spokesman into its most incisive judge. He penetrated beneath the surface of their life to reveal its worthlessness.

Fitzgerald never truly belonged in the life of America's wealthy class, which he both longed for and mistrusted. He wanted to have the appearance of belonging to the upper crust, believing that the appearance would give him the freedom to conduct his life just as he wished. However, he found that wealth altered people's characters, making them mean and destructive. Money bought only tragedy and remorse. In his best novels, he both condemned and pitied the rich.

Fitzgerald dealt most astutely with the double theme of love and money. He understood the corrupting relationship between the two better than any other American novelist. Fitzgerald also understood, from his own experience, the constant need for more money which drove these men and women to unscrupulousness.

He did not like the rich. He resented their undeserved privileges, their vulgarity, and their secret belief in their own superiority. He saw that the rich boys could buy more than luxuries—they could attract the affection of any girl they wanted. He believed that the wealthy class corrupted the whole of American society because it became everybody's ideal to join it. He wrote from true experience, for he himself was fatally attracted to it. A deep attitude of morality underlies his stories.

Later in his life, Fitzgerald wrote, "I would have gone on writing musical comedies, but I am too much of a moralist at heart, and really want to preach at people in some acceptable form rather than entertain them." He found an admirably "acceptable form" in the modern novel.

His style of writing is closely related to his theme. It relies on an accumulation of well-chosen and ironic detail, carefully observed from life. He exactly reproduces the language and conversation of the time. In his chapters, he moves rapidly from one brightly presented scene to the next, leaving the tedious process of transition to the reader's imagination.

3. His Works

Fitzgerald's first highly successful novel, *This Side of Paradise* (1920), can now be seen as an immature work describing the wild, rebellious young men and women after the First World War. In this novel, Fitzgerald spoke as one of them, at the age of 23. He made a true portrait of the very young, with their new way of dressing, their disregard of manners and propriety. He caught the glamour which they saw in themselves, and made his readers see them as glamorous and important, also.

His second novel, *The Beautiful and Damned* (1921) followed a similar theme and increased Fitzgerald's popularity even more. The book describes a handsome young man and his beautiful wife, undoubtedly modeled after himself and Zelda. The couple enjoy a frivolous life among their wealthy friends while waiting to inherit a large fortune, but they degenerate into jaded middle age before they can get the money.

The Great Gatsby (1925) is considered by many to be Fitzgerald's best novel. It is a lively, deeply moral book, which shows the two sides of his character. The narrator is a decent Middle Western graduate from an eastern university (like Fitzgerald) who observes the life of his rich neighbor, Gatsby. This young man has grown rich quickly and illegally as a "bootlegger" in order to join the wealthy class and recapture a beautiful but shallow girl who slighted him when he was poor. Gatsby entertains other rich people at fabulous parties but his death is brought about by the carelessness of others and all his so-called friends abandon him in the end. The book is a severe criticism of the whole society and a book that studies the failure of American dream.

Tender Is The Night (1934) is Fitzgerald's second important novel, in which he condemns the wasted energy of misguided youth. The hero is a psychiatrist who marries a rich patient but he sacrifices all his talent and energy to maintain an illusion of love with a wife who abandons him anyway. The book passes a harsh judgment on the false values of the 1920's.

The Last Tycoon (1941) was Fitzgerald's unfinished novel, which told about a film-producer trying to maintain his honesty in the corrupt environment of Hollywood. The book was edited and published by a literary friend of Fitzgerald after his death.

Fitzgerald wrote many short stories. One of his best is "Babylon Revisited", the story of an American's return to Paris in the 1930's and his regretful realization that the past was beyond his reach, where he could neither alter it nor make amends.

4. Introduction to *The Great Gatsby*

1) Plot Overview

Nick Carraway, a quiet young man from the Mid-west, comes to work on the New York stock exchange. Though inclined to reserve his personal judgments on others, Nick is eager to experience life in the East and is ready to work hard to make a successful career. He rents a modest bungalow house, next to a pretentious and vulgar mansion built in the style of a French castle, owned by the ridiculously wealthy Jay Gatsby. West Egg is the home of people like Gatsby, who have made quick money and huge fortunes but who lack the traditions related with inherited wealth and titles.

Nick is invited to dine with his cousin, Daisy, and her husband, Tom Buchanan, who is also a midwesterner and has recently come east. They live in East Egg, where people like the Buchanans with inherited wealth make their homes. As a sophisticated observer of character and surroundings, Nick notices that the home of the Buchanans is lavish, and the young couple enjoy arrogant leisure. Tom is muscular, handsome and proud of his house and horses. Daisy and her friend, Jordan Baker, laze around in stylish dresses to kill the time. Daisy is charming and graceful in her social manners and always murmurs in a magical voice which "was full of money" so that the listener finds it pleasant to lean forward to catch her meaning. She also takes great delight in mentioning her three-year-old daughter. When Nick chances to mention Gatsby, the millionaire neighbor he does not know himself, Daisy asks, "What Gatsby?" Their living style is so lazy and cozy that Daisy is puzzled about what to plan for entertainment. Yet there is a tense moment when Tom goes out to answer the phone and Jordan Baker wants to listen to Tom's conversation: Tom is speaking to his mistress, Myrtle Wilson. Daisy later confesses to Nick that she is not happy but sophisticated since "she has been everywhere and seen everything and done everything." Nick feels disgusted and disturbed when he leaves the Buchanans. Tom's keeping another woman is an obvious result of dissatisfaction with his life.

Gatsby hosts a succession of fabulous parties at his house where he treats his guests to his motor-boats and private beach, apart from the endless flow of cocktails.

Nick is invited to one of these parties. He doesn't see his neighbor in person, but meets Jordan Baker there and they begin to develop a mild romance. Jordan tells Nick of Gatsby's love affair with Daisy five years ago. Daisy was said to have broken off with Gatsby with the intervention of her family which has been very rich. But soon Daisy recovered from the loss of Gatsby and became engaged to Tom. They married the following year.

Jordan also reveals that Gatsby has bought his house in West Egg just to be across the bay from Daisy. For Gatsby, Daisy is the promise of fulfillment that lies beyond the green light gleaming all night on her dock. Gatsby's hidden motivation of "purposeless splendor" is to capture the woman who has come to represent his ideal. Gatsby believes that he can win his woman back with his wealth, that he can attain the ideal she stands for through material success. Now he wants Nick to invite Daisy to tea so that he can meet her again. Up to the present moment, everything Gatsby owns exists only for the attainment of his vision: to repeat the past and win his woman back.

Hostility explodes when Tom forces Gatsby to tell the truth about what is going on between him and Daisy. At last, Gatsby blurts out that Daisy has never loved Tom. But Daisy corrects him by declaring that she has loved them both. Tom points out that Gatsby's accumulation of wealth is connected with criminal activities. Daisy now is lost to Gatsby forever, despite his frantic attempts to revitalize the "dead dream."

On the way back to West Egg, Gatsby's big yellow ear hits Myrtle Wilson and Daisy drives away. From Gatsby's father, Nick learns how rigidly Gatsby had worked towards self-fulfillment from youth. Nick can no longer tolerate the moral chaos that lies beneath the wealth and sophistication of Eastern society. So he decides to return to the Midwest. Months later, he meets Tom Buchanan and realizes that it was he who told Wilson where to find Gatsby and he and Daisy had fled to New York before Gatsby was murdered.

2) Brief Comment

①The themes of the novel

One theme of the novel is the atmosphere and reality of the Jazz Age. In the much quoted Chapter Three, the author, through a lot of details at the party, shows that the age is one with material wealth but spiritual poverty.

The more important theme is the emptiness and failure of American dream. Daisy stands for American dream in Gatsby's eyes. His efforts to win Daisy stands for his efforts in realization of American dream. When Daisy betrays Gatsby, it means that he is actually betrayed by the dream he pursues. Nick realizes the failure of Gatsby's dream, when he comments, "I thought of Gatsby's wonder when he first picked out the green light at the end of Daisy's dock...His dream must have seemed so close that he could hardly fail to grasp it. He did not know that it was already behind him, ...".

②Writing Techniques used in this novel

The narrator in this novel Nick Carraway is a reliable narrator. He is an inside character who has relations with every major character so that he is able to participate in the events happening in the story. At the same time, he is also an outsider in the story in that he is from the west and is not involved in the events emotionally, which makes it possible for him to observe calmly. He is also the writer's spokesman.

Symbolism is used in this book. There are many symbols. The green light symbolizes Gatsby's dream. The eyes of the doctor symbolize the eyes of the God.

Impressionistic technique is also used. The author used colors to create the atmosphere, like "blue garden" and "yellow bug". Details are also helpful in bringing out the effect of the age.

5. Selected Reading

The Great Gatsby

CHAPTER Ⅸ

After two years I[1] remember the rest of that day, and that night and the next day, only as an endless drill of police and photographers and newspapermen in and out of Gatsby's front door. A rope stretched across the main gate and a policeman by it kept out the curious, but little boys soon discovered that they could enter through my yard, and there were always a few of them clustered open-mouthed about the pool. Someone with a positive manner, perhaps a detective, used the expression "madman" as he bent over Wilson's body[2] that afternoon, and the adventitious authority of his voice set the key for the newspaper reports next morning.

Most of those reports were a nightmare—grotesque, circumstantial, eager, and untrue. When Michaelis'[3] testimony at the inquest brought to light Wilson's suspicions of his wife I thought the whole tale would shortly be served up in racy pasquinade—but Catherine[4], who might have said anything, didn't say a word. She showed a surprising amount of character about it too—looked at the coroner with determined eyes under that corrected brow of hers, and swore that her sister had never seen Gatsby, that her sister was completely happy with her husband, that her sister had been into no mischief whatever. She convinced herself of it, and cried into her handkerchief, as if the very suggestion was more than she could endure. So Wilson was reduced to a man "de-ranged by grief" in order that the case might remain in its simplest form. And it rested there.

But all this part of it seemed remote and unessential. I found myself on Gatsby's side, and alone. From the moment I telephoned news of the catastrophe to West Egg Village[5], every surmise about him, and every practical question, was referred to me. At first I was surprised and confused; then, as he lay in his house and didn't move or breathe or speak, hour upon hour, it grew upon me that I was responsible, because no one else was interested-interested, I mean, with that intense personal interest to which everyone has some vague right at the end.

I called up Daisy[6] half an hour after we found him, called her instinctively and without hesitation. But she and Tom[7] had gone away early that afternoon, and taken baggage with them.

"Left no address?"

"No."

"Say when they'd be back?"

"No."

"Any idea where they are? How I could reach them?"

"I don't know. Can't say."

I wanted to get somebody for him. I wanted to Bo into the room where he lay and reassure him: "I'll get somebody for you, Gatsby. Don't worry. Just trust me and I'll get somebody for you—"

Meyer Wolfsheim's[8] name wasn't in the phone book. The butter gave me his office address on Broadway, and I called Information, but by the time I had the number it was long after five, and no one answered the phone.

"Will you ring again?"

"I've rung them three times."

"It's very important."

"Sorry. I'm afraid no one's there."

I went back to the drawing room and thought for an instant that they were chance visitors, all these official people who suddenly filled it. But, as they drew back the sheet and looked at Gatsby with unmoved eyes, his protest continued in my brain:

"Look here, old sport, you've got to get somebody for me. You've got to try' hard. I can't go through this alone."

Someone started to ask me questions, but I broke away and going upstairs looked hastily through the unlocked parts of his desk—he'd never told me definitely that his parents were dead. But there was nothing—only the picture of

Dan Cody [9], a token of forgotten violence, staring down from the wall.

Next morning I sent the butler to New York with a letter to Wolfsheim, which asked for information and urged him to come out on the next train. That request seemed superfluous when T wrote it. I was sure he'd start when he saw the newspapers, just as T was sure there'd be a wire from Daisy before noon-but neither a wire nor Mr. Wolfsheim arrived; no one arrived except more police and photographers and newspapermen. When the butler brought back Wolfsheim's answer I began to have a feeling of defiance, of scornful solidarity between Gatsby and me against them all.

Dear Mr. Carraway. This has been one of the most terrible shocks of my life to me I hardly can believe it that it is true at all. Such a mad act as that man did should make us all think. I cannot come down now as I am tied up in some very important business and cannot get mixed up in this thing now. If there is anything I can do a little. Later let me know in a letter by Edgar. I hardly know where I am when I hear about a thing like this and am completely knocked down and out.

Yours truly

MEYER WOLFSHEIM

And then hasty addenda beneath:

Let me know about the funeral etc do not know his family at all.

When the phone rang that afternoon and longdistance said Chicago was calling I thought this would be Daisy at last. But the connection came through as a man's voice, very thin and far away.

"This is Slagle [10] speaking..."

"Yes?" The name was unfamiliar.

"Hell of a note, isn't it? Get my wire?"

"There haven't been any wires."

"Young Parke's [11] in trouble," he said rapidly. "They [12] picked him up when he handed the bonds over the counter. They got a circular from New York giving'em the numbers just five minutes before. What d'you know about that, hey? You never can ten in these hick towns."

"Hello!" I interrupted breathlessly. "Look here—this isn't Mr. Gatsby.

Mr. Gatsby's dead."

There was a long silence on the other end of the wire, followed by an exclamation...then a quick squawk as the connection was broken.

I think it was on the third day that a telegram signed Henry C. Gatz arrived from a town in Minnesota. It said only that the sender was leaving immediately and to postpone the funeral until he came.

It was Gatsby's father, a solemn old man, very helpless and dismayed, bundled up in a long cheap ulster against ale warm September day. His eyes leaked continuously with excitement, and when I took the bag and umbrella from his hands he began to pun so incessantly at his sparse gray beard that I had difficulty in getting off his coat. He was on the point of collapse, so I took him into the music room and made him sit down while I sent for something to eat. But he wouldn't eat, and the glass of milk spilled from his trembling hand.

"I saw it in the Chicago newspaper," he said. "It was all in the Chicago newspaper. I started right away."

"I didn't know how to reach you."

His eyes, seeing nothing, mowed ceaselessly about the room.

"It was a madman," he said. "He must have been mad."

"Wouldn't you like some coffee?" I urged him.

"I don't want anything. I'm all right now, Mr. —"

"Carraway."

"Well, I'all right now. Where have they got Jimmy?"

I took him into the drawing room, where his son lay, and left him there. Some little boys'had come up on the steps and were looking into the hall; when I told them who had arrived, they went reluctantly away.

After a little while Mr. Gatz opened the door and came out, his mouth ajar, his face flushed slightly, his eyes leaking isolated and unpunctual tears. He had reached an age where death no longer has the quality of ghastly surprise, and when he looked around him now for the first time and saw the height and splendor of the hall and the great rooms opening out from it into other rooms, his grief began to be mixed with an awed pride. I helped him to a bedroom upstairs; while he took off his coat and vest I told him that all arrangements had been deferred until he came.

"I didn't know what you'd want, Mr. Gatsby—"

"Gatz is my name."

"—Mr. Gatz. I thought you might want to take the body West."

He shook his head.

"Jimmy always liked it better down East. He rose up to his position in the East. Were you a friend of my boy's, Mr. —?"

"We were close friends."

"He had a big future before him, you know. He was only a young man, but he had a lot of brain power here."

He touched his head impressively, and I nodded.

"If he'd of lived, he'd of been a great man.[13] A man like James J. Hill[14]. He'd of helped build up the country."

"That's true," I said, uncomfortably.

He fumbled at the embroidered coverlet, trying to take it from the bed, and lay down stiffly—was instantly asleep.

That night an obviously frightened person called up, and demanded to know who I was before he would give his name.

"This is Mr. Carraway," I said.

"Oh!" He sounded relieved. "This is Klipspringer[15]."

I was relieved too, for that seemed to promise another friend at Gatsby's grave. I didn't want it to be in the papers and draw a sight-seeing crowd, so I'd been calling up a few people myself. They were hard to find.

"The funeral's tomorrow," I said. "Three o'clock, here at the house. I wish you'd tell anybody who'd be interested."

"Oh, I win," he broke out hastily. "Of course I'm not likely to see anybody, but if I do."

His tone made me suspicious.

"Of course you'll be there yourself."

"Well, I'll certainly try. What I called up about is—"

"Wait a minute," I interrupted. "How about saying you'll come?"

"Well, the fact is—the truth of the matter is that I'm staying with some people up here in Greenwich [15], and they rather expect me to he with them tomorrow. In fact, there's a sort of picnic or something. Of course I'll do my very best to get away."

I ejaculated an unrestrained "Huh!" and he must have heard me, for he went on nervously:

"What I called up about was a pair of shoes I left there. I wonder if it'd be too much trouble to have the butler send them on. You see, they're tennis shoes, and I'm sort of helpless without them. My address is care of B. F. —"

I didn't hear the rest of the name, because I hung up the receiver. After that I felt a certain shame for Gatsby—one gentleman to whom I telephoned implied that he had got what he deserved. However, that was my fault, for he was one of those who used to sneer most bitterly at Gatsby on the courage of Gatsby's liquor, and I should have known better than to call him.

The morning of the funeral I went up to New York to see Meyer Wolfsheim; I couldn't seem to reach him any other way. The door that I pushed open, on the advice of an elevator boy, was marked "The Swastika Holding Company," and at first there didn't seem to be anyone inside. But when I'd shouted "hello" several times in vain, an argument broke out behind a partition, and presently a lovely Jewess appeared at an interior door and scrutinized me with black hostile eyes.

"Nobody's in," she said. "Mr. Wolfsheim's gone to Chicago."

The first part of this was obviously untrue, for someone had begun to whistle "The Rosary," tunelessly, inside.

"Please say that Mr. Carraway wants to see him."

"I can't get him back from Chicago, can I?"

At this moment a voice, unmistakably Wolfsheim's, called "Stella!" from the other side of the door.

"Leave your name on the desk," she said quickly. "I'll give it to him when he gets back."

"But I know he's there."

She took a step toward me and began to slide her hands indignantly up and down her hips.

"You young men think you can force your way in here any time," she scolded. "We're getting sickantired [17] of it. When I say he's in Chicago, he's in Chicago." I mentioned Gatsby.

"Oh—h!" She looked at me over again. "Will you just—what was your name?"

She vanished. In a moment Meyer Wolfsheim stood solemnly in the doorway, holding out both hands. He drew me into his office, re-marking in a reverent voice that it was a sad time for all of us, and offered me a cigar.

"My memory goes back to when first I met him," he said. "A young major just out of the army and covered over with medals he got in the war. He was so hard up he had to keep on wearing his uniform because he couldn't buy some regular clothes. First time I saw him was when he come [18] into Winebrenner's poolroom at Forty-third Street and asked for a job. He hadn't eat [19] anything for a couple of days. 'Come on have some lunch with me,' I said. He ate more than four dollars' worth of food in half an hour."

"Did you start him in business?" I inquired.

"Start him! I made him."

"Oh."

"I raised him up out of nothing, right out of the gutter. I saw right away he was a fine-appearing, gentlemanly young man, and when he told me he was an Oggsford [20] I knew I could use him good. I got him to join up in the American Legion [21] and he used to stand high there. Right off he did some work for a client of mine up to Albany [22]. We were so thick like that in everything" —he held up two bulbous fingers— "always together."

I wondered if this partnership had included the world's series transaction in 1919. [23]

"Now he's dead," I said after a moment. "You were his closest friend, so I know you'll want to come to his funeral this afternoon."

"I'd like to come."

"Well, come then."

The hair in his nostrils quivered slightly, and as he shook his head his eyes filled with tears.

"I can't do it—I can't get mixed up in it," he said.

"There's nothing to get mixed op in. It's all over now."

"When a man gets killed I never like to get mixed up in it in any way. I keep out. When I was a young man it was different—if a friend of mine died, no matter how, I stuck with them to the end. You may think that's sentimental, but I mean it—to the bitter end."

I saw that for some reason of his own he was determined not to come, so I stood up.

"Are you a college man?" he inquired suddenly.

For a moment I thought he was going to suggest a "gonnegtion[24]", but he only nodded and shook my hand.

"Let us learn to show our friendship for a man when he is alive and not after he is dead," he suggested. "After that, my own rule is to let everything alone."

When I left his office the sky had turned dark and I got back to West Egg in a drizzle. After changing my clothes I went next door and found Mr. Gatz walking up and down excitedly in the hall. His pride in his son and in his son's possessions was continually increasing and now he had something to show me.

"Jimmy sent me this picture." He took out his wallet with trembling fingers. "Look there."

It was a photograph of the house, cracked in the corners and dirty with many hands. He pointed out every detail to me eagerly. "Look there!" and then sought admiration from my eyes. He had shown it so often that I think it was more real to him now than the house itself.

"Jimmy sent it to me. I think it's a very pretty picture. It shows up well."

"Very well. Had you seen him lately?"

"He come out[25] to see me two years ago and bought me the house I live in now. Of course we was broke up when he run off from home[26], but I see now there was a reason for it. He knew he had a big future in front of him. And ever since he made a success he was very generous with me."

He seemed reluctant to put away the picture, held it for another minute, lingeringly, before my eyes. Then he returned the wallet and pulled from his pocket a ragged old copy of a book called *Hopalong Cassidy* [27].

"Look here, this is a book he had when he was a boy. It just shows you."

He opened it at the back cover and turned it around for me to see. On the last flyleaf was printed the word SCHEDULE [28], and the date September 12, 1906. And underneath:

Rise from bed ······	6: 00	A. M.
Dumbbell exercise and wall-scaling... ······	6: 15—6: 30	A. M.
Study electricity, etc. ······	7: 15—8: 15	A. M.
Work ······	8: 30—4: 30	P. M.
Baseball and sports ······	4: 30—5: 00	P. M.
Practice elocution, poise and how to attain it ······	5: 00—6: 00	P. M.
Study needed inventions ······	7: 00—9: 00	P. M.

GENERAL RESOLVES

No wasting time at Shafters or [a name, indecipherable]

No more smokeing or chewing.

Bath every other day

Read one improving book or magazine per week

Save $5.00 [crossed out] $3.00 per week

Be better to parents

"I come across [29] this book by accident," said the old man. "It just shows you, don't it?"

"Jimmy was bound to get ahead. He always had some resolves like this or something. Do you notice what he's got about improving his mind? He was always great for that. He told me I et [30] like a hog once, and I beat him for it."

He was reluctant to close the book, reading each item aloud and then looking eagerly at me. I think he rather expected me to copy down the list for my own use.

NOTES

①I：Nick Carraway，the narrator of the story 故事的叙述人。

②Wilson's body：George Wilson runs a garage. His wife died in a car accident. He believed his wife's lover Tom's lie and mistakenly believed that Gatsby was the murderer. He shot Gatsby and killed himself. 威尔逊的尸体。Wilson 即乔治·威尔逊。他经营一个汽车买卖和修理业务的汽车修理行，其妻因车祸丧生。他听信妻子的情夫汤姆的谎言，误认为盖茨比为肇事者，因此将他杀死，后自尽。

③Michaelis：a young Greek who managed a coffeehouse. He is the neighbor of Wilson and witnessed the car accident. 一个开咖啡馆的年轻的希腊人，乔治·威尔逊的邻居，曾目睹汽车撞死乔治的妻子默特尔。

④Catherine：Myrtle's sister，Myrtle 的妹妹。

⑤West Egg Village：the place where Gatsby and Nick Carraway lived. 西卵镇，是书中主人公盖茨比（Gatsby）和故事叙述者尼克·卡拉韦住的地方。

⑥Daisy：a beautiful girl from a rich family. She had been Gatsby's lover，but later married Tom. 黛西，出身富家的漂亮小姐，原为盖茨比的情人，后嫁给花花公子汤姆。

⑦Tom：Tom Buchanan，Daisy's husband 即汤姆·布坎南，黛西的丈夫。

⑧Meyer Wolfsheim：Gatsby's partner in his illegal business 一个与盖茨比合伙做非法生意的人。

⑨Dan Cody：Gatsby worked for him when he was young. He got rich by opening up gold and silver mines. 小说中一个数次被提到但从未露面的人物。他靠开发金银矿发迹。盖茨比年轻时曾在他手下工作过。Dan Cody 这一名字使人想起西部的著名人物 Daniel Boone 和 Buffalo Bill Cody 及他们所代表的开拓精神。

⑩Slagle：Gatsby's partner in his illegal business 盖茨比做非法生意的伙伴。

⑪Parke：Gatsby's partner in his illegal business 盖茨比做非法生意的伙伴。

⑫They：police station，指警察局。

⑬If he'd of lived，…a great man：If he'd lived，he'd have been a great man. 口语中或未受过教育者的话中常有不合语法的句子。

⑭James J. Hill：America railroad magnate 詹姆斯. J. 希尔（1838—1916），美国的铁路

大王。

⑮Klipspringer：the one who often lived in Gatsby's home. 一个常到盖茨比家长住的人，有盖茨比家的“寄宿者”之称。

⑯Greenwich：a city in Southeast Connecticut 格林尼治，美国康涅狄格州西南部一城市，濒临长岛海峡。

⑰sickantired：应为 sick and tired。

⑱when he come：应为 when he came。

⑲He hadn't eat：应为 He hadn't eaten。

⑳an Oggsford：应为 an Oxford，牛津大学毕业生。

㉑The American Legion：美国退伍军人协会。

㉒Albany：the Capital of New York State 奥本尼，美国纽约州的首府。

㉓the world's series transaction in 1919：1919 年世界棒球赛的那项交易，小说的第四章曾提到此事。盖茨比曾对尼克说，“He's the man who fixed the world's series back in 1919.”（“他是远在 1919 年操纵过世界棒球比赛的人。”）

㉔gonnegtion：应为 connection。

㉕He come out：应为 He came out。

㉖of course we was broke up when he run off from home：应为 Of course we were broken up when he ran off from home.

㉗Hopalong Cassidy：the name of a cartoon book，书名，《牛仔卡西迪》。Hapalong 意为“跛子”；Cassidy 为人名。

㉘SCHEDULE：Timetable. 作息时间表。这个作息时间表及后面的个人总守则与本杰明·富兰克林《自传》中所谈的修身要求极相似。富兰克林认为通过艰苦劳动、节约和诚实，穷人可以从贫困中解放自己。盖茨比的故事很有美国成功故事的意味。然而时过境迁，富兰克林一生所体现的“美国梦”到盖茨比时代业已破灭。

㉙come across：应为 came across。

㉚I et：应为 I ate。

Topic Discussion

1. What's the significance of Gatsby's schedule? What does it tell us?
2. What does Gatsby represent in Jazz Age?

第五节　20世纪30年代与斯坦贝克

每节导读

本节简要介绍美国的20世纪30年代文学和斯坦贝克。

本节的主要内容包括20世纪30年代美国大萧条时期的这段历史背景和被誉为“美国抗议作家”的约翰·斯坦贝克的生平、作品介绍、作家的创作思想、写作手法以及他的代表作，即反映美国大萧条时期的史诗般的作品《愤怒的葡萄》。20世纪初的美国，随着机械化和工业化的出现，小农场被大农场所取代，资本和财富越来越 集中在少数人手中。随着大人物与为他们干活的小人物之间的差距的加大，不满情绪有所增加，最终在全国激化为1929年的股市大崩溃以及随之而来的经济大萧条。在经济大萧条时期，美国作家关注人民大众的生活，成为其代言人，斯坦贝克就是其中之一。斯坦贝克的代表作《愤怒的葡萄》体现了作家对当时那些小人物悲惨生活、命运的关注以及作家极力倡导的博爱的人文主义思想和集体主义的共产主义思想。

Ⅰ. Background of the 1930s

With the Stock Market crash of 1929, America moved into the Great Depression. The economic structure in the U. S. A. changed, as small farms were replaced by larger ones and the financial picture enlarged to include corporations, large investments and amassing fortunes. The gap between the rich and the poor lengthened. More and more people lost their jobs. So unemployment and poverty were the main social problems. At this time, the post-war period ended and a new pre-war period began. The new mood of the nation called forth a new type of class-conscious, proletarian writing. The new writers identified their point of view closely with the suffering of farmers and workers, and novels such as John Steinbeck's *The Grapes of Wrath* were highly influential in raising the nation's social conscience. Social concern became the biggest thing in writers' mind and they served as the spokesmen of the suffering people. Although the young writers of the 1930's were severely influenced by the Depression, there were many excellent writers in the 1930's, and they had far greater literary resources than ever before thanks to the new freedoms of style, method and technique, and to reforms in the language, which had been experimented with and explored by the writers of the previous period. Faulkner continued to experiment with style. He examined the disintegrating old society of the South, limiting the scope of many of his books to one southern country in order to describe the social forces at work there.

Ⅱ. John Steinbeck (1902—1968)

John Steinbeck published his first book *Cup of Gold* in 1929, the year of America's stock market crash, and he is recognized as the foremost writer of the Great Depression. He wrote sympathetically about poor, oppressed California farmers, migrants, laborers, and the unemployed, making their lives and sorrows very understandable to his readers. His theme was usually that simple human virtues such as kindness and fair treatment were far superior to official hard-heartedness, or the dehumanizing cruelty of exploiters for their own commercial advantage.

1. His Life and Literary Career

John Steinbeck was born in Salinas, California, in a long valley between two mountain ranges, which he used as the setting for many of his stories. His father was a well-to-do flour miller who also served as a county official, and his mother was a schoolteacher. With his three older sisters, they were a family who enjoyed books. So Steinbeck did well at school. He attended a university in California on and off for five years, studying literature and taking courses in writing. Between terms of study, he worked at various unskilled jobs, acquiring knowledge about the lower levels of society and gaining admiration for the human qualities of the humble people he worked with. He wrote stories about them which he sent to magazines, but his stories were always rejected. In the 1920's, people were not interested in reading about such things.

In 1925, Steinbeck got tired of studying. Without graduating, he went to New York with $3 in his pocket, hoping to make his living there as a writer.

His uncle helped him find a job as a reporter, but he was not good at newspaper work and he was soon dismissed. Discouraged, he returned to California where he went back to doing odd jobs, moving from town to town. But he still continued to write as much as he could, in his spare time and between jobs.

Finally, in 1929, a publisher accepted his first book. It was a romantic, fictional biography of a pirate, which did not bring him much money, but nevertheless, he decided to get married and continue writing. He published two more books *The Pastures of Heaven and To a God Unknown*, which were not very successful, and he sold a few stories to magazines. Fortunately, Steinbeck's father had given the young couple a small house and an allowance of $25 a month so they were able to live during these lean years.

In 1935, Steinbeck published *Tortilla Flat*, a book which vividly described the life of poor Mexican-Americans with affection and humor. This book was an immediate success, and Steinbeck was never poor again. Each book that he wrote thereafter became a best seller. The following year, he wrote *In Dubious Battle* in a far different, grimmer mood. It was the story of a farm workers' strike, which, in later times, has been called the best "strike novel" in the English language.

In 1937, he wrote *Of Mice and Men*, a short novel which established Steinbeck's reputation among literary critics as a major American writer. This story told of the strange, tragic friendship between two migrant workers, the homeless people who wandered from place to place during the Depression, looking for work as agricultural laborers. The book was turned into a play in the same year, and then into a film, both of which were highly successful. In 1939, he wrote his masterpiece, *The Grapes of Wrath*, of which more will be said later. This book was turned into an unforgettable film, which is still considered a great classic.

At the beginning of his success, in 1935, Steinbeck visited Mexico, the first of many trips which he took to foreign lands. After the huge success of *The Grapes of Wrath* in 1939, he was seldom at home. Perhaps this was why his wife divorced him in 1942. He soon married again, and this second marriage marked a dividing line in Steinbeck's career. He only wrote one more book, *Cannery Row* (1945) about the poor people of California whom he loved and understood. From that time onward, he ceased to be a Californian. He and his wife moved to New York and Steinbeck's writing never again achieved the powerful quality of the books he wrote during the 1930s. Soon after his wedding, he went to Europe to cover the Second World War for a big New York newspaper. His post-war novel *The Pearl* (1947) reflected his bitter feelings against those greedy, rapacious elements of society which made the war possible. In 1948, his second marriage ended in divorce. His third marriage fortunately turned out to be a very happy one.

During the 1950's, Steinbeck wrote several books, all of which were very popular with the public, but which literary critics all compared unfavorably with his earlier work. He wrote scripts for several films based on his own stories, and also original film scripts, the best-remembered of which is *Viva Zapata*, the life of a Mexican revolutionary leader. His last notable book was *Travels with Charley In Search of America*, published in 1962. It told of his journey across America with his pet dog, and it was a runaway best seller. However, by that time Steinbeck seemed to have lost his fiery concern about the lives of poor and oppressed people. While traveling with his dog in New Orleans, in the Deep South, there were riots and protest demonstrations on behalf of the black Civil Rights Movement. But Steinbeck avoided them and did not mention them in his book. He felt strong anger against the injustice to farm laborers in the 1930s, but he did not feel the same sympathy for poor, oppressed city workers and blacks, thirty years later.

In 1962, Steinbeck was awarded the Nobel Prize for Literature for his lifetime work, but primarily for the great works which he produced in the 1930s. He died in New York, in 1968.

2. His Style and Point of View

Steinbeck's prose style is noted for a poetic quality which heightens the realism of his naturalistic writing—relieving and brightening the grim subjects which he often wrote about. Steinbeck frequently set a scene, of the mood for a chapter, in short, abrupt passages which were almost like the stage directions for a play, as though the author wanted his reader to see the story clearly in his imagination. This habit was undoubtedly what encouraged many film producers to turn his novels into films. Steinbeck, like Eugene O'Neill, nearly always wrote the dialogue of his books just as it should sound, using strange spelling to denote the regional accent, and inserting many words of slang and dialect. By reproducing the exact speech patterns of his characters, Steinbeck made his reader feel as though he knew them personally. Steinbeck's best writing was produced by outrage at the injustices of society and by his admiration for the strong spirit of the poor.

During the Depression years, his fiction combined warm humor, regionalism, and violence with a realistic technique which produced a unique kind of social protest. His influence was very wide in arousing public sympathy for the subjects of his novels.

3. His Major Works

Steinbeck wrote eighteen novels as well as many short stories, works of non-fiction, plays and film scripts. His most important books are the following:

1935—Tortilla Flat is a collection of short stories about an imaginary Mexican-American town in California. The same group of characters appears in different stories, so the form of the book resembles Sherwood Anderson's Winesburg, Ohio. But Steinbeck treats his characters in a much more light-hearted vein.

1936—*In Dubious Battle* is a naturalistic, objective novel about Jim, a young, unemployed communist who, with an old, experienced Party member, sets out to organize the poor migrant fruit-pickers in California in a strike. The workers' union is crushed by the landowners and Jim is killed. But at the end of the book, the farm workers continue their struggle, led on by the old Party member.

1937—*Of Mice and Men* is a short novel, written almost like a play with six chapters, each of which represents a scene. It tells of the tragic friendship between a migrant farm worker and his enormously strong, feebleminded friend whom he is finally forced to kill, as an act of kindness, to save him from a worse death at the hands of his oppressors.

1939—*The Grapes of Wrath* is Steinbeck's masterpiece. It is the story of a family from Oklahoma who are evicted from their small farm when they cannot pay their debts. They set out as migrants for California, to start a new life. Cruel police and employers mistreat them, some of them die, but the family somehow survives by all helping one another.

1945—*Cannery Row* centers the story around a group of characters who live on the waterfront of a California town given over to fish canneries. It is a satire, ridiculing both those who try to gain wealth and social position, and also the Communist Party, reflecting Steinbeck's changed attitude toward social problems after the Second World War.

1962—*Travels with Charley in Search Of America* is a work of non-fiction, recounting his impressions and adventures as he traveled through America in a truck with his dog. It is amusing but not profound.

4. Introduction to *The Grapes of Wrath*

1) Plot Overview

The *Grapes of Wrath* is of course Steinbeck's epic masterpiece of social consciousness in its picture of helpless people crushed by drought and depression, and is one of the classic documents of the Depression.

The thirteen people, members of the three generations of the Joad family and Jim Casy, impoverished victims of the "Dustbowl" drought in Oklahoma, set out in an old automobile they bought for all their family property for California, in which they believe they could seek their "promised land". Grampa and Granma cannot stand bumping during the hard journey and died.

After arriving at California, they do not find a land of plenty, but exploitative migrant labor camps instead, which compound the misery of their poverty and dislocation. In one conflict with sheriffs, Jim Casy, an ex-preacher and rustic socialist coming together with the Joads, is jailed. He actively leads strikes after being released and has an effect on Tom Joad, who becomes his unconscious "disciple".

During an attack by vigilantes Casy is killed, and Tom in turn kills his murderer. While hiding Tom, the Joads work at picking cotton exhaustedly and fearfully, and Rose of Sharon, Tom's sister, gives birth to a stillborn child. Finally Ma, being patient in her determination to keep down fear and encourage joy in her family and a powerful though unassuming figure in the Joad clan, sends Tom away, who is determined to carry on Casy's work as a labor organizer. Not by heroic individualism but by cooperation and adaptation are the Joads able to survive.

2) Brief Comment

①The Themes of the Novel

The novel reflects such a theme as that strength comes from unity (changes from I to We). It also reflects people's faith in life, people's will and people's struggle to live a better life.

②Writing Style in this Novel

Firstly, the use of interchapters contributes greatly to the book's success as a social document and literary masterwork. The use of interchapters is one of the structural features of the book, the other structural feature is that the book is Bible-dictated, based on the story of "Exodus". Next, Symbols are used in it, e. g. "grapes" symbolizes people's anger; "The turtle" symbolizes people's will and faith; "The tractors" symbolize destructive forces; the Biblical symbol, for example, Jim Casy is a Christ figure with the same initials J. C. and he is the guiding principle of the Joads, etc. As for Steinbeck's language, he invented a lot of spellings and made them sound just like the language spoken in that place.

Ⅲ. Selected Reading

The Grapes of Wrath

CHAPTER Ⅳ

WHEN Joad heard the truck get under way, gear climbing up to gear and the ground throbbing under the rubber beating of the tires, he stopped and turned about and watched it until it disappeared. When it was out of sight he still watched the distance and the blue air-shimmer. Thoughtfully he took the pint from his pocket, unscrewed the metal cap, and sipped the whisky delicately, running his tongue inside the bottle neck, and then around his lips, to gather in any flavor that might have escaped him. He said experimentally, "There we spied a nigger—" and that was all he could remember. At last he turned about and faced the dusty side road that cut off at right angles through the fields. The sun was hot, and no wind stirred the sifted dust. The road was cut with furrows where dust had slid and settled back into the wheel tracks. Joad took a few steps, and the flourlike dust spurted up in front of his new yellow shoes, and the yellowness was disappearing under gray dust.

He leaned down and untied the laces, slipped off first one shoe and then the other. And he worked his damp feet comfortably in the hot dry dust until little spurts of it came up between his toes, and until the skin on his feet tightened with dryness. He took off his coat and wrapped his shoes in it and slipped the bundle under his arm. And at last he moved up the road, shooting the dust ahead of him, making a cloud that hung low to the ground behind him.

The right of way ① was fenced, two strands of barbed wire on willow poles. The poles were crooked and badly trimmed. Whenever a crotch came to the proper height the wire lay in it, and where there was no crotch the barbed wire was lashed to the post with rusty baling wire. Beyond the fence, the corn lay beaten down by wind and heat and drought, and the cups where leaf joined stalk were filled with dust.

Joad plodded along, dragging his cloud of dust behind him. A little bit ahead he saw the high-domed shell of a land turtle, crawling slowly along through the dust, its legs working stiffly and jerkily. Joad stopped to watch it, and his shadow fell on the turtle. Instantly head and legs were withdrawn and the short thick tail clamped sideways into the shell. Joad picked it up and turned it over. The back was browngray, like the dust, but the underside of the shell was creamy yellow, clean and smooth. Joad shifted his bundle high under his arm and stroked the smooth undershell with his finger, and he pressed it. It was softer than the back. The hard old head came out and tried to look at the pressing finger, and the legs waved wildly. The turtle wetted on Joad's hand and struggled uselessly in the air. Joad turned it back upright and rolled it up in his coat with his shoes. He could feel it pressing and struggling and fussing under his arm. He moved ahead more quickly now, dragging his heels a little in the fine dust.

Ahead of him, beside the road, a scrawny, dusty willow tree cast a speckled shade. Joad could see it ahead of him, its poor branches curving over the way, its load of leaves tattered and scraggly as a molting chicken ②. Joad was sweating now. His blue shirt darkened down his back and under his arms. He pulled at the visor of his cap and creased it in the middle, breaking its cardboard lining so completely that it could never look new again. And his steps took on new speed and intent toward the shade of the distant willow tree. At the willow he knew there would be shade, at least one hard bar of absolute shade thrown by the trunk, since the sun had passed its zenith. The sun whipped the back of his neck now and made a little humming in his head. He could not see the base of the tree, for it grew out of a little swale that held water longer than the level places. Joad speeded his pace against the sun, and he started down the declivity. He slowed cautiously, for the bar of absolute shade was taken. A man sat on the ground, leaning against the trunk of the tree. His legs were crossed and one bare foot extended nearly as high as his head. He did not hear Joad approaching, for he was whistling solemnly the tune of "Yes, Sir, That's My Baby." ③ His extended foot swung slowly up and down in the tempo. It was not dance tempo. He stopped whistling and sang in an easy thin tenor:

"Yes, sir, that's my Saviour,
Je — sus is my Saviour,
Je-sus is my Saviour now.
On the level ④
'S not the devil,
Jesus is my Saviour now."

Joad had moved into the imperfect shade of the molting leaves before the man heard him coming, stopped his song, and turned his head. It was a long head, bony, tight of skin, and set on a neck as stringy and muscular as a celery stalk. His eyeballs were heavy and protruding; the lids stretched to cover them, and the lids were raw and red. His cheeks were brown and shiny and hairless and his mouth full-humorous or sensual. The nose, beaked and hard, stretched the skin so tightly that the bridge showed white. There was no perspiration on the face, not even on the tall pale forehead. It was an abnormally high forehead, lined with delicate blue veins at the temples. Fully half of the face was above the eyes. His stiff gray hair was mussed back from his brow as though he had combed it back with his fingers. For clothes he wore overalls and a blue shirt. A denim coat with brass buttons and a spotted brown hat creased like a pork pie lay on the ground beside him. Canvas sneakers, gray with dust, lay near by where they had fallen when they were kicked off.

The man looked long at Joad. The light seemed to go far into his brown eyes, and it picked out little golden specks deep in the irises. The strained bundle of neck muscles stood out.

Joad stood still in the speckled shade. He took off his cap and mopped his wet face with it and dropped it and his rolled coat on the ground.

The man in the absolute shade uncrossed his legs and dug with his toes at the earth.

Joad said,"Hi. It's hotter'n hell on the road."

The seated man stared questioningly at him. "Now ain't you young Tom Joad—ol' Tom's boy?"

"Yeah," said Joad. "All the way. Goin' home now."

"You wouldn' remember me. I guess," the man said. He smiled and his full lips revealed great horse teeth. "Oh, no, you wouldn't remember. You was always too busy pullin' little girls' pigtails when I give you the Holy Sperit. You was all wropped up in yankin' that pigtail' out by the roots. ⑤You maybe don't recollect, but I do. The two of you come to Jesus at once' cause of that pigtail yankin'. Baptized both of you in the irrigation ditch at once. Fightin' an' yellin' like a couple a cats."

Joad looked at him with drooped eyes, and then he laughed. "Why, you're the preacher." You're the preacher. I jus' passed a recollection about you to a guy not an hour ago.

"I was a preacher," said the man seriously. "Reverend Jim Casy—was a Burning Busher ⑥. Used to howl out the name of Jesus to glory. And used to get an irrigation ditch so squirmin' full of repented sinners half of'em like to drownded. But not no more," he sighed. "Just Jim Casy now. Ain't got the call no more. ⑦Got a lot of sinful idears—but they seem kinda sensible."

Joad said,"You're bound to get idears if you go thinkin' about stuff. Sure I remember you. You use ta give a good meetin'. I recollect one time you give a whole sermon walkin' around on your hands yellin' your head off. Ma favored you more than anybody. An' Granma says you was just lousy with the spirit." Joad dug at his rolled coat and found the pocket and brought out his pint. The turtle moved a leg but he wrapped it up tightly. He unscrewed the cap and held out the bottle. "Have a little snort?"

Casy took the bottle and regarded it broodingly. "I ain't preachin' no more much. The sperit ain't in the people much no more; and worse'n that, the sperit ain't in me no more. 'Course now an' again the sperit gets movin' an' I rip out a meetin', or when folks sets out food I give'em a grace ⑧, but my heart ain't in it. I on'y do it' cause they expect it."

Joad mopped his face with his cap again. "You ain't too damn holy to take a drink, are you?" he asked.

Casy seemed to see the bottle for the first time. He tilted it and took three big swallows. "Nice drinkin' liquor," he said.

"Ought to be," said Joad. "That's fact'ry liquor. Cost a buck."

Casy took another swallow before he passed the bottle back. "Yes, sir!" he said. "Yes, sir!"

Joad took the bottle from him, and in politeness did not wipe the neck with his sleeve before he drank. He squatted on his hams and set the bottle upright against his coat roll. His fingers found a twig with which to draw his thoughts on the ground. He swept the leaves from a square and smoothed the dust. And he drew angles and make little circles. "I ain't seen you in a long time," he said.

"Nobody seen me," said the preacher. "I went off alone, an' I sat and figured. The sperit's strong in me, on'y it ain't the same. I ain't so sure of a lot of things." He sat up straighter against the tree. His bony hand dug its way like a sqairrel into his overall pocket, brought out a black, bitten plug of tobacco. Carefully he brushed off bits of straw and gray pocket fuzz before he bit off a corner and settled the quid into his cheek. Joad waved his stick in negation when the plug was held out to him. The turtle dug at the rolled coat. Casy looked over at the stirring garment. "What you got there—a chicken? Yor'll smother it."

Joad rolled the coat up more tightly. "An old turtle," he said. "Picked him up on the road. An old bulldozer. Thought I'd take'im to my little brother. Kids like turtles."

The preacher nodded his head slowly. "Every kid got a turtle some time or other. Nobody can't keep a turtle though. They work at it and work at it, and at last one day they get out and away they go-off somewheres. It's like me. I wouldn' take the good ol' gospel that was just layin' there to my hand. I got to be pickin' at it an' workin' at it until I got it all tore down. Here I got the sperit sometimes an' nothin' to preach about. I got the call to lead the people, an' no place to lead'em."

"Lead'em around and around," said Joad. "Sling' em in the irrigation ditch.[9] Tell'em they[10]'ll burn in hell if they don't think like you. What the hell you want to lead'em someplace for? Jus' lead' em." The straight trunk shade had stretched out along the ground. Joad moved gratefully into it and squatted on his hams and made a new smooth place on which to draw his thoughts with a stick. A thick-furred yellow shepherd dog came trotting down the road, head low, tongue lolling and dripping. Its tail hung limply curled, and it panted loudly. Joad whistled at it, but it only dropped its head an inch and trotted fast toward some definite destination. "Goin' someplace," Joad explained, a little piqued. "Goin' for home maybe."

The preacher could not be thrown from his subject. "Goin' someplace," he repeated. "That's right, he's goin' someplace. Me—I don't know where I'm goin'. Tell you what—I use ta get the people jumpin' an' talkin' in tongues,[11] an' glory—shoutin' till they just fell down an' passed out. An' some I'd baptize to bring'em[12] to. An' then—you know what I'd do? I'd take one of them girls out in the grass, an' I'd lay with her. Done it ever' time. Then I'd feel bad, an' I'd pray an' pray, but it didn't do no good. Come the nex' time, them an' me was full of the sperit, I'd do it again. I figgered there just wasn't no hope for me, an' I was a damned ol' hypocrite. But I didn't mean to be."

Joad smiled and his long teeth parted and he licked his lips. "There ain't nothing like a good hot meetin' for pushin'em over," he asid. "I done that myself."

Casy leaned forward excitedly. "You see," he cried, "I seen it was that way, an' I started thinkin'." He waved his bony big-knuckled hand up and down in a patting gesture. "I got to thinkin' like this—'Here's me preachin' grace. An' here's them people gettin' grace so hard they're jumpin' an' shoutin'. Now they say layin' up with a girl comes from the devil. But the more grace a girl got in her, the quicker she wants to go out in the grass. An' I got to thinkin' how in hell, s'cuseme [13], how can the devil get in when a girl is so full of the Holy Sperit that it's spoutin' out of her nose an' ears. You'd think that'd be one time when the devil didn't stand a snowball's chance [14] in hell. But there it was." His eyes were shining with excitement. He worked his cheeks for a moment and then spat into the dust, and the gob of spit rolled over and over, picking up dust until it looked like a round dry little pellet. The preacher spread out his hand and looked at his palm as though he were reading a book. "An' there's me," he went on softly. "There's me with all them people's souls in my han'—responsible an' feelin' my responsibility—an' ever' time, I lay with one of them girls." He looked over at Joad and his face looked helpless. His expression asked for help.

Joad carefully drew the torso of a woman in the dirt, breasts, hips, pelvis. "I wasn't never a preacher," he said. "I never let nothin' get by when I could catch it. An' I never had no idears about it except I was goddarmn glad when I got one."

"But you wasn't a preacher," Casy insisted. "A girl was just a girl to you. They wasn't nothin' to you. But to me they was holy vessels. I was savin' their souls. An' here with all that responsibility on me I'd just get' em frothin' with the Holy Sperit, an' then I'd take'em out in the grass."

"Maybe I should of been a preacher [15]," said Joad. He brought out his tobacco and papers and rolled a cigarette. He lighted it and squinted through the smoke at the preacher. "I been a long time without a girl," he said. "It's gonna take some catchin' up."

Casy continued, "It worried me till I couldn't get no sleep. Here I'd go to preachin' and I'd say, By God, this time I ain't gonna do it. And right while I said it, I knowed I was."

"You should a got a wife," said Joad. "Preacher an' his wife stayed at our place one time. Jehovites [16] they was. Slep' upstairs. Held meetin's in our barnyard. Us kids would listen. That preacher's missus took a godawful poundin' after ever' night meetin'."

"I'm glad you tol' me," said Casy. "I use to think it was jus' me. Finally it give me such pain I quit an' went off by myself an' give her a damn good thinkin' about." He doubled up his legs and scratched between his dry dusty toes. "I says to myself, 'What's gnawin' you? Is it the screwin'?' An' I says, 'No, it's the sin.' An' I says, 'Why is it that when a fella ought to be just about mule-ass proof against sin [17], an' all full up of Jesus [18], why is it that's the time a fella gets fingerin' his pants buttons?'" He laid two fingers down in his palm in rhythm, as though he gently placed each word there side by side. "I says, 'Maybe it ain't a sin. Maybe it's just the way folks is. Maybe we been whippin' the hell out of ourselves for nothin'.' An' I thought how some sisters [19] took to beatin' theirselves with a three-foot shag of bobwire. An' I thought how maybe they liked to hurt themselves, an' maybe I liked to hurt myself. Well, I was layin' under a tree when I figured that out, and I went to sleep. And it come night, an' it was dark when I come to. They was a coyote squawkin' near by. Before I knowed it, I was sayin' out loud, 'The hell with it! There ain't no sin and there ain't no virtue. There's just stuff people do. It's all part of the same thing. And some of the things folks do is nice, and some ain't nice, but that's as far as any man got a right to say.'" He paused and looked up from the palm of his hand, where he had laid down the words.

Joad was grinning at him, but Joad's eyes were sharp and interested, too. "You give her a goin'over," he said "You figured her out."

Casy spoke again, and his voice rang with pain and confusion. "I says, 'What's this call, this sperit?' An' I says, 'It's love. I love people so much I'm fit to bust, sometimes.' An' I says, 'Don't you love Jesus?' Well, I thought an' thought, an' finally I says, 'No, I don't know nobody name' Jesus. I know a bunch of stories, but I only love people. An' sometimes I love'em fit to bust, an' I want to make'em happy, so I been preachin' somepin I thought would make'em happy.' An' then—I been talkin' a hell of a lot. Maybe you wonder about me using bad words. Well, they ain't bad to me no more. They're jus' words folks use, an' they don't mean nothing bad with'em. Anyways, I'll tell you one more thing I thought out; an' from a preacher it's the most unreligious thing, and I can't be a preacher no more because I thought it an' I believe it."

"What's that?" Joad asked.

Casy looked shyly at him. "If it hits you wrong, don't take no offense at it, will you?"

"I don't take no offense'cept a bust in the nose," said Joad. "What did you figger?"

"I figgered about the Holy Sperit and the Jesus road. I figgered, 'Why do we got to hang it on God or Jesus? Maybe,' I figgered, 'maybe it's all men an' all women we love; maybe that's the Holy Sperit—the human sperit-the whole shebang. Maybe all men got one big soul ever'body's a part of.' Now I sat there thinkin' it, an' all of a suddent—I knew it. I knew it so deep down that it was true, and I still know it."

Joad's eyes dropped to the ground, as though he could not meet the naked honesty in the preacher's eyes. "You can't hold no church [20] with ideas like that," he said. "People would drive you out of the country with idears like that. Jumpin' an' yellin'. That's what folks like. Makes'em feel swell. When Granma got to talkin' in tongues, you couldn't tie her down. She could knock over a full-growed deacon with her fist."

Casy regarded him broodingly. "Somepin I like to ast you," he said. "Somepin that been eatin' on me."

"Go ahead. I'll talk, sometimes."

"Well," —the preacher said slowly— "here's you that I baptized right when I was in the glory roof-tree. Got little hunks of Jesus jumpin' outa my mouth [21] that day. You won't remember'cause [22] you was busy pullin' that pigtail."

"I remember," said Joad. "That was Susy Little. She bust my finger a year later."

"Well—did you take any good outa that baptizin'? Was your ways better?"

Joad thought about it. "No—o—o, can't say as I felt anything."

"Well—did you take any bad from it? Think hard."

Joad picked up the bottle and took a swig. "They wasn't nothing in it, good or bad. I just had fun." He handed the flask to the preacher. He sighed and drank and looked at the low level of the whisky and took another tiny drink. "That's good," he said. "I got to worryin' about whether in messin' around maybe I done somebody a hurt."

Joad looked over toward his coat and saw the turtle, free of the cloth and hurrying away in the direction he had been following when Joad found him. Joad watched him for a moment and then got slowly to his feet and retrieved him and wrapped him in the coat again. "I ain't got no present for the kids," he said. "Nothin' but this ol' turtle."

"It's a funny thing," the preacher said. "I was thinkin' about ol' Tom Joad when you come along. Thinkin' I'd call in on him. I used to think he was a godless man. How is Tom?"

NOTES

①the right of way: a public path subject to a right to pass over another person's land. 通过私人土地的公共通道。

②a molting chicken: a chicken losing feathers before growth 一只脱毛小鸡

③Yes, Sir, That's my baby: it is a popular song. Casy changed its words into that's my Saviour and so on. 一首流行歌曲。凯西借用它的曲调，改换歌词，把"这是我的宝贝"改成"这是我的救世主"等。

④On the level: honest, reliable 诚实，可靠

⑤You was all wropped up in Yankin' that pigtail out by the roots: you were trying to pull up that pigtail out by the roots. 当时，你一个劲儿地揪着那条辫子，想把它连根揪掉。

⑥a Burning Busher: 一簇熊熊燃烧的灌木丛。语出《圣经·出埃及记》第三章。

⑦Ain't got the call no more: I am no more a preacher. 不再担任牧师的职务了。

⑧I give'em a grace: I give them a prayer. 我给他们做了一次感恩祷告。

⑨Sling'em in the irrigation ditch: here refers to baptize them in the ditch 在灌溉水渠里洗涤他们，指施行洗礼。

⑩They: Here refers to the police station 指警察局。

⑪talkin' in tongues：talking noisily 嘈杂地说话。

⑫An' some I'd baptize to bring'em to：And some people I had baptized them to bring them to consciousness. 有一些人我给他们受洗礼，使他们苏醒过来。

⑬S'cuse me：即 excuse me。

⑭the devil didn't stand a snowball's chance：the devil did not have a chance. 魔鬼碰不到一点机会。

⑮I should of been a preacher：即 I should have been a preacher 我应当是一位牧师。

⑯Jehovites：基督教的一个派别，相当于 Jehovits，是 Jehovah 的派生词。

⑰mule-ass proof against sin：mule-ass 用来加强语气，污秽语。

⑱full up of Jesus：he believes in Jesus. 满脑子是耶稣基督的信条。

⑲some sisters：some nuns 某些修女

⑳you can't hold no church：you can not hold a post in church. 你不能在教堂中任职。

㉑Got little hunks of Jesus jumpin' outa my mouth：Got little hunks of Jusus jumping out of my mouth. 耶稣基督的只言片语，脱口而出。

㉒cause：because 因为

Topic Discussion

1. What is the symbolic meaning of the turtle connected with the theme?
2. What is the function of Jim Casy in the whole story?

第六节 南方文学与福克纳

每节导读

本节需要掌握南方文学与福克纳代表作品和艺术特色。

南方文学兴起于 20 世纪 30 年代，是动荡的南方社会的产物，也称为“南方文艺复兴”。南方文学的主要成就在于小说，福克纳是最杰出的代表。南方小说的主要特点在于：1）作家对南方家乡炽热的爱；2）对南方历史的一种复杂态度；3）对人物扭曲心理的刻画等。

威廉·福克纳是最杰出的带有浓厚地方色彩的美国南方作家，是美国文学史上一位承上启下的重要作家。他在其南方小说中创造了“约克纳帕塔法县”，并在艺术技巧上有诸多创新，大量使用现代技巧，如“意识流”、“多重视角”。

Ⅰ. Southern Literature

The American South includes the southeastern states and the southern states along the Gulf of Mexico. This is a unique region where people have their distinctive culture, viewpoint and history. In the southern history, the southern whites kept slaves since 1621 until the end of Civil War. So the south had quite special tradition different from the north. First, the southerners have a strong sense of the past, a strong feeling of history. They had high opinions on family tie. And the southerners are also known as a hot-blooded people, because they had more interest in guns and hunting. They are usually considered as violent people. Besides violence, they firmly believed in revision. The south is known as the Bible Belt. Finally, the south is a land of oratory. Those great American speakers were all from the south.

In fact, southern literature can find its origin in Edgar Allan Poe. The early expressions of the 20th century southern literature came from James Branch Cabell, Ellen Glasgow and Erskine Caldwell who denounced the wicked nature of southern aristocracy. Many women writers represent the realist tradition of the southern literature. They are Katherine Anne Porter, Eudora Wetly and Flannery O'Connor.

Southern Literature reached its peak with the appearance of the two giants: Thomas Wolfe (1900—1938) and William Faulkner (1897—1962).

Although southern writers focus their literary creation on the southern society with southern setting, southern characters, and southern subject matters, they are not just concerned with the South but the human situation in general. The spiritual deterioration which characterizes modern life stems directly from the loss of love and want of emotional response. Southern writers use the South as a microcosm, a miniature world for exploring problems of America, as well as the universe itself.

The basic features of Southern Literature can be summarized as: (1) love of south. All the writers show their affection and concern for the region they come from and write about. (2) a sense of history. The writers have ambivalent feelings toward their history and also describe southern people's decision and hesitation in front of social change. (3) creation of Gothic world in human heart.

Ⅱ. William Cuthbert Faulkner (1897—1962)

1. Life

Faulkner was born on September 25, 1897 in New Albany, Mississippi, and brought up in nearby Oxford. He came from an old, white upper class family. It was from his own family history that Faulkner drew the material for most of his fiction. His family history represented the typical southern region's characteristics of white social status, racial violence, honor codes, and tradition moral values.

In 1925, Faulkner went to New Orleans where some of his early poems, articles and sketches were published and where he came in touch with Freud's psychology and James Joyce's fiction.

In at least three aspects Faulkner stood out as a very important literary figure. First, he was one of the Nobel Prize winners; second, he is considered the most representative and influential writer in southern literature; third, he was a master of stream of consciousness.

2. Literary Career

Faulkner's first novel Soldier's Pay was accepted by the publishers in 1926. The story tells about the return of a soldier disabled in World War I. His second novel Mosquitoes is a satirical story about a group of southern artists and intellectuals. During the time from 1929 to 1942, Faulkner produced a lot of literary works, including *The Sound and the Fury* (1929) and *As I Lay Dying* (1930). And those novels are made powerful but difficult by the use of convoluted sentences, strange vocabulary and other extraordinary elements of composition.

In 1949, Faulkner was awarded the Nobel Prize for his literary achievement. And in 1940s and 1950s, his works won a popular readership as well as critical appreciation. In 1955, he received the National Book Award and the Pulitzer Prize for A Fable.

His major works took Yoknapatawpha County and Jefferson town as setting, which resembled his native Oxford in Lafayette County, Mississippi. These works include *Sartoris* (1929), *The Sound and the Fury* (1929), *As I Lay Dying* (1930), *Sanctuary* (1931) *Light in August* (1932) *Absalom, Absalom!* (1936) and *Go down, Moses* (1942), which are characterized by a series of events and activities as well as families that appear as the central focus in one novel, but as a minor plot in another. In this sense, Faulkner made his novels reflect the whole process of southern development on different levels.

The imaginary place of Yoknapatawpha functions as an allegory or a parable of the South. In this mythical kingdom, Faulkner explored the society on different levels, from plantation owners to the blacks, the townspeople, the poor whites and even the native Indians. He presented conflicts between generations, classes, races, man and environment, and man and himself. He believed that in the long run the brotherhood of man would triumph.

Faulkner, as the foremost southern writer of the 20th century altogether produced nineteen novels, four collections of about seventy short stories, and two volumes of poetry. He depicted the bitterness of southern history with poetic expression. His important subjects are childhood, families, sex, obsessions, the past and the modern southern memory, myth and reality, race and alienation.

3. Features

Faulkner used the South to embody all human beings in terms of the violence and evil. He presented setting and characters in rather ambiguous way. He stressed on symbolic approach to literature in order to discover the truth of human heart. There are three emphases in Faulkner's writing: history and race; folk humor of the South; horror, violence and the abnormal to cause moral outrage.

Faulkner was a great experimenter. He successfully applied some modern literary techniques. He used the device of stream of consciousness. He also used the floating or multiple point of view and circular form which make it difficult for the reader to reach a true judgment. He stressed authorial transcendence to avoid authorial intrusion in narration. He applied an original narrative method giving confusing information. The violation of chronology in the narrative structure is combined with a violation of everyday language habits. His prose varies from colloquial, regional to formal diction and cadences of American speech.

Faulkner also probed the inner lives of the southerners when he provided the reader with external events. He created images to convey the mood, atmosphere of his fictional world. His artistic techniques include the exploration of psychological reality, the nature of time, and the relation of the past to the present. He also created the anti-hero, who was weak and ineffective.

The Sound and the Fury is a good example to illustrate Faulkner's concern in creative writing. The novel is a complex account of the breakdown of the once distinguished and honored Compson family. Mr. Compson is disenchanted with life and the society he lives in. Unable to find meaning in the moral verities he was brought up with, he escapes into alcoholism and cynicism. Mrs. Compson is spiritually effete and has little love to spare for her children. Of the four children, Caddy is the only one capable of loving, but she loses her virginity. The youngest brother, Benjy, is an idiot, a curse on the family. Another, Quentin, lives in the ideal world of his youth with his dreams of love, honor, and integrity, and, when he fails to keep off the intrusion of the "loud, harsh world," he destroys himself. The life of another brother, Jason, is empty and meaningless. Love is alien to him, and so are other traditional humanistic values. The book is divided into four sections, largely reliant on stream of consciousness. The first section (April 7, 1928) is narrated by Benjy, the youngest member of the family. Like his brothers Quentin and Jason, he is chiefly preoccupied with his sister Caddy. For Benjy, her disappearance amounts to the loss of the center of his universe. The second section is told by Quentin, a Harvard freshman, on the day (July 2, 1910) he commits suicide. In the third section (April 6, 1928) Jason, reveals his bitterness and anger at the opportunities he has lost because of the irresponsibility and selfishness which he feels predominate in his family. The final section (April 8, 1928, Easter Sunday) concentrates on the Compsons' black servant, Dilsay, and her grandson, Luster. This section provides some objective information to unify the previous subjective narrations into an organic entity.

The Sound and the Fury tells a story of deterioration from the past to the present. It is actually about the downfall of the old south. The past is idealized to form a striking contrast with the loveless present. An acute feeling of nostalgia toward the happy past prevails in the whole book. In Quentin's section this feeling is the most keenly felt. Unable to adapt to the modern world, Quentin frequently casts a backward glance at the time of his childhood when life was innocent, romantic, and secure. He just cannot bring himself to come to terms with the purposeless, futile and valueless present, in which life is not worth living. His suicide then is but inevitable, a complete negation of the present. In a sense, Quentin's value system may represent Faulkner's own idea of an ideal way of life, that of an ante-bellum society. The fact that Benjy's section begins the book is perhaps a purposeful arrangement on the part of the author, for it is Benjy who feels most keenly the loss of love. Benjy lives on the emotional support of love. Although an idiot with no sense of time, he knows who loves him best. When Caddy is gone, his world of love vanishes with her; and nobody can take her place, not even Dilsey. Thus this section helps to dramatize the theme of loss from the very beginning of the story. With the story of Jason whose life embodies all the evils and problems of the modern world, the contrast between the ante-bellum society and the present one is demonstrated as clearly as possible.

4. Selected Reading: *Dry September*

1) Introduction

As a Southern writer, Faulkner draws upon the mores and prejudices of his own regional culture to create unforgettable characters and settings for his novels and short stories. "Dry September" clearly shows the horrible miscarriages of justice that prejudice can cause. Although the story revolves around the killing of Will Mayes, the actual act of killing is omitted in order to keep our attention focused on the causes of the violence, and on the mental and physical atmospheres that breed such senseless and random acts of cruelty.

First published in the January 1931 edition of Scribner's *Magazine*, "Dry September" was reprinted in Faulkner's *Collected Stories* (1950) and in the

Selected Short Stories of William Faulkner (1961). This powerful study of a cultural mentality that promotes rash, swift killings of black men is based on the Southern White Goddess concept. To understand fully the themes and setting of the story, we need to have some knowledge of this White Goddess concept, which applies not only to "Dry September," but also to any Southern story dealing with womanhood and rape, including Faulkner's Light in August and Harper Lee's popular *To Kill a Mockingbird*.

In its simplest form, the White Goddess concept refers to any "lily-white" Southern woman, who is raised in a society that protects her from any unpleasantries. Because she is white, the culture sets her atop a mythical pedestal, creating an imaginary, protective shield through which the Southern aristocracy lets nothing pass that might endanger—both physically and emotionally—its women. While the Southern white male will allow a woman to fib or tell "white lies" about insignificant matters, he believes adamantly that a Southern lady could never outright lie; even if she did, a Southern gentleman would never confront her with the lie. Instead, it is obligatory that the white man act upon the premise that a Southern woman can tell nothing but the truth. Psychologically, this complete deference to a woman's integrity is based on the belief that she could never be attracted to a black man; consequently, she would never lie about such a matter.

"Dry September", short though it may be, addresses many aspects of this Southern culture. Rather than emphasize the violence of Will Mayes' death, the story focuses on the causes leading up to that violence and the mentality that breeds such monstrous behavior. Closely related to this sadism is a sense of insecurity. For example, John McLendon, the leader of the murderous mob, might be skilled in killing defenseless blacks, but he is anything but successful in his private life. He physically abuses his wife, and his house is described as "a birdcage and almost as small..." Unable to face personal failure, he turns to various acts of sadism, whether they be against Will Mayes or his passive, timid wife.

Faulkner treats many of his characters as victims of various societal forces. Of course, Will Mayes is the most obvious victim. The only character who evokes our complete sympathy, he does nothing to make us believe that he is guilty of raping his accuser, Miss Minnie Cooper. But Miss Minnie is also a victim, a victim of her own sexual frustration. She is driven to desperation by her "idle and empty days": She has no occupation, no social position, and no intellectual interests. Trapped by her advancing age, she fantasizes, hoping that the mere hint of rape will prove her still sexually desirable. McLendon is also somewhat of a victim—his problem stems from an insecurity that he compensates for with violent actions. Note that every description of McLendon emphasizes his violence: His face is "furious," and his movements are described as violent and barely under his control. After striking his wife, he tears through the house "ripping off his shirt" and then hunting "furiously" for it.

The story is divided into five sections: Sections I and Ⅲ. show the town's reaction to the rumor that Miss Minnie, a spinster, has been attacked by Will Mayes, a black man; Parts II and IV familiarize us with Miss Minnie's history and give us an inside view of her emotional state; and Section V provides us with a glimpse of McLendon's home life and his rebellious tyranny over his wife. In fact it is the last section that deepens the theme of human conflicts at different levels.

2) Selected Reading

Dry September

I

Through the bloody September twilight, aftermath of sixty-two rainless days, it had gone like a fire in dry grass—the rumor, the story, whatever it was[①]. Something about Miss Minnie Cooper and a Negro. Attacked, insulted, frightened: none of them, gathered in the barber shop on that Saturday evening where the ceiling fan Stirred, without freshening it, the vitiated air, sending back upon them, in recurrent surges of stale pomade and lotion, their own stale breath and odors, knew exactly what had happened.

"Except it wasn't Will Mayes," a barber said. He was a man of middle age; a thin, sand-colored man with a mild face, who was shaving a client. "I know Will Mayes. He's a good nigger. And I know Miss Minnie Cooper, too."

"What do you know about her?" a second barber said.

"Who is she?" the client said. "A young girl?"

"No," the barber said. "She's about forty, I reckon. She ain't married. That's why I don't believe—"

"Believe hell!" a hulking youth in a sweat-stained silk shirt said. "Won't you take a white woman's word before[2] a nigger's?"

"I don't believe Will Mayes did it," the barber said. "I know Will Mayes."

"Maybe you know who did it, then. Maybe you already got him out of town, you damn niggerlover."

"I don't believe anybody did anything. I don't believe any thing happened. I leave it to you fellows if them ladies that get old without getting married don't have notions that a man can't—"

"Then you are a hell of a white man," the client said. He moved under the cloth. The youth had sprung to his feet.

"You don't?" he said. "Do you accuse a white woman of lying?"

The barber held the razor poised above the half-risen client. He did not look around.

"It's this durn weather[3]," another said. "It's enough to make a man do anything. Even to her."

Nobody laughed. The barber said in his mild, stubborn tone: "I ain't accusing nobody of nothing. I just know and you fellows know how a woman that never—"

"You damn niggerlover!" the youth said.

"Shut up, Butch," another said. "We'll get the facts in plenty of time to act."

"Who is? Who's getting them?" the youth said. "Facts, hell! I—"

"You're a fine white man," the client said. "Ain't you?" In his frothy beard he looked like a desert rat in the moving pictures. "You tell them, Jack," he said to the youth. "If there ain't any white men in this town, you can count on me, even if I ain't only a drummer and a stranger."

"That's right, boys," the barber said. "Find out the truth first. I know Will Mayes."

"Well, by God!" the youth shouted. "To think that a white man in this town—"

"Shut up, Butch," the second speaker said. "We got plenty of time."

The client sat up. He looked at the speaker. "Do you claim anything excuses a nigger attacking a white woman? Do you mean to tell me you are a white man and you'll stand for it? You better go back North where you came from. The South don't want you kind here."

"North what?" the second said. "I was born and raised in this town."

"Well, by God!" the youth said. He looked about with a strained, baffled gaze, as if he was trying to remember what it was he wanted to say or to do. He drew his sleeve across his sweating face. "Damn if I'm going to let a white woman—"

"You tell them, Jack," the drummer said. "By God, if they—"

The screen door crashed open. A man stood in the floor, his feet apart and his heavy-set body poised easily. His white shirt was open at the throat; he wore a felt hat. His hot, bold glance swept the group. His name was McLendon. He had commanded troops at the front in France and had been decorated for valor.

"Well," he said, "are you going to sit there and let a black son rape a white woman on the streets of Jefferson?"

Butch sprang up again. The silk of Ms shirt clung flat to his heavy shoulders. At each armpit was a dark halfmoon. "That's what I been telling them! That's what I—"

"Did it really happen?" a third said. "This ain't the first man scare [4] she ever had, like Hawkshaw says. Wasn't there something about a man on the kitchen roof, watching her undress, about a year ago?"

"What?" the client said. "What's that?" The barber had been slowly forcing him back into the chair; he arrested himself reclining, his head lifted, the barber still pressing him down.

McLendon whirled on the third speaker. "Happen? What the hell difference does it make? Are you going to let the black sons get away with it until one really does it? [5]"

"That's what I'm telling them!" Butch shouted. He cursed, long and steady, pointless.

"Here, here," a fourth said. "Not so loud. Don't talk so loud."

"Sure," McLendon said; "no talking necessary at all. I've done my talking. Who's with me?" He poised on the balls of his feet, roving his gaze.

The barber held the drummer's face down, the razor poised. "Find out the facts first, boys. I know Willy Mayes. It wasn't him. Let's get the sheriff and do this thing right."

McLendon whirled upon him his furious, rigid face. The barber did not look away. They looked like men of different races. The Other barbers had ceased also above their prone clients. "You mean to tell me," McLendon said, "that you'd take a nigger's word before a white woman's? Why, you damn niggerloving—"

The third speaker rose and grasped McLendon's arm; he too had been a soldier. "Now, now. Let's figure this thing out. Who knows anything about what really happened?"

"Figure out hell!" McLendon jerked his arm free. "All that're with me get up from there. The ones that ain't—" He roved his gaze, dragging his sleeve across his face.

Three men rose. The drummer in the chair sat up. "Here," he said, jerking at the cloth about his neck; "get this rag off me. I'm with him. I don't live here, but by God, if our mothers and wives and sisters—" He smeared the cloth over his face and flung it to the floor. McLendon Stood in the floor and cursed the others. Another rose and moved toward him. The remainder sat uncomfortable, not looking at one another, then one by one they rose and joined him.

The barber picked the cloth from the floor. He began to fold it neatly. "Boys, don't do that. Willy Mayes never done it. I know."

"Come on," McLendon said. He whirled. From his hip pocket protruded the butt of a heavy automatic pistol. They went out. The screen door crashed behind them reverberant in the dead air.

The barber wiped the razor carefully and swiftly, and put it away, and ran to the rear, and took his hat from the wall. "I'll be back as soon as I can," he said to the other barbers. "I can't let—" He went out, running. The two other barbers followed him to the door and caught it on the rebound, leaning out and looking up the street after him. The air was flat and dead. It had a metallic taste at the base of the tongue.

"What can he do?" the first said. The second one was saying "Jees Christ[⑥], Jees Christ" under his breath "I'd just as lief [⑦] be Will Mayes as Hawk, if he gets McLendon riled."

"Jees Christ, Jees Christ," the second whispered.

"You reckon he really done it to her?" the first said.

Ⅱ

She was thirty-eight or thirty-nine. She lived in a mall frame house with her invalid mother and a thin, sallow, unflagging aunt, where each morning between ten and eleven she would appear on the porch in a lace-trimmed boudoir cap, to sit swinging in the porch swing until noon. After dinner she lay down for a while, until the afternoon began to cool. Then, in one of the three or four new voile dresses which she had each summer, she would go downtown to spend the anteroom in the stores with the other ladies, where they would handle the goods and haggle over the prices in cold, immediate voices, without any intention of buying.

She was of comfortable people—not the best in Jefferson, but good people enough-and she was still on the slender of ordinary looking [⑧], with a bright, faintly haggard manner and dress. When she was young she had had a slender, nervous body and a sort of hard vivacity which had enabled her for a time to ride upon the crest of the town's social life [⑨] as exemplified by the high school party and church social period of her contemporaries while still children enough to be unclassconscious.

She was the last to realize that she was losing ground; that those among whom she had been a little brighter and louder flame than any other were beginning to learn the pleasure of snobbery-male—and retaliation-female [⑩]. That was when her face began to wear that bright, haggard look. She still carried it to parties on shadowy porticoes and summer lawns, like a mask on a flag, with that battlement of furious repudiation of truth in her eyes. One evening at a party she heard a boy and two girls, all schoolmates, talking. She never accepted another invitation.

She watched the girls with whom she had grown up as they married and got homes and children, but no man ever called on her steadily until the children of the other girls had been calling her "aunty" for several years, the while their mothers told them in bright voices about how popular Aunt Minnie had been as a girl. Then the town began to see her driving on Sunday afternoons with the cashier in the bank. He was a widower of about forty—a high-colored man, smelling always faintly of the barber shop or of whisky. He owned the first automobile in town, a red runabout; Minnie had the first motoring bonnet and veil the town ever saw. Then the town began to say: "Poor Minnie." "But she is old enough to take care of herself," others said. That was when she began to ask her old schoolmates that their children call her "cousin" instead of "aunty."

It was twelve years now since she had been relegated into adultery by public opinion, and eight years since the cashier had gone to a Memphis bank, returning for one day each Christmas, which he spent at an annual bachelors' party at a hunting club on the river. From behind their curtains the neighbors would see the party pass, and during the over-the-way Christmas day visiting they would tell her about how well he looked, and how they heard that he was prospering in the city, watching with bright, secret eyes her haggard, bright face. Usually by that hour there would be the scent of whisky in her breath. It was supplied her by a youth, a clerk at the soda fountain: "Sure; I buy it for the old gal. I reckon she's entitled to a little fun."

Her mother kept to her room altogether now; the gaunt aunt ran the house. Against that background Minnie's bright dresses, her idle and empty days, had a quality of furious unreality. She went out in the evenings only with women now, neighbors, to the moving pictures. Each afternoon she dressed in one of the new dresses and went downtown alone, where her young "cousins" were already strolling in the late afternoons with their delicate, silken heads and thin, awkward arms and conscious hips, clinging to one another or shrieking and giggling with paired boys in the soda fountain when she passed and went on along the serried store fronts, in the doors of which the sitting and lounging men did not even follow her with their eyes any more.

Ⅲ

The barber went swiftly up the street where the sparse lights, insects-swirled, glared in rigid and violent suspension in the lifeless air. The day had died in a pall of dust; above the darkened square, shrouded by the spent dust, the sky was as clear as the inside of a brass bell. Below the east was a rumor of the twice-waxed moon [11].

When he overtook them McLendon and three others were getting into a car parked in an alley. McLendon stooped his thick head, peering out beneath the top. "Changed your mind, did you?" he said. "Damn good thing; by God, tomorrow when this town heard about how you talked tonight—"

"Now, now," the other ex-soldier said. "Hawkshaw's all right. Come on, Hawk; jump in."

"Will Mayes never done it, boys," the barber said. "If anybody done it. Why, you all know well as I do there ain't any town where they got better niggers than us. And you know how a lady will kind of think things about men when there ain't any reason to, and Miss Minnie anyway—"

"Sure, sure," the soldier said. "We're just going to talk to him a little; that's all."

"Talk hell!" Butch said. "When we're through with the—"

"Shut up, for God's sake!" the soldier said. "Do you want everybody in town—"

"Tell them, by God!" McLendon said. "Tell every one of the sons that'll let a white woman—"

"Let's go; let's go: here's the other car-" The second car slid squealing out of a cloud of dust at the alley mouth. McLendon started his car and took the lead. Dust lay like fog in the street. The street lights hung nimbused as in water. They drove on out of town.

A rutted lane turned at right angles. Dust hung above it too, and above all the land. The dark bulk of the ice plant, where the Negro Mayes was night watchman, rose against the sky. "Better stop here, hadn't we?" the soldier said. McLendon did not reply. He hurled the car up and slammed to a stop, the headlights glaring on the blank wall.

"Listen here, boys," the barber said; "if he's here, don't that prove he never done it? Don't it? If it was him, he would run. Don't you see he would?" The second car came up and stopped. McLendon got down; Butch sprang down beside him. "Listen, boys," the barber said.

"Cut the lights off!" McLendon said. The breathless dark rushed down. There was no sound in it save their lungs as they sought air in the parched dust in which for two months they had lived; then the diminishing crunch of McLendon's and Butch's feet, and a moment later McLendon's voice:

"Will! ...Will!"

Below the east the wan hemorrhage of the moon [12] increased. It heaved above the ridge, silvering the air, the dust, so that they seemed to breathe, live, in a bowl of molten lead. There was no sound of nightbird nor insect, no sound save their breathing and a faint ticking of contracting metal about the cars. Where their bodies touched one another they seemed to sweat dryly, for no more moisture came. "Christ!" a voice said, "let's get out of here."

But they didn't move until vague noises began to grow out of the darkness ahead; then they got out and waited tensely in the breathless dark. There was another sound: a blow, a hissing expulsion of breath and McLendon cursing in undertone. They stood a moment longer, then they ran forward. They ran in a stumbling clump, as though they were fleeing something. "Kill him, kill the son," a voice whispered. McLendon flung them back.

"Not here," he said. "Get him into the car." "Kill him, kill the black son!" the voice murmured. They dragged the Negro to the car. The barber had waited beside the car. He could feel himself sweating and he knew he was going to be sick at the stomach.

"What is it, captain?" the Negro said. "I ain't done nothing. Fore God [13], Mr John." Someone produced handcuffs. They worked busily about the Negro as though he were a post, quiet, intent, getting in one another's way. He submitted to the handcuffs, looking swiftly and constantly from dim face to dim face. "Who's here, captains?" he said, leaning to peer into the faces until they could feel his breath and smell his sweaty reek. He spoke a name or two. "What you all say I done, Mr John?"

McLendon jerked the car door open. "Get in!" he said.

The Negro did not move. "What you all going to do with me, Mr John? I ain't done nothing. White folks, captains, I ain't done nothing: I swear'fore

God." He called another name.

"Get in!" McLendon said. He struck the Negro. The others expelled their breath in a dry hissing and struck him with random blows and he whirled and cursed them, and swept his manacled hands across their faces and slashed the barber upon the mouth, and the barber struck him also. "Get him in there," McLendon said. They pushed at him. He ceased struggling and got in and sat quietly as the others took their places. He sat between the barber and the soldier, drawing his limbs in so that not to touch them, his eyes going swiftly and constantly from face to face. Butch clung to the running board. The car moved on. The barber nursed his mouth with his handkerchief.

"What's the matter, Hawk?" the soldier said.

"Nothing," the barber said. They regained the highroad and turned away from town. The second car dropped back out of dust. They went on, gaining speed; the final fringe of houses dropped behind.

"Goddamn, he stinks!" the soldier said.

"We'll fix that," the drummer in front beside McLendon said. On the running board Butch cursed into the hot rush of air. The barber leaned suddenly forward and touched McLendon's arm.

"Let me out, John," he said.

"Jump out, niggerlover," McLendon said without turning his head. He drove swiftly. Behind them the sourceless lights of the second car glared in the dust. Presently McLendon turned into a narrow road. It was rutted with disuse. It led back to an abandoned brick kiln-a series of reddish mounds and weed-and vine-choked vats without bottom. It had been used for pasture once, until one day the owner missed one of his mules. Although he prodded carefully in the vats with a long pole, he could not even find the bottom of them.

"John," the barber said.

"Jump out, then," McLendon said, hurling the car along the ruts. Beside the barber the Negro spoke:

"Mr Henry."

The barber sat forward. The narrow tunnel of the road rushed up and past.

Their motion was like an extinct furnace blast: cooler, but utterly dead. The car bounded from rut to rut.

"Mr Henry," the Negro said.

The barber began to tug furiously at the door. "Look out there!" the soldier said, but the barber had already kicked the door open and swung on to the running board. The soldier leaned across the Negro and grasped at him, but he had already jumped. The car went on without checking speed.

The impetus hurled him crashing through dust-sheathed weeds, into the ditch. Dust puffed about him, and in a thin, vicious crackling of sapless stems he lay choking and retching until the second car passed and died away. Then he rose and limped on until he reached the highroad and turned toward town, brushing at his clothes with his hands. The moon was higher, riding high and clear of the dust at last, and after a while the town began to glare beneath the dust. He went on, limping. Presently he heard the glow of them grew in the dust behind him and he left the road and crouched again in the weeds until they passed. McLendon's car came last now. There were four people in it and Butch was not on the running board.

They went on; the dust swallowed them; the glare and the sound died away. The dust of them hung for a while, but soon the eternal dust absorbed it again. The barber climbed back onto the road and limped on toward town.

Ⅳ

As she dressed for supper on that Saturday evening, her own flesh felt like fever. Her hands trembled among the hooks and eyes, and her eyes had a feverish look, and her hair swirled crisp and crackling under the comb. While she was still dressing the friends called for her and sat while she donned her sheerest underthings and stockings and a new voile dress. "Do you feel strong enough to go out?" they said, their eyes bright too with a dark glitter. "When you have had time to get over the shock, you must tell us what happened. What he said and did; everything."

In the leafed darkness, as they walked toward the square, she began to breathe deeply, something like a swimmer preparing to dive, until she ceased trembling, the four of them walking slowly because of the terrible heat and out of solicitude for her. But as they neared the square she began to tremble again, walking with her head up, her hands clenched at her sides, their voices about her murmurous, also with that feverish, glittering quality of their eyes.

They entered the square, she in the center of the group, fragile in her fresh dress. She was trembling worse. She walked slower and slower, as children eat ice cream, her head up and her eyes bright in the haggard banner of her face, passing the hotel and the coatless drummers in chairs along the curb looking around at her: "That's the one: see? The one in pink in the middle." "Is that her? What did they do with the nigger? Did they—?" "Sure. He is all right." "All right, is he?" "Sure. He went on a little trip." Then the drug store, where even the young men lounging in the doorway tipped their hats and followed with their eyes the motion of her hips and legs when she passed.

They went on, passing the lifted hats of the gentlemen, the suddenly ceased voices, deferent, protective. "Do you see?" the friends said. Their voices sounded like long, hovering sighs of hissing exultation. "There's not a Negro on the square. Not one."

They reached the picture show. It was like a miniature fairyland with its lighted lobby and colored lithographs of life caught in its terrible and beautiful mutations. Her lips began to tingle. In the dark, when the picture began, it would be all right; she could hold back the laughing so it would not waste away so fast and so soon. So she hurried on before the turning faces, the undertones of low astonishment, and they took their accustomed places where she could see the aisle against the silver glare and the young men and girls coming in two and two against it.

The lights flicked away; the screen glowed silver, and soon life began to unfold, beautiful and passionate and sad, while still young men and girls entered, scented and sibilant in the half dark, their paired backs in silhouette delicate and sleek, their slim, quick bodies awkward, divinely young, while beyond them the silver dream accumulated, inevitably on and on. She began to laugh. In trying to suppress it, it made more noise than ever; heads began to turn. Still laughing, her friends raised her and led her out, and she stood at the curb, laughing on a high, sustained note, until the taxi came up and they helped her in.

They removed the pink voile and the sheer underthings and the stockings, and put her to bed, and cracked ice for her temples, and sent for the doctor. He was hard to locate, so they ministered to her with hushed ejaculations, renewing the ice and fanning her. While the ice was fresh and cold she stopped laughing and lay still for a time, moaning only a little. But soon the laughing welled again and her voice rose screaming.

"Sh! Sh!" they said, freshening the icepack, smoothing her hair, examining it for gray; "Poor girl!" Then to one another: "Do you suppose anything really happened?" their eyes darkly aglitter secret and passionate. "Sh! Poor girl! Poor Minnie!"

V

It was midnight when McLendon drove up to his neat new house. It was trim and fresh as a birdcage and almost as small, with its clean, green-and-white paint. He locked the car and mounted the porch and entered. His wife rose from a chair beside the reading lamp. McLendon stopped in the floor and stared at her until she looked down.

"Look at that clock," he said, liftng his arm, pointing. She stood before him, her face lowered, a magazine in her hands. Her face was pale, strained, and weary-looking. "Haven't I told you about sitting up like this, waiting to see when I come in?"

"John," she said. She laid the magazine down. Poised on the balls of his feet, he glared at her with his hot eyes, his sweating face.

"Didn't I tell you?" He went toward her. She looked up then. He caught her shoulder. She stood passive, looking at him.

"Don't, John. I couldn't sleep ... The heat; something. Please, John. You're hurting me."

"Didn't I tell you?" He released her and half struck, half flung her across the chair, and she lay there and watched him quietly as he left the room.

He went on through the house, ripping off his shirt, and on the dark, screened porch at the rear he stood and mopped his head and shoulders with the shirt and flung it away. He took the pistol from his hip and laid it on the table beside the bed, and sat on the bed and removed his shoes, and rose and slipped his trousers off. He was sweating again already, and he stooped and hunted furiously for the shirt. At last he found it and wiped his body again, and, with his body pressed against the dusty screen, he stood panting. There was no movement, no sound, not even an insect. The dark world[14] seemed to lie stricken beneath the cold moon and the lidless stars.

NOTES

①the rumor, the story, whatever it was: No one knows whether it is true or not that Miss Minnie was assaulted by a Negro. 没有人知道这究竟是事实还是谣言。

②before: in stead of

③durn weather: damn weather 该死的天气

④man scare: frightened by black men 意为受到黑人奸污的危险。

⑤Are you going to let the black sons get away...: 这里种族主义者不打自招地说出这件黑人强奸白人妇女的事情纯属乌有。

⑥Jees Christ: Jesus Crist 发誓语

⑦as life: (古) as gladly

⑧on the slender of ordinary looking: not really beautiful, but kind of good-looking. 相貌平平，略有几分姿色。

⑨ride upon the crest of the...social life: a bit popular in social life. 在小城社会生活中颇露风头。

⑩that those among whom she had...: 先前认为她比别人漂亮的人们暗中感到高兴，男人出于势利心理，女人则出于报复心理。

⑪twice-waxed moon: the moon that is round twice in a month. 月亮一月两圆。

⑫wan hemorrhage of the moon: the moon in the color of red like blood, meanwhile it is pale as well. 血红色的月亮，时值清晨，又呈苍白色。

⑬Fore God: before God 上帝在上

⑭The dark world: a pun, on the one hand, it is dark night; on the other hand, it refers to the dark society. 双关语，既指夜色，也指黑暗的社会。

Topic Discussion

1. What is the major theme of the story?
2. What are the symbolic meanings of the characters' names?

第四章
当代美国文学

第一节　当代美国文学历史背景简介

每节导读

本章主要涉及20世纪五六十年代以来的当代美国文学。第二次世界大战以及战后美国工业的迅猛发展对人们的社会生活产生了深刻的影响，人们开始重新认识世界，审视自我。对这一阶段的美国生活和文学产生重要影响的事件很多，例如，麦卡锡主义、民权运动、越南战争等等。这一时期的文学创作无论在主题还是形式上都较以往有很大的不同，所以通常被称为"后现代主义"，主要代表有"垮掉的一代"，以黑色幽默著称的约瑟夫·海勒和代表后现代主义潮流的托马斯·品钦。

After World War Ⅱ, the peace seemingly restored in 1945 proved not to have been restored at all. Far from being able to relax and enjoy the fruits of victory, America faced more serious and more intractable problems than ever before in her history. First of all, the dropping of an atomic bomb over Hiroshima in Japan shocked the world and made many Americans doubt about the function of science and technology in human progress. And then the Cold War led to a problem of another kind. It is true that the country was richer and more powerful than ever before. But the prosperity was accompanied by acute tensions and divisions; and world leadership did not come easily to a nation that had so long prided itself on being exempt from the conflicts and alliances of the Old World. Intelligent Americans urged their fellow-countrymen to accept their new responsibilities. Less intelligent and more bigoted Americans, finding a spokesman in the late Senator McCarthy, sought a simple explanation for their problems. With him, they believed that they were the victims of a conspiracy—the conspiracy of world Communism, acting inside the very centers of American life: the federal government, the schools, Hollywood, even within the churches. Witch-hunts and spy-manias swept the country. Caution and conformity became epidemic. It was difficult for writers and other intellectuals, while the mood lasted, to maintain their dignity. Some claimed, a little exaggeratedly, that they were being persecuted: it became almost a point of pride, for some, to insist that their telephones were being tapped. Others hastened to apologize in public for past errors in their thinking. Others again, insensibly, abandoned their interest in political ideas in favor of a kind of apolitical conservatism. The national mood was nervous, aggressive, defensive, lost. Americans looked back nostalgically to the supposed certainties of the early Republic, or to the highly colored drama of the Civil War (the subject of score upon score of books), or to the informalities of the 1920s and the dedications of the 1930s. In retrospect, each of these eras seemed to be enviably self-possessed and extraordinarily remote. Americans felt cut off from their own past.

Shock upon shock continued to buffet the America of the 1960s. No sooner did one crisis die away than another claimed the headlines. The courage and growing militancy of the Civil Rights Movement, the disciplined intransigence of the Black Muslims and the killing of their chief spokesman, Malcolm X; the reluctant discovery that the nation's affluence was accompanied by widespread and perhaps growing poverty; the murder of President Kennedy, in circumstances of weird confusion; the involvement in Vietnam: all these outran conjecture so swiftly that it began to seem that the old division of history into generations of twenty or thirty years would have to be replaced by some shorter unit, say, a lustrum of five years. One consequence was an intense desire to know exactly what was going on. More than ever Americans discussed their identity, personal and national.

After the war, it was not fiction by young writers which flourished, but rather literary criticism. New methods were applied, old masterpieces were re-examined, and 20th Century literature was reassessed in relation to what had gone before. Universities took on this work on a grand scale. The most influential critics and leading poets became professors. The relationship between Faulkner and Hawthorne was clarified. Hemingway's prose style was traced back through Mark Twain to earlier writers. The social realist writers of the

1930's were seen to have roots in the 1890's. A kind of pompousness and unadventurousness settled over American intellectual life which was centered in the universities during much of the 1950's. And there is a reason for this phenomenon.

The dropping of the atomic bombs on Japan caused great fear in America and Europe. It made the destruction of Western civilization a possibility and it led to serious questioning by intellectuals of science's role in human progress. Added to this uneasiness was the Cold War, a mutual fear and hostility between capitalist and communist nations, led by America and Russia.

In the United States, Senator Joseph McCarthy began an official persecution of Communists, and all Popular Front left-wingers, which included almost all intellectuals who had been active in the 1930's. Writers, playwrights, film-makers, movie stars, teachers, were called to Washington, investigated, questioned and branded as "Red" or "Pink". Some went to prison; many lost their jobs or went into exile. In such an intellectual climate, the only safety was to be found in the universities and in non-political writing. Senator McCarthy met his downfall in 1952, but the climate of caution, dullness and fear continued for several years more.

The average citizens enjoyed a time of prosperity during the 1950's. The returned soldiers settled down to get married, have large families, physical comforts, a car and a TV. People wanted to behave, look and think like their neighbors, and avoid trouble. It was, in general, a self-satisfied, dull decade, but under the surface, movements were forming which would explode in the 1960's and shatter America's complacency for good.

In the 1950's, many books were published which popularized new theories of psychology, religion and philosophy. The books were often superficial and over-simplified, but they were easy to understand. In many ways they opened people's minds and introduced them to ideas which unsettled their traditional ways of thinking. The new ideas led toward a growing emphasis on individuality and discontent with the society.

American writers became more and more alienated, feeling like foreigners in their own land. This process, which began with McCarthy's persecutions and the Korean War, continued as many of them joined the rebellions of the 1960's.

The gulf between the American government and a sizable portion of the population, including many groups of intellectuals, grew steadily wider. However, there was no unifying movement among writers. Rather, they wrote from the point of view of a particular region or a particular "interest group". But by the end of the 1950's, the writers were being heard and literature took on a vigorous new life.

In the South, a special type of writing developed using themes similar to Faulkner's. Some of the best Southern writers were women, of whom Flannery O'Connor is considered the best. They often wrote about extremes of abnormal behavior, grotesque characters and violence, as symbolic of their own twisted history. In the North, especially in New York, Jewish writers wrote about American city life, using Jewish subjects. Two Nobel Prize winners in the 1970's for literature were American Jews: Saul Bellow and Isaac Bashevis Singer.

Other writers wrote on behalf of sections of the society which felt alienated from the mainstream. Salinger and Vonnegut wrote for the youth who were too young to remember the war and who did not share the same attitudes as their parents. Ellison, Baldwin and many other black writers expressed the anger and desire for full equality and real freedom of African-Americans.

In 1958, Norman Mailer wrote a pamphlet, *The White Negro*, repudiating the obedient, self-satisfied, unthinking way in which Americans accepted an unjust, rotten society. He named the conformists "square" and called on disenchanted whites to join the blacks in rejecting a "square" way of life, advising them to live boldly and dangerously. Other writers, such as Paul Goodman in his book Growing Up Absurd (1959) joined Mailer in demanding reforms which would put Americans in charge of their own lives again, to bring them closer to Jefferson's ideal, rather than being swept helplessly along by absurd economic and commercial forces.

But the literary expression of disaffection which received the most public attention came from a group of San Francisco writers who called themselves the Beat Generation. The Beats wrote and behaved exactly as they felt, which was frequently outrageous. They cultivated qualities of spontaneity and freedom from all formality. They respecteded Walt Whitman and practiced Zen Buddhism. Led by Allen Ginsberg and Jack Kerouac, they read their works in coffee houses and bars, while their comic, unpredictable antics shocked the public. The literature of the Beats constituted a challenge to the carefully constructed poetry and fiction which were most characteristic of the 1950's.

The year 1960 represented the beginning of a new era. Young President John Kennedy's election brought a new generation to power. He first alleviated the Cold War, temporarily, by agreeing with the Russians to stop nuclear tests. He promised social justice, and set an example by including several prominent blacks in his government. He loosened the laws of censorship and permitted many books to be read which had formerly been banned as pornographic (including modern English classics by James Joyce and D. H. Lawrence). The liberation from official standards of correctness gave rise to a burst of satirical, bizarre, ribald novels by new American writers who specialized in "black humor" as a way to criticize the Army, the bureaucracy and other inflexible, repressive aspects of American society.

Kennedy's assassination in 1963 coincided with the beginning of riots and uprisings by poor people and blacks in the cities. Unrest and rebellions began to sweep the nation, and the 1960's are now remembered as a time of widespread social disturbances. In the South, Dr. Martin Luther King organized the black Civil Rights Movement, demanding fully equal treatment for blacks under the law. Many students, young people and older open-minded whites went to the South to join the movement. Throughout America, students and youth rebelled against the Vietnam War, which partly led to the popularity of anti-war novels in this period. Writers and intellectuals, among them Norman Mailer and Robert Lowell, led some of the protests and defied the authority of the government. Students seized control of many universities. America was split between supporters of "the American way of life" and the customary capitalist system, and those who rejected all authority, dropping out of the society to form a "counterculture". The violence culminated in the assassinations of Robert Kennedy, the brother of the late President, and Dr. Martin Luther King in 1968.

In the same year, President Nixon was elected because of his promise to restore law and order in America. He failed to do so. On the contrary, his policy to bomb Cambodia in 1970 caused such protests that white students at Kent State University and black students at Jackson State University were killed by government troops. In time, Nixon withdrew the American army from Vietnam and the rebellions subsided. He made great achievements in foreign policy, notably his friendly approach to China, but at home he failed to win the confidence of the people. When he resigned in disgrace in 1974 the authority of the government was weakened and disunity in the society was made worse by a common dislike and distrust of all national leaders.

The violence of the 1960's was replaced by disgust with social affairs in the 1970's and a rampant kind of selfish individualism which one popular writer dubbed the "Me Generation". The single important social movement of the 1970's has been the Feminist, or Women's Liberation Movement, commonly known as Women's Lib. Although it has met with strong opposition, it has brought about remarkable changes in American life. It has given rise to a new feminist literature and a feminist school of literary criticism which has strongly influenced intellectuals. Like many other writers, these women writers feel driven to extremes of expression by the chaotic world they live in.

It is difficult to sum up the state of American literature in the 1980's. Less fiction and poetry are being written than in earlier times. A new form of "journalistic fiction" has emerged, in which major writers examine true, often shocking events, with exhaustive care, and produce works of high literary value, which seek the underlying truths of present-day existence in America. Perhaps the unstable society has reached a point where the truth is stranger than fiction.

To sum up, the social events and changes after World War Two have had great impact on American belief, life and literary expression. People started to question the function of science and technology in human progress and fear that science and technology might be misused to bring disaster to human beings. Religion was not as important as before and people began to think that life was really an absurdity. The society has become disordered and fragmented and people, more alienated and estranged.

These, together with other concerns, become the major subject matter of American writers in this period.

第二节 垮掉的一代

每节导读

“垮掉的一代”指一群在20世纪50年代中期写作的诗人和小说家。他们反对规章制度，反对政治，反对知识，否定公认的文化道德和价值观念，赞同无拘无束的自我实现和自我表达。他们的特点是反主流文化。他们的作品向人们呈现了美国社会各种光怪陆离的景象，如抢劫、打架、吸毒、嬉皮士、性泛滥等等，反映了这一代人厌倦、沮丧、疲乏的精神状态，以及他们在正统体制压抑下的反叛和愤怒。他们的作品具有以下特征：1）反对当时受麦卡锡主义影响的美国社会中保守的政治氛围；2）摒弃中产阶级生活方式；3）在写作方法上一反当时流行的式样，提倡一种自发的形式。代表作家有诗人A·金斯堡（Allan Ginsburg）和小说家J·凯鲁亚克（Jack Kerouac），前者的诗歌《嚎叫》（*Howl*，1956）和后者的小说《在路上》（On the Road，1958）被公认为这一派文学具有代表性的作品。

Ⅰ. Emergence

Many people associate the Beat Generation rising in the middle of the 1950s with crime, delinquency, immorality, and amorality. Even some professors and critics feel sorry that the high ideal of the Beats became very degenerate in practice. Although the Beat Generation is all history now, it remains an important chapter in American literature.

It is Jack Kerouac who first used the term “Beat Generation” in his talk with John Clellon Holmes (1926—1988) about the implications of the Lost Generation and existentialism in 1948. The New York Times carried an article entitled “This Is the Beat Generation” in 1952. This is the origin of the term, though not all the Beats liked it. The word “Beat” is originally a jazz term for rhythm. When it applies to the Beats, the word is used as a pun. First of all, it can mean beaten down, destroyed, demolished. The Beats were beaten down. They were not wealthy people. They gave up good jobs and lived a very poor life. They preferred to beg rather than to work so that they had the experience of poverty. So they were beaten down. But in being beaten down they had an experience of beatitude, and beatitude means blessedness. So the shortened form of beatitude is beat, and thus "Beat" means "beatific". The term itself carries the idea of mystical inspiration. "Beat" means being inspired with the wonder of life. In essence, the word "Beat" represents a nonconformist, rebellious spirit toward conventional values concerning sex, religion, education, politics, and the American way of life in general.

From "Beat" derives "Beats", "Beatest", "Beatific", "Beatness", "Beatniks", and the related words such as "Jazzniks", "Bopniks", "Bugniks", and "Hippies". Some terms used by the Beats carry special meanings. The word "hip" means "rise", or "aware of advanced tastes". A hipster is a person who rebels against conventions. So a hip person is a rebel against conventions. The word "cool" means very good, excellent or superior, for instance, cool jazz. The word "square" means conventional. To be square is to be rigid. A square is a rigid conformist who fits into a proper slot, does everything just right, conventional, probably dull, and probably has no personality.

The Beat Generation was a generation of men and women in their teens and early twenties who affected an alienation from general society because they rejected conventional social and moral values. They emphasized the free expression of emotions. Their activities were marked by an experimental quest for new way of life. The Beat Generation was made up of Bohemians. A Bohemian is a person who lives in an unconventional life style. Whitman was called a Bohemian. Bohemians in the 1950s included jazz musicians, artists, painters, and other kinds of writers. They were centered for the most part in San Francisco. They would often wander from place to place. There were groups of Beatniks living in New York and Boston. Some of them went to the small villages in Mexico so as to drop out from society. Some went to live along the beaches of southern California, and became beachcombers. Some went to the Rocky Mountains, way up into the little cabins in the woods. Some went to the smoky mountains of the American South, again going far away from urban civilization.

Many of the Beats lived in San Francisco for an economic reason. During 1934 and 1936, there had been workers' strikes that were quite successful in San

Francisco. They were successful in raising the wage level of manual laborers in that area. So San Francisco had a very high wage for people who did manual work; for people who did office work, the wage was not competitive to the rest of the country. Many of these young people would drop out of school, go to San Francisco where they could get very well-paid jobs, doing manual labor, construction, shipping, and some other kind of work. They would work for four months, or two months, earn enough money to live and then quit their jobs. Many artists did this. They worked for a month or so, had enough money to pay the rent and buy some food, then they would quit working, and they would devote their time to painting or writing. When they needed money, they would go back to work. San Francisco then was a good place for them to live. The climate was mild, so they did not have to worry about keeping their house, to worry about buying a winter coat.

The Beat Generation was a product of the time. Social and intellectual changes of the 1950s in America catalyzed the Beat Movement. The 1950s, the years of presidency of Dwight David Eisenhower (1890—1969), were extremely conventional years. It was an era of easy compliance with authority. Men who had come back from serving in World War Ⅱ were eager to start their families, to move out of the city into the suburbs. The 1950s also witnessed a widespread discontentment among the postwar generation. Its voice was one of protest against the frightened, conservative political mood created by Senator Joseph McCarthy (1909—1957), against the greedy, money seeking "respectable" life of the dominant middle class, against the literary formalism of American writing after World War Ⅱ. This was a time when many intellectuals tried to avoid controversies and hid safely inside colleges and research institutions as they believed that people were fighting a hopeless battle against everything. The general mood of the time was that of despair, and the Beat Movement was in essence a reaction to a dullness in the culture they felt at that time.

The Beat Generation was a social phenomenon rather than an artistic one. The great emphasis was on the way people lived, the way the Beats lived. They also produced important literature, but the rebellion in life style of these people was an important part of the time. Without any knowledge of the way they lived, people would not understand the literature they produced. The 1950s and early 1960s were in the social tradition of American romantic revolt. American romantic revolt means the individual as opposed to society. The basic trust was in the power of the individual, and anything that was done by society as a group was down-graded. The Beats just wanted to drop out from society. They did not accept any conventions or general rules because they believed that the power should go to the individual.

Ⅱ. Characteristics

1. The Beats were fed up with the official explanations of why things happened. They denied the ready-made interpretation of human behavior, and they were drawn to aspects of human experiences that were ignored by all the sciences or condemned by society. They protested against what they felt was an inadequate conception of the nature of man. They were not going to accept the given conditions but seek another way of conducting their lives with the kind of joy and illusion of freedom. They were drawn to the idea of breaking control and getting out of one's ordinary head, partly for joy, partly for the sake of new perception.

2. The Beats rejected middle class values, commercialism, and conformity. They scorned the middle class by adopting an "unrespectable" way of life, growing their hair and beards very long, deliberately remaining poor and dressing like paupers, living in an unconventional and undisciplined way. They were enthusiastic for visionary states produced by religious meditation, sexual experience, jazz or drug. They wanted to get lost on drugs to enjoy a mystical experience. The Beats found nothing wrong with the use of drugs, a crime without a victim, and this is reflected in their literary works. The Beats accepted all forms of sexual behavior. This of course broke the codes of middle class life. The Beats had a great sense of the street because they held that street knowledge meant functioning in the world. To the Beats, madness was a kind of retreat for those who wanted to stay privately sane. The Beats liked Jazz which began in African-American society. To the Beats, jazz was "a call from the dark, it was the euphoria of joy, dance, let loose". They would get high while they listened to jazz. The Beats were interested in excessive experiences, in the

extreme, because they held that a man who puts himself outside the law is a man who puts himself into himself.

3. The Beats withdrew from politics and from the obligations of citizenship. By and large they were in favor of peace. They involved themselves in the civil rights and peace movements and in campus anti- "multiversity" free speech demonstrations. They did not support candidates for Congress. They did not work within a political system. They just did not care.

4. The Beats rejected universities and the academic tradition. They favored complete reliance on the individual efforts that they gave up on formal institutions. They preferred to learn and teach themselves instead of going to a school to receive a meaningless academic degree. They did not want to go to the universities to learn how to be a poet, but they wanted to go to the people. So it was a more democratic attitude. There is no positive or negative side of rejecting the university. For the most part it is healthy because the Beats did bring new life into American writing by going back to the people instead of staying in the university.

5. The Beats evolved a free, non-materialistic religion with no formal church, but based loosely on the teaching of Buddha, comprising love, gay, and anarchy. Their philosophy of life was based on Zen Buddhism, an oriental mysticism. It is an entire anti-rational form of Buddhism that stresses vegetation and personal inspiration rather than reading the sacred scriptures. So the emphasis of these people was mystical inspiration from meditation. They had a feeling for the holy and the sacred parts of life. They had a feeling of the presence of the divinity in the material world. This led to an attitude of a wonder and delight in life when they would reach a spiritual insight, a moment of illumination. Evidently, this draws from people like Thoreau and Whitman. Their objects of veneration were Whitman, Buddha, and Eastern religions generally.

6. The Beats regarded modern American life as so cruel, selfish, and impersonal that writers and artists were being driven to madness. They wanted to create an alternative, free, loving way of life, a "counterculture," which could replace it. They were drawn in politically-minded onslaughts. The Beats read their outrageously critical poetry to the public in the coffee houses and bars.

Poetry and jazz became very popular art forms in coffee houses first in San Francisco, New York, and then in Chicago and finally expanding to many small cities. Someone would play a guitar while the poets recited their poetry in turn. And the people in the room were drinking tea, or coffee, listening to the words of the poets. When it was over, everybody clapped and passed the basket and put in some small change as a thank-you for listening to their poems. They did not have a market for their poetry, so they would read it aloud to their friends, and sometimes they would print their poems on a hand press or they would make a small book of 10—20 pages and sell it for a few pennies.

Ⅲ. Beat Writers

The most publicized literary expression of disaffection with "official" American life was made by the "Beat" writers. They counted Kenneth Rexroth (1905—1982), Kenneth Patchen (1911—1972), and Henry Miller (1891—1980) among their immediate precursors. The beginning of the Beat Movement can be dated to a poetry reading at the Six Gallery in San Francisco in the fall of 1955. Kenneth Rexroth was master of the ceremonies. The readers included Allen Ginsberg (1926—1997), Philip Lamantia (1927—), Michael McClure (1932—), Gary Snyder (1930—), Lew Welsh (1926—1971), and Philip Whalen (1923—); with Neal Cassady (1926—1968), Jack Kerouac (1922—1969), Lawrence Ferlinghetti (1919—) in audience. Except for Gregory Corso (1930—) and William Everson (1912—), all the major Beat poets were there. John Clellon Holme, Herbert Huncke, John Tytell, Carl Solomon, and Peter Orlovsky are also well-known names associated with the Beat Movement. Starting about 1957, Norman Mailer (1923—) became sympathetic to the Beat Movement.

This group of writers put on a concerted and well-publicized rebellion against "official" American life and culture. They struggled in their art and in their lives to discover valid responses in an anxious time without simply escaping in nihilism. In literature, they showed the renewed interest in Walt Whitman because Walt Whitman had broken all the conventional rules of his time and lived an exuberant life. The Beats rejected the constricting literary forms of their contemporary writers. Instead, they wanted to write with complete spontaneity and honesty, even if the effect was slap-dash. They preferred to express emotions "raw", exactly as it was felt, rather than "cooked" through memory and translation into art.

In form and style Beat writings range from the oral "breath-length" line to a highly controlled prosody, but nearly all Beat writers followed the tradition of Ezra Pound. Beat poetry exhibits a high degree of improvisation, "cut-up" effects, a juxtaposition of seemly unrelated images, and an erotic orientation. Beat prose is characteristic of the disappearance of the "story line". Beat literature uses new forms both in prose and in poetry. Their most enduring works are represented by Jack Kerouac's On the Road and Willian Burroughs's *Naked Lunch* in prose and Allen Ginsberg's "Howl" and Lawrence Ferlinghetti's *Pictures from the Gone World* in poetry. "Howl" and *On the Road* became the pocket Bibles of the Beat Generation. The Beats were somewhat softened by the knocks of time and chose to live quietly in the more rebellious late 1950s and 1960s. They wrote happily like archangels "lying around in the woods gloomy and laughing, but at least devoted to life and not camping around rearranging social moral ideas etc.", as Allen said.

Ⅳ. Selected Reading of On the Road

1. Introduction to the writer and the novel

Jack Kerouac's role in the Beat Movement is manifold. He was a novelist who did the most to spread the philosophy of the Beat Movement. He gave the movement its mane. His novels told about the Beat life-style of poverty, freedom and aimlessness. His pioneering search for new ways of living and new ways of writing made him, the man and the writer, the symbol of the Beat Generation.

He was born into a French Canadian worker's family in Massachusetts in 1922. He went to school in New York and attended Columbia University where he got to know Ginsberg. He did not graduate from the university. Later he served in the Navy during World War Two, but was dismissed because he was considered crazy. After that he roamed around the USA and Mexico between

1943 and 1950, doing all kinds of jobs and writing down his experience. He also recorded the conversations he heard in order to catch people's actual speech.

All through his life, he lived a wandering and degenerate life and published altogether 18 novels. He died at 47 from drugs and alcohol.

His masterpiece *On the Road* was published in 1957. It was based on his traveling experience mentioned above. He wrote the novel in three weeks. It is said that he just put paper to the typewriter and typed what he experienced. The publishers rejected the book for six years and when it was finally published it became successful at once. It is a book that painted a complete picture of the whole Beat Generation, thus making him one of the spokesmen of the Beat Generation.

The subject of the novel is the life of various kinds of people-penniless poets, hipsters, dropouts and so on-that Kerouac met on his travels. In fact, nearly everything he wrote is somewhat autobiographical, exhibiting a quality of being emotional and confessional. The hero Sal is actually the author himself transformed. The title is a pun meaning both literally on the road as homeless and aimless travelers and symbolically on the road to enlightenment and freedom. In style it is the first novel written in his spontaneous style-unedited, without reflection or interpretation, trying to capture experience in its original form. The language demonstrates a quality of being colloquial, fresh, flexible and dynamic.

The following is taken from this novel. It is about the hero Sal's ride on the back of a truck with a group of strangers who have been picked up by two farmers driving an empty truck to Los Angeles. Some have destinations and others are just aimless.

2. Selected reading

On the Road

Excerpt from Part Four

The greatest ride in my life was about to come up, a truck, with a flatboard at the back, with about six or seven boys sprawled out on it, and the drivers, two young blond farmers from Minnesota, were picking up every single soul [①] they found on that road—the most smiling, cheerful couple of handsome bumpkins [②] you could ever wish to see, both wearing cotton shirts and overalls, nothing else; both thick-wristed and earnest, with broad howareyou smiles for anybody and anything that come across their path. I ran up, said, "Is there room?" They said, "Sure, hop on, 'sroom for everybody."

I wasn't on the flatboard before the truck roared off; I lurched, a rider grabbed me, and I sat down. Somebody passed a bottle of rotgut [③], the bottom of it. I took a big swig in the wild, lyrical, drizzling air of Nebraska. "Whooee, here we go!" yelled a kid in a baseball cap, and they gunned up [④] the truck to seventy and passed everybody on the road. "We been riding this sonofabitch [⑤] since De Moines. These guys never stop. Every now and then you have to yell for pisscall [⑥], otherwise you have to piss off the air, and hang on, brother, hang on."

I looked at the company. There were two young farmer boys from North Dakota in red baseball caps, which is the standard North Dakota farmer-boy hat, and they were headed for the harvests; their old man [⑦] had given them leave to hit the road [⑧] for a summer. There were two young city boys from Columbus, Ohio, high-school football players, chewing gum, winking, singing in the breeze, and they said they were hitchhiking around the United States for the summer. "We are going to LA!" they yelled.

"What are you going to do there?"

"Hell, we don't know. Who cares?"

Then there was a tall slim fellow who had a sneaky look. "Where you from?" I asked. I was lying next to him on the platform; you couldn't sit without bouncing off, it had no rails. And he turned slowly to me, opened his mouth, and said, "Mon-ta-na."

Finally there were Mississippi Gene and his charge [⑨]. Mississippi Gene was a little dark guy who rode freight trains around the country, a thirty-year-old hobo but with a youthful look so you couldn't tell exactly what age he was. And he sat on the board crosslegged, looking out over the fields without saying anything for hundreds of miles, and finally at one point he turned to me and said, "Where you headed?"

I said Denver.

"I got a sister there but I ain't seed [10] her for several couple years." His language was melodious and slow. He was patient. His charge was a sixteen-year-old tall blond kid, also in hobo rags; that is to say, they wore old clothes that had been turned black by the soot of railroads and the dirt of boxcars and sleeping on the ground. The blond kid was also quiet and he seemed to be running away from something, and it figured to be the law the way he looked straight ahead and wet his lips in worried thought. Montana slim spoke to them occasionally with a sardonic and insinuating smile. They paid no attention to him. Slim was all insinuation [11]. I was afraid of his long goofy grin that he opened up straight in your face and held there half-moronically.

"You got any money?" he said to me.

"Hell no, maybe enough for a pint of whisky till I got to Denver. What about you?"

"I know where I can get some."

"Where?"

"Anywhere. You can always folly a man down an alley [12], can't you?"

"Yeah, I guess you can."

"I ain't beyond doing it when I really need some dough [13]. Headed up to Montana to see my father. I'll have to get off this rig [14] at Cheyenne and move up some other way. These crazy boys are going to Los Angeles."

"Straight?"

I mulled this over; the thought of zooming all night across Nebraska, Wyoming, and the Utah desert in the morning, and then most likely the Nevada desert in the afternoon, and actually arriving in Los Angeles within a foreseeable space of time [15] almost made me change my plans. But I had to go to Denver. I'd have to get off at Cheyenne too, and hitch south ninety miles to Denver.

I was glad when the two Minnesota farmboys who owned the truck decided to stop in North Platte and eat; I wanted to have a look at them. They came out of the cab and smiled at all of us. "Pisscall!" said one. "Time to eat!" said the other. But they were the only ones in the party who had money to buy food. We all shambled after them to a restaurant run by a bunch of women, and sat around over hamburgers and coffee while they wrapped away enormous meals just as if they were back in their mother's kitchen. They were brothers; they were transporting farm machinery from Los Angeles to Minnesota and making good money at it. So on they trip to the Coast empty they picked up everybody on the road. They'd done this about five times now they were having a hell of a time ⑯. They liked everything. They never stopped smiling. I tried to talk to them—a kind of dumb attempt on my part to befriend the captain of our ship ⑰—and the only responses I got were two sunny smiles and large corn-fed teeth.

NOTES

①every single soul: every person 每一个人

②bumpkins: simple person from the country 乡巴佬

③rotgut: liquor of poor quality 劣质酒

④gunned up: drive the truck at a high speed 加大油门

⑤sonofabitch: the truck. 这里是对卡车的谑称。

⑥pisscall; ask to pass urine. 要求上厕所小便。

⑦their old man: their father. 这里指他们的父亲。

⑧to hit the road: start on a journey 上路

⑨Mississippi Gene and his charge: the man from Mississippi and the person he takes charge of. 来自密西西比州的人以及他监护的人。

⑩ain't seed: haven't seen. 不规范英语。

⑪Slim was all insinuation: This thin person was always suggesting something unpleasantly. 这个瘦长的人总是旁敲侧击。

⑫folly a man down an alley: get money out of some stupid person. 指骗某人钱。

⑬dough: (sl.) money. (俚) 钱。

⑭rig: Here it means the truck. 指卡车。

⑮within a foreseeable space of time: in a short period of time. 在可预见的短时间内。

⑯having a hell of a time: having a wonderful time 过得十分愉快

⑰befriend the captain of our ship: to make friends with the driver. 这里 captain of our ship 是一个比喻，指司机。

Topic Discussion

1. Discuss the meaning of the title of the novel.
2. Comment on the language style of the selection.

第三节　黑色幽默与海勒

每节导读

学习本节需要掌握黑色幽默与海勒其代表作品《第二十二条军规》。

黑色幽默在20世纪60年代达到顶峰，在20世纪70年代逐渐衰落，但作为一种写作方式仍在影响着许多作家。黑色幽默的理论基础主要是法国哲学家、作家萨特的存在主义，以及现代主义反理性的种种哲学思潮和社会思想。其艺术特征主要为：1）以喜剧的形式处理悲剧的题材；2）小说主人公不再是传统意义上的英雄；3）小说的结构也不同于传统小说按时间顺序发展的结构。

约瑟夫·海勒的《第二十二条军规》(*Catch-22*，1961）是黑色幽默文学的杰出代表。作者采用了荒诞不经的手法来表现现代社会的杂乱无章、人性的扭曲和人生的荒谬。他所塑造的反英雄人物行为乖僻，言行可笑且命运坎坷，任人摆布。为了强调荒诞、不符合逻辑的主题，海勒不以故事发展的时间顺序为主线，使事件看上去互不联系。他还运用一些语言技巧，如“循环式谈话”和“套语”，以达到一系列令人啼笑皆非的效果。

Ⅰ. Black Humor

In the decade of the sixties of 20th century, America took the international leadership in terms of global strategy and economic development for the West. It gradually entered into a postindustrial society. However, the American writers began to doubt the very reality of the modern life, particularly the reality of the political events they witnessed: the blunders of the Johnson Administration, the lies of the Nixon administration, the Vietnam War, etc. They thought the universe is absurd, the world is chaotic, and human existence is absurd and meaningless. It is in this historical background that the rise and popularity of Black Humor was witnessed.

Black Humor can be defined as a type of modern humor caused by anger. It combines absurdity with humor often describing horrible or sad events in words normally associated with pleasant or light-hearted occasions, thus producing the absurd effect needed for humor. It makes the reader laugh at the darkness in human life and laugh in face of tragic situation. Therefore it is humor out of despair and laughter out of tears. Theoretically, Black Humor was chiefly influenced by French philosopher and writer Sartre's Existentialism and the theory of psychology. The major artistic features are as follows: 1) the tragic content is dealt with in comic style; 2) the protagonist is no longer the hero in traditional sense, rather, he is an anti-hero; 3) the structure of the fiction is not chronologically and clearly organized any more, but fragmented and disorderly. Black humor reached its peak in the 1960s and declined in 1970s. The acknowledged representative writers of Black Humor include Joseph Heller and Kurt Vonnegut, Jr. (1922—).

Among the writers of Black Humor in the 1960s, Joseph Heller (1923—) provided the readers with an excellent example of dealing with the absurdity themes in *Catch-22* (1961). This book exposes the absurdity of World War II and protests against the absurdity of modern America. The story takes place in a United States Air Force Base in Italy. Here the lives of the wretched bomber pilots are in the hand of a military hierarchy, which draws up a "rule" known as "Catch-22". With this rule, those pilots, who fear flying and wish to be grounded and escape death, can never stop flying. One of them, Orr, is crazy and can be grounded. But as soon as he starts asking to be grounded, he is no longer considered crazy and thus must fly more bombing missions. This is the simple logic of Catch-22. Everybody knows that Catch-22 does not exist, but all think that it exists and therefore obey its absurd logic.

Joseph Heller depicted his characters in a different way from traditional sense. Yossarian, the hero of *Catch-22*, is no longer a brave and respectable heroic character.

Afraid of death in the mission, he pretends to be ill and escapes into the hospital. Till then the traditional sense of glorious war disappears completely. Joseph Heller also uses an absurd linguistic surface to reflect the tragic content of modern life. He employs devices like "circular conversations", comic, unexpected responses, the "wrenched cliche", to convey the illogicality and the unpredictability of a crazy world. Another remarkable feature of this book is its "formlessness". It means from a traditional point of view this book seems a structural failure. Because Heller writes it in a way which deliberately confounds the notion of coherent time and does not follow a chronological order of coherent time and does not follow a chronological order of the events, Yet, to Heller, in a world where life is no longer rational and orderly and nothing like a chronological development is possible, this is just the way to expose the absurdity.

In brief, Heller's narrative is fragmented, discontinuous, ironic and full of black humor in the use of the morbid and the absurd for darkly comic purposes. It carries the tone of anger and bitterness in the grotesque situations of suffering, anxiety and death. It makes readers laugh at the dark side of modern life.

Ⅱ. Joseph Heller (1923—1999)

1. Life and Works

Joseph Heller is a famous contemporary American novelist, who was born in Brookline, New York. After graduation from high school, he joined American Air Force as a bomber in World War Two. He considered the war beneficial to himself in that it not only gave him the opportunity to go to university but also provided him with the experience and material for his famous novel *Catch-22*. In 1948 he received MA degree in Columbia University and later he went to Oxford University for a year to study English literature. In 1950s, he taught English at Pennsylvania State University but soon left to work for various national magazines including Times, writing advertisement.

In 1961, Heller published is major book *Catch-22*, which is usually regarded as one of the best postwar protest literal works. Through the description of a story taking place in a united states Air Force base, Heller exposes and criticizes the corruption of American bureaucracy as well as the inhumanity of the whole capitalist world, This novel was particularly popular with young people during Vietnam War, In 1974, Heller's another book *Something Happened* came out, telling a story about family confects. Then in 1979, he produced *Good as Gold*, which is about a professor who hates power but desires to be secretary of state. His last work is *Closing Time* published in 1994. In addition, Heller wrote some plays, such as we *Bombed Ness Haven* (1967) and *Clevenger's Trial* (1974).

2. Introduction to *Catch-22*

Catch-22 tells a story which took place in a United States Air Force base in war-state Italy. The absurd relation between officers and common pilots reveals the tyranny and corruption of American military authority, and mirrors various absurd things in modern society.

The protagonist, pilot Yossarian, always feels his life is endangered, and the threat comes much more from the bureaucracy existing in American military and industry than from the mad war. In such a system, "reason", "patriotism" and "justice" are all fake. They are only used as a tool with which to control people. According to the military rule, pilots have the right to get rewired and go back to America if they finish 25 flight missions. However, they can never do it, because colonel Cathcart and colonel Kern constantly raise the times of flying so that they can have the chance of promotion. Completely hopeless, Yossarian has to choose hospital as refuge and finally he runs to Sweden.

The world of Yossarian is an absurd one, where people still alive are declared dead and dead people are kept alive. One officer welcomes visitors in his office only when he is out. And in such a place only those who never ask questions are allowed to attend "educational sessions", even worse, a traitor is set free because he has made money. All these absurd things are based on a "rule" known as "catch-22", Although everybody knows that this "rule" does not exist, they all have to obey its absurd logic. Their life is in the grip of the power of absurdity which rules and ruins modern existence. Joseph Heller makes his novel different from traditional ones in terms of theme, character and form, The novel is not written chronologically and plots are seemingly fragmented and unrelated, which reflects the chaos of modern world. Characters are anti-hero kind. They do not believe in the traditional notion of glorious war and doubt authority. So they are desperate and tragic. Heller deals with the tragic content in a comic way, and critics see his *Catch-22* as a milestone in the history of the American novel.

Ⅲ. Selected Reading

Catch-22

FORTY [1]

There was, of course, a catch.

"Catch-22," inquired Yossarian.

"Of course," Colonel Korn answered pleasantly, after he had chased the mighty guard of massive M. P. s out with an insouciant flick of his hand and a slightly contemptuous nod-most relaxed, as always, when he could be most cynical. His rimless square eyeglasses glinted with sly amusement as he gazed at Yossarian. "After all, we can't simply send you home for refusing to fly more missions and keep the rest of the men here, can we? That would hardly be fair to hem."

"You're goddam right!" Colonel Cathcart blurted out, lumbering back and forth gracelessly like a winded bull, puffing and pouting angrily. "I'd like to tie him up hand and foot and throw him aboard a plane on every mission. That's what I'd like to do."

Colonel Korn motioned colonel Cathcart to be silent and smiled at Yossarian. "You know, you really have been making things terribly difficult for Clolnel Cathcart," he observed with flip good humor, as though the fact did not displease him at all. "The men are unhappy and morale is beginning to deterioriate. And it's all your fault."

"It's your fault," Yossarian argued, "for raising the number of missions."

"No, it's your fault for refusing to fly them," Colonel Korn retorted. "The men were perfectly content to fly as many mission as we asked as long as the thought they had no alternative. Now you've given them hope, and they're unhappy. So the blame is all yours."

"Doesn't he know there's a war going on? Colonel Cathcart, still stamping back and forth, demanded morosely without looking at Yossarian."

"I'm quite sure he does," Colonel Korn answered, "That's probably why he refuses to fly them."

"Doesn't it make any difference to him?"

"Will the knowledge that there's a war going on weaken your decision to refuse to participate in it?" Colonel Korn inquired with sarcastic seriousness, mocking Colonel Cathcart.

"No, sir," Yossarian replied, almost returning Colonel Korn's smile.

"I was afraid of that," Colonel Korn remarked with an elaborate sigh, locking his fingers together comfortably on top of his smooth, bald, broad, shiny brown head. "You know, in all fairness, we really haven't treated you too badly, have we? We've fed you and paid you on time. We gave you a medal and even made you a captain."

"I never should have made him a captain," Colonel Cathcart exclaimed bitterly. "I should have given him a courtmartial after he loused up that Ferrara② mission and went around twice."

"I told you not to promote him," said Colonel Korn, "but you wouldn't listen to me."

"No you didn't. You bold me to promote him, didn't you?"

"I told you not to promote him. But you just wouldn't listen."

"I should have listened."

"You never listen to me," Colonel Korn persisted with relish. "That's the reason we're in this spot."

"All right, gee whiz. Stop rubbing it in, will you?" colonel Cathcart burrowed his fists down deep inside his pockets and turned away in slouch. "Instead of picking on me, why don't you figure our what we're going to do about him?"

"We're going to send him home, I'm afraid." Colonel Korn was chuckling triumphantly when he turned away from Colonel Cathcart to face Yossarian. "Yossarian, the war is over for you. We're going to send you home. You really don't deserve it, you know, which is one if one of the reasons I don't mind doing it. Skince there's nothing else we can risk doing to you at this time, we've decided to return you to the States. We've worked out this little deal to—"

"What kind of deal?" Yossarian demanded with defiant mistrust.

Colonel Korn tossed his head back and laughed. "Oh, a thoroughly despicable deal, make no mistake about that. It's absolutely revolting. But you'll accept it quickly enough."

"Don't be too sure."

"I haven't the slightest doubt you will, even though it stinks to high heaven. Oh, by the way. You haven't told any of the men you've refused to fly more missions, have you?"

"No, sir," Yossarian answered promptly.

Colonel Korn nodded approvingly. "That's good. I like the way you lie. You'll go far in this world if you ever acquire some decent ambition."

"Doesn't he know there a war going on?" Colonel Cathcart yelled out suddenly, and blew with vigorous disbelief into the open end of his cigarette holder.

"I'm quite sure he does," Colonel Korn replied acidly, "since you brought that identical point to his attention just a moment ago." Colonel Korn frowned wearily for Yossarian's benefit, his eyes twinkling swarthily with sly and daring scorn. Gripping the edge of Colonel Cathcart's desk with both hands, he lifted his flaccid haunches far back on the corner to sit with both short legs dangling freely, His shoes kicked lightly against the yellow oak wood, his sludgebrown socks, garterless, collapsed in sagging circles below ankles that were surprisingly small and whit. "You know, Yossarian," he mused affably in a manner of casual reflection that seemed both derisive and sincere, "I really do admire you a bit. You're an intelligent person of great moral character who has taken a very courageous stand. I'm an intelligent person with no moral character at all, so I'm in an ideal position to appreciate it."

NOTES

①This chapter deeply exposes the nature of Catch-22 through that Cathcart and Korn tempted Yossarian to get retired and return to their country. 这一章通过卡思卡特和克恩设法诱使尤索林复员回国，深刻揭露第二十二条军规的本质。尤索林拒绝飞行任务，在卡思卡特和克恩看来，他的行为在其他飞行员中间造成极坏影响，成了他们实现将军梦的一大障碍。因此，他们决定将尤索林送回美国，一旦他离开空军基地，其余的飞行员就不会再给他们制造麻烦。而且将尤索林打扮成荣归故里的英雄还可以鼓舞别的飞行员去执行更多的飞行任务。但尤索林必须答应一个条件，即他必须“从心里喜欢”卡思卡特和克恩他们。“喜欢我们，加入我们一伙，成为我们的朋友。不论在这里，还是回美国，都要说我们的好话。”尤索林若能答应这个条件，他就能回到美国，就能像百万富翁一样享受富贵荣华，原先被指控为怯懦而被责难的行为也可被当作英雄业绩而受嘉奖。否则，他就要受到军事法庭的审判，被关进监狱。当然，尤索林既不愿无缘无故将自己交给军事法庭，在监狱里度过一生，也不会违心地去“喜欢”他不喜欢的人，更不会替他们去说好话。

为了从长计议，为了逃脱死亡的命运，他权且接受了这个交易，但他并不准备履行他的许诺。最后，他没有回到美国，而是逃往北欧的瑞典，去寻找先他到达那里的奥尔。至于尤索林是否逃跑成功，对小说的主题无关紧要。

②Ferrara：a place name 地名。卡思卡特为了升官，主动应允在 24 小时内将弗雷拉大桥炸掉。他派尤索林和阿尔菲执行任务。因驾驶员阿尔菲没有弄清轰炸目标，尤索林心中胆怯，未能投弹，只好又一次返回目的地，才把大桥炸毁。这样一个事实在本章里被卡思卡特和克恩随心所欲地作了两种截然不同的解释。

Topic Discussion

What are the writing features of the novel?

第四节　后现代主义与品钦

每节导读

学习本节需要掌握后现代主义小说与品钦的写作特色及代表作品。

西方评论界对后现代主义的含义有种种不同解释，我们可以将其视为一个总称，用以概括二战后新出现的反传统、反文学主流的“现代派”。总的来看，美国后现代主义从非理性、虚无的人生哲学出发，将文学看做个人主观精神的表现，因此主张作家应该用自己的天赋和才能，在作品里另外创造一个世界，或用荒诞笔法对现实世界进行夸张和扭曲。不同作家的后现代主义小说从内容到形式有可能是不同的，但他们的写作都有一些共同特征，如意义的不确定性、内容的荒诞性、结构的无序性、文本自我反映等。

托马斯·品钦是后现代主义文学的主要代表人物之一。同样是描写荒诞主题，品钦则有自己独特的视角，他对物理学理论十分着迷，在作品中他大量借用物理学原理，以说明在机械文明的影响下，人将变得越来越非人化，人的个性特征将迷失在无生命的自动化中。正是因为他的作品中充斥着现代自然科学的内容，所以对于读者来说阅读比较困难。其作品里的中心思想是“热寂说”，将此理论应用于社会，就是说社会在日趋混乱、衰竭以致死亡。

Ⅰ. Postmodern Fiction

1. Background

American writers saw two great developments in their own country in the postwar era. On the one hand, the United States took the international leadership in terms of global strategy and economic development for the West. On the other hand, the U. S. gradually entered a postindustrial social structure.

But American writers were extremely skittish about political labels. Even those who tackled political and social issues seldom announced their political affiliations or accepted political classification. Most writers treated politics as taboo. However, one of the main themes of literature in this period was just to show the interrelatedness of American politics and the new social mores. Many novels written during the 1950s eulogized World War Two as a glorious war, but during the 1960s there emerged novels which mocked this war and recent American history to the point of reducing it to an absurd farce. *V* (1963) by Thomas Pynchon (1937—), *Mother Night* (1961) and *Slaughterhouse Five* (1968) by Kurt Vonnegut, Jr., *The Painted Bird* (1965) by Jerzy Kosinski (1933—), and *Giles Goat-Boy* (1966) by John Barth are all such examples.

In the 1960s and 1970s American writers were doubting the very reality of the political events they were witnessing: the blunders of the Johnson administration, the lies of the Nixon administration, the Vietnam War, the Watergate debacle, the proliferation of the nuclear weapons, etc. All the official versions were being mistrusted. The blurring of fact and fiction brought about a new mode of writing which filled the linguistic gap created by the disarticulation of the official discourse. American fiction began to question, mock, parody the official discourse. Thus the line between the real and the imaginary was erased, meaning collapsed, and absurdity permeated on all levels of social life. For instance, Joseph Heller (1923—) provided an excellent example in *Catch-22* (1961), which explores the absurdity of World War Two and protests against the absurdity of modern America. The narrative became fragmented, discontinuous, ironic, and full of black humor.

Black humor refers to the use of the morbid and the absurd for darkly comic purposes. It carries the tone of anger and bitterness in the grotesque situations of suffering, anxiety and death. It makes readers laugh at the blackness of modern life. The black humorists feel amused at their characters' vain attempt to create order in their absurd world.

2. Emergence

In literature, postmodernism has its origins in the rejection of traditional mimetic fiction in favor of a heightened sense of artifice, a delight in games and verbal pyrotechnics, a suspicion of absolute truth and a resulting inclination to stress the fictionality of fiction. All these traits are already present in the publications of *Lolita* (1955) by Nabokov, *The Recognitions* (1955) by William Gaddis (1922—), and *Naked Lunch* (1959) by William Burroughs (1914—). They ushered in the postmodern fiction in America.

Although postmodern fiction is often identified as peculiarly American and

Larry MaCaffery has identified November 22, 1963—the day Kennedy was shot—as the beginning of postmodernism, it owed much of the founding influence of Nabokov, Samuel Beckett (1906—1989), and Jorge Luis Borges (1899—1986) who were born outside America. These writers denied the feasibility of any literary art to represent or bring order to reality because they believed that reality was multiple, elusive and uncertain. They tried to upset all tradition and create confusion so that readers would come to terms with the absurd reality. Hence, they brought home the sense of pervasive skepticism, of sharpened absurdity and narcissistic self-awareness to American fiction. Postmodern fiction did not form a unified movement with a coherent theory. It was characterized by a multiplicity of individual voices. They did share a common sense that a crisis was at hand for society and for literature and that all forms of dogma, convention, ideology needed to be reexamined and replaced if necessary by fresher systems more suitable to the times.

3. Major Concepts

1) As Burroughs states in *Naked Lunch*, "The world cannot be expressed, it can perhaps be indicated by mosaics of juxtaposition, like objects abandoned in a hotel room, defined by negatives and absence." Postmodern writers brooded over what they perceived to be absence of answers and continuity by emphasizing randomness, discontinuity, and by blurring the distinction between author and fictional character. They insisted on drawing the reader into the confidence that the text was the only reality.

2) As postmodern writers rejected the traditional referential of art, they produced self-reflexive works. The self-reflexive text explicitly concerns itself with the process of narration, with writing, and with composition. It is characteristic of gimmicks, playfulness, and narcissism through parody and burlesque. It is a kind of grotesque comedy treated as a cosmic joke. Postmodern fiction sought to show the form rather than the content of American reality. It tried to render concrete and even visual in its language, in its syntax, in its typography and topology, the disorder, the chaos, the violence, the incongruity, but also the energy and vitality, of American reality.

3) It seems that the fundamental rule of the postmodern fiction is the absurd

and the arbitrary. Postmodern fiction seems to turn in a void, but not without clinging irony and black humor. At the end of the postmodern fiction there is no real message, no order, no easy resolution, no false moral statement, only a text that offers itself as a kind of nonsense delirium that, to a great extent, reflects the nonsense of historical events and the delirium, of the language recounting these events. It is no longer a question of representing or explaining or even justifying American reality, but a question of denouncing the very vehicle that expressed and represented that reality: discursive language and the traditional form of fiction. In other words, postmodern writers confronted their own writing, placed themselves in front of or inside their own texts in order to question the very act of using language and of writing fiction, even at the risk of alienating the reader.

4) Postmodern writers held that the reality of modern life was too elusive and uncertain for people to rationalize and idealize. Any attempt to impose order on a disordered reality was artificial and falsifying. Therefore, they chose the play of irrationality, the free play of language over discursive coherence and formalistic unity. As a result, postmodern text is disintegrated into a form of deliberate unreadability. By rendering language irrational, and even unreadable, postmodern writers neutralized the fiasco of reality and the imposture of history and suggested participation in the chaos and absurdity of the world as the only meaningful way of life. They believed that this was the way to come closer to the truth of the world.

5) The distrust of traditional mimetic genres, allied to the philosophical climate of structuralism and deconstruction, has encouraged postmodernism to embrace popular forms, such as detective fiction, science fiction, and fairy tale. Equally postmodernistic is the blurring of boundaries between the novel and journalism in Robert Pirsig's *Zen and the Art of Motorcycle Maintenance* (1974). The postmodern fiction extricated itself from realism and naturalism, and from metaphoric and symbolic representation of reality as modernists had done. By using pastiche, parody, irony, digression, and playfulness, it created a rupture in order to revive an "exhausted" genre-a genre that could no longer accommodate and express the extravagant notions of time and space of the

postindustrial reality. Hence, disorder, deliberate chaos, fragmentation, violation, disruption, dislocation, decentering, contradiction, confrontation, multiplicity, and indetermination comprise and accompany the postmodern text.

4. Reaction against Modernism

Postmodern writers challenged the terms that defined modernist fiction such as stream of consciousness, interior monologue, psychological depth, and syncopated syntax. Postmodern fiction undermined the modernist tradition and rejected its mimetic function. While reflecting upon itself, upon its own means and possibilities, postmodern fiction offered itself as a collection of fragments, as a puzzling catalogue of lists, as a montage or collage of disparate elements both in space and time.

Unlike modernism, which suggested a historic period, postmodernism described a sensibility, a feeling for innovation, for experiment with conventional ways of framing experience. Modernists tried to control the fragmented society through the agency of art and give it an art form, but postmodern writers were too nihilistic to trust their own ability to give shape or significance to the absurd world. Whereas modern consciousness developed a number of responses that created a sense of underlying coherence and order, as in the mythological structures in forming Ulysses and *The Sound and the Fury*, postmodern consciousness could no longer find a response adequate to the situation in which it found itself. Whereas modernist literature manipulated ancient myths and stable symbols, postmodern fiction confronted and exploded contemporary myths and clichés. Modernism emphasized the subjective apprehension of experience, but postmodernism found itself unable to structure and ordering ideas of reality and so conceived of reality as itself unreal. Rather than observing the modernist slogan "Make It New," postmodern writers repeated, parodied, and slowed things down. They appropriated other genres, both high and popular, longing for a both/and situation rather than one of either/or. Perhaps the most typical recent partitioner is Don DeLillo (1936—), who, by returning to the Kennedy assassination in *Libra* (1988), links postmodernism's latest phase to what is arguably its first cause.

Ⅱ. Thomas Pynchon (1937—)

Thomas Ruggles Pynchon, Jr. was born to Thomas Ruggles Pynchon, Sr. and Katherine Frances Bennett Pynchon on May 8, 1937 in Glen Cove, Long Island, New York. They moved to East Norwich when Thomas, Jr. was just a child. His father became town supervisor of Oyster Bay and later an industrial surveyor. He has two siblings, sister, Judith and brother, John.

Pynchon is an American novelist and short-story writer whose works combine black humor and fantasy to depict human alienation in the chaos of modern society.

After earning his B. A. in English from Cornell University in 1958, Pynchon spent a year in Greenwich Village writing short stories and working on a novel. In 1960 he was hired as a technical writer for Boeing Aircraft Corporation in Seattle, Washington. Two years later he decided to leave the company and write full-time. In 1963 Pynchon won the Faulkner Foundation Award for his first novel, V (1963), a whimsical, cynically absurd tale of a middle-aged Englishman's search for "V", an elusive, supernatural adventuress appearing in various guises at critical periods in European history. V cannot be understood by reference to convenient fictional signposts. Although it showed an indebtedness to Faulkner and Joyce (an indebtedness shared by most ambitious American novelists), Pynchon's style—or rather, styles—was already wholly his own. In writing that was by turns, labyrinthine, eloquent, and colloquial, Pynchon showed a particular fondness for imitating other styles. But these imitations and parodies instead of disparaging or minimizing their subjects radiated a generous spirit of exuberance which extended to the many characters who people *V* and whose individual paranoias—Pynchon's word to characterize the human attempt to make connections between events—propel them into unbelievably complicated and absurd plots. The interest of V was largely in the remarkably unending inventiveness with which Pynchon developed those plots, which might involve anything from diplomatic spy stories in nineteenth-century Africa to the bombing of Malta during World War Ⅱ, to surgical reconstruction of a young woman's nose, or a hunt for alligators in the sewers of New York City.

The comic talent shown in various New York episodes from V was also evident in *The Crying of Lot 49* (1966). This short, perfectly controlled novel teases us and itself with questions about the meaning of our American heritage, as embodied in the form of the mysterious legacy left to its heroine, Oedipa Maas. (The joky yet portentous name exemplifies Pynchon's teasing way of playing at "significance.") What is the connection between this legacy and the mysterious alternative to the U. S. Postal System on which Oedipa believes she has stumbled? Is there a secret network of alienated citizens carrying on their lives outside the ordinary systems and institutions of American life? Or is it all Oedipa's delusion, her private paranoia? These questions are considered through a style which continually surprises and unsettles us, though it is less discontinuous than V's. In Pynchon's world everything serious has its silly aspects (the Marx Brothers, among countless other comic acts, are in the background), while bits of trivia and foolery are suddenly elevated, through the style, into objects of sublime contemplation—as the novel's end when Oedipa thinks of "squatters" who...slept in junkyards in the stripped shells of wrecked Plymouths, or even more daring, spent the night up some pole in a lineman's tent like caterpillars. swung among a web of telephone wires, living in the very copper rigging and secular miracle of communication, untroubled by the dumb voltages flickering their miles, the night long, in the thousand of unheard messages.

Here his sentences enact the daring freedom he admires, in contrast to the institutions of a technological society.

Pynchon's longest and most daring and exhaustive effort came with the publication, in 1973, of *Gravity's Rainbow*. This encyclopedic fantasy operates through brilliant improvisations, tall tales, obscene parables, and burlesque stage routines, all of which work together into a story of supersonic capabilities and annihilative retributions. A huge cast of characters, each with a crazy name and a plot to unravel, is located all over the map, but mainly in World War II London and in postwar Germany. As the tour, main plot and the countless subsidiary plots take shape, characters—and the reader as well—attempt to "read" the messages flickering, the dumb intent to communicate, in the most casual as well as the most portentous sign. Pynchon's knowingness and fascination with popular culture is overwhelmingly evident in *Gravity's Rainbow*, as is his preoccupation with the lore of theoretical science, of obscure historical tales, or of contemporary comic books. No one denies the formidably encyclopedic nature of this astonishing effort; the question is, as Warner Berthoff has asked it, whether that effort may not also be "encyclopedically monotonous and static". More readers begin *Gravity's Rainbow* than finish it. Since 1973 all has been silence on the Pynchon front, although his early stories have been published as a collection (*Slow Learner*, 1984). But if there is still no consensus of his stature as an enduring American writer, there is general recognition of the quirky, uncanny exactitude of his imagination. Pynchon's theatrical spellbindings as a man of metaphor, his feats of association (in Robert Frost's phrase) are employed on subjects—like the rocket in *Gravity's Rainbow*—which were thought to be beyond words. For daring, wit, and exuberance, there is no contemporary writer who excels him.

Thomas Pynchon is concerned with death as a salient feature of the sense of the absurd. His is what has come to be known as the entropic vision. Entropy is a technical term in physics, denoting the tendency of the universe toward uniformity. Modern physics says that the universe forever moves in a leveling or decaying process in which the distribution of energy (or heat) is becoming the same everywhere. When a state of total equilibrium is reached, the death of the universe will come. Pynchon is also fascinated with the quantum theory which holds that all things contain a measure of uncertainty, and that, by extension, man's knowledge is inaccurate. Pynchon borrows the theories and employs them in his novels as an informing principle. Under the impact of the mechanical civilization, Pynchon feels, man is being dehumanized. He is fast losing his individual distinction to become part of the gray mass of "inanimate automation." He is deteriorating. A reading of Pynchon's short story, "Entropy," reveals the protagonist's and also Pynchon's obsession with keeping his world distinct and separate and immune from the conforming forces of the actual world around him.

Pynchon's novel, *V.*, brings forth his entropic vision and his sense of the world being uncertain. The search for the true meaning of the letter V serves as a good illustration of our point here. Each of the identities of Vin the novel represents a stage in the entropic evolution of man toward dehumanization and disintegration. Either as Victoria, a young convent dropout, who helps to kill a British spy in Egypt, or as a high-priced prostitute in Florence, or a voluptuous patroness of the theater in Paris, or the cruel Veronica Manganese in Malta, or Vera Meroving in Southwest Africa or in Valletta, V. has advanced in her non-humanity as well as in her years. Denying the humanity of others, she becomes inanimate herself. When she is dead, she is found wearing false hair, with a clock-iris eye, a gold foot, and a gold leg. Her process toward entropy is complete. And it is appalling to know the V. is not the only case of such death and inanimation: death lies at the core of earth's reality, and all seem to run to their annihilation. The uncertain and multiple nature of reality is best illustrated by the letter V. Its meaning is obscure and protean. It can be names such as Victoria, Vera, and Veronica. It can be places like Valletta of Malta or Venezuela. And it can be a good many other things, the "V" shape of spread thighs, say, or the Virgin Mother. There is an amount of truth in all these suggestions which fall, nonetheless, short of the whole truth. Its obscurity is further increased by the ambiguous way of narrative of the novel. The reader is often placed in a quandary where he is hard put to it to tell fact from fiction. Pynchon is a talented writer, able to see into the nature of contemporary life and to present his vision in an impressive way. In addition to his widely acclaimed V, his second book, *The Crying of Lot-49* should be placed on any reading list of contemporary American literature. It should be noted here that Pynchon is very difficult to read.

第五节　犹太文学与贝娄

每节导读

学习本节需要掌握犹太文学与贝娄及其代表作品《赫索格》。

犹太文学是美国现代文学一个重要组成部分，其主要特点如下：1）犹太文学深受古老的犹太文化及文学传统的影响；2）比较集中地描写异化社会；3）作品以犹太人为主人公；4）当代美国犹太小说家受欧洲现实主义传统影响比较大。犹太作家作品描写的虽是犹太人，反映的却是整个美国社会中普通人的处境。

战后最杰出的美国犹太作家是索尔·贝娄。其作品表现出人道主义的关怀和喜剧的风格。1976年贝娄由于“他的作品中融合了对人性的理解和对当代文化细致的分析”而荣获诺贝尔文学奖。《赫索格》的题材是犹太知识分子的感情纠葛，表现了当代美国人的困境。

Ⅰ. Jewish Literature

American Literature draws from the diverse cultures of all immigrants, ethnic and religious groups in the country. Jewish Literature is a unique part of American Literature. It refers to the published writings by American Jews about their American experiences, which were described from a Jewish perspective self-consciously. But one thing to mention here is that it is not necessarily that the work written by a Jewish writer can be definitely classified as Jewish literature. It is true that there is a lack of uniformity in thoughts and techniques even in the works of representative Jewish writers, however, we can still find some basic similarities that might be called features of Jewish literature. 1) Jewish literature is strongly influenced by Jewish culture and literary tradition. 2) Jewish literature tends to center on the description of alienation, which is resulted from the Jews historical background. 3) Jews, be he an unimportant small potato or economically better-off intellectual, will be the major characters, the heroes. 4) Jewish writers are influenced more by European realists.

The Jews originally lived in the Middle East in ancient times. Around 44B. C., they were driven out of their homeland by the Roman Empire. As a result they became homeless and had to wander around, some of whom settled down in many countries in Asia, Africa and Europe. They suffered from racial discrimination and persecution all the time until the 19th century when Jews, through hard working, became successful in society.

1881—1924 was the years of the great immigration of Jews from Eastern Europe to America. Unlike other immigrants from countries like Germany, Ireland etc, Jewish people tended to live in the cities and mainly in the Northeast. That is why Jewish literature always reveals a crowded urban background around the turn of 20th century, Jews came to America with a desire for learning. They were fascinated and enchanted by the new world, where their life changed from a Middle-Age sort, close-knit traditional community into an open and liberal world of modernity. Another wave of immigration occurred on the eve of World War Two due to Nazi persecution of Jews. And their situation in America was changed by two historical events, the holocaust during the war and the founding of Israel in 1948. Since then they won sympathy and acceptance. They have gradually assimilated themselves into American culture.

The true arrival of competent mature Jewish literature appeared by the end of World War Two, when many talented Jewish writers have been in the spotlight of American literature. Since Saul Bellow (1915—2005) and Isaac Bolshevik Singer (1904—1991) received Nobel Prizes in 1976 and 1978 respectively, the status of Jewish literature as an important part of America literature has been firmly established. Their common attitude derives from their common cultural background, a common history of being persecuted and discriminated as people rather than individuals.

Ⅱ. Saul Bellow (1915—2005)

1. Life and literary career

Bellow was born in Lachine, Quebec, Canada on June 10, 1915two years after his parents had emigrated from Russia. He grew up in the Jewish ghetto of Montreal. Under the influence of his mother, he learned Hebrew, Yiddish, French and English. In 1924 he moved to Chicago with his family and later in 1933 he attended the University of Chicago. In 1935 he studied at the Northwestern University and obtained a Bachelor of Science degree in anthropology and sociology two years after.

Being a thorough intellectual, he read widely in many subjects. During World War Two he served in the Merchant Marine and settled down to teach and write.

Bellow's first book, Dangling Man, came out in 1944. Then in the following four decades, a good number of novels, short stories and plays were published and won him awards. After *The Victim* (1947), he published *The Adventures of Augie March* (1953), which won the first of his three National Book Awards. In 1956 Bellow's another book, *Seize the Day* came out, to be followed by *Henderson the Rain King* (1959). In 1960 he won the Friends of Literature Fiction Award. His next book, *Herzog* (1964), received four awards including the James L. Dow Award and the National Book Award (1965). His collection of short stories, *Mosby's Memoirs* (1968) was awarded the French Croix de Chevalier des Arts et letters, and *Mr. Sammler's Planet* (1970) won his third National Book Award (1971). His *Humboldt's Gift* appeared in print in 1975, then *The Dean's December* in 1982. His career reaches its climax in 1976, in which year he was a warded the Pulitzer Prize and the Nobel Prize for literature. He died on April 5, 2005. Hearing his death, another Jewish writer Philip Roth commented that William Faulkner and Saul Bellow were the two most important writers in the 20th century American literature.

2. Comment

Bellow's works are in essence affirmatively humanistic. In his eyes, modern man has suffered frustration and defeat. Managing to get rid of pressures, man strives for truth, freedom and wisdom. So most of Saul Bellow's heroes are Jewish intellectuals, who try to discover the queerness of existence and overcome it. It is easy for us to see a typical Bellovian protagonist in his works, Tommy Wilhelm (*Seize the Day*), Asa Leventhal (*The Victim*), or Herzog (*Herzog*), who is usually in a suffering situation and behaves in an impotent, tragic-comic way. Despite the wretchedness and absurdity of man's existence, Bellow has a faith in his power and ability. Thus his novels usually end on an affirmative note.

Bellow is famous for depicting and interpreting the struggle of city dwellers to define their roles and responsibilities in the modern world. His themes are displacement, alienation and searching for identity. He follows the realistic tradition in literature and stresses the truthful representation of life as it is. At the same time he is influenced by modernistic literature and thus realism, romanticism and existentialism as well have all left their imprint on his works.

3. Selected Reading

1) Introduction to *Herzog*

Herzog (1964) is Saul Bellow's masterpiece, which won him the National Book Award and three other awards. It depicts a 47-year-old, sort of neurotic, alienated professor of literature who experiences an emotional, intellectual and moral crisis. He suffers the lonely feeling of estrangement from his two ex-wives, his Japanese mistress, his current lover, and his children as well. He is in a terrible condition where he has difficulty in dealing with women on the one hand, yet cannot live without them. He tries to recover his stability by analyzing his own false illusions and pretensions. His mentality is revealed in the form of brilliant and funny letters either in his head or on paper, to friends, relatives, politicians, philosophers, psychiatrists, the public and even God. These letters are actually an important way of expressing Professor Herzog's desire for communication with others and his failure to establish any real contact with outside world. Herzog's story also suggests the futility of attempts to establish one's identity through sex.

Bellow's fiction is dominated by the marginal man, an alienated and absurd character caught between his own disability and the pressure imposed by his friends and society. Bellow's protagonists are often uncommon thinkers who long for transcendental existence as they are estranged from the world. They laugh at their deficiency with bitter irony for it relieves despair. They hunger for communication, yet they hold back lest that would but betray the sanctity of their private self. Therefore, they are driven even deeper into their inner recesses. Bellow, however, is by no means pessimistic because he firmly believes in human reason. A man cannot shape his own destiny, but he can control the manner in which he faces it and denies absurdity by his efforts.

2) Selected Reading

Herzog

If I am out of my mind, it's all right with me, thought Moses Herzog.

Some people thought he was cracked and for a time he himself had doubted that he was all there. But now, though he still behaved oddly, he self confident, cheerful, clairvoyant, and strong. He had fallen under a spell and was writing letters to everyone under the sun. He was so place with a valise full of papers. He had carried this valise from New York to Martha's Vineyard ①, but returned from the Vineyard immediately; two days later he flew to Chicago, and from Chicago he went to a village in western Massachusetts. Hidden in the country, he wrote endlessly, fanatically, to the newspapers, to people in public life, to friends and relatives and at last to the dead, his own obscure dead, and finally the famous dead.

It was the peak of summer in the Berkshires②. Herzog was alone in the big old house. Normally particular about food, He now ate Silver cup bread③ from the paper package, beans from the can, and American cheese④. Now and then he picked raspberries in the overgrown garden, lifting up the thorny canes with absent-minded caution. As for sleep, he slept on a mattress without sheets—it was his abandoned marriage bed—or in the hammock, covered by his coat. Tall bearded grass and locust and maple seedlings surrounded him in the yard. When he opened his eyes in the night, the starts were near like spiritual bodies. Fires, of course; gases-minerals, heat, atoms, but eloquent at five in the morning to a man lying in a hammock, wrapped in his overcoat.

When some new thought gripped his heart he went to the kitchen, his headquarters, to write it down. The white paint was scaling from the table with his sleeve, calmly wondering why field mice should have such a passion for wax and paraffin. They made holes in paraffin-sealed preserves; they gnawed birthday candles down to the wicks. A rat chewed into a package of bread, leaving the shape of its body in the layers of slices. Herzog ate the other half of the loaf spread with jam. He could share with rats too.

All the while, one corner of his mind remained open to the external world. He heard the crows in the morning. Their harsh call was delicious. He heard the thrushes at dusk. At night there was a barn owl. When he walked in the garden, excited by a mental letter ⑤, he saw roses winding about the rain spout; or mulberries-birds gorging in the mulberry tree. The days were hot, the evenings flushed and dusty. He looked keenly at everything but he self half blind.

His friend, his former friend, Valentine, and his wife, his ex-wife of his face in a gray, webby window, He looked weirdly tranquil. A radiant line went from mid-forehead over his straight nose and full, silent lips.

Late in spring Herzog had been overcome by the need to explain, to have it out, to justify, to put in perspective, to clarify, to make amends.

At that time he had been giving adult-education lectures in a New York night school. He was clear enough in April but by the end of May he began to ramble. It became apparent to his students that they would never learn much about the roots of Romanticism but that they would see and hear odd things. One after another, the academic formalities dropped away. Professor Herzog had the unconscious frankness of a man deeply preoccupied. And toward the end of the term there were long pauses in his lectures. He would stop, muttering, "Excuse me," reaching inside his pen. The table creaking, he wrote on scraps of paper with a great pressure of eagerness in his hands; he was absorbed, his eyes darkly circled. His white face showed everything-everything. He was reasoning, arguing, he was suffering, he had thought of a brilliant alternative—he was wide-open, he was narrow; his eyes, his mouth made everything silently clear-longing, bigotry, bitter anger. One could see it all. The class waited three minutes, five minutes, utterly silent.

At first there was no pattern to the notes he made. They were fragments—nonsense syllables, exclamations, twisted proverbs and quotations of, in the Yiddish of his long-dead mother, Trepverter—retorts that came too late, when you were already on your way down the stairs.

NOTES

①Martha's Vineyard: an island in the southeast of Massachusetts. 马萨诸塞州东南的一

个岛屿，夏季旅游的胜地。

②Berkshires：a mountain in Massachusetts. 马萨诸塞州境内的伯克希尔山。

③Silver cup bread：a trademark of bread 银杯面包（面包的商标名称）

④American Cheese：美式干酪

⑤a mental letter：a designed letter in one's mind 一封信的腹稿

Topic Discussion

What is the theme of the novel?

第五章
少数族裔文学

第一节　非裔美国文学简介

每节导读

本节学习需要掌握非裔美国文学作品背景、发展历史及其代表作家、作品。

非裔美国文学不同于美国主流文学。非裔美国文学由非裔美国作家创作，描写非裔美国人的经历、遭遇和生活等。对自由、平等的向往是贯穿于非裔美国文学的主旨。它以《圣经》中的“出埃及记”为其发端。

非裔美国文学的发展也经历了不同阶段。在白人文学发展的同时，非裔美国文学就以口头形式开始出现。到20世纪，非裔美国文学更加蓬勃发展。20年代后期到30年代初，居住在纽约哈莱姆贫民区的黑人作家以大量作品表现黑人的悲惨生活，形成“哈莱姆文艺复兴”。休斯、卡伦等是那一时期代表作家。四五十年代，赖特、艾利森、鲍德温在美国文坛崛起，创作了《土生子》、《看不见的人》、《向苍天呼吁》等经典之作，黑人文学出现第二次高潮。70年代以来，美国黑人文学进入一个新的发展阶段，沃克、莫里森等人取得令人瞩目的成就。并且，莫里森成为获得诺贝尔文学奖的第一位非裔美国作家。

Ⅰ. General introduction

African-American literature has to be considered separately for the reason that it is all tied up with the bitter experience of the African-American people. It has a different tradition from the mainstream American literature we have been talking about so far, which is generally white. Certainly, many American white writers created images of the African-Americans in American literature, for example, Stowe created the images of Tom in *Uncle Tom's Cabin*; Mark Twain created Jim in *The Adventures of Huckleberry Finn*, etc., however, all the images created by the whites cannot be free of prejudice of themselves. African-

American literature differs in kind from all these.

First of all, African-American literature is one created by African-American writers themselves and it is a literature concerned with the experience, life and struggle of African-American people.

It also centers on a biblical myth, like the mainstream American literature, but it is a quite different myth from that on which white American literature is based. Whereas the latter has been inspired from the very beginning by the myth of the Garden of Eden, African-American literature is patterned on that of deliverance from slavery, that of the Hebrew prophet Moses leading the Jews in their flight from the bondage of Egypt, that is, the Exodus. This is in a way the key to understanding this literature. The African-American people often try to express their feelings and aspirations in biblical terms, possibly for want of a better medium. They have found in Jews' flight a parallel to their own struggle for freedom and equality. The literature is African-American writers' way of expressing their longing for "freedom" and "emancipation." This is the essential spirit running through Black American literature.

Ⅱ. Development of African-American literature

African-American literature underwent a long process of evolution. Oral tradition came first in the form of songs, ballads and spirituals, in short, folk literature in its various manifestations.

Then in the 18th century, African-American poets like Jupiter Hammon (1720—1800) and Phillis Wheatley (1753—1894) appeared on the scene. The Abolitionist Movement and the Civil War gave some of African-Americans a chance for education and brought a new impetus to African-American literature. Paul Laurence Dunbar (1872—1906) and James Weldon Johnson (1871—1938) produced substantial works of poetry and won national recognition. African-American novel developed at the turn of the twentieth century, but really nothing significant appeared until the publication of the widely acclaimed novel, Cane (1923), by Jean Toomer (1894—1967) who was essentially a poet. The 1920s saw a new upsurge of African-American literature in what has come to be known as the Harlem Renaissance which is so called because it first started in

Harlem a district inhabited mostly by African-Americans. African-American authors like Langston Hughes, Gwendolyn Brooks, and many others contributed a lot to the development of African-American literature. Hughes is probably the most prominent among them. African-American poetry became an indispensable part of American literature.

By far the most important person in the Harlem Renaissance was Langston Hughes (1902—1967) known as Black America's poet laureate, who ultimately outgrew the movement, and developed into one of the major African-American authors to help to make African-American culture. Hughes loved literature. When still in school, he began to write and publish. Around 1925 he was working as a busboy in a hotel in Washington D. C. when he met the then well-known and influential white poet, Vachel Lindsay. Lindsay was so struck by the poems which Hughes had submitted to him for advice that he encouraged the boy to devote himself to writing. Hughes became known as "the busboy poet". The next year he put his poems together in a book, entitled *The Weary Blues*. This collection marks a stage in Hughes' development as an author. The poems, like the blues songs, are sad in tone, describing the fact of having to live in a very cruel and oppressive world. But there is no fight in them. Merely describing how things are, they read as if Hughes were trying to relieve himself and his race of a mental load and to achieve a degree of reconciliation with the wicked world. His collection of short stories, *The Ways of White Folks*, appeared in 1934. Hughes' contribution to African-American literature can be seen in many aspects one of which is that he established African-American theater almost single-handedly, writing plays for the actors.

From the 1930s onward the African-American novel assumed an ever increasing importance writing to bring the bleeding heart out of hiding with more fighting spirit. This decade also witnessed the publication of an important novel by Zora Neale Hurston, entitled *Their Eyes Were Watching God* (1937) which, though criticized and neglected at first, has received favorable comments later on and has influenced later writers.

In 1940s African-American literature reached maturity, which was called protest literature. The representative is the *Native Son* by Richard Wright. In 1950s, Ralph Ellison's *Invisible Man* marked a higher level of maturity for

African-American literature. In Ellison's work, we can sense the plight of the hero both as an African-American and as a modern man. Together with him, James Baldwin (1924—1987) also showed concern not only about the problems faced by African-Americans but also about the conditions of man. *Go Tell It on the Mountain is* his masterwork. African-American theatre was slower in developing. It was bleak in the 19th century and nothing of importance appeared until the early 1960s when James Baldwin came up with their militant plays to arouse the African-American audience to action. The 1960s proved to be a turbulent period for the United States' when the African-Americans seemed, all of a sudden, inspired by the Civil Rights Movement, to awaken to the need for power, Black power, and it proved to be a period of spectacular growth in African-American literature.

The representative of this period is Toni Morrison, whose works included *The Bluest Eye*, *Song of Solomon*, *beloved* and so on. Toni Morrison, who received a Nobel Prize for literature in 1993, was the first African-American author to be so honored in the United States, which marked the new and higher stage that African-American literature has developed into. Another contemporary African-American author worth mentioning is Alice Walker (1944—) Whose The *Color Purple* won her the Pulitzer Prize. African-American literature is still developing with new authors appearing; for example, Maya Angelou (1928—) who was invited by President Clinton to read her poem at his inauguration, became the first African-American author to be so honored.

第二节　重要非裔美国作家及作品

每节导读

学习本节需要掌握美国作家赖特及其《土生子》、艾利森及其《看不见的人》，以及莫里森及其《所罗门之歌》。

20 世纪四五十年代，赖特、艾利森在美国文坛崛起，创作了《土生子》、《看不见的人》等经典之作，黑人文学出现第二次高潮。

赖特是20世纪美国杰出的黑人作家。他不仅写小说、短篇故事，还写杂文戏剧和诗歌等。他以深刻的笔触和充满激情的叙述再现了挣扎在贫困、恐惧、耻辱和仇恨之中的黑人生活，愤怒声讨了种族歧视现象和种族隔离政策。1940年，《土生子》的发表轰动美国文坛，该书描写了一个家境贫寒的黑人青年别格因无意中杀死了富有的白人小姐玛丽被判处死刑的故事。这是一部抗议小说，它暴露了美国黑人被压抑的仇恨和被压迫的痛苦。许多评论家认为该书的出版标志着非裔美国文学走向成熟。

艾里森立志要创作出一部美国文学的经典之作才写了《看不见的人》。经过7年的努力，1952年该书出版。它讲述的是一个黑人在白人社会寻找自我的故事。书中不乏对种族歧视的揭露和抗议，然而它更着重探讨“寻找自我”这样一个具有普遍意义的命题。因此，该书被认为是代表着非裔美国文学在更高层次上的成熟。

20世纪60年代，随着人权运动的深入发展，非裔美国文学也进入了一个新的发展阶段。莫里森是这一阶段的杰出代表之一。其《所罗门之歌》被认为是继《土生子》、《看不见的人》之后最好的非裔美国小说。它讲述了一个非裔美国青年寻找自己的文化以及自我的过程。莫里森的作品中融进了黑人的文化及传说，代表着非裔美国文学发展的新方向。

Ⅰ. Richard Wright（1908—1960）

1. Life and Works

The most important author to appear in the 1940s was Richard Wright who became a powerful writer and a big influence though with a small productivity. Richard Wright's boyhood was a miserable memory. He was not happy at home with his stern mother and grandmother, he also suffered from the racial discrimination of the American south of the time. Eventually he fled to Chicago, where in contact with left-wing friends and finally with the Communist Party, he began to see the African-American situation as part of the general human situation of the oppressed and to gain a growing sense of social awareness. His first book, *Uncle Tom's Children: Four Novellas* came out in 1938, followed two years later by his masterwork, *Native Son*. For the first time in American history a book by an African-American author about the life of African-Americans made such an impact on the consciousness of the nation that Richard Wright became famous nationwide. In 1944 he broke with the Communist Party, and the next year published his second powerful book, *Black Boy*, an autobiography relating the bitter experience of his youth. The racial discrimination of the country becoming increasingly intolerable to him, Wright left for Europe, where he settled down in France. Thus, cut off from the reality of African-American experience, he was seriously unable to create his work; thus, none of his works later, whether they were novels, stories or essays, ever again touched his best work in power and critical acclaim.

Native Son is an extremely fascinating book. It, in a sense, simply shocked the American reading public. Dealing with one of the problems with which America had been involved-the racial question, the book pushed it into the reader's mind in a manner no one had ever done before. African-American readers got the message that they are human beings and should be treated as such, and that if nothing else can help to assert their dignity and identity, then the only way to deal with the situation is to resort to violence. The whites can also read out a message, that is, the moment has arrived when they have to come to terms with their African-American fellowmen, and if not, they will have to take the consequences. Bigger Thomas, the hero of the book, represents a new type of African-American personality. Rebellious and aggressive by nature, he is both the murderer and the victim of the society. Thus Bigger Thomas, more than any other African-American characters, represents a higher level of racial awareness. In him and his actions, the African-Americans saw their identity and the whites their folly and obligation. Richard Wright has contributed to African-American literature as well as American literature in the following three aspects: the first is his naturalistic vision of urban African-American characters and culture; the second is his creation of the best-known character in African-American fiction by a combination of white and black myths of "bad Nigger"; and the third is his projection of African-American as the metaphor for American modern man. Richard Wright's influence over subsequent African-American writers has been great. It is no exaggeration to say that he began the contemporary literary tradition of violent self-assertion and that it is in his Native Son that African-American literature began to mature.

2. Introduction to Native Son

1) Plot Overview

The plot is divided into three parts: 1) Fear; 2) Flight; 3) Fate.

Bigger Thomas, no father, lived with his mother, brother and sister in a kitchen net.

One morning, his sister found a big rat and Bigger was asked to beat it to death. The rat was facing death and had a death struggle. It ran up into Bigger's trousers. He was so angry that he still beat it though it was already dead.

Bigger went to work in the white Daltons as a driver. Mrs. Daltons was blind and often encouraged him to finish his education. One day, Mary, Mrs. Daltons' daughter, asked him to send her to her boyfriend who was a communist. Mary got overdrunk. Bigger carried her to her bedroom. Just then Mrs. Daltons appeared, he put a pillow on Mary's mouth in order that his owner couldn't misunderstand him. As a result, Mary died after Mrs. Daltons left. He put Mary into a furnace to burn her body.

After that, Bigger Thomas escaped. Bigger's girlfriend persuaded him to go to the police office. However, he killed his girlfriend in case that she might betray him. Mary's boyfriend sent a lawyer to defend Bigger. But no matter how hard, Bigger was still sentenced to electric chair. Ironically, he was more condemned for killing white Mary incidentally rather than his purposely killing his black girlfriend.

2) Characterization of Bigger Thomas

① Bad nigger: African-Americans are always the victims; they are persecuted and lynched in other writings. However, Bigger is a rebellious figure, because he is someone who kills and who is violent.

②A victim of society: The rat's confrontation with Bigger is the metaphor of Bigger's confrontation with society. In the latter part, Bigger is weaker. That's why the last chapter is called Fate. He is so powerless compared to the white society. Violence is his way of self-affirmation. Here we can see the author's theme.

③Bigger is modern American. Bigger is a product of America, or the native son of the land. He is dispossessed and disinherited man. Modern world is a world of alienation not only to African-Americans but also to the white. Bigger's experience can be everybody's experience in a sense.

3. Selected Reading:

Native Son

BOOK I FEAR

Brinng! ①

An alarm clock clanged in the dark and silent room. A bed spring creaked.

A woman's voice sang out impatiently: "Bigger, shut that thing off!"

A surly grunt sounded above the tinny ring of metal. Naked feet swished dryly across the planks in the wooden floor and the clang ceased abruptly.

"Turn on the light, Bigger."

"Awright," came a sleepy mumble.

Light flooded the room and revealed a black boy standing in a narrow space between two iron beds, rubbing his eyes with the backs of his hands. From a bed to his right the woman spoke again:

"Buddy, get up from there! I got a big washing on my hands today and I want you—all out of here."

Another black boy rolled from bed and stood up. The woman also rose and stood in her nightgown.

"Turn your heads so I can dress," she said.

The two boys averted their eyes and gazed into a far corner of the room. The woman rushed out of her nightgown and put on a pair of step—ins. She turned to the bed from which she had risen and called:

"Vera! Get up from there!"

"What time is it, Ma?" asked a muffled, adolescent voice from beneath a quilt.

"Get up from there, I say!"

"O. K., Ma."

A brown—skinned girl in a cotton gown got up and stretched her arms above her head and yawned. Sleepily, she sat on a chair and fumbled with her stockings. The two boys kept their faces averted while their mother and sister put on enough clothes to keep them from feeling ashamed; and the mother and sister did the same while the boys dressed. Abruptly, they all paused, holding their clothes in their hands, their attention caught by a light tapping in the thinly plastered walls of the room They forgot their conspiracy against shame and their eyes strayed apprehensively over the floor.

"There he is again, Bigger!" ② the woman screamed, and the tiny one-room apartment galvanized into violent action. A chair toppled as the woman, half-dressed and in her stocking feet, scrambled breathlessly upon the bed. Her two sons, barefoot, stood tense and motionless, their eyes searching anxiously under the bed and chairs. The girl ran into a corner, half stooped and gathered the hem of her slip into both of her hands and held it tightly over her knees.

"Oh! Oh!" she wailed.

"There he goes!"

The woman pointed a shaking finger. Her eyes were round with fascinated horror.

"Where?"

"I don't see'im!"

"Bigger, he's behind the trunk!" the girl whimpered.

"Vera!" the woman screamed. "Get up here on the bed! Don't let that thing bite you!"

Frantically, Vera climbed upon the bed and the woman caught hold of her. With their arms entwined about each other, the black mother and the brown daughter gazed open-mouthed at the trunk in the corner.

Bigger looked round the room wildly, then darted to a curtain and swept it aside and grabbed two heavy iron skillets from a wall above a gas stove. He whirled and called softly to his brother, his eyes glued to the trunk.

"Buddy!"

"Yeah? ..."

"Here; take this skillet."

"O. K."

"Now, get over by the door!"

"O. K."

Buddy crouched by the door and held the iron skillet by its handle, his arm flexed and poised. Save for the quick, deep breathing of the four people, the room was quiet. Bigger crept on tiptoe toward the trunk with the skillet clutched stiffly in his hand, his eyes dancing and watching every inch of the wooden floor in front of him. He paused and, without moving an eye or muscle, called:

"Buddy!"

"Hunh?"

"Put that box in front of the hole so he can't get out!"

"O. K."

Buddy ran to a wooden box and shoved it quickly in front of a gaping hole in the molding and then backed again to the door, holding the skillet ready. Bigger eased to the trunk and peered behind it cautiously. He saw nothing. Carefully, he stuck out his bare foot and pushed the trunk a few inches.

"There he is!" the mother screamed again.

A huge black rat squealed and leaped at Bigger's trouserleg and snagged it in his teeth, hanging on.

"Goddamn!" Bigger whispered fiercely, whirling and kicking out his leg with all the strength of his body. The force of his movement shook the rat loose and it sailed through the air and struck a wall. Instantly, it rolled over and leaped again.

Bigger dodged and the rat landed against a table leg. With clenched teeth, Bigger held the skillet; he was afraid to hurl it, fearing that he might miss. The rat squeaked and turned and ran in a narrow circle, looking for a place to hide; it leaped again past Bigger and scurried on dry rasping feet to one side of the box and then to the other, searching for the hole. Then it turned and reared upon its hind legs.

"Hit'im, Bigger!" Buddy shouted.

"Kill'im!" the woman screamed.

The rat's belly pulsed with fear. Bigger advanced a step and the rat emitted a long thin song of defiance, its black beady eyes glittering, its tiny forefeet pawing the air restlessly. Bigger swung the skillet; it skid-ded over the floor, missing the rat, and clattered to a stop against a wall.

"Goddamn!"

The rat leaped. Bigger sprang to one side. The rat stopped under a chair and let out a furious screak. Bigger moved slowly backward toward the door.

"Gimme that skillet, Buddy," he asked quietly, not taking his eyes from the rat. Buddy extended his hand. Bigger caught the skillet and lifted it high in the air. The rat scuttled across the floor and stopped again at the box and searched quickly for the hole; then it reared once more and bared long yellow fangs, piping shrilly, belly quivering.

Bigger aimed and let the skillet fly with a heavy grunt. There was a shattering of wood as the box caved in. The woman screamed and hid her face in her hands. Bigger tiptoed forward and peered.

"I got'im," he muttered, his clenched teeth bared in a smile. "By God, I got'im." He kicked the splintered box out of the way and the flat black body of the rat lay exposed, its two long yellow tusks showing distinctly. Bigger took a shoe and pounded the rat's head, crushing it, cursing hysterically:

"You son of a bitch!"

The woman on the bed sank to her knees and buried her face in the quilts and sobbed:

"Lord, Lord, have mercy..."

"Aw, Mama," Vera whimpered, bending to her. "Don't cry. It's dead now."

The two brothers stood over the dead rat and spoke in tones of awed admiration.

"Gee, but he's a big bastard."

"That son of a bitch could cut your throat."

"He's over a foot long."

"How in hell do they get so big?"

"Eating garbage and anything else they can get."

"Look, Bigger, there's a three—inch rip in your pant—leg."

"Yeah; he was after me, all right."

"Please, Bigger, take'im out," Vera begged.

"Aw, don't be so scary," Buddy said.

The woman on the bed continued to sob. Bigger took a piece of newspaper and gingerly lifted the rat by its tail and held it out at arm's length.

"Bigger, take'im out," Vera begged again.

Bigger laughed and approached the bed with the dangling rat, swinging it to and fro like a pendulum, enjoying his sister's fear.

"Bigger!" Vera gasped convulsively; she screamed and swayed and closed her eyes and fell headlong across her mother and rolled limply from the bed to the floor.

"Bigger, for God's sake!" the mother sobbed, rising and bending over Vera. "Don't do that! Throw that rat out!"

He laid the rat down and started to dress.

"Bigger, help me lift Vera to the bed," the mother said.

He paused and turned round.

"What's the matter?" he asked, feigning ignorance.

"Do what I asked you. Will you, boy?"

He went to the bed and helped his mother lift Vera. Vera's eyes were closed. He turned away and finished dressing. He wrapped the rat in a newspaper and went out of the door and down the stairs and put it into a garbage can at the corner of an alley.

When he returned to the room his mother was still bent over Vera, placing a wet towel upon her head. She straightened and faced him, her cheeks and eyes wet with tears and her lips tight with anger.

"Boy, sometimes I wonder what makes you act like you do."

"What I do now?" he demanded belligerently.

"Sometimes you act the biggest fool I ever saw."

"What you talking about?"

"You scared your sister with that rat and she fainted! Ain't you got no sense at all?"

"Aw, I didn't know she was that scary."

"Buddy!" the mother called.

"Yessum."

"Take a newspaper and spread it over that spot."

"Yessum."

Buddy opened out a newspaper and covered the smear of blood on the floor where the rat had been crushed. Bigger went to the window and stood looking out abstractedly into the street. His mother glared at his back.

"Bigger, sometimes I wonder why I birthed you," she said bitterly.

Bigger looked at her and turned away.

"Maybe you oughtn't've. Maybe you ought to left me where I was."

"You shut your sassy mouth!"

"Aw, for chrissakes!" Bigger said, lighting a cigarette.

"Buddy, pick up them skillets and put'em in the sink," the mother said.

"Yessum."

Bigger walked across the floor and sat on the bed. His mother's eyes followed him.

"We wouldn't have to live in this garbage dump if you had any manhood in you," she said.

"Aw, don't start that again."

"How you feel, Vera?" the mother asked.

Vera raised her head and looked about the room as though expecting to see another rat.

"Oh, Mama!"

"You poor thing!"

"I couldn't help it. Bigger scared me."

"Did you hurt yourself?"

"I bumped my head."

"Here; take it easy. You'll be all right."

"How come Bigger acts that way?" Vera asked, crying again.

"He's just crazy," the mother said. "Just plain dumb black crazy."

"I'll be late for my sewing class at the Y. W. C. A.," Vera said.

"Here; stretch out on the bed. You'll feel better in a little while," the mother said.

She left Vera on the bed and turned a pair of cold eyes upon Bigger.

"Suppose you wake up some morning and find your sister dead? What would you think then?" she asked. "Suppose those rats cut our veins at night when we sleep? Naw! Nothing like that ever bothers you! All you care about is your own pleasure! Even when the relief offers you a job you won't take it till they threaten to cut off your food and starve you! Bigger, honest, you the most no—countest man I ever seen in all my life!"

"You done told me that a thousand times," he said, not looking round.

"Well, I'm telling you agin! And mark my word, some of these days you going to set down and cry. Some of these days you going to wish you had made something out of yourself, instead of just a tramp. But it'll be too late then."

"Stop prophesying about me," he said.

"I prophesy much as I please! And if you don't like it, you can get out. We can get along without you. We can live in one room just like we living now, even with you gone," she said.

"Aw, for chrissakes!" he said, his voice filled with nervous irritation.

"You'll regret how you living some day," she went on. "If you don't stop running with that gang of yours and do right you'll end up where you never thought you would. You think I don't know what you boys is doing, but I do. And the gallows is at the end of the road you traveling, boy. Just remember that." ③ She turned and looked at Buddy.

"Throw that box outside, Buddy."

"Yessum."

There was silence. Buddy took the box out. The mother went behind the curtain to the gas stove. Vera sat up in bed and swung her feet to the floor.

"Lay back down, Vera," the mother said.

"I feel all right now, Ma. I got to go to my sewing class."

"Well, if you feel like it, set the table," the mother said, going behind the curtain again. "Lord, I get so tired of this I don't know what to do," her voice floated plaintively from behind the curtain. "All I ever do is try to make a home for you children and you don't care."

"Aw, Ma," Vera protested. "Don't say that."

"Vera sometimes I just want to lay down and quit."

"Ma, please don't Say that."

"I can't last many more years, living like this."

"I'll be old enough to work soon, Ma."

"I reckon I'll be dead then. I reckon God'll call me home."

Vera went behind the curtain and Bigger heard her trying to comfort his mother. He shut their voices out of his mind. He hated his family because he knew that they were suffering and that he was powerless to help them. He knew that the moment he allowed himself to feel to its fullness how they lived, the shame and misery of their lives, he would be swept out of himself with fear and despair. So he held toward them an attitude of iron reserve; he lived with them, but behind a wall, a curtain. And toward himself he was even more exacting. He knew that the moment he allowed what his life meant to enter fully into his consciousness, he would either kill himself or someone else. So he denied himself and acted tough. He got up and crushed his cigarette upon the window sill. Vera came into the room and placed knives and forks upon the table.

"Get ready to eat, you—all," the mother called.

He sat at the table. The odor of frying bacon and boiling coffee drifted to him from behind the curtain. His mother's voice floated to him in song.

Life is like a mountain railroad
With an engineer that's brave
We must make the run successful
From the cradle to the grave....

The song irked him and he was glad when she stopped and came into the room with a pot of coffee and a plate of crinkled bacon. Vera brought the bread in and they sat down. His mother closed her eyes and lowered her head and mumbled,

"Lord, we thank Thee for the food you done placed before us for the nourishment of our bodies. Amen." She lifted her eyes and without changing her tone of voice, said, "You going to have to learn to get up earlier than this, Bigger, to hold a job."

He did not answer or look up.

"You want me to pour you some coffee?" Vera asked.

"Yeah."

"You going to take the job, ain't you, Bigger?" his mother asked.

He laid down his fork and stared at her.

"I told you last night I was going to take it. How many times you want to ask me?"

"Well, don't bite her head off," Vera said. "She only asked you a question."

"Pass the bread and stop being smart."

"You know you have to see Mr. Dalton at five-thirty," his mother said.

"You done said that ten times."

"I don't want you to forget, son."

"And you know how you can forget," Vera said.

NOTES

①Brinng!: The ringing bell of an alarm clock is a symbol. Bigger's life is filled with worry, shame and hatred. Today, he begins to come close to death. 闹钟声的象征意义在于，比格的每一天都充满了困扰、耻辱与仇恨，今天则是他走向死亡的开始。

② "There is he is again, Bigger!": "he" refers to the rat. The rat makes the family feel unrest and even fearful. The rat is just as afraid of Bigger as Bigger is of the white world. The death of the rat symbolizes the death of Bigger. 这个"he"指老鼠。老鼠的出现一方面说明比格一家人经常被老鼠搅得不得安宁；另一方面也有寓意，老鼠之于比格一家犹如比格之于白人社会，老鼠的死预示比格的死。

③ "You' ll regret…Just remember that.": In appearance, the mother is cursing her son. Actually, she is cursing the white world. 母亲表面上诅咒儿子，实则诅咒白人社会。

Topic Discussion

1. What's the characterization of Bigger Thomas like?
2. What's the characteristic in language as can be seen from this part?

Ⅱ. Ralph Ellison (1914—1994)

1. Life and works

Ralph Ellison was born in Oklahoma; his father was a construction worker who died when his son was only three. However, his life is much better than Richard Wrights'. After his father died in 1917, his mother worked as a housemaid where she could bring some thrown-away books and magazines for her son. He attended school regularly. In 1933, he won a state scholarship and went to Tuskegee Institute, a famous Negro university, majoring in music. Later he went to New York and met Hughes and Wrights who introduced him to the works of other literary masters and encouraged him to write himself. In 1952, *Invisible Man* came out, which he took seven years to write. This novel marked a higher level of maturity for African-American literature. In 1953,

Ellison won the National Book Award. Book Weeks (1965) considered Invisible Man as the best book published after the Second World War.

2. Introduction to *Invisible Man*

The hero has no name. He was an obedient black boy in the South. He got a scholarship because of his obedience and went to a university. One day, a white benefactor visited the school, and he was asked to show the white benefactor around. Later he was expelled because he had shown the black ghettos and something unpleasant to the white man. He had to go to the North to find a job but he could only do lower jobs because the recommendation letter written by the president of the university said something very bad about him. First, he worked in a paint factory and got wounded. When he came out of the hospital he saw an old African-American couple driven out of a flat and immediately he made a radical speech and was appreciated by the leader of brotherhood association. Later he joined the brotherhood and was driven out of it because of different opinion. After that he stayed in the underground for twenty years with 1369 lights on to show his visibility.

The novel is about the hero's dual experience as an African-American and as a modern man: as an African-American, the hero is invisible to the white. As a modern man, he suffers from alienation and loss of self in modern society.

The novel is full of symbols and images some of which are related to the idea of being invisible and blind. The style also changes as the setting of the story changes.

3. Selected Reading

Invisible Man

PROLOGUE ①

I am an invisible man. No, I am not a spook like those who haunted Edgar Allan Poe; nor am I one of your Hollywood—movie ectoplasms. I am a man of substance, of flesh and bone, fiber and liquids—and I might even be said to possess a mind. I am invisible, understand, simply because people refuse to see me. Like the bodiless heads you see sometimes in circus sideshows, it is as though I have been surrounded by mirrors of hard, distorting glass. When they approach me they see only my surroundings, themselves, or figments of their imagination—indeed, everything and anything except me.

Nor is my invisibility exactly a matter of a bio—chemical accident to my epidermis. That invisibility to which I refer occurs because of a peculiar disposition of the eyes of those with whom I come in contact. A matter of the construction of their inner eyes, those eyes with which they look through their physical eyes upon reality. I am not complaining, nor am I protesting either. It is sometimes advantageous to be unseen, although it is most often rather wearing on the nerves. Then too, you're constantly being bumped against by those of poor vision. Or again, you often doubt if you really exist. You wonder whether you aren't simply a phantom in other people's minds. Say, a figure in a nightmare which the sleeper tries with all his strength to destroy. It's when you feel like this that, out of resentment, you begin to bump people back. And, let me confess, you feel that way most of the time. You ache with the need to convince yourself that you do exist in the real world, that you're a part of all the sound and anguish, and you strike out with your fists, you curse and you swear to make them recognize you. And, alas, it's seldom successful.

One night I accidentally bumped into a man, and perhaps because of the near darkness he saw me and called me an insulting name. I sprang at him, seized his coat lapels and demanded that he apologize. He was a tall blond man, and as my face came close to his he looked insolently out of his blue eyes and cursed me, his breath hot in my face as he struggled. I pulled his chin down sharp upon the crown of my head, butting him as I had seen the West Indians do, and I felt his flesh tear and the blood gush out and I yelled, "Apologize! Apologize!" But he continued to curse and struggle, and I butted him again and again until he went down heavily, on his knees, profusely bleeding. I kicked him repeatedly, in a frenzy because he still uttered insults though his lips were frothy with blood. Oh yes, I kicked him! And in my outrage I got out my knife and prepared to slit his throat, right there beneath the lamplight in the deserted street, holding him by the collar with one hand, and opening the knife with my teeth—when it occurred to me that the man had not seen me, actually; that he, as far as he knew, was in the midst of a walking nightmare! And I stopped the blade, slicing the air as I pushed him away, letting him fall back to the street. I stared at him hard as the lights of a car stabbed through the darkness. He lay there, moaning on the asphalt; a man almost killed by a phantom. It unnerved me. I was both disgusted and ashamed. I was like a drunken man myself, wavering about on weakened legs. Then I was amused. Something in this man's thick head had sprung out and beaten him within an inch of his life. I began to laugh at this crazy discovery. Would he have awakened at the point of death? I ran away into the dark, laughing so hard I feared I might rupture myself. The next day I saw his picture in the Daily News, beneath a caption stating that he had been "mugged." Poor fool, poor blind fool, I thought with sincere compassion, mugged by an invisible man!

Most of the time (although I do not choose as I once did to deny the violence of my days by ignoring it) I am not so overtly violent. I remember that I am invisible and walk softly so as not to awaken the sleeping ones. Sometimes it is best not to awaken them; there are few things in the world as dangerous as sleepwalkers. I learned in time though that it is possible to carry on a fight against them without their realizing it. For instance, I have been carrying on a fight with Monopolated Light and Power [2] for some time now, I use their serice and pay them nothing at all, and they don't know it. Oh, they suspect that power is being drained off, but they don't know where. All they know is that according to the master meter back there in their power station a hell of a lot of free current is disappearing somewhere into the jungle of Harlem. The joke, of course, is that I don't live in Harlem but in a border area. Several years ago (before I discovered the advantage of being invisible) I went through the routine process of buying service and paying their outrageous rates. But no more. I gave up all that, along with my apartment, and my old way of life: That way based upon the fallacious assumption that I, like other men, was visible. Now, aware of my invisibility, I live rent-free in a building rented strictly to whites, in s section of the basement that was shut off and forgotten during the nineteenth century, which I discovered when I was trying to escape in the night from Ras the Destroyer [3]. But that's getting too far ahead of the story, almost to the end, although the end is in the beginning and lies far ahead.

The point now is that I found a home—or a hole in the ground, as you will. Now don't jump to the conclusion that because I call my home a "hole" it is damp and cold like a grave; there are cold holes and warm holes. Mine is a warm hole. And remember, a bear retires to his hole for the winter and lives until spring; then he comes strolling out like the Easter chick breaking from its shell. I say all this to assure you that it is incorrect to assume that, because I'm invisible and live in a hole, I am dead. I am neither dead nor in a state of suspended animation. Call me Jack—the—Bear, for I am in a state of hibernation.

My hole is warm and full of light. Yes, full of light. I doubt if there is a brighter spot in all New York than this hole of mine, and I do not exclude Broadway. Or the Empire State Building on a photographer's dream night. But that is taking advantage of you. Those two spots are among the darkest of our whole civilization—pardon me, our whole culture (an important distinction, I've heard) —which might sound like a hoax, or a contradiction, but that (by contradiction, I mean) is how the world moves: Not like an arrow, but a boomerang. (Beware of those who speak of the spiral of history; they are preparing a boomerang. Keep a steel helmet handy.) I know; I have been boomeranged across my head so much that I now can see the darkness of lightness[④]. And I love light. Perhaps you'll think it strange that an invisible man should need light, desire light, love light. But maybe it is exactly because I am invisible. Light confirms my reality, gives birth to my form. A beautiful girl once told me of a recurring nightmare in which she lay in the center of a large dark room and felt her face expand until it filled the whole room, becoming a formless mass while her eyes ran in bilious jelly up the chimney. And so it is with me. Without light I am not only invisible, but formless as well; and to be unaware of one's form is to live a death. I myself, after existing some twenty years, did not become alive until I discovered my invisibility.

That is why I fight my battle with Monopolated Light & Power. The deeper reason, I mean: It allows me to feel my vital aliveness. I also fight them for taking so much of my money before I learned to protect myself. In my hole in the basement there are exactly 1369 lights. I've wired the entire ceiling, every inch of it. And not with fluorescent bulbs, but with the older, more-expensive-to-operate kind, the filament type. An act of Sabotage, you know. I've already begun to wire the wall. A junk man I know, a man of vision, has supplied me with wire and sockets. Nothing, storm of flood, must get in the way of our need for light and ever more and brighter light. The truth is the light and light is The truth. When I finish all four walls, then I'll start on the floor. Just how that will go, I don't know. Yet when you have lived invisible as long as I have you develop a certain ingenuity. I'll solve the problem. And maybe I'll invent a gadget to place my coffeepot on the fire while I lie in bed, and even invent a gadget to warm my bed-like the fellow I saw in one of the picture magazines who made himself a gadget to warm his shoes! Though invisible, I am in the great American tradition of tinkers. That makes me kin to Ford ⑤, Edison ⑥ and Franklin ⑦. Call me, since I have a theory and a concept, a "thinker-tinker." Yes, I'll warm my shoes; they need it, they're usually full of holes. I'll do that and more.

Now I have one radio-phonograph; I plan to have five. There is a certain acoustical deadness in my hole, and when I have music I want to feel its vibration, not only with my ear but with my whole body. I'd like to hear five recordings of Louis Armstrong ⑧ playing and singing "what Did I Do to Be so Black and Blue" —all at the same time. Sometimes now I Listen to Louis while I have my favorite dessert of vanilla ice cream and sloe gin. I pour the red liquid over the white mound, watching it glisten and the vapor rising as Louis bends that military instrument into a beam of lyrical sound. Perhaps I like Louis Armstrong because he's made poetry out of being invisible. I think it must be because he's unaware that he is invisible. And my own grasp of invisibility aids me to understand his music. Once when I asked for a cigarette, some jokers gave me a reefer, which I lighted when I got home and sat listening to my phonograph. It was a strange evening. Invisibility, let me explain, gives one a slightly different sense of time. You're never quite on the beat. Sometimes you're ahead and sometimes behind. Instead of the swift and imperceptible flowing of time, you are aware of its nodes, those points where time stands still or from which it leaps ahead. And you slip into the breaks and look around. That's what you hear vaguely in Louis' music.

Once I saw a prizefighter boxing a yokel. The fighter was swift and amazingly scientific. His body was one violent flow of rapid rhythmic action. He hit the yokel a hundred times while the yokel held up his arms in stunned surprise. But suddenly the yokel, rolling about in the gale of boxing gloves, struck one blow and knocked science, speed and footwork as cold as a well-digger's posterior. The smart money hit the canvas ⑨. The long shot got the nod ⑩. The yokel had simply stepped inside of his opponent's sense of time. So under the spell of the reefer ⑪ I discovered a new analytical way of listening to music. The unheard sounds came through, and each melodic line existed of itself, stood out clearly from all the rest, said its piece, and waited patiently for the other voices to speak. That night I found myself hearing not only in time, but in space as well. I not only entered the music but descended, like Dante into its depths.

NOTES

①Prologue: The Prologue and the Epilogue make the structure of the novel unique. In both of the two parts, the protagonist looks back at what has happened to him when he is pursued by the black nationalists and falls into the hole. The protagonist also makes comment on the questions such as "good and evil","love and hatred","light and dark","illusion and reality", "freedom","truth" and "social responsibilities". "I myself, after existing some twenty years, did not become alive until I discovered my invisibility." 小说《看不见的人》的结构独具特色，除故事主体之外，开头有一个"前言"，末尾有一个"结束语"。这两部分都是故事接近尾声时，主人公在黑人民族主义者拉斯一伙的追逐下掉进"洞"里以后，回顾以往走过的道路，对"善"与"恶"、"爱"与"恨"、"光明"与"黑暗"、"幻想"与"现实"以及"自由"、"真理"和"社会责任"等问题有所领悟而发的议论，"直到发现自己是个看不见的人，才意识到自己是个活人"。

②Monopolated Light and Power: The company from which the protagonist steals electricity to fill his "hole" with light. 电力公司名称。

③Ras the Destroyer: He is one of the main characters in this novel. He is the leader of the black nationalists in Harlem. The protagonist hides underground just because of his pursuit. 毁灭者拉斯，小说主要人物之一，纽约市哈莱姆区黑人民族主义者领导人。主人公就是在他追逐下躲进地下室的。

④the darkness of lightness: The blow on his head makes the protagonist see stars. This is also a pun, which means to mix up black and white. 指头部被撞击以后眼冒金花的状态，双关语，意指黑白混淆。

⑤Ford: Henry Ford (1863—1947), American automobile manufacturer. 亨利·福特，美国汽车工业大王。

⑥Edison: Thomas Alva Edison (1847—1931), American inventor. 托马斯·艾尔瓦·爱迪生，美国发明家。

⑦Franklin: Benjamin Franklin (1706—1790), who was the outstanding statesman, litterateur and inventor during the age of American Revolution. 本杰明·富兰克林，美国革命时期杰出政治家、文学家和发明家。

⑧Louis Armstrong: (1900—1971) a famous American Jazz musician. 路易斯·阿姆斯特朗，美国著名黑人爵士乐演奏家。

⑨The smart money hit the canvas: (*slang*) The conceited person falls on the ground. (俚) 自负的家伙倒在地上。

⑩The long shot got the nod: (*slang*) The person with the least prospect of success turns out to be the winner. (俚) 没有希望的人得胜了。

⑪under the spell of the reefer: to be intoxicated by the cigarette containing marijuana. 在大麻叶烟卷的迷醉下。

Topic Discussion

1. What are conditions of the African-Americans as seen through the hero in *Invisible Man*?
2. What are the features of the hero in *Invisible Man*?

Ⅲ. Toni Morrison (1931—)

1. Life and Major Works

Morrison was born Chloe Anthony Wofford on February 18, 1931 in Lorain, Ohio. She was the second of four children of George Wofford, a shipyard welder and Hamah Willis Wofford. Her parents moved to Ohio to find better opportunities and to escape the racist attitudes that had plagued African-Americans in the South. At home, she heard many songs and tales of Southern black folklore. She was brought up to be proud of her heritage and rich historical background. She grew up in Lorain, Ohio, and changed her name into Toni after finishing school there. Lorain was a small industrial town populated with immigrant Europeans, Mexicans and Southern African-Americans coexisting among one another. She attended an integrated school and in first grade, she was the only African-American student in the class and the only one who could read. She was friends with many of her white schoolmates and did not encounter discrimination until she grew older.

In 1949, she went East to Howard, a university for African-American students in Washington, DC, majoring in English and got her BA there in 1953. Then she continued her graduate study in Cornell University and took her MA in 1955. She taught first in Texas Southern University and then in Howard University until 1964. She married Harold Morrison but got divorced later.

She started writing in 1960s and published her first novel *The Bluest Eye* in 1970. Her other works include *Sula* (1973), *Song of Solomon* (1977), *Tar Baby* (1981), *Beloved* (1987) and so on. She was awarded the Pulitzer Prize in 1988 and the Nobel Prize in 1993. Thus she became the first African-American author to be so honored.

2. Introduction to *Song of Solomon*

1) Plot Overview

The publication of *Song of Solomon* firmly established Morrison's position in American literature as a great author. The novel is considered the best African-American novel published after *Native Son and Invisible Man*. It marks the maturity of Morrison's literary creation.

The novel centers on an African-American family, the Deads, through the story of which the author traces the history of African-Americans from the Civil War to 1960s. The hero of the novel, Macon Dead Ⅲ. or Milkman, is the son of Macon Dead II and Ruth. Taught by his father, Milkman at first is selfish and cares for nobody but himself. His aunt, the sister of his father, Pilate tells Milkman to be kind and sympathetic. Later Milkman leaves the little town in Michigan for the South in search of the gold he believes that his father and aunt hid in a cave in Virginia. In his journey, he meets a lot of fellow African-Americans who keep their own culture and customs even though they live a poor life. Milkman finds no gold; instead, he discovers his own family history and the story of his great-grandfather Solomon in folk songs. He changes from a man in pursuit of material things into one who is spiritually and morally better than before.

2) Analysis of the Theme

Song of Solomon is a story of search. First of all it is a search for the true name. Milkman has lost his name. "Milkman" is a nickname which shows the twisted relationship between him and his mother. His surname "Dead" is a mistake of a white man who was drunk when filling in his grandfather's surname. Name means identity and loss of one's name means loss of identity. In Milkman's search for gold, he finds by accident the true names of his ancestors. Thus, by regaining his true name Milkman regains his true identity.

Second, it is also a search for cultural tradition. Milkman's search for his ancestors' name and family history is also a search for his origin-African cultural tradition. The novel is based on the myth that Africans could fly. This myth embodies African-Americans' desire to escape slavery and their pursuit of freedom. After Milkman learns the culture of his ancestors, he becomes one that can fly-a spiritually free man.

Third, it is also a search for human nature. Milkman is brought up in a wealthy middle class family by a selfish and greedy father. Naturally he himself becomes someone without love for others and he believes that money is the only important thing in the world. He takes but never gives. He, in a sense, is not a human being by nature. In the novel, Milkman starts his search for gold but ends his search by finding his human nature. He gives up his material pursuit, feels ashamed for his selfish behaviors before and learns to take responsibility. He is able to love and becomes a truly free man.

3. Selected Reading

Song of Solomon

Chapter XII

At four o'clock he knocked on the door of the only house back of the ridge with a brick front. Fresh and shining in the army fatigues Sweet [1] had washed and pressed, he had tramped along feeling ready for anything. But he didn't think Guitar would jump him in the daytime on a winding path (which they called a road) that cut through hilly land that was nevertheless tilled and had a smattering of houses and people. If he did confront him (with anything other than a gun) Milkman was sure he could take him, but it would be best to get back before nightfall. He didn't know what was on Guitar's mind, but he knew it had something to do with the gold. If he knows I'm here and where I have been and what I did in each place, then he must know that I'm trying to get it, doing just what I said I would do. Why would he try to kill me before I got it or even found out what happened to it? ② Most of it was a total mystery to him, but the part that was clear was enough to keep him alert and jittery all the way.

The Byrd ③ house sat on a neat lawn separated by a white picket fence from the field grass on either side if the property. A child's swing dangled from a cedar tree; four little steps painted blue led up to the porch, and from the window, between fluttering curtains, came the smell of gingerbread baking.

A woman who looked to be about his mother's age answered the door.

"Miss Byrd?" Milkman asked her.

"Yes?"

"How are you? My name is, uh, Macon, and I'm visiting here for a few days. I'm from Michigan and I think some of my people lived here a long time ago. I was hoping you'd be able to help me."

"Help you what?" She sounded arch and Milkman had the distinct impression that this lady did not like the color of his skin.

"Find them. I mean find out about them. We're all split up, my family, and some folks in town thought you might know some of them."

"Who's that, Susan?" Another woman's voice came from behind her.

"Somebody to see me, Grace."

"Well, why don't you ask him in? Don't make him state his business on the steps."

Miss Byrd sighed. "Please come in, Mr. Macon."

Milkman followed her into a pleasant living room full up with sunshine. "Excuse me," She said. "I didn't mean to be rude. Please have a seat." She motioned to a gray velvet wing-back chair. A woman in a two-piece print dress came into the room, clutching a paper napkin in her hand and chewing on something.

"Who'd you say?" She addressed her question to Miss Byrd, but ran inquisitive eyes over Milkman.

Miss Byrd held out a hand. "This is a friend of mine—Miss Long. Grace Long—Mr.... "

"How do you do?" Grace held out her hand to him.

"Fine, thank you."

"Mr. Macon, is it?"

"Yes."

"Susan, perhaps Mr. Macon would like some refreshment." Miss Long smiled and sat on the sofa facing the gray chair.

"Well, he just stepped foot in the door, Grace. Give me time" Miss Byrd turned to Milkman. "Would you like a cup of coffee on some tea?"

"Sure. Thanks."

"Which one?"

"Coffee's all right."

"You've got butter cookies, Susan. Give him some of those butter cookies."

Miss Byrd gave her friend a tired frown. "I'll just be a minute," she said to Milkman, and left the room.

"Yes, well. Did I hear you say you were visiting in these parts? We don't see to many visitors." Grace crossed her ankles. Like Susan Byrd, she wore black laced shoes and cotton stockings. As she made herself comfortable, she inched her dress up a little.

"Yes, visiting."

"You in the service?"

"Ma'am? Oh, no. I was hunting last night. Some friends lent me these." He smoothed the seam Sweet had made in the fatigues.

"Hunting? Oh, Lord, don't tell me you're one of them. I can't stand those hunting people. They make me sick, always prowling round other people's property. Day and night they're shooting up the world. I tell my students—I'm a schoolteacher, you know, I teach over at the normal school. Have you seen it yet?"

"No, not yet."

"Well, there's nothing to see, really. Just a school, like any other. But you're welcome to stop by. We'd be pleased to have you. Where you from again?"

"Michigan."

"I thought so. Susan!" She turned around. "He's from up North." Then back to Milkman: "Where are you staying?"

"Well, nowhere yet. I just met a few people in town and..."

Susan Byrd came in with a tray of coffee cups and a plate of wide pale cookies.

"He's from Michigan," said Grace.

"I heard him. How do you take your coffee?"

"Black."

"Black? No cream or sugar at all?" asked Grace. "Wish I could do that; maybe I could get back into twelve. But it's never going to happen now." She pressed one hand on her hip and smiled at Milkman.

"What did you want to see me about?" Susan Byrd placed a mild but clear stress on the word "me."

"I'm trying to locate anybody who might have known my grandmother. Her name was Sing."

Grace clapped her hands to her mouth and gave a little squeal. "Relatives! You all are relatives!" Milkman put his cup down. "Well, I'll be!" Grace's eyes were lit and dancing.

"You've come to the right place," said Susan, "But I doubt if I can help you any."

"What are you talking about, Susan? Your mother was named Sing, wasn't she?"

"No, she wasn't Grace, and if you let me finish a sentence you might learn something you don't know too."

"I thought you said—"

"My mother's name was Mary. M—a—r—y, Mary."

"Well, excuse me."

Susan turned to Milkman. "My father, Crowell Byrd, had a sister named Sing." ④

"That must be her! My grandmother! Sing. Did she marry a man named—"

"I knew there was somebody in your family named Sing!"

"She didn't marry anybody that I know of." Susan interrupted them both.

"Oh, this is really something. A stranger walks right into your house and he's your own...what? Cousin? I hate to say it, but this is a small world. Isn't it? You have got to visit my class, Mr. Macon."

Milkman joined Susan Byrd in ignoring Grace Long. "Where did she live?" he asked her.

"The last time my father saw her, she was on a wagon headed for Massachusetts to a private school up there. A Quaker school."

"Your people Quakers? You never told me that. See, Mr. Macon, what your friends hide from you? I bet she'd hide you too."

"And she never married?" Milkman couldn't take the time to acknowledge Grace's attentions.

"Not anybody we heard of. After she went to that Quaker school they lost track of her. I believe they tried to locate her, mostly because my grandmother—her name was Heddy—she was so torn up about it. I always believed the same thing my father believed: that she didn't want to be found after she left that school."

"You know darn well she didn't," said Grace. "She probably started passing ⑤ like the rest of'em, that's what." She leaned toward Milkman. "There used to be a lot of that. A lot of it. Not so much nowadays, but there used to be a lot of'em did it—if they could." She shot a glance at Susan. "Like your cousins, Susan. They're passing now. Lilah, John. I know John is, and he knows I know he is."

"Everybody knows that, Grace."

"Mr. Macon doesn't know it. I saw John on the street in Mayville—"

"Mr. Macon doesn't need to know it. He's not even interested."

"How do you know he's not?"

"Because he said the woman he's looking for was his grandmother, and if she's his grandmother she'd be too dark to..." Susan Byrd hesitated. "Well, too dark to pass. Wouldn't she?" She flushed a little.

Milkman ignored the question. "And you say she lived in Massachusetts, right?"

"Yes, Boston."

"I see." It looked like a dead end, so he decided to follow another line. "Did you ever know or hear of a woman around here named Pilate?"

"Pilate. No. Never. Have you, Grace?"

Grace shook her head. "No, and I've been here most of my life."

"I've been here *all* of mine," said Susan. "Both my parents were born her and so was I. Never been farther away than St. Phillips County. I have people in South Carolina, but I've never even been to visit them."

"That's because they're passing too. Just like John. You couldn't visit them if you wanted to." Grace leaned over the plate of cookies and selected one.

"They're not the only family I have left." Susan was indignant.

"I hope not. It's a sad thing, Mr. Macon, when you're left without any people to claim you. I keep up with my family. I'm not married, you know, not yet anyway, but my family is very close." She gave him a meaningful look. Milkman turned his wrist and looked down to see what time it was.

"Oh, look at that." Grace pointed to his hand. "What a good-looking watch. May I see it?" Milkman stood up to hand it to her and remained standing. "Look, Susan, it doesn't have a single number on it. Just dots. Now, how can any body figure out what time it is from those dots?"

Susan rose too. "You ever been sown here before, Mr. Macon?"

"No. This is my first visit."

"Well, I hope it won't be your last. How long will you be here?"

"Oh, I think I'll get on back tonight or tomorrow at the latest." He looked out the window. The sun was dropping.

"That soon?" asked Grace. "Why don't you give him something to take with him, Susan? Would you like to take some butter cookies with you, Mr. Macon?"

"No, thank you."

"You'll be happy to have them later." The woman was wearing him down.

He smiled, though, and said, "If you like."

"I'll fix a little package for you. Okay, Susan?" She fled from the room.

Susan managed a small smile. "Wish you could stay and visit with us awhile." He words were as mechanical as her smile.

"So do I," he said, "but, well, maybe I'll be back."

"That'd be nice. Sorry I couldn't be of any help to you."

"You have been."

"Have I?"

"Oh, sure. You have to know what's wrong before you can find what's right."

She smiled a genuine smile then. "It's important to you, is it, to find your people?"

Milkman thought about it. "No. Not really. I was just passing through, and it was just—just an idea. It's not important."

Grace returned with a little parcel wrapped in white paper napkins. "Here you are," she said. "You'll appreciate this later on."

"Thank you. Thank you both."

"Nice meeting you."

"And you."

NOTES

①Sweet: An African-American woman whom Milkman met while looking for his ancestors in Shalimar. Milkman has lived in her home. She treated him warmheartedly. 奶娃在萨里马尔寻访自己祖先时遇到的一个黑人妇女，奶娃曾住在她家，她热情地接待过他。（见本书第11章）。

②Why would he... what happened to it?: Guitar and Milkman are still friends on the surface. In fact, Guitar has begun to take Milkman as his enemy because they came from different classes. 吉他和奶娃表面上是朋友，实际上，因为他们来自不同的社会阶层，吉他已经把奶娃看做敌人。吉他加入激进的黑人复仇组织"七日社"（Seven Days）以后，他们在"爱"与"恨"的问题上有过激烈的争论，存在着很大的分歧。奶娃甩开吉他一个人到南方去寻找他以为仍然藏在那里的金子，表现出他是一个自私贪婪的人，因此，吉他决定杀死他。

当奶娃和萨里马尔村的猎人们一起在森林里打猎时，吉他已经向他开了冷枪。

③Byrd：Susan Bryd，an Indian woman. She is Milkman's relative，the daughter of Sing Bird's brother Crowell. 印第安妇女，她和奶娃是亲戚，是辛厄·伯德的哥哥克罗韦尔的女儿。

④Sing Bird and Crowell Bird are the children of an Indian old woman Heddy who adopted Jake，Milkman's grandfather. 辛厄·伯德和克罗韦尔·伯德都是印第安老妇人海地的孩子，即收养杰克（奶娃的祖父）的海地。

⑤passing：Here it refers to the phenomenon that some African-American or those who have black blood in their veins take themselves as the white. 指黑人或有黑人血统的人把自己当做白人。

Topic Discussion

1. What is the theme of the novel?
2. Comment on the name of the hero Milkman.

第三节　华裔美国文学简介

每节导读

本节重点学习华裔美国文学从20世纪初至今的发展历史，熟悉其中重要作家及作品，了解华裔美国文学的发展变化趋势。

华裔美国文学指的是在美国的华裔移民所著的关于在美华裔生活的文学作品。它所涵盖的内容不仅仅局限于移民们在不同历史阶段的经历，也包括种族主义对亚裔的影响。本节首先回顾早期移民历史和中国文化对华裔文学的影响，之后介绍华裔文学发展史以及不同阶段代表作家和作品。第一位用英语进行创作的华裔女作家是艾迪丝·伊顿（Edith Maud Eaton，1865—1914），笔名水仙花（Sui Sin Far）。从20世纪30年代起旅居纽约的华人作家林语堂向美国人传播了独特的中国文化，令美国人耳目一新。四五十年代出现了一些以自传体形式反映第二代华裔移民生活的作品，如刘裔昌（帕迪·刘 Pardee Lowe）的《父亲和荣耀的后代》、黄玉雪（Jade Snow）的《第五个中国女儿》，步其后尘描写唐人街生活的还有黎锦扬（Chin

Yang Lee）的《花鼓歌》和朱路易（Louis Chu）的《吃一碗茶》。1976年，汤亭亭（Maxine Hong Kingston）的《女勇士》揭开了华裔文学重新崛起的序幕。新崛起的华裔作家有赵健秀（弗兰克·金 Frank Chin）、叶添祥（劳伦斯·迈克尔·叶 Laurence Michael Yep）、黄哲伦（David Henry Hwang）、谭恩美（艾米·谭 Amy Tan），任碧莲（Gish Jen）等。他们描写中西文化的差异和碰撞、老一辈和新一代的代沟，力图以优秀的作品扩展华裔文学的空间，使它从边缘文学逐步进入美国主流文学。

Ⅰ. Introduction

Chinese-American literature can be defined as literature by and about Chinese immigrants in America.

It covers not only the immigrant experience across different historical periods but also the influence of the history of racism on Chinese-Americans.

This chapter begins with the Chinese cultural backgrounds and the early immigrant experiences across the Pacific Ocean. Then it traces the development of Chinese-American literature. Finally, general trends and developments are outlined with a historical view of the development in this field.

Ⅱ. Immigrant History

The Chinese came to the United States in large numbers, about 20, 026 by 1852, as gold rush prospectors in the mid-nineteenth century. They were driven by the political and economic disturbances in rural southern China after the Opium War. They joined gold mining in the Sierra Nevada and established numerous small Chinatowns there. Competition and the declining profits in gold mines led to widespread white hostility and racist violence. The Chinese were driven out, tortured, and lynched, their living quarters burned down. The Californian legislature passed laws imposing taxes on the Chinese and discouraging Chinese immigration. From the mid-1860s, the Chinese turned to work on the construction of the Central Pacific Railway. After the completion of the first transcontinental railway in 1869 and with the economic crisis in America, they found themselves competing in a racist job market. They were not only exploited as cheap labor but also more and more singled out as scapegoats in politicians' racist propagandas and white mobs' riots. The 1882 Chinese Exclusion Act banned all Chinese labor immigration to the United States and prohibited Chinese immigrants from becoming naturalized citizens.

The American exclusionary immigration laws led to the creation of a bachelor society for Chinese-American men, who could not bring their wives and sons over nor marry the whites here due to anti-miscegenation laws. After the 1906 San Francisco earthquake, which destroyed government documents, many Chinese had a chance to falsely claim native-born citizenship status and manage to send for their family members. The immigrants were kept for screening on Angel Island off the coast of San Francisco. They underwent racist humiliations and suffered from loneliness and anxiety for months or even years.

The Chinese in America remained mainly an urban population. They were forced by white racism to work in menial jobs. They concentrated mainly in Chinese restaurants, corner stores, and laundries, where the family members and Chinese employees worked long hours at low wages. During the long years of racist exclusion, the Chinese formed various organizations within Chinatowns to take care of each other and develop their own community. During the Second World War, the Chinese actively participated in military service and war efforts, and their contributions helped to induce the U. S. Congress to abolish the Chinese exclusion acts in 1943.

Since the Second World War, the U. S. immigration policies for the Chinese have been subjected to changes in political and economic climates. After 1943, the quota for the Chinese immigration was only 105 a year. The liberation of mainland China in 1949 led to the Refugee Acts, allowing Chinese political refugees to immigrate to America. The Immigration and Naturalization Act of 1965 replaced the national-origin quota system (much biased against Asians) with hemispheric quotas at 170, 000 for the Eastern Hemisphere and 20, 000 annual maximum per country. Thousands of students and scholars from Taiwan in the 1960s and 1970s and from China in the 1980s and 1990s came to USA. Taiwan and Hong Kong business entrepreneurs have also moved to America for a "First World" passport and a Western education for their children. Besides, there are also illegal immigrants smuggled into America and working underground in the strict control of gangs and criminals.

Chinese immigrants are a diverse community with a long history in America. Writers have been trying to uncover and explore various aspects of the Chinese immigrant experience, which has not been properly recognized in official American history.

Ⅲ. Literary-cultural History

Chinese culture influences Chinese-American literature. The most familiar in the field is the warrior traditions, male and female, advanced by Frank Chin and Maxine Hong Kingston. In Chin's version, the warrior tradition in Chinese popular culture is best represented by Chinese classic novels like *Water Margin* (《水浒传》) and *The Romance of the Three Kingdoms* (《三国演义》). It is a tradition of universal brotherhood, of taking justice into one's own hands when the country is ruled by a tyrant, of opposing the rich and powerful on behalf of the poor and downtrodden. Frank Chin resurrected this tradition in the late 1960s in order to recover Chinese masculinity against the white emasculation of Asian America. Here the Chinese heroism serves to shatter the white myth of the effeminate Chinamen. The Chinese-American woman writer Maxine Hong Kingston's work *The Woman Warrior* invents the tradition of the woman warrior from a famous classical narrative poem Fa Mulan (《木兰词》). The common emphasis on warrior in both types of cultural invention shows the urgency of Chinese-American writers waging a war of pens for minority rights.

Chinese culture is marked by geographical and historical diversity. Confucianism as a dominant ideology of Chinese culture is a humanist philosophy, a secular ethics of reason and fairness (情, 理) governing human relations. Taoism and Buddhism also influence Chinese culture with their Oriental mysticism, yin/yang dialectics, and transcendentalism. There are also various folk traditions such as Chin's Cantonese opera and Kingston's "talk story". They are unofficial, alternative cultures deeply embedded in the immigrants' daily life and traceable to their roots across the Pacific. Most of the early immigrants represented by Chin and Kingston came from the Cantonese-speaking rural southern China. The immigrants in the works of Gish Jen and Amy Tan spoke Mandarin and Shanghai dialect and came from an urban background. China in this century has witnessed a history of Westernization, colonialism, and modernity. Cultural mixing often makes it difficult to tell the East from the West, a convenient division that has often led to racial stereotypes.

Chinese immigrants came to America in the mid-nineteenth century as gold miners, railway builders, factory workers, and agricultural laborers. Racial stereotypes are what whites define the "yellow" other. Morally and physically, Chinese were the same as the animalistic and rude blacks and deserve the same fate as the American Indians. They were a source of more efficient labor than the blacks and cheaper than the white workers. This unique position translated into many threats in the racial fantasies of whites: cheap competitors against white workers, greedy hoarders of wealth, armed with sly cunning and low-wage competition, Chinese would overwhelm America.

Chinese American writers are influenced by Chinese culture and make efforts to break the racial stereotypes of Chinese in their works.

Ⅳ. Dominant Concerns and Major Authors

Chinese-American literature in its early days has diverse concerns and structures of sensibilities.

One of the earliest spokeswomen in English for the Chinese immigrant community is Sui Sin Far (水仙花, Edith Maud Eaton, 1867—1914). Born of a Chinese mother and an English father, Sui Sin Far grew up amid poverty. She felt she was a stranger between cultures and races. During the years of mounting white racism against the Chinese, She wrote in newspapers fighting for the rights of the Chinese and published many stories about Chinese immigrant experiences. In 1916, the collection of her works *Mrs Spring Fragrance* (《春香夫人》) was published. Most of her stories are autobiographical, depicting her personal experiences. More than mere realism or protest, Sui Sin Far's voice explores deeply the split psyche of double consciousness in immigrant life. Her highly personal autobiographical writings and fiction are always informed with an antiracist political position. She has a noble vision of transcending racial barriers for a common humanity while carefully noting cultural differences in concrete details of daily life.

There were many Chinese scholar-travelers writing their experiences and impressions of America and carrying on a high-level cultural dialogue between Chinese and Western traditions. Lin Yutang(林语堂，1895—1976) is the most prominent among them. He is a professor of philosophy. He was educated first in missionary schools and universities in China and then in graduate schools in the West. He was well read both in Western and Chinese cultures and well known for his humorous essays. After he came to live in America in 1930, he wrote and published many books introducing Chinese culture and people to the American readers, including *My Country and My People* (《吾国吾民》, 1935), *The Importance of Living* (《生活的艺术》, 1937), *and Chinatown Family*: *On the Wisdom of America* (《唐人街家庭》, 1948). These books introduce Chinese culture and Chinese character and express a Chinese literary gentleman's pride about his own cultural tradition.

In the forties and the fifties of the twentieth century, some Chinese-American autobiographical novels were published. Pardee Lowe's(刘裔昌) *Father and Glorious Descendant*(《父亲和荣耀的后代》,1942)and Jade Snow Wong's(黄玉雪，1922—) *Fifth Chinese Daughter* (《第五个中国女儿》, 1945) contained autobiographies of second-generation Chinese Americans. They grew up torn between their immigrant parents' culture and the American mainstream culture. In their novels, on one hand, there is much self-hatred and self-contempt. On the other hand, there is also much complaint about the self's not being accepted and assimilated by the mainstream culture. That is because at that time the Chinese were just beginning to be taken as American allies and were still confined to Chinatown.

Chin Yang Lee's(黎锦扬，1917—) *Flower Drum Song* (《花鼓歌》, 1957) and Louis Chu' s(朱路易)*Eat a Bowl of Tea*(《吃一碗茶》, 1961) portrays Chinatown on the verge of change. These novels weren't popular among the Western readers because the relationship between People's Republic of China and the United States got worse in the Cold War climate of 1950s.

From Sui Sin Far to Louis Chu, pre-1960s Chinese-American literature is marked by a series of firsts, first novel, first woman writer, first second-generation writer. The pre-1960s literature remains a cultural legacy for later writers and critics. The pre-1960s literature, especially the more popular books in the mainstream market, helped invent and solidify a Chinese identity between black and white, a composite of images defined through certain descriptions of passivity and endurance and a series of differences in the American context. This sliding of identities provides the background for new uncertainties and attempts at new beginnings in the post-1960s creative and critical awareness of ethnic identity and political alliance.

The era of the Vietnam War and the Civil Rights Movement in America was marked by increased awareness of racial and cultural identity.

Chinese-American writers Frank Chin (赵健秀, 1940—) and later, Maxine Hong Kingston (汤亭亭) proved to be the most influential in shaping the sensibilities of Chinese-American culture, gender, and ethnicity in this period.

Frank Chin has been called the "godfather" of Asian American writing. His works up to this moment include poems, short stories, plays, and two novels. The plays are *The Chickencoop Chinaman* (《鸡笼中国佬》, 1971), *The Year of the Dragon* (《龙年》, 1974). The novels are *Donald Duk* (《唐老亚》, 1991) and *Gunga Din Highway* (《甘加丁之路》, 1994).

Frank Chin's works show a wide-ranging view of cultural and racial problems. He is concerned with what he perceives as the decline of Chinatown in America. Most of the protagonists in his stories are alienated young men dissatisfied with the stultifying quaint costumes and old-age decay of Chinatown and yet unable to gain acceptance in racist mainstream society.

Chin has explored various traditions of the Chinese-American subject, producing a strange company: on one hand, Chin embraces the heroic tradition in Chinese culture; on the other hand, he would call himself a cowboy; yet on a more historical level, he would declare the tradition of Chinese forefathers who came to America to build railways as pioneers. In his novel, *Donald Duk*, one white child and one Chinese child learn to appreciate Chinese culture and the history of Chinese Americans. This work explores the daily community life of Chinatown and bridging gaps between whites and Chinese, between different generations.

Maxine Hong Kingston made a major literary event in Chinese-American literature with the publication of her work *The Woman Warrior* (《女勇士》) in 1976. It traces a Chinese woman's tradition with a modern feminist stance and carries the bewilderment of a Chinese American girl lost between two cultures. Her second book is *China Men* (《中国佬》, 1980). It explores the history of Chinese male immigrants as they worked on the railways and farms amid racist oppression. In both works, the hard line between fiction and nonfiction is blurred. Her latest book, *Tripmaster Monkey* (《孙行者》), came out in 1989. It is a post-modern novel that breaks in style from her earlier works and mixes ethnicity amid myriads of intertextual references and images of a multiracial America.

The certainty about one's Chinese cultural identity may be more illusory than real in these novels and stories, since they are all set in modern America, where the culture and the race still suffer from discrimination and neglect. Yet paradoxically, the immigrant characters all cling to that culture as the only real spiritual support, even in a critical sense. While this sentiment may not be politically effective, it should not be used in any way as a justification for white racist charges of Chinese unassimilability. On the contrary, the failure of assimilation for certain ethnic minorities points to the racist shadow right at the heart of the mainstream culture. In an age of multiculturalism and cultural difference, a sense of exile should not be denied as a part of the immigrant experience and sensibilities.

Ⅴ. Multiplicity of Literary Explorations since the 1980s

Chinese-American literature has undergone a booming period since the beginning of the 1980s, not only in scholarly research and university curriculum but also in the variety of literary creations and experiments. While certain concerns and themes persist, more spaces are opened for various kinds of literary explorations of identity, politics, and cultural expressions.

Chinese immigrant history continues to be a fascinating subject. Laurence Yep's (叶添祥) play *Pay the Chinaman* (1987) is based on the playwright's research into the history of early Chinese immigrants' gold mining and pioneering in the West and the eventual wiping out of many small Chinatowns during the ensuing racist waves. The play explores the trickster figure as an immigrant survivor who has to lie and change himself and his lifestyle in order to make a living in a hostile and volatile environment.

In his play *FOB* (《新移民》, 1979), David Henry Hwang (黄哲伦) telescopes Kwan Kung (关公), the early immigrant protector god, with the contemporary context of new immigrants from Hong Kong. Thereby he seeks a way to solve the contradictions between the second-generation, American-born Chinese with troubled racial feelings and the new arrivals who find themselves targets of a new kind of racism. In the interstices of generations, histories, cultures, and genders, identities are scattered and shattered in a multiplicity of disguises. Histories and traditions are both explored for inspiration and inheritance and subjected to invention and modification.

Amy Tan's(谭恩美)novel *The Joy Luck Club*(《喜福会》,1989)explores the tensions, jealousies, and love-hate relationship between immigrant mothers and their American-born daughters. All the four mothers have gone through many hardships in China. They survive and become pioneers in coming to America and making a new life. The novel opens up a space for the daughters to recognize and embrace a female tradition in their ethnic culture that they need to treasure in their own life.

The depiction of Chinese students/immigrants apparently secure in their cultural identity is a theme usually found in immigrant literature in Chinese. Gish Jen's(任碧莲)*Typical American*(《典型的美国佬》,1991)portrays the loss of idealism in Chinese students/immigrants as their American dream fails.

The contemporary scene of Chinese immigrant literature is marked by diversity in subjects and rapid change in political and aesthetic concerns, over-determined by American race politics, minority discourses, feminisms, and post-modern sensibilities. The Chinese-American writers are developing new languages and adopting new perspectives to fulfill the task of challenging racism and dismantling patriarchy.

第四节 汤亭亭与谭恩美

每节导读

本节重点学习华裔美国文学优秀作家汤亭亭和谭恩美，通过对他们的生平及各自的代表作，汤亭亭的《女勇士》，谭恩美的《喜福会》的介绍，了解这两位作家的写作特点和作品主题。

汤亭亭著有《女勇士》、《中国佬》、《孙行者》等作品。《女勇士》是其成名作。作者真实而生动地描写了一些中国的社会习俗和花木兰的神话故事，也揭露了封建社会对中国妇女的残酷迫害，表现了老一代移民在中美文化碰撞下的困惑和奋斗，新一代对中国文化传统的重新认识。它是自传与神话的巧妙结合。

谭恩美以其处女作《喜福会》一举成名。小说用拼贴手法描绘四个中国妇女在旧中国的坎坷遭遇，她们到美国后感到孤独和苦闷，与子女产生代沟，中西文化在她们家里产生了撞击。小说心理描写细腻，文笔机智幽默，获得评论界的好评。

Ⅰ. Maxine Hong Kingston(1940—)

1. Life and Works

Maxine Hong Kingston(汤亭亭)is a highly acclaimed writer of both fiction and nonfiction. She was one of the first Asian Americans to make it to the top of the literary world in America. Her first book, a memoir published in 1976 called *The Woman Warrior: Memoirs of a Girlhood Among Ghosts*(《女勇士》), won the National Book Critic's Circle Award and made her a literary celebrity at the age of 36. Kingston has since written two other critically hailed books. *China Men*(《中国佬》), was published in 1980 and also received the National Book Critic's Circle Award. These two books were published as nonfiction. In 1989 Kingston published her first novel, *Tripmaster Monkey: His Fake Book*(《孙行者》).

Kingston's father, Tom Hong, and her mother, Chew Ling Yan, were both Chinese immigrants. They operated a gambling house in Stockton, California, when Maxine was born in 1940. Shortly after her birth, the family opened a laundry where she and her five brothers and sisters joined their parents in working long, arduous hours. Kingston attended public schools, where she was an excellent student. After graduation, with the help of scholarships, she was enrolled in the University of California at Berkeley, one of the finest public colleges in the country. She at first intended to study engineering, but changed her major to English literature.

Kingston graduated with a bachelor's degree in 1962. In November of that year, she married Earl Kingston, whom she had met in an English course. She earned a teaching certificate from the state of California and in 1965 taught high school for a year in Hayward. In 1967, the Kingstons moved to Hawaii, where Kingston took various teaching posts. From 1970 to 1977, she taught at the Mid-

Pacific Institute, a private boarding school. Since 1991, she teaches English Writing in University of California.

In 1976, her first book *The Woman Warrior* was published and became an immediate success. In the memoir, Kingston writes of the conflicting cultural messages she received as the daughter of Chinese immigrants growing up in the America of the 1950s. The book also tells the story of the generations of Chinese women that preceded her. The subtitle of the book, Memoirs of a Girlhood Among Ghosts, suggests to the ghosts of Kingston's female relatives and the tragedy of many of their lives, lives lived in the extremely male-dominated society of China.

The Woman Warrior received excellent reviews. Newsweek called it "thrilling" and "a book of fierce clarity and originality." The New York Times termed it "a brilliant memoir." It became a bestseller, was awarded the National Book Critic's Circle Award. It is taught in high schools and colleges all over the country.

Kingston's next book, *China Men*, was published in 1980. In many ways, it is a companion to her first. In it she describes the Chinese American experience as it was felt by the men in her family. This book, too, received glowing reviews. The New York Times deemed the volume "a triumph of the highest order, of imagination, of language, of moral perception," Kingston was awarded the National Book Critic's Circle Award again.

In 1989, Kingston published her third book, *Tripmaster Monkey*: His Fake Book. This is her first novel. The story is set in San Francisco in the 1960s and tells of Wittman Ah Sing, a manic, playful, highly verbal young man who is one year out of college. After being fired from his job at a toy store, the irreverent Wittman turns his enormous energies to writing a contemporary epic based on an old Chinese novel. The book was a startling departure for Kingston and confused many readers. Still, critics praised it. The Nation called Tripmaster "less charming [than her memoirs] but more exuberant. Instead of falling into pattern or turning on wheel-there's something inevitable about everything in [her memoirs], something fated-this language bounces, caroms and collides; abrades and inflames. Instead of Mozart, Wittman's rock and roll." Other reviewers compared the main character to Holden Caulfield of J. D. Salinger's landmark *The Catcher in the Rye* and Mark Twain's Huck Finn.

2. Introduction to *The Woman Warrior*

1) Plot Overview

The Woman Warrior focuses on the stories of five women-Kingston's long-dead aunt, "No-Name Woman"; a mythical female warrior, Fa Mu Lan; Kingston's mother, Brave Orchid; Kingston's aunt, Moon Orchid; and finally Kingston herself-told in five chapters. The chapters integrate Kingston's lived experience with a series of talk-stories-spoken stories that combine Chinese history, myths, and beliefs-her mother tells her.

The first chapter, "No-Name Woman," begins with one such talk-story, about an aunt Kingston never knew she had. Because this aunt had brought disgrace upon her family by having an illegitimate child, she killed herself and her baby by jumping into the family well in China.

The second chapter "White Tigers" is based on another talk-story, one about the mythical female warrior Fa Mu Lan. She pretends to be a man herself and leads an army of men against the forces of a corrupt baron and emperor.

The third chapter "Shaman" focuses on Kingston's mother, Brave Orchid, and her old life back in China. To a young Kingston, Brave Orchid's past is as astounding. Many of the images from her mother's talk-story-Chinese babies left to die, slave girls being bought and sold, a woman stoned to death by her villagers-haunt Kingston's dreams for years to come. At the end of the chapter, Maxine visits her mother after being away for many years. The two arrive at some kind of understanding after many years of disagreement and conflict.

The title of the forth chapter "At the Western Palace" refers to another of Brave Orchid's talk-stories, about an emperor who had four wives. Kingston's aunt Moon Orchid's story is told in this part. Deserted by her husband, she can't live on her own in Los Angeles. She proves wholly unable to adjust to American life and slowly goes insane.

The final chapter of the memoir, "A Song for a Barbarian Reed Pipe," is about Kingston herself. This section focuses mainly on her childhood and teenage years, depicting her anger and frustration in trying to express herself and attempting to please an unappreciative mother. Later in her life, however,

Kingston comes to appreciate her mother's talk-stories. It is a fitting conclusion to a text in which Kingston combines very different worlds and cultures and creates a harmony of her own.

2）Themes

The themes of The *Woman Warrior* are the role of women in Chinese society and growing up Chinese-American.

①The Role of Women in Chinese Society：

Men are conspicuously, intentionally absent from *The Woman Warrior*. Each chapter focuses on a woman that affects Kingston's life, and in most cases depicts how that woman relates to the male-dominated society around her. However, it is often not the men themselves who are most oppressive in the memoir, but rather the power of tradition as carried through women. It is women who utter phrases like "better to have geese than girls" to Kingston, women who are pictured destroying the house of No-name Woman, girls who torment each other on the playground in the final chapter. The subtext of Kingston's relationship with her mother and her mother's talk-stories in particular is both empowerment and disempowerment. Her mother tells her stories of female swordswomen and shamans, and is herself an accomplished, intelligent doctor, but she also reinforces the notion that girls are disappointments to their parents, despite what they may accomplish. As a little girl, Kingston feels haunted by the images or ghosts of little Chinese girls whose parents left them to die because they wanted sons instead. Given such conflicting messages, it is no surprise that in Kingston's fantasy retelling of the story of Fa Mu Lan the warrior manages to be everything to everyone, able to satisfy the role of wife and mother while still leading her people to victory in battle. It is the only way-besides leaving home-that Kingston is able to reconcile what she has been taught.

②Growing Up Chinese-American：

Though Kinston claims elsewhere that she does not want her memoir to be "representative," it is clear that she is also reaching out to other Chinese-Americans who share her feelings of displacement and frustration. For the first generation born in America, it is especially difficult to reconcile the heavy-handed and often restrictive traditions of the immigrants with the relative freedom of life in America. Being Chinese-American often means that one is torn between both worlds without really being part of either. Indeed, Kingston feels as different from her American classmates as she does from her own relatives. For a woman, this frustration is heightened because many of the typical traits of Chinese women, such as a loud speaking voice, are not considered "American-feminine". Another difficulty in being Chinese-American is that one's cultural heritage is always second-hand, filtered through the lens-or talk-story-of someone else. At the time Kingston wrote her memoir she had never even been to China. Much of the memoir is about the attempt to sort out the difference between what is Chinese and what is peculiar to her family, what is real and what is just "the movies."

3. Select Reading

The Woman Warrior

Chapter Ⅰ. No Name Woman

"You must not tell anyone," my mother said, "what I am about to tell you. In China your father had a sister who killed herself. She jumped into the family well. We say that your father has all brothers because it is as if she had never been born."

"In 1924 just a few days after our village celebrated seventeen hurry-up weddings — to make sure that every young man who went 'out on the road' would responsibly come home—your father and his brothers and your grandfather and his brothers and your aunt's new husband sailed for America, the Gold Mountain. It was your grandfather's last trip. Those lucky enough to get contracts waved goodbye from the decks. They fed and guarded the stowaways and helped them off in Cuba, New York, Bali, Hawaii. We'll meet in California next year, they said. All of them sent money home.

"I remember looking at your aunt one day when she and I were dressing; I had not noticed before that she had such a protruding melon of a stomach. But I did not think, She's pregnant, until she began to look like other pregnant women, her shirt pulling and the white tops of her black pants showing. She could not have been pregnant, you see, because her husband had been gone for years. No one said anything. We did not discuss it. In early summer she was ready to have a child, long after the time when it could have been possible.

"The village had also been counting. On the night the baby was to be born the villagers raided out house. Some were crying. Like a great saw, teeth strung with lights, files of people walked zigzag across our land, tearing the rice. Their lanterns doubled in the disturbed black water, which drained away through the broken bunds. As the villagers closed in, we could see that some of them, probably men and women we knew well, wore white masks. The people with long hung hair hung it over their faces. Women with short hair made it stand up on end. Some had tied white bands around their foreheads, arms, and legs.

"At first they threw mud and rocks at the house. Then they threw eggs and began slaughtering our stock. We could hear the animals scream their deaths—the roosters, the pigs, a last great roar from the ox. Familiar wild heads flared in our night windows, the villagers encircled us. Some of the faces stopped to peer at us, their eyes rushing like searchlights. The hands flattened against the panes, framed heads, and left red prints.

"The villagers broke in the front and the back doors at the same time, even though we had not locked the doors against them. Their knives dripped with the blood of our animals. They smeared blood on the doors and walls. One woman swung a chicken, whose throat she had slit, splattering blood in red arcs about her. We stood together in the middle of our house, in the family hall with the pictures and tables of the ancestors around us, and looked straight ahead.

"At that time the house had only two wings. When the men came back, we would build two more to enclose our courtyard and a third one to begin a second courtyard. The villagers pushed through both wings, even your grandparents' rooms, to find your aunt's, which was also mine until the men returned. From this room a new wing for one of the younger families would grow. They ripped up her clothes and shoes and broke her combs, grinding them underfoot. They tore her work from the loom. They scattered the cooking fire and rolled the new weaving in it. We could hear them in the kitchen breaking our bowls and banging the pots. They overturned the great waist-high earthenware jugs; duck eggs, pickled fruits. Vegetables burst out and mixed in acrid torrents. The old woman from the next field swept a broom through the air and loosed the spirits-of-the-broom over our heard. 'Pig.' 'Ghost.' 'Pig.' they sobbed and scolded while they ruined our house.

"When they left, they took sugar and oranges to bless themselves. They cut pieces from the dead animals. Some of them took bowls that were not broken and clothes that were not torn. Afterward we swept up the rice and sewed it back up into sacks. But the smells from the spilled preserves lasted. Your aunt gave birth in the pigsty that night. The next morning when I went for the water, I found her and the baby plugging up the family well.

"Don't let your father know that I told you. He denies her. Now that you have started to menstruate ①, what happened to her could happen to you. Don't humiliate us. You wouldn't like to be forgotten as if you had never been born. The villagers are watchful."

Whenever she had to warn us about life, my mother told stories that ran like this one, a story to grow up on. She tested our strength to establish realities. Those in the emigrant generations who could not reassert brute survival died young and far from home. Those of us in the first American generations have had to figure out how the invisible world the emigrants built around our childhoods fits in solid America ②.

The emigrants confused the gods by diverting their curses, misleading them with crooked streets and false names. They must try to confuse their offspring as well, who, I suppose, threaten them in similar ways—always trying to get things straight, always trying to name the unspeakable. The Chinese I know hide their names—sojourners ③, take new names when their lives change and guard their real names with silence.

Chinese-Americans, when you try to understand what things in you are Chinese, how do you separate what is peculiar to childhood, to poverty, insanities ④, one family, your mother who marked your growing with stories, from what is Chinese? What is Chinese tradition and what is the movie?

NOTES

①menstruate：discharge blood，etc from the uterus，usually once a month. ［生理］月经，月经期间。

②solid America：China is "invisible，" an intangible place that Kingston only hears about；America is "solid，" not only because she physically lives in it，but because she interacts daily with other Americans and necessarily wants to fit in. 具体的美国。

③sojourner：people who stay in a place for a time 旅居者，寄居者

④insanity：madness；being mad 精神错乱，疯狂，愚顽

Topic Discussion

Kingston is frequently frustrated by the ambiguity of her mother's talk-stories. In what ways，however，might she be said to use talk-story to her advantage?

Ⅱ. Amy Tan（1952—　）

1. Life and Works

Amy Tan（谭恩美）is the author of *The Joy Luck Club*（《喜福会》，1989），an internationally bestselling novel which explores the relationships between Chinese women and their Chinese-American daughters. She is also the author of *The Kitchen God's Wife*（《灶神娘娘》），*The Hundred Secret Senses*（《通灵女孩》），and two children's books. Recent works include the novel *The Bonesetter's Daughter*（《正骨师的女儿》）.

Amy Tan was born in 1952 in Oakland，California. Both of her parents were Chinese immigrants. Her father，John Tan，was an electrical engineer and Baptist minister who came to America to escape the turmoil of the Chinese Civil War. The harrowing early life of her mother，Daisy，inspired Amy Tan's novel *The Kitchen God's Wife*. In China，Daisy had divorced an abusive husband but lost custody of her three daughters.

Tragedy struck the Tan family when Amy's father and oldest brother both died of brain tumors within a year of each other when Amy was fifteen. Mrs. Tan moved her surviving children to Switzerland, where Amy finished high school, but by this time mother and daughter were in constant conflict.

Mother and daughter did not speak for six months after Amy Tan left the Baptist College her mother had selected for her to follow her boyfriend to San Jose City College. Tan studied English and linguistics. She received her bachelor's and master's degrees in these fields at San Jose State University. In 1974, she and her boyfriend, Louis DeMattei were married. Later they settled in San Francisco.

Tan studied for a doctorate in linguistics, first at the University of California at Santa Cruz, later at Berkeley. By this time, she had developed an interest in the problems of the developmentally disabled. She left the doctoral program in 1976 and took a job as a language development consultant to the Alameda County Association for Retarded Citizens and later directed a training project for developmentally disabled children.

With a partner, she started a business writing firm, providing speeches for salesmen and executives for large corporations. Amy Tan prospered as a business writer. The work had become a compulsive habit and she sought relief in creative efforts. She studied jazz piano. She also began to write fiction.

Her first story "Endgame," won her admission to the Squaw Valley writer's workshop taught by novelist Oakley Hall. The story appeared in *FM*, a literary magazine, and was reprinted in *Seventeen*. A literary agent, Sandra Dijkstra, was impressed enough with Tan's second story "Waiting Between the Trees," to take her on as a client. Dijkstra encouraged Tan to complete an entire volume of stories.

Just as she was working on this new career, Tan's mother fell ill. Amy Tan promised herself that if her mother recovered, she would take her to China, to see the daughter who had been left behind almost forty years before. Mrs. Tan regained her health and mother and daughter departed for China in 1987. The trip was a revelation for Tan. It gave her a new perspective on her often-difficult relationship with her mother, and inspired her to complete the book of stories she had promised her agent.

On the basis of the completed chapters and a synopsis of the others, Dijkstra found a publisher for the book, now called *The Joy Luck Club*. With a $50, 000 advance from G. P. Putnam's Sons, Tan quit business writing and finished her book in a little more than four months. Upon its publication in 1989, Tan's book won enthusiastic reviews and remained for eight months on the New York Times best-seller list, paperback rights sold for $1. 23 million. The book has been translated into 17 languages, including Chinese. The novel was selected as a finalist for the National Book Award and the National Book Critics Circle Award. It received the Bay Area Book Reviewers Award for Fiction and the Commonwealth Club Gold Award. The book has been made into a major motion picture.

Her subsequent novel, *The Kitchen God's Wife* (1991) confirmed her reputation and enjoyed excellent sales. Since then Amy Tan has published two books for children, *The Moon Lady* and *The Chinese Siamese Cat* and two novels *The Hundred Secret Senses* (1998) and her latest, *The Bonesetter's Daughter* (2001). Tan wrote beautifully, being incredibly sensitive with her descriptions of the contrast between two very different cultures. Those who are open-minded to the diverse world would thrive inside these stories. Those with mixed backgrounds would be filled with complete understanding.

2. Introduction to The Joy Luck Club

1) Plot Overview

The plot of *The Joy Luck Club* is both loose and complex. It is really a group of separate stories woven around the members of a ladies' club, located in San Francisco Chinatown. The book begins and ends with Jing-Mei telling the story of her mother, Suyuan; she also narrates two additional chapters within the novel. Jing-Mei's story becomes related to all the others in the novel, for she takes the place of Suyuan in the Joy Luck Club and learns about the past of An-Mei, Ying-ying, and Lindo. Jing-Mei also knows the other daughters.

After her mother Suyuan's death, thirty-six year old Jing-mei (June) Woo joins The Joy Luck Club. The club, which Suyuan founded in China during the war, consists of four women playing mahjong, eating good dinners, and gambling. She restarted the club with three other women her age: An-mei Hsu, Lindo Jong, and Ying-ying St. Clair in San Francisco Chinatown. The four women and their daughters, who are about the same age, grow older together, and each mother and daughter relationship is full of sadness, anger and joy.

The mothers remember their childhood in China. An-mei lived with her grandmother and was forbidden to even speak her mother's name. Lindo's marriage was arranged when she was very young. Lindo made up a story about an angry ancestor who would kill her husband if they stayed married. She was given enough money to go to America and told to keep her mouth shut about their curse. Ying-ying remembers going to a moon festival as a young girl and finding out that the magic and ceremony is often just an act.

The daughters remember growing up with Chinese mothers in California. Sometimes they felt like they weren't Chinese at all, and didn't know how to deal with the Chinese culture in their homes. Waverly was a chess champion, but she quit when she and Lindo fought and Lindo told her it was not as easy to play or not play as she believed. Lena remembers her mother Ying-ying as a meek woman who always wondered what bad thing would happen next. Rose Jordan has some of the same problems with lack of confidence. June Woo remembers that her mother was never satisfied with her: she always wanted June to be a genius, so June was determined to waste any talent she had, just to spite her mother.

The mothers think about their pasts. An-mei remembers that her mother killed herself to make a better life for her children, because in a marriage with four other wives, that was the only way for her children to have any of the benefits from her rich husband (who she was forced to marry, contrary to what her family believed). Ying-ying remembers how she gave up her strength, her will, so that she would no longer be hurt when bad things happened to her. She now realizes that in doing this she has made her daughter weak as well, and resolves to teach her daughter to be strong. Lindo remembers how she came to America, and, looking at her adult daughter Waverly, she sees how similar they are—both inside and out. The book ends with June going to China to meet her half-sisters. Her father is happily reunited with his family. June is at first nervous, but when she meets first her father's family and then her sisters, she sees that part of her is Chinese after all: her blood.

2) The major theme

The major theme in the novel is the difficulty of preserving one's heritage and culture when one immigrates to a foreign country. Although all four of the mothers (Suyuan, Ying-ying, An-Mei, and Lindo) have terrible experiences in China, they love their native land even after they come to America. When they have children, they try to teach them about China and its customs and traditions. The children, however, are not really interested in the past. Born in America, Jing-Mei, Lena, Rose, and Waverly all want to minimize their Chinese appearance and heritage. They all want to look like and be accepted as Americans. During the course of the novel, each of the daughters realizes the strength and dignity of her mother and, to differing degrees, learns to appreciate her Chinese heritage.

The four mothers all want the best for their daughters. They want them to have all the advantages that America has to offer, but they also want them to live their Chinese heritage and exemplify the Chinese values. All four mothers, however, feel that their daughters have become so Americanized that they have lost their ways. The mothers realize that the daughters struggle with who they are because they have never had to fight or suffer. Life has been easy for them; as a result, they have not built the strength or character that Suyuan, An-Mei, Ying-ying, and Lindo were forced to build because of what they endured in China and what they had to endure as first generation immigrants to America.

The mothers finally tell their daughters about their suffering in hopes of inspiring them and giving them strength. When the daughters begin to appreciate the spirits of their mothers and their Chinese heritage, they become stronger and happier women. In accepting their past and blending it with their present identity, Jing-Mei, Waverly, Lena, and Rose all become more whole people.

3. Selected Reading

The Joy Luck Club

Chapter 2

My mother believed you could be anything you wanted to be in America. You could open a restaurant. You could work for the government and get good retirement. You could buy a house with almost no money down. You could become rich. You could become instantly famous.

"Of course you can be prodigy ①, too," my mother told me when I was nine. "You can be best anything. What does Auntie Lindo know? Her daughter, she is only best tricky."

America was where all my mother's hopes lay. She had come here in 1949 after losing everything in China: her mother and father, her family home, her first husband, and two daughters, twin baby girls. But she never looked back with regret. There were so many ways for things to get better.

We didn't immediately pick the right kind of prodigy. At first, my mother thought I could be a Chinese Shirley Temple ②. We'd watch Shirley's old movies on TV as though they were training films. My mother would poke my arm and say, "Ni Kan" — You watch. And I would see Shirley tapping her feet, or singing a sailor song, or pursing her lips into a very round while saying, "Oh my goodness."

"Ni Kan," said my mother as Shirley's eyes flooded with tears. "You already know how. Don't need talent for crying!"

Soon after my mother got this idea about Shirley Temple, she took me to a beauty training school in the Mission district and put me in the hands of a student who could barely hold the scissors without shaking. Instead of getting big fat curls, I emerged with an uneven mass of crinkly black fuzz ③. My mother dragged me off to the bathroom and tried to wet sown my hair.

"You look like Negro Chinese," she lamented ④, as if I had done this on purpose.

The instructor of the beauty training school had to lop off these soggy clumps to make my hair even again ⑤. "Peter Pan ⑥ is very popular these days," the instructor assured my mother. I now had hair the length of a boy's, with straight-across bangs that hung at a slant two inches above my eyebrows. I liked the haircut and it made me actually look forward to my future fame.

In fact, in the beginning, I was just as excited as my mother, maybe even more so, I pictured this prodigy part of me as many different images, trying each on for size. I was a dainty ballerina girl standing by the curtains, waiting to hear the right music that would send me floating on my tiptoes. I was like the Chris child lifted out of the straw manger, crying with holy indignity. I was Cinderella ⑦ stepping from her pumpkin carriage with sparkly cartoon music filling the air.

In all of my imaginings, I was filled with a sense that I would soon become perfect. My mother and father would adore me. I would be beyond reproach. I would never feel the need to sulk ⑧ for anything.

But sometimes the prodigy in me became impatient. "If you don't hurry up and get me out of here, I'm disappearing for good," it warned. "And then you'll always be nothing."

Every night after dinner, my mother and I would sit at the Fornica kitchen table. She would present new tests, taking her examples from stories of amazing children she had read in Ripley's Believe it or Not, or Good Housekeeping, Reader's Digest, and a dozen other magazines she kept in a pile in our bathroom. My mother got these magazines from people whose houses she cleaned. And since she cleaned many houses each week, we had a great assortment. She would look through them all, searching for stories about remarkable children.

The first night she brought out a story about a three-year-old boy who knew the capitals of all the states and even most of the European countries. A teacher was quoted as saying the little boy could also pronounce the names of the foreign cities correctly.

"What's the capital of Finland?" my mother asked me, looking, at a magazine story.

All I knew was the capital of California, because Sacramento was the name of the street we lived on in Chinatown. "Nairobi!" I guessed, saying the most foreign world I could think of. She checked to see if that was possibly one way to pronounce "Helsinki" before showing me the answer.

The tests got harder-multiplying numbers in my head, finding the queen of hearts in a deck of cards, trying to stand on my head without using my hands, predicting the daily temperatures in Los Angeles, New York, and London.

One night I had to look at a page from the Bible for three minutes and then report everything I could remember. "Now Jehoshaphat had riches and honor in abundance and ... that's all I remember, Ma," I said. And after seeing my mother's disappointed face once again, something inside of me began to die. I hated the tests, the raised hopes and failed expectations. Before going to bed that night, I looked in the mirror above the bathroom sink and when I saw only my face staring back—and that it would always be this ordinary face—I began to cry. Such a sad, ugly girl! I made high-pitched noises like a crazed animal, trying to scratch out the face in this mirror.

And then I saw what seemed to be the prodigy side of me— because I had never seen that face before. I looked at my reflection, blinking so I could see more clearly. The girl staring back at me was angry, Powerful. This girl and I were the same. I had new thoughts, willful thoughts, or rather thought filled with lots of won'ts. I won't let her change me, I promised myself. I won't be what I'm not.

So now on nights when my mother presented her tests, I performed listlessly, my head propped on one arm. I pretended to be bored. And I was. I got so bored that I started counting the bellows of the foghorns out on the bay while my mother drilled me in other areas. The sound was comforting and reminded me of the cow jumping over the moon. And the next day, I played a game with myself, seeing if my mother would give up on me before eight bellows. After a while I usually counted only one, maybe two bellows at most. At last she was beginning to give up hope.

NOTES

①prodigy: people with unusual or remarkable qualities or abilities 奇才，神童

②Shirley Temple: famous American child actress. 秀兰·邓波，美国著名童星。

③an uneven mass of crinkly black fuzz: black curls of hair in irregular shape 一头乱糟糟参差不齐的黑色卷毛。

④lament: feel or express great sorrow or regret for somebody or something 悲叹，痛惜

⑤lop off these soggy clumps to make my hair even again: cut the wet curls of hair and make the hair neat again. 剪掉这些湿漉漉的发卷，把我的头发弄整齐。

⑥Peter Pan: Peter Pan is a fictional character created by J. M. Barrie, and the name of a stage play, a children's book, and various adaptations of them. The character is a little boy who refuses to grow up, and spends his time having magical adventures. 彼得·潘，以其名字命名的儿童故事书中的调皮男孩。

⑦Cinderella: a beautiful girl in fairy tale. She is ill-treated by her stepmother. Later, with the help of a fairy, she is married to a prince. 童话中的灰姑娘。

⑧sulk: be silent or unsociable as a result of bad temper or resentment 生气，愠怒

Topic Discussion

The major theme in the novel is the difficulty of preserving one's heritage and culture when one immigrates to a foreign country. How is this theme expressed in the selected chapter?

第六章 美国戏剧

第一节 美国戏剧发展简介

每节导读

通过本节的学习，了解美国戏剧总体发展及各个时期发展状况。重点掌握二战后的美国戏剧，认识该时期戏剧创作的基本特征及其对美国戏剧的影响。

美国戏剧的历史较短。从殖民地时代起到19世纪初，戏剧在成就上远逊于同时期的散文、诗歌和小说。直到20世纪初才渐趋成熟，在两次世界大战之间赶上了世界水平而进入黄金时代。

美国19世纪的戏剧并不发达，剧本缺乏文学价值。19世纪美国剧作家创作的戏剧大部分是作为商品提供给著名演员和新兴的剧院。公众要看的是娱乐性节目和心中喜爱的演员的表演，盛行情节剧，而对严肃的戏剧毫无兴趣，因此不少剧作未能流传下来。19世纪末美国戏剧开始步入成熟阶段，剧作家注意使美国戏剧摆脱欧洲古典戏剧模式的影响以实现民族化。

第一次世界大战以后，美国戏剧开始多样化，并逐步赶上了世界水平。大学里设立了戏剧课，小剧场雨后春笋般出现，冲击了戏剧界的商业习气。百老汇本身也进行了一些改革。奥尼尔是新戏剧运动的主力。当时还涌现出一大批优秀的剧作家，有的用新奇手法揭示机器对人的压迫，有的用爵士乐般喧闹的节奏表现下层社会复杂多样的生活，有的写出了有心理深度的社会批判剧，有的通过小人物日常生活发掘善良的人性。这个时期是美国戏剧的“黄金时代”。

第二次世界大战使美国戏剧发展停止了一段时间。二战后，尽管麦卡锡主义猖獗一时，文坛沉寂，仍然涌现出T·威廉斯（1911—1983）和A·米勒（1915—2005）等剧作家。

自60年代起，美国国内反越战运动、民权运动、黑人运动、女权运动风起云涌，青年普遍对传统的价值观念产生怀疑而采取抗拒或蔑视的态度。美国剧坛也随着社会思潮起了新的变化，一些反传统的流派，如荒诞派和先锋派等，盛极一时。新崛起的剧作家中以E·阿尔比（1928—）最富盛名。他以《谁害怕弗吉尼亚·伍尔夫?》（1960）一剧成名，成为美国荒诞派戏剧的主要代表。

美国公众的文化情趣往往随着社会思潮而相应转变。他们在60年代对一些宣传鼓动的戏甚感兴趣，70年代后则对一些单纯说教的戏失去兴趣，进入80年代更要求剧作家如实反映各阶层人士的想法和作为，而不要以剧中人物作为剧作家本人意见的跳板施加给观众。他们愿意看过戏后通过自己的思考作出各自的判断。美国严肃的剧作家正在朝这个方向努力。

二战后美国戏剧也逐渐进入了多元化发展的阶段，不仅仅是在主题与技巧上，而且在多种族剧作方面都展现出百花齐放的局面，如亚裔美国剧作家黄哲伦的《声音之响》，叶添祥的《给中国佬付钱》；非裔美国剧作家及剧作有在20世纪50年代影响非常大的洛雷因·汉斯伯雷及其《太阳下的一颗葡萄干》(1952)，著名非裔小说家鲍德温在1964年创作的《唱给查理先生听的布鲁士》等等。

Professor Chang Yaoxin said in his *A Survey of American Literature* (2003): "To say that American drama began in 1916 when the Provincetown Players produced Eugene O'Neill's first play, *Bound East for Cardiff*, is to write off the efforts of the nineteenth-century playwrights too ruthlessly to be just." However, we have to admit that it is true that there were no great masters in the American theatre before 20th century, even though there were writers who contributed to the rise of American drama. Compared with notable accomplishments in other literary fields, drama was distinctly inferior. Compared with the drama of other countries, American drama before the 20th century was also inferior. Limitations mainly resided in the inherent structure of melodrama, where contrived plots drove the action. The purpose of melodrama was to entertain the audience, not really for the purpose of artistic creation.

Real development in American drama started around 1910s with "Little Theatre Movement". "Little Theatre Movement" marks the maturity of American Drama. Different from the "big theatres" on Broadway, the purpose of these little theatres was for art, not for profit. Two of the best-known of such little theatres are Provincetown Players in Massachusetts and Washington Square Players in New York City.

In 1920s, there appeared a renaissance of drama in the United States. The features of drama in this period were psychological depth and experimental techniques. It is in this period that great dramatists like O'Neill started to produce their great works.

Responding to the changes that were occurring around the world after World War I, Eugene O'Neill (1888—1953) was the foremost American playwright of the time. His earliest plays stayed within the rules of the realistic play, but in his later plays *The Great God Brown* (1926), *The Iceman Cometh* (1946) and *Long Day's Journey into Night* (1956), he began to experiment with ways of expanding the theater beyond the realistic structure. O'Neill's major subject matter is the family with tension. His major theme is the power of illusion. It is fair to say, as one critic did, that O'Neill alone advanced the American drama by at least one generation. His plays, especially *Beyond the Horizon* (1920) and *Desire Under the Elms* (1924), are considered to be the first modern American plays. Another famous playwright on the American stage in this period was Elmer Rice (1892—1967) whose *The Adding Machine* (1923) is a completely expressionistic play showing its hero as a victim of the machine age.

Following O'Neill's successes, Thornton Wilder (1897—1975) also began bringing powerful drama to the American stage. However, Wilder demanded his audience to accept the fact that they were watching actors and actresses on the stage. The characters often speak directly to the people in the audience. Wilder only wrote a few plays, but they will be remembered for their expressionism. His best plays are *Our Town* (1938) and *The Skin of Our Teeth* (1942). The success of these playwrights encouraged others, and the American theater was suddenly alive and exciting.

The Great Depression did not stop the development of American Drama. The central concern of this period was social problems and people's sufferings. Clifford Odets (1906—1963) (*Waiting for Lefty*), Sidney Kingsley (1906), and Lillian Hellman (1905—1984) (*Watch on the Rhine*) all wrote some very good plays for the American theater before the next great disturbance in the peaceful existence of the world, World War II.

After World War II, Tennessee Williams (1911—1983) and Arthur Miller (1915—) emerged as the prominent American playwrights. Both playwrights made effective use of both Ibsen's realism and Strindberg's expressionism. Williams' most acclaimed play is *The Glass Menagerie* (1945). The title refers to the collection of glass animals that Laura Wingfield has on the shelf in her room. They are fragile little animals and represent not only the girl, who is withdrawn from daily life, but all the characters in the play. The visual effects and poetic dialogue of the play are very good. Another important play of his is *A Streetcar Named Desire* (1947), a play about the decline and tragic end of

Blanche DuBois, a southern lady, who, as she herself says, has "always depended on the kindness of strangers."

Arthur Miller's best contribution to American drama is *Death of a Salesman* (1949), a play about Willy Loman, a salesman and the values we all have in our lives. Willy finds himself unwanted at his job because of his age so he kills himself. A notable speech by a character Charley at the end of the play is: "Willy was a salesman. ...riding on a smile and a shoeshine. A salesman is got to dream, boy. It comes with the territory." Though it is a very traditional play, it makes extensive use of expressionistic techniques, especially in the scenes when Willy Loman talks with his dead brother, Ben. Other plays by Miller include *All My Sons* (1947), *The Crucible* (1953), and *After the Fall* (1964), which tells the story about his marriage to film star Marilyn Monroe.

The star dramatist of the 1960s was Edward Albee, the great representative of the Theatre of the Absurd, whose first work, *The Zoo Story* (1958), was presented off Broadway in 1960, followed by three more Off Broadway one-acts and, in 1962, by *Who's Afraid of Virginia Woolf?* (1962) on Broadway. Particularly in his attacks on upper-middle class complacency in a style blending absurd humor, rhetorical pomposity and existential musings in a usually naturalistic context, Albee helped to reflect American society as it pulled apart in the wake of political assassinations, the Civil Rights and Women's Movements, and the Vietnam War.

After World War Two, American drama also shows the feature of diversity, not only in subject matter and techniques, but also in multiethnic drama. In Asian-American drama, for example, there are David Henry Hwang's *The Sound of a Voice* (1983) and Laurence Yep's *Pay the Chinaman* (1987). In African-American drama, in 1950s there was already a well-known play by Lorraine Hansberry (1930—1965) entitled *A Raisin in the Sun* (1952). In 1964, famous African-American Novelist James Baldwin also wrote a play called Blues for Mister Charlie. Plays by other ethic minority writers have been produced too.

In the recent history of American drama there have been a good number of playwrights trying to offer, on Broadway or off it, a variety of productions, which have invigorated the theatre. A new generation of authors appeared in the

1960s such as Jack Richardson and Arthur Kopit, etc. As to which of these people will eventually emerge as the greatest, it is too early to judge yet: it is indeed wise to leave it for time to decide.

第二节 重要剧作家与作品

每节导读

本节学习要求了解该时期主要作家的文学生涯、艺术特色及其代表作品的主题结构、人物刻画和语言风格等。同时结合注释，读懂所选作品，了解其思想内容和写作特色，培养理解和分析文学作品的能力。

奥尼尔被称为美国戏剧之父，又有“美国的莎士比亚”之称。他的特点是把枯燥乏味的日常生活与美好的梦想加以对照，同时用大胆创新的戏剧手法表现出来，以达到哲理、心理的高度。他在形式和内容上都做了大胆的探索和试验，运用现实主义、象征主义、表现主义、神秘主义和意识流等不同手法创作出《琼斯皇帝》(1920)、《毛猿》(1922)、《榆树下的欲望》(1924) 和《布朗大神》(1926) 等名剧。奥尼尔对美国社会的合理性产生怀疑，在剧中深刻地探讨了人际关系、人神之间的关系以及现代生活中存在的悲剧。

威廉斯以《玻璃动物园》(1944)、《欲望号街车》(1947) 和《热铁皮屋顶上的猫》(1955) 三剧赢得了国际声誉。其中，《玻璃动物园》被认为是二战之后美国戏剧重新发展的开端之作。

米勒以《推销员之死》(1944)、《炼狱》(1953) 和《桥头眺望》(1957) 等剧在国际上声名大震。尤其是《推销员之死》一剧是继杰克·伦敦和菲兹杰拉德之后又一部深刻研究美国梦破灭的作品。

Ⅰ. Eugene O'Neill (1888—1953)

1. His life and his works

Eugene O'Neill was born in New York City on October 16, 1888. His father, James, was a successful touring actor and Eugene O'Neill's mother, Ella, accompanied her husband touring around the country. Eugene was born in a hotel room and spent most of his childhood on the road with his family. O'Neill was educated at boarding schools in his early years and then attended Princeton University for a year, from 1906 to 1907. After Eugene left school he began an education in, what he later called,"life experience." Over the next six years he shipped to sea, lived destitute on the waterfronts of New York, Buenos Aires and Liverpool, became alcoholic and attempted suicide. At age twenty-four, O'Neill finally began to recover from this state and held a job as a reporter for the New London Daily Telegraph. Eugene was forced to quit his reporting job when he became extremely ill with tuberculosis and was subsequently hospitalized in Gaylord Farm Sanitarium in Wallington, Connecticut for six months. While in the hospital, Eugene began to reevaluate his life in what he later termed his "rebirth." After his hospitalization, O'Neill studied the techniques of playwriting at Harvard University from 1914 to 1915 under the famous theater scholar George Pierce Baker.

In the summer of 1916, O'Neill made his first appearance as a playwright in a tiny playhouse on the wharf of Provincetown, MA. The playhouse was started as a new experimental theater by a group of young writers and painters. The playhouse produced *Bound East for Cardiff*, O'Neill's first play. This same group of writers formed the Playwrights' Theater in New York's Greenwich Village, eventually Provincetown Players, where O'Neill made his New York debut. For ten years O'Neill worked as a dramatist and playwright for this company. O'Neill's first full-length endeavor was produced on Broadway on February 2, 1920 at the Morosco Theater. *Beyond the Horizon* won the Pulitzer Prize for drama, the first of four awarded to O'Neill in his lifetime. O'Neill was later awarded Pulitzers for *Anna Christie*, *Strange Interlude*, *and Long Day's Journey into Night*. O'Neill was also the first and the only American playwright to receive the Nobel Prize for literature. *Long Day's Journey into Night* is somewhat autobiographical. The Tyrones of the play are in fact modeled on the O'Neill family. The four major characters include James Tyrone, the father, a famous actor, anxious to become rich at the expense of his own talent; Mary Tyrone, the mother, a drug addict; Jamie Tyrone, their elder son, and Edmund Tyrone, their younger son seriously ill with consumption. All the four suffer frustrations and wish to escape from the harsh reality, James and Jamie looking for relief in their cups, while Mary and Edmund seek the protection of the fog which they hope would keep them away from the intrusion of the world outside. The long day thus journeys into night when the tragedy of the family is finally enacted. Love gives way to hate, day to night, and hope to despair. In a figurative sense, *Long Day's Journey into Night* is a metaphor for O'Neill's lifelong endeavor to find truth and the way to acceptance.

Between 1920 and 1943, O'Neill completed twenty long plays and many shorter ones. All of O'Neill's plays are written from a personal point of view and reflect on the tragedy of the human condition. There is no doubt that O'Neill's early life experience contributed to his writing. Like O'Neill as a boy, many of his characters are caught in destructive situations and paths that they cannot escape. Before O'Neill, most American plays were farce or melodrama. O'Neill embraced the theater as a venue to work out serious social issues and ideas. He transformed the American Theater into a serious and important cultural institution.

O'Neill has been compared to virtually every literary figure in the Western world and is considered the first great American playwright. His plays deal specifically with the American tragedy, rooted in American history and social movements. O'Neill had broad vision and was sometimes criticized when this vision seemed to exceed his skill. Some critics even believed that O'Neill aimed too consciously at greatness. His dramas are marked by expressionistic theatrical techniques and symbolic devices that function to express religious and philosophical ideas. O'Neill even used the Ancient Greek Chorus as a device to comment on the action of many of his plays. By bringing psychological depth, poetic symbolism and expressionistic technique to the American theatre, O'Neill raised the standards of American theatre.

The last twenty years of his life, O'Neill battled a crippling nervous disorder similar to Parkinson's disease. He died in 1953.

2. Technique

1) O'Neill was a tireless experimentalist in dramatic art. He took drama away from the old traditions of the last century and rooted it deeply in life. He borrowed from the best traditions of European drama and from modern literary

techniques and then combined these with his original art form. In this way he turned American drama into a form of literature.

2) He is good at using setting. He conveys many symbolic meanings through the setting. For example, in *The Hairy Ape*, cage is a very important setting. It symbolizes that the modern society is like a cage that imprisons people. The characters are just like imprisoned animals moving from one cage to another.

3. Introduction to *The Hairy Ape*

1) Plot Overview

The hero in this drama is Yank who is a stoker on a luxury liner. Yank is happy with life until the day when he is forced to realize that he does not "belong" anywhere. He is disconcerted, becomes violent, and is even rejected by the radical workers. In his quest for self-identity, he wanders to the zoo where he finds affinity with the great ape there. He goes over to it, only to be crushed by its outstretched arms. Yank dies, without ever finding his place of "belonging". The general feeling is one of despair: Man is rootless in an indifferent and impersonal universe.

2) Themes

①Human Regression by Industrialization

The resounding theme of *The Hairy Ape* is the effect of industrialization and technological progress on the worker. Industrialization has reduced the human worker into a machine. The men are programmed to do one task, are turned on and off by whistles, and are not required to think independently. Today, the job of the coal stoker is actually done by a machine. Workers are thus forced into jobs that require nothing but grunt work and physical labor, which has caused a general deterioration of the worker into an animal or Ape. This is made clear by O'Neill's stage direction, which indicates that the Firemen actually look like apes and one of the oldest workers, Paddy, as "extremely monkey-like." The longer the Firemen work, the further back they fall on the human evolutionary path-thus Paddy, one of the oldest, is especially "monkey-like." As a whole, the play is a close investigation of this regressive pattern through the character Yank-the play marks his regression from an ape-like man on the ship to an actual ape at the zoo.

②The Frustration of Class

Mildred and Yank are representatives of the highest and lowest societal classes-the bourgeois and the proletariat. However, while Mildred and Yank's lifestyles are extremely different, they share similar complaints about class. Mildred describes herself as the "waste product" of her father's steel company. She has reaped the financial benefits of the company, but has felt none of the vigor or passion that created it. Mildred yearns to find passion to touch "life" beyond her cushioned, bourgeois world. Yank, on the other hand, has felt too much of the "life" Mildred describes. Yank desires to topple the class structure by re-inscribing the importance and necessity of the working class. Yank defines importance as "who belongs." Class restricts and determines both Mildred and Yank's financial resources, educational opportunities, outlook on life, and culture. *The Hairy Ape* reveals how deeply and rigidly class is inscribed into American culture and the cultural and financial boundaries it erects.

③Belonging

The idea of "belonging" is continually reinforced throughout *The Hairy Ape*. Yank equates "belonging" with power and importance and uses "belonging" as a way to reverse societal power structures. In Scene One, Yank claims that he "belongs" to the ship, as opposed to the passengers in first class who are merely "baggage." Yank also associates "belonging" with an individual's usefulness and functionality. The Firemen "belong" because they make the ship run and are essential to its workings. Yank thinks that he belongs to the industrial world-the "steel" but is especially affected by Mildred because she presents a world and class to which he cannot belong. After their meeting, the play essentially follows Yank in his quest to find belonging, with the workers first, and finally leading him to the monkey-house at the zoo, and then to death.

3) Symbols

①Apes

Apes are everywhere in *The Hairy Ape*: Yank is called an ape; Yank thinks he is an ape, Mildred thinks she sees an ape. The ape may symbolize man in a primitive state in which technology, complex language structures, complex thought or money were not necessary. The ape may also represent man that is not only behind in an evolutionary sense, but is free of class, technology and other elements of modern society. The ape is only concerned with survival. The ape, however, can also stand for modern man who is imprisoned in cage, that is, the modern society.

②Steel

Steel is both a symbol of power and oppression in *The Hairy Ape*. While Yank exclaims in Scene One that he is steel, "the muscles and the punch behind it," he is all the while penned in a virtual cage of steel created by the ship around him. Steel creates other cages in the play—Yank's jail cell and the cell of the ape. Steel is also oppressive because it creates jobs like Yank's; it is symbolic of the technology that forces Yank and the Firemen into slave-like jobs.

③The ship

The ship can be a symbol of modern society with the ruling class on top while the working class at the bottom.

4. Selected Reading:

The Hairy Ape

Scene 8

Twilight of the next day. The monkey house at the Zoo. One spot of clear gray light falls on the front of one cage so that the interior can be seen. The other cages are vague, shrouded in shadow from which chatterings pitched in a conversational tone can be heard. On the one cage a sign from which the word "Gorilla" stands out. The gigantic animal himself is seen squatting on his haunches on a bench in much the same attitude as Rodin's

"Thinker." [①] YANK [②] enters from the left. Immediately a chorus of angry chattering and screeching breaks out. The gorilla turns his eyes but makes no sound or move.

YANK: [With a hard, bitter laugh.] Welcome to your city, huh? Hail, hail, de gang's all here! [③] [At the sound of his voice the chattering dies away into an attentive silence. YANK walks up to the gorilla's cage and, leaning over the railing, stares in at its occupant, who stares back at him, silent and motionless. There is a pause of dead stillness. Then YANK begins to talk in a friendly confidential tone, half-mockingly, but with a deep undercurrent of sympathy.] Say, yuh're some hard-lookin' guy, ain't yuh? I seen lots of tough nuts dat de gang called gorillas, but yuh're de foist real one I ever seen. Some chest yuh got, and shoulders, and dem arms and mits! I bet yuh got a punch in eider fist dat'd knock'em all silly! [This with genuine admiration. The gorilla, as if he understood, stands upright, swelling out his chest and pounding on it with his fist. YANK grins sympathetically.] Sure, I get yuh. Yuh challenge de whole woild, huh? Yuh got what I was sayin' even if yuh muffed de words. [Then bitterness creeping in.] And why wouldn't yuh get me? Ain't we both members of de same club—de Hairy Apes? [They stare at each other—a pause—then YANK goes on slowly and bitterly.] So yuh're what she seen when she looked at me, de white-faced tart! I was you to her, get me? On'y outa de cage—broke out—free to moider her, see? Sure! Dat's what she tought. She wasn't wise dat I was in a cage, too—worser'n yours—sure—a damn sight—'cause you got some chance to bust loose—but me— [He grows confused.] Aw, hell! It's all wrong, ain't it?

[A pause.] I s'pose yuh wanter know what I'm doin' here, huh? I been warmin' a bench down to de Batter—ever since last night. Sure. I seen de sun come up. Dat was pretty, too—all red and pink and green. I was lookin' at de skyscrapers—steel—and all de ships comin' in, sailin' out, all over de oith—and dey was steel, too. De sun was warm, dey wasn't no clouds, and dere was a breeze blowin'. Sure, it was great stuff. I got it aw right-what Paddy said about dat bein' de right dope—on'y I couldn't get in it, see? I couldn't belong in dat. It was over my head. And I kept tinkin'—and den I beat it up here to see what youse was like. And I waited till dey was all gone to git yuh alone. Say, how d'yuh feel sittin' in dat pen all de time, havin' to stand for'em comin' and starin' at yuh—de white-faced, skinny tarts and de boobs what marry'em—makin' fun of yuh, laughin' at yuh, gittin' scared of yuh—damn'em! [He pounds on the rail with his fist. The gorilla rattles the bars of his cage and snarls. All the other monkeys set up an angry chattering in the darkness. YANK goes on excitedly.] Sure! Dat's de way it hits me, too. On'y yuh're lucky, see? Yuh don't belong wit'em and yuh know it. But me, I belong wit'em—but I don't, see? Dey don't belong wit me, dat's what. Get me? Tinkin' is hard— [He passes one hand across his forehead with a painful gesture. The gorilla growls impatiently. YANK goes on gropingly.] It's dis way, what I'm drivin' at. Youse can sit and dope dream in de past, green woods, de jungle and de rest of it. Den yuh belong and dey don't. Den yuh kin laugh at'em, see? Yuh're de champ of de woild. But me—I ain't got no past to tink in, nor nothin' dat's comin', on'y what's now—and dat don't belong. Sure, you're de best off! Yuh can't tink, can yuh? Yuh can't talk neider. But I kin make a bluff at talkin' and tinkin'—a'most git away wit it—a'most! —and dat's where de joker comes in. [He laughs.] I ain't on oith and I ain't in heaven, get me? I'm in de middle tryin' to separate'em, takin' all de woist punches from bot' of'em. Maybe dat's what dey call hell, huh? But you, yuh're at de bottom. You belong! Sure! Yuh're de on'y one in de woild dat does, yuh lucky stiff! [The gorilla growls proudly.] And dat's why dey gotter put yuh in a cage, see? [The gorilla roars angrily.] Sure! Yuh get me. It beats it when you try to tink it or talk it—it's way down—deep—behind—you'n' me we feel it. Sure! Bot' members of dis club! [He laughs-then in a savage tone.] What de hell! T' hell wit it! A little action, dat's our meat! Dat belongs! Knock'em down and keep bustin''em till dey croaks yuh wit a gat-wit steel! Sure! Are yuh game? Dey've looked at youse, ain't dey-in a cage? Wanter git even? Wanter wind up like a sport'stead of croakin' slow in dere? [The gorilla roars an emphatic affirmative. YANK goes on with a sort of furious exaltation.] Sure! Yuh're reg'lar! Yuh'll stick to de finish! Me'n' you, huh? —bot' members of this club! We'll put up one last star bout dat'll knock'em offen deir seats! Dey'll have to make de cages stronger after we're trou! [The gorilla is straining at his bars, growling, hopping from one foot to the other. YANK takes a jimmy from under his coat and forces the lock on the cage door. He throws this open.] Pardon from de governor! Step out and shake hands! I'll take yuh for a walk down Fif' Avenoo. We'll knock'em off de oith and croak wit de band playin'. Come on, Brother. [The gorilla scrambles gingerly out of his cage. Goes to YANK and stands looking at him. YANK keeps his mocking tone—holds out his hand.] Shake—de secret grip of our order. [Something, the tone of mockery, perhaps, suddenly enrages the animal. With a spring he wraps his huge arms around YANK in a murderous hug. There is a crackling snap of crushed ribs—a gasping cry, still mocking, from YANK.] Hey, I didn't say, kiss me. [The gorilla lets the crushed body slip to the floor; stands over it uncertainly, considering; then picks it up, throws it in the cage, shuts the door, and shuffles off menacingly into the darkness at left. A great uproar of frightened chattering and whimpering comes from the other cages. Then YANK moves, groaning, opening his eyes, and there is silence. He mutters painfully.] Say—dey oughter match him—wit Zybszko. He got me, aw right. I'm trou. Even him didn't tink I belonged. [Then, with sudden passionate despair.] Christ, where do I get off at? Where do I fit in? [Checking himself as suddenly.] Aw, what de hell! No squakin', see! No quittin', get me! Croak wit your boots on! [He grabs hold of the bars of the cage and hauls himself painfully to his feet—looks around him bewilderedly—forces a mocking laugh.] In de cage, huh? [In the strident tones of a circus barker.] Ladies and gents, step forward and take a slant at de one and only— [His voice weakening] —one and original—Hairy Ape from de wilds of— [He slips in a heap on the floor and dies. The monkeys set up a chattering, whimpering wail. And, perhaps, the Hairy Ape at last belongs.]

NOTES

①Rodin's "Thinker": a famous French sculpture by Rodin. 罗丹的"思想者"，一尊法国雕像。

②YANK: The play's antagonist. Yank works as a Fireman on a Transatlantic Ocean Liner. The play follows his quest to find a sense of belonging in modern, industrial society. Yank, whose real name is Bob Smith, was born in New York City and was brought up in a lower class family. Yank is a burly, sometimes menacing figure who has difficulty with thought. He is known to take the physical position of Rodin's "The Thinker" when processing information or dealing with a problem. 本剧中的主要角色。

③de gang's all here! 他经常使用非标准语言，如把 them 读成 em，把 looking 读成 lookin。此句相当于：The gang's all here.

Topic Discussion

Can you see any symbols in the play?

Ⅱ. Tennessee Williams (1911—1983)

1. His life and works

Tennessee Williams was born in Columbus, Mississippi, in 1911. The name given to him at birth was Thomas Lanier Williams Ⅲ. He did not acquire the nickname Tennessee until college, when classmates began calling him that in honor of his Southern accent and his father's home state. The Williams family had produced several illustrious politicians in the state of Tennessee, but Williams's grandfather had squandered the family fortune. Until Williams was seven, he lived in Mississippi. After that, the family moved to St. Louis. The family moved sixteen times in ten years, and the young Williams, always shy and fragile, was ostracized and taunted at school. During these years, he and his sister, Rose, became extremely close. Rose, the model for Laura in *The Glass Menagerie*, suffered from mental illness later in life.

An average student and social outcast in high school, Williams turned to the movies and writing for solace. At sixteen, Williams won five dollars in a national competition for his answer to the question "Can a good wife be a good sport?" his answer was published in *Smart Set* magazine. The next year, he published a horror story in a magazine called *Weird Tales*, and the year after that he entered the University of Missouri as a journalism major. While there, he wrote his first plays. Before Williams could receive his degree, however, his father forced him to withdraw from school and go to work at a shoe company.

Williams worked at the shoe factory for three years. After that, he returned to college, this time at Washington University in St. Louis. While he was studying there, a St. Louis theater group produced his play *The Fugitive Kind and Candles to the Sun*. Personal problems led Williams to drop out of Washington University and enroll in the University of Iowa. While he was in

Iowa, his sister, Rose, underwent a lobotomy, which left her institutionalized for the rest of her life. Despite this trauma, Williams finally graduated in 1938. In the years that followed, he lived a bohemian life, working menial jobs and wandering from city to city. He continued to work on drama, however, receiving a Rockefeller grant and studying playwriting at the New School in New York. During the early years of World War Ⅱ, Williams worked in Hollywood as a scriptwriter.

Around 1941, Williams began the work that would become *The Glass Menagerie*. The play evolved from a short story entitled "Portrait of a Girl in Glass," which focused more completely on Laura than the play does. In December of 1944, The Glass Menagerie was staged in Chicago, with the collaboration of a number of well-known theatrical figures. When the play first opened, the audience was sparse, but the Chicago critics raved about it, and eventually it was playing to full houses. In March of 1945, the play moved to Broadway, where it won the prestigious New York Drama Critics' Circle Award. This highly personal, explicitly autobiographical play earned Williams fame, fortune, and critical respect, and it marked the beginning of a successful run that would last for another ten years. The staging of this play marked the development of American drama after World War Two. Two years after The Glass Menagerie, Williams won another Drama Critics' Circle Award and a Pulitzer Prize for *A Streetcar Named Desire*. Williams won the same two prizes again in 1955, for *Cat on a Hot Tin Roof*.

Alcoholism, depression, thwarted desire, loneliness in search of purpose, and insanity were all part of Williams' world. Since the early 1940s, he had been a known homosexual, and his experiences in an era and culture unfriendly to homosexuality certainly affected his work. After 1955, Williams began using drugs. He continued to write though most critics agree that the quality of his work diminished in his later life. His life's work adds up to twenty-five full-length plays, five screenplays, over seventy one-act plays, hundreds of short stories, two novels, poetry, and a memoir; five of his plays were also made into movies. Williams died from choking in a drug-related incident in 1983.

2. Features in His Writing

1) He was influenced by his southern background. His plays are basically based on the southern setting. His plays have a "gothic" flavor in that situations and characters are distorted and also in that his tragedies happen in a reality distorted by the author's imagination. His plays are called "Gothic tragedies" because they show the horrors of the soul.

2) He often uses a lot of symbols in his plays. For example in *The Glass Menagerie* glass menagerie is easily broken, so it symbolizes fragile Laura, the family, the reality, and the world.

3) He used images（舞台旁银幕上的映像）and legends（舞台旁银幕上的题文）to help reinforce and emphasize the theme that he wanted to express.

3. Introduction to *The Glass Menagerie*

1) Plot Overview

The Glass Menagerie is a memory play, and its action is drawn from the memories of the narrator, Tom Wingfield.

Amanda, originally from a genteel Southern family, talks her children frequently with tales of her idyllic youth and the scores of suitors who once pursued her. She is disappointed that Laura, who wears a brace on her leg and is painfully shy, does not attract any gentleman callers. Amanda then decides that Laura's last hope must lie in marriage and begins selling newspaper subscriptions to earn the extra money she believes will help to attract suitors for Laura. Meanwhile, Tom, who dislikes his warehouse job, finds escape in liquor, movies, and literature.

Amanda and Tom discuss Laura's prospects, and Amanda asks Tom to keep an eye out for potential suitors at the warehouse. Tom selects Jim O'Connor, a casual friend, and invites him to dinner. Amanda quizzes Tom about Jim and is delighted to learn that he is a young man with his mind set on career advancement. She prepares an elaborate dinner and insists that Laura wear a new dress. At the last minute, Laura learns the name of her caller; as it turns out, she had a devastating crush on Jim in high school. When Jim arrives, Laura answers the door, on Amanda's orders, and then quickly disappears, leaving Tom and Jim alone. Tom confides to Jim that he has used the money for his family's electric bill to join the merchant marine and plans to leave his job and family in search of adventure. Laura refuses to eat dinner with the others, feigning illness. Amanda, wearing an ostentatious dress from her glamorous youth, talks vivaciously with Jim throughout the meal.

As dinner is ending, the lights go out as a consequence of the unpaid electric bill. The characters light candles, and Amanda encourages Jim to entertain Laura in the living room while she and Tom clean up. Laura is at first paralyzed by Jim's presence, but his warm and open behavior soon draws her out of her shell. She confesses that she knew and liked him in high school but was too shy to approach him. They continue talking, and Laura reminds him of the nickname he had given her: "Blue Roses," a word he used for Laura's medical condition, pleurisies. He reproaches her for her shyness and low self-esteem but praises her uniqueness. Laura then ventures to show him her favorite glass animal, a unicorn. Jim dances with her, but in the process, he accidentally knocks over the unicorn, breaking off its horn. Laura is forgiving, noting that now the unicorn is a normal horse. Jim then kisses her, but he quickly draws back and apologizes, explaining that he was carried away by the moment and that he actually has a serious girlfriend. Resigned, Laura offers him the broken unicorn as a souvenir.

Amanda enters the living room, full of good cheer. Jim hastily explains that he must leave because of an appointment with his fiancée. Amanda sees him off warmly but, after he is gone, turns on Tom, who did not know that Jim is engaged. Amanda accuses Tom of being an inattentive, selfish dreamer and then throws herself into comforting Laura. From the fire escape outside of their apartment, Tom watches the two women and explains that, not long after Jim's visit, he gets fired from his job and leaves Amanda and Laura behind. Years later, though he travels far, he finds that he is unable to leave behind guilty memories of Laura.

2) Themes

①The Difficulty in Accepting Reality

Among the most prominent and urgent themes of *The Glass Menagerie* is the difficulty the characters have in accepting and relating to reality. Each member of the Wingfield family is unable to overcome this difficulty, and each, as a result, withdraws into a private world of illusion where he or she finds the comfort and meaning that the real world does not seem to offer. Of the three Wingfields, reality has by far the weakest grasp on Laura. The private world in which she lives is populated by glass animals-objects that, like Laura's inner life, are incredibly fanciful and dangerously delicate. Unlike his sister, Tom is capable of functioning in the real world, as we see in his holding down a job and talking to strangers. But, in the end, he has no more motivation than Laura does to pursue professional success, romantic relationships, or even ordinary friendships, and he prefers to retreat into the fantasies provided by literature and movies and the stupor provided by drunkenness. Amanda's relationship to reality is the most complicated in the play. Unlike her children, she is partial to real-world values and longs for social and financial success. Yet her attachment to these values is exactly what prevents her from perceiving a number of truths about her life. She cannot accept that she is or should be anything other than the pampered belle she was brought up to be, that Laura is peculiar, that Tom is not a budding businessman, and that she herself might be in some ways responsible for the sorrows and flaws of her children. Amanda's retreat into illusion is in many ways more pathetic than her children's, because it is not a willful imaginative construction but a wistful distortion of reality. Even Jim, who represents the "world of reality," is banking his future on public speaking and the television and radio industries—all of which are means for the creation of illusions and the persuasion of others that these illusions are true. *The Glass Menagerie* identifies the conquest of reality by illusion as a huge and growing aspect of the human condition in its time.

②The Impossibility of True Escape

At the beginning of Scene Four, Tom regales Laura with an account of a magic show in which the magician managed to escape from a nailed-up coffin. Clearly, Tom views his life with his family and at the warehouse as a kind of coffin-cramped, suffocating, and morbid-in which he is unfairly confined. The promise of escape, represented by Tom's missing father, the Merchant Marine Service, and the fire escape outside the apartment, haunts Tom from the beginning of the play, and in the end, he does choose to free himself from the confinement of his life.

The play takes an ambiguous attitude toward the moral implications and even the effectiveness of Tom's escape. As an able-bodied young man, he is locked into his life not by exterior factors but by emotional ones—by his loyalty to and possibly even love for Laura and Amanda. Escape for Tom means the suppression and denial of these emotions in himself, and it means doing great harm to his mother and sister. The magician is able to emerge from his coffin without upsetting a single nail, but the human nails that bind Tom to his home will certainly be upset by his departure. One cannot say for certain that leaving home even means true escape for Tom. As far as he might wander from home, something still "pursue [s]" him. Like a jailbreak, Tom's escape leads him not to freedom but to the life of a fugitive.

Not only Tom, but also Amanda and Laura, in fact, are escapists. The former refuses to face the present reality by escaping into the past memories or by escaping into the imagination of future while the latter escapes into her collection of glass animals seeing in them a better life and an ideal world. But, like Tom, they fail in their escape and are forced to face reality again at the end of the play.

③The Unrelenting Power of Memory

According to Tom, *The Glass Menagerie* is a memory play—both its style and its content are shaped and inspired by memory. As Tom himself states clearly, the play's lack of realism, its high drama, its overblown and too perfect symbolism, and even its frequent use of music are all due to its origins in memory. Most fictional works are products of the imagination that must convince their audience that they are something else by being realistic. A play drawn from memory, however, is a product of real experience and hence does not need to drape itself in the conventions of realism in order to seem real.

The story that the play tells is told because of the inflexible grip it has on the narrator's memory. Thus, the fact that the play exists at all is a testament to the power that memory can exert on people's lives and consciousness. The narrator, Tom, is not the only character haunted by his memories. Amanda too lives in constant pursuit of her bygone youth, and old records from her childhood are almost as important to Laura as her glass animals. For these characters, memory is a crippling force that prevents them from finding happiness in the present or the offerings of the future. But it is also the vital force for Tom, prompting him to the act of creation that culminates in the achievement of the play.

3) Symbols

①Laura's Glass Menagerie

As the title of the play informs us, the glass menagerie, or collection of glass animals, is the play's central symbol. Laura's collection of glass animal figurines represents a number of facets of her personality. Like the figurines, Laura is delicate, fanciful, and somehow old-fashioned. Glass is transparent, but, when light is shone upon it correctly, it refracts an entire rainbow of colors. Similarly, Laura, though quiet and bland around strangers, is a source of strange, multifaceted delight to those who choose to look at her in the right light. The menagerie also represents the imaginative world to which Laura devotes herself—a world that is colorful and enticing but based on fragile illusions.

②The Glass Unicorn

The glass unicorn in Laura's collection—significantly, her favorite figure—represents her peculiarity. As Jim points out, unicorns are "extinct" in modern times and are lonesome as a result of being different from other horses. Laura too is unusual, lonely, and ill-adapted to existence in the world in which she lives. The fate of the unicorn is also a smaller-scale version of Laura's fate in Scene Seven. When Jim dances with and then kisses Laura, the unicorn's horn breaks off, and it becomes just another horse. Jim's advances endow Laura with a new normalcy, making her seem more like just another girl, but the violence with which this normalcy is thrusted upon her means that Laura cannot become normal without somehow shattering. Eventually, Laura gives Jim the unicorn as a "souvenir." Without its horn, the unicorn is more appropriate for him than for her, and the broken figurine represents all that he has taken from her and destroyed in her.

③ "Blue Roses"

Like the glass unicorn, "Blue Roses," Jim's high school nickname for Laura, symbolizes Laura's unusualness yet allure. The name is also associated with Laura's attraction to Jim and the joy that his kind treatment brings her. Furthermore, it recalls Tennessee Williams's sister, Rose, on whom the character of Laura is based.

Ⅲ. Arthur Miller (1915—2005)

1. His Life and Works

Arthur Miller, the son of a women's clothing company owner, was born in 1915 in New York City. His father lost his business in the Depression and the family was forced to move to a smaller home in Brooklyn. After graduating from high school, Miller worked at jobs ranging from radio singer to truck driver to clerk in an automobile-parts warehouse. Miller began writing plays as a student at the University of Michigan, joining the Federal Theater Project in New York City after he received his degree. His first Broadway play, *The Man Who Had All the Luck*, opened in 1944 and his next play, *All My Sons*, received the Drama Critics' Circle Award. Arthur Miller's first success came in 1947 with *All My Sons* for which he won the New York Drama Critics' Circle award. Although it lacked the originality of some of his later works, this family drama, which told the story of a factory owner who caused the death of several American pilots during World War I by selling defective parts to the government, dealt with issues of guilt and dishonesty that Miller would revisit and expand upon in some of his more memorable plays.

His next play, *Death of a Salesman* (1949), stunned audiences with its brilliance and was quickly regardeded as a classic of the modern theatre. It also sparked heated debates over the true nature of tragedy. Some critics criticized Miller for infusing the play with a deep sense of pity for the commonplace salesman Willy Loman. They insisted that Willy was a "little man" and therefore not worthy of the pathos reserved for such tragic heroes as Oedipus and Medea. Miller, however, argued that the tragic feeling is invoked whenever we are in the presence of a character, any character, who is ready to sacrifice his life, if need be, to secure one thing—his sense of personal dignity. And the "little" salesman was determined to do just that, no matter what the cost. Arthur Miller was awarded the Pulitzer Prize in 1949 for *Death of a Salesman*, which he directed at the People's Art Theatre in Beijing in 1983. He has come to be considered one of the greatest dramatists in the history of the American

Theatre, and his plays, a fusion of naturalistic and expressionistic techniques, continue to be widely produced.

In 1956 and 1957, Miller was summoned by the House Un-American Activities Committee and was convicted of contempt of Congress for his refusal to identify writers believed to hold Communist sympathies. The following year, the United States Court of Appeals overturned the conviction. In 1959 the National Institute of Arts and Letters awarded him the Gold Medal for Drama. Miller married three times: to Mary Grace Slattery in 1940, Marilyn Monroe in 1956, and photographer Inge Morath in 1962, with whom he lived in Connecticut. He and Inge have a daughter, Rebecca. Among his works are *A view from the Bridge*, *The Misfits*, *After the Fall*, *The Price*, *The American Clock*, *Broken Glass and Timebends*: *A life*, his autobiography. Miller's writing has earned him a lifetime of honors, including the Pulitzer Prize, seven Tony Awards, two Drama Critics Circle Awards, an Obie, an Olivier, the John F. Kennedy Lifetime Achievement Award, and the Dorothy and Lillian Gish prize. He held honorary doctorate degrees from Oxford University and Harvard University.

Throughout his life and work, Miller remained socially engaged and had written with conscience, clarity, and compassion. As Chris Keller says to his mother in All My Sons,"Once and for all you must know that there's a universe of people outside, and you're responsible to it." Miller's work is infused with his sense of responsibility to humanity and to his audience. "The playwright is nothing without his audience," he wrote. "He is one of the audience who happens to know how to speak."

Because of his concern with social problems and because of his social morality plays, he was called the "American Ibsen".

2. Introduction to *Death of a Salesman*

1) Plot Overview

The drama focuses on the life of an aging salesman, Willy Loman, who, at the outset of the play is on the verge of a nervous breakdown. He lives with his adoring but over protective wife, Linda, who acts as a buffer between her husband and their two adult sons, Biff and Happy, whose relationship with their father is permanently under tension. Loman wants to change his job as a traveling salesman into an office one, but fails. What's more, he is fired by his boss. Unable to pursue his American dream, he hopes that his sons will continue the pursuit. In order to leave his insurance money to his sons, he commits suicide.

The play plots the tragic collapse of a man who cannot face up to his moral responsibilities in a society whose false values attach a dangerous importance to success as measured in such transient terms as income and material possessions. Living according to these values means that failure is likewise defined in economic terms.

2) Major Theme—a Sad Version of American Dream

In the play, Willy has a brother called Ben, who goes to make his own fortune and then becomes rich. Willy also admires a salesman Singleman by name who does business by phone calls at the age of 84. Inspired by Ben's and Singleman's success, Willy also believes that it is possible to become wealthy and popular through his own efforts. But all through his life, he achieves neither at all. At the last moment of his life, he clings to his dream, but still fails to realize it.

3) Techniques

①Setting

The stage setting is half-transparent with a kind of frame. Therefore, it gives characters more freedom in space. On the stage the audience sees a house which in a way is frame-like. The actors and actresses may have actions in the house and observe the walls and doors, but they can also walk out of it freely without being prevented by the walls when required by the stage directions.

②Use of Light

The artful manipulation of light helps to change the setting in time and space in a highly flexible manner when different parts of the setting—the house, garden, offices and restaurant—are lit up as the actors move from place to place and move back and forth in time.

③Music

To some extent, music helps to make the play more expressionistic than realistic. To be specific, it seems to break the line between reality and illusion, and between present and past. The music has two functions in the play. One is to help the transition in time and place and the other is to help in the creation of atmosphere.

④Use of Past

Similar to Anderson's moment of illumination, in the play, the past has a direct effect on the present. Besides, it also forms the sharp contrast between the past and the present. Miller learned from Ibsen the technique of giving the audience information about the past events little by little and the new information about the past changes the way the audience sees the present situation.

3. Selected Reading

Death of a Salesman

Act Ⅱ

Music is heard, gay and bright. The curtain rises as the music fades away. Willy, in shirt sleeves, is sitting at the kitchen table, sipping coffee, his hat in his lap. Linda is filling his cup when she can.

Willy: Wonderful coffee. Meal in itself.

Linda: Can I make you some eggs?

Willy: No. Take a breath.

Linda: You look so rested, dear.

Willy: I slept like a dead one. First time in months. Imagine, sleeping till ten on a Tuesday morning. Boys left nice and early, heh?

Linda: They were out of here by eight o'clock.

Willy: Good work!

Linda: It was so thrilling to see them leaving together. I can't get over the shaving lotion in this house.

Willy, smiling: Mmm—

Linda: Biff was very changed this morning. His whole attitude seemed to be hopeful. He couldn't wait to get downtown to see Oliver.

Willy: He's heading for a change. There's no question, there simply are certain men that take longer to get—solidified. How did he dress?

Linda: His blue suit. He's so handsome in that suit. He could be a-anything in that suit!

Willy gets up from the table. Linda holds his jacket for him.

Willy: There's no question, no question at all. Gee, on the way home tonight I'd like to buy some seeds.

Linda, laughing: That'd be wonderful. But not enough sun gets back there. Nothing' ll grow any more.

Willy: You wait, kid, before it's all over we're gonna get a little place out in the country, and I'll raise some vegetables, a couple of chickens...

Linda: You'll do it yet, dear.

Willy walks out of his jacket. Linda follows him.

Willy: And they'll get married, and come for a weekend. I'd build a little guest house. 'Cause I got so many fine tools, all I'd need would be a little lumber and some peace of mind.

Linda joyfully: I sewed the lining...

Willy: I could build two guest houses, so they'd both come. Did he decide how much he's going to ask Oliver for?

Linda, getting him into the jacket: He didn't mention it, but I imagine ten or fifteen thousand. You going to talk to Howard today?

Willy: Yeah. I'll put it to him straight and simple. He'll just have to take me off the road. ①

Linda: And Willy, don't forget to ask for a little advance, because we've got the insurance premium. It's the grace period now.

Willy: That's a hundred...?

Linda: A hundred and eight, sixty-eight. Because we're a little short again.

Willy: Why are we short?

Linda: Well, you had the motor job on the car...②

Willy: That goddam Studebaker ③!

Linda: And you got one more payment on the refrigerator...

Willy: But it just broke again!

Linda: Well, it's old, dear.

Willy: I told you we should've bought a well-advertised machine. Charley bought a General Electric [4] and it's twenty years old and it's still good, that son-of-a-bitch.

Linda: But, Willy—

Willy: Whoever heard of a Hastings refrigerator? Once in my life I would like to own something outright before it's broken! I'm always in a race with the junkyard! I just finished paying for the car and it's on its last legs [5]. The refrigerator consumes belts like a goddam maniac. They time those things. They time them so when you finally paid for them, they're used up.

Linda, buttoning up his jacket as he unbuttons it: All told, about two hundred dollars would carry us, dear. But that includes the last payment on the mortgage. After this payment, Willy, the house belongs to us.

Willy: It's twenty-five years!

Linda: Biff was nine years old when we bought it.

Willy: Well, that's a great thing. To weather a twenty-five year mortgage is—

Linda: It's an accomplishment.

Willy: All the cement, the lumber, the reconstruction I put in this house! There ain't a crack to be found in it any more.

Linda: Well, it served its purpose.

Willy: What purpose? Some stranger' ll come along, move in, and that's that. If only Biff would take this house, and raise a family... He starts to go. Good-by, I'm late.

Linda, suddenly remembering: Oh, I forgot! You're supposed to meet them for dinner.

Willy: Me?

Linda: At Frank's Chop House [6] on Forty-eighth near Sixth Avenue.

Willy: Is that so! How about you?

Linda: No, just the three of you. They're gonna blow you to a big meal!

Willy: Don't say! Who thought of that?

Linda: Biff came to me this morning, Willy, and he said, "Tell Dad, we want to blow him to a big meal." Be there six o'clock. You and your two boys are going to have dinner.

Willy: Gee whiz! [7] That's really somethin'. I'm gonna knock Howard for a loop, kid. I'll get an advance, and I'll come home with a New York job. Goddammit, now I'm gonna do it!

Lind: Oh, that's the spirit, Willy!

Willy: I will never get behind a wheel the rest of my life.

Linda: It's changing, Willy, I can feel it changing.

Willy: Beyond a question. G'by, I'm late. He starts to go again.

Linda, calling after him as she runs to the kitchen table for a handkerchief: You got your glasses?

Willy, feels for them, then comes back in: Yeah, yeah, got my glasses.

Linda, giving him the handkerchief: And a handkerchief.

Willy: Yeah, handkerchief.

Linda: And your saccharine?

Willy: Yeah, my saccharine.

Linda: Be careful on the subway stairs.

She kisses him, and silk stocking is seen hanging from her hand. Willy notices it.

Willy: Will you stop mending stockings? At least while I'm in the house. It gets me nervous. I can't tell you, please.

Linda hides the stocking in her hand as she follows Willy across the forestage in front of the house.

Linda: Remember, Frank's Chop House.

Willy, passing the apron: Maybe beets would grow out there.

Linda, laughing: But you tried so many times.

Willy: Yeah. Well, don't work hard today. *He disappears around the right corner of the house.*

Linda: Be careful!

As Willy vanishes, Linda waves to him. Suddenly the phone rings. She runs across the stage and into the kitchen and lifts it.

Linda: Hello? Oh, Biff! I'm so glad you called, I just...Yes, sure, I just told him. Yes, he'll be there for dinner at six o'clock, I didn't forget. Listen, I was just dying to tell you. You know that little rubber pipe I told you about? That he connected to the gas heater? I finally decided to go down the cellar this morning and take it away and destroy it. But it's gone! Imagine? He took it away himself, it isn't there! *She listens.* When? Oh, then you took it. Oh—nothing, its just that I'd hoped he'd taken it away himself. Oh I'm not worried, darling, because this morning he left in such high spirits, it was like the old days! I'm not afraid any more. Did Mr. Oliver see you? ... Well, you wait there then. And make a very nice impression on him, darling. Just don't perspire too much before you see him. And have a nice time with Dad. He may have big news too! ... That's right, a New York job. And be sweet to him tonight, dear. Be loving to him. Because he's only a little boat looking for a harbor. *She is trembling with sorrow and joy.* Oh, that's wonderful, Biff, you'll save his life. Thanks, darling. Just put your arm around him when he comes to the restaurant. Give him a smile. That's the boy...Good-by, dear... You got your comb? ...that's fine. Good-by. Biff dear.

In the middle of her speech, Howard Wagner, thirty-six, wheels on a small typewriter table on which is a wire-recording machine and proceeds to plug it in. This is on the left forestage. Light slowly fades on Linda as it rises on Howard. Howard is intent on threading the machine and only glances over his shoulder as Willy appears.

Willy: Pst! Pst!

Howard: Hello, Willy, come in.

Willy: Like to have a little talk with you, Howard.

Howard: Sorry to keep you waiting. I'll be with you in a minute.

Willy: What's that, Howard?

Howard: Didn't you ever see one of these? Wire recorder.

Willy: Oh. Can we talk a minute?

Howard: Records things. Just got delivery yesterday. Been driving me crazy, the most terrific machine I ever saw in my life. I was up all night with it.

Willy: What do you do with it?

Howard: I bought it for dictation, but you can do anything with it. Listen to this. I had it home last night. Listen to what I picked up. The first one is my daughter. Get this. *He flicks the switch and "Roll out the Barrel" is heard being whistled.* Listen to that kid whistle.

Willy: That is lifelike, isn't it?

Howard: Seven years old. Get that tone.

Willy: Ts, ts. Like to ask a little favor if you...

The whistling breaks off, and the vice of Howard's daughter is heard.

His Daughter: "Now you, Daddy."

Howard: She is crazy for me! Again the same song is whistled. That's me! Ha! He winks.

Willy: You're very good.

The whistling breaks off again. The machine runs silent for a moment.

Howard: Sh! Get this now, this is my son.

His Son: "The capital of Alabama is Montgomery; the capital of Arizona is Phoenix; the capital of Arkansas is Little Rock; the capital of California is Sacramento..." and on, and on.

Howard, holding up five fingers: Five years old, Willy!

Willy: He'll make an announcer some day!

His Son, continuing: "the capital..."

Howard: Get that—alphabetical order! The machine breaks off suddenly.

Wait a minute. The maid kicked the plug out.

Willy: It certainly is a—

Howard: Sh, for God's sake!

His Son: It's nine o'clock, Bulova watch time. [8] So I have go to sleep.

Willy: That really is—

Howard: Wait a minute! The next is my wife.

They wait.

Howard's voice: *"Go on, say something." Pause. "Well, you gonna talk?"*

His Wife: I can't think of anything.

Howard's Voice: *"Well, talk—it's turning."*

His Wife, shyly, beaten: "Hello." Silence. "Oh, Howard, I can't talk into this..."

Howard, snapping the machine off: That was my wife.

Willy: That is a wonderful machine. Can we—

Howard: I tell you, Willy, I'm gonna take my camera, and my bandsaw, and all my hobbies, and out they go. This is the most fascinating relaxation I ever found.

Willy: I think I'll get one myself.

Howard: Sure, they're only a hundred and a half. You can't do anything without it. Supposing you wanna hear Jack Benny, see? But you can't be at home at that hour. So you tell the maid to turn the radio on when Jack Benny comes on, and this automatically goes on with the radio...

Willy: And when you come home you...

Howard: You can come home twelve o'clock, one o'clock, any time you like, and you get yourself a Coke and sit yourself down, throw the switch, and there's Jack Benny's program in the middle of the night!

Willy: I'm definitely going to get one. Because lots of time I'm on the road, and I think to myself, what I must be missing on the radio!

Howard: Don't you have a radio in the car?

Willy: Well, yeah, but who ever thinks of turning it on?

Howard: Say, aren't you supposed to be in Boston?

Willy: That's what I want to talk to you about, Howard. You got a minute? *He draws a chair in from the wing.*

Howard: What happened? What're you doing here?

Willy: Well...

Howard: You didn't crack up again, did you?

Willy: Oh, no. No...

Howard: Geez, you had me worried there for a minute. What's the trouble?

Willy: Well, tell you the truth, Howard. I've come to the decision that I'd rather not travel any more.

Howard: Not travel! Well, what'll you do?

Willy: Remember, Christmas time, when you had the party here? You said you'd try to think of some spot for me here in town.

Howard: With us?

Willy: Well, sure.

Howard: Oh, yeah, yeah. I remember. Well, I couldn't think of anything for you, Willy.

Willy: I tell ya, Howard. The kids are all grownup, y' know. I don't need much any more. If I could take home—well, sixty five dollars a week, I could swing it ⑨.

Howard: yeah, but Willy, see I—

Willy: I tell ya why, Howard. Speaking frankly and between the two of us, y'know—I'm just a little tired.

Howard: Oh, I could understand that, Willy. But you're a road man, Willy, and we do a road business. We've only got a half-dozen salesmen on the floor here.

Willy: God knows, Howard, I never asked a favor of any man. But I was with the firm when your father used to carry you in here in his arms.

Howard: I know that, Willy, but—

Willy: Your father came to me the day you were born and asked me what I thought of the name of Howard, may he rest in peace.

Howard: I appreciate that, Willy, but there just is no spot here for you. If I had a spot I'd slam you right in, but I just don't have a single solitary spot.

He looks for his lighter. Willy has picked it up and gives it to him. Pause.

Willy, with increasing anger: Howard, all I need to set my table is fifty dollars a week.

Howard: But where am I going to put you, kid?

Willy: Look, it isn't a question of whether I can sell merchandise, is it?

Howard: No, but it's a bushiness, kid, and everybody's gotta pull his own weight.

Willy, desperately: Just let me tell you a story, Howard—

Howard: 'Cause you gotta admit, business is business.

Willy, angrily: Business is definitely business, but just listen for a minute. You don't understand this. When I was a boy—eighteen, nineteen—I was already on the road. And there was a question in my mind as to whether selling had a future for me. Because in those days I had a yearning to go to Alaska. See there were three gold strikes in one month in Alaska, and l felt like going out. Just for the ride, you might say.

Howard, barely interested: Don't say.

Willy: Oh, yeah, my father lived many years in Alaska. He was an adventurous man. We've got quite a little streak of self-reliance in our family. I thought I'd go out with my older brother and try to locate him, and maybe settle in the North with the old man. And I was almost decided to go, when I met a salesman in the Parker House. His name was David Singleman. And he was eighty-four years old, and he'd drummed merchandise in thirty-one states. And old Dave, he'd go up to his room, y'understand, put on his green velvet slippers—I'll never forget—and pick up his phone and call the buyers, and without ever leaving his room, at the age of eighty-four, he made his living. And when I saw that, I realized that selling was the greatest career a man could want. 'cause what could be more satisfying than to be able to go, at the age of eighty-four, into twenty or thirty different cities, and pick up a phone, and be remembered and loved and helped by so many different people? Do you know? When he died—and by the way he died the death of a salesman, in his green velvet slippers in the smoker of the New York, New Haven and Hartford, going into Boston—when he died, hundreds of salesmen and buyers were at his funeral. Things were sad on a lotta trains for months after that. *He stands up. Howard has not looked at him.* In those days there was personality in it, Howard. There was respect, and comradeship, and gratitude in it. Today, it's s all cut and dried, and there's no chance for bringing friendship to bear—or personality. You see what I mean? They don't know me any more.

Howard, moving away, to the right: That's just the thing, Willy.

Willy, If I had forty dollars a week—that's all I'd need. Forty dollars, Howard.

Howard: Kid, I can't take blood from a stone, I—

Willy, desperation is on him now: Howard, the year Al Smith was nominated, your father came to me and—

Howard, starting to go off: I've got to see some people, kid...

NOTES

①He'll just have to take me off the road：He won't let me travel about. 他不能再让我东跑西颠了。

②Well，you had the motor job on the car...：You spent money getting the car repaired. 你修汽车还花了钱呢。

③Studebaker：the trademark of Willy's car 威利的汽车牌号

④a General Electric：an engine made by the General Electric，一台通用电器公司生产的发动机。

⑤it's on its last legs：The car has worn out. 车已经快磨损了。

⑥Frank's Chop House：a restaurant in New York City 纽约市一饭馆名

⑦Gee whiz：expressing surprise or enthusiasm 表达惊奇或热情

⑧It's nine o'clock，Bulova watch time：It's the ad words of Bulova clock company in America. 这是美国 Bulova 钟表公司的广告语。

⑨swing it：hold out；maintain 维持下去

Topic Discussion

Do some introduction about Willy Loman，please.

主要参考书目

1. 常耀信. 美国文学简史. 天津：南开大学出版社，1990.
2. 胡荫桐，刘树森. 美国文学教程. 天津：南开大学出版社，1995.
3. 林缃华. 西方现代派文学评论. 上海：上海人民出版社，1987.
4. 李宜燮，常耀信. 美国文学选读（上册）. 天津：南开大学出版社，1991.
5. 李宜燮，常耀信. 美国文学选读（下册）. 天津：南开大学出版社，1991.
6. 吴定柏. 美国文学大纲. 上海：上海外语教育出版社，1998.
7. 王松年. 美国文学作品选读. 上海：上海交通大学出版社，2003.
8. 吴伟仁. 美国文学史及选读. 北京：外语教学与研究出版社，2003.
9. 张伯香. 英美文学选读. 北京：外语教学与研究出版社，1998.
10. 张颖. 自学考试题典——英美文学选读. 长春：吉林大学出版社，2002.
11. 李翠亭，李正栓. 美国文学学习指南. 北京：清华大学出版社，1998.
12. 杨任敬. 20世纪美国文学史. 青岛：青岛出版社，2000.
13. 秦小孟. 当代美国文学——概述及作品选读.（上、中、下）. 上海：上海译文出版社，1986.
14. 李公昭. 20世纪美国文学导论. 西安：西安交通大学出版社，2000.
15. 董衡巽. 美国文学简史（修订本）. 北京：人民文学出版社，2003.
16. 史志康. 美国文学背景概观. 上海：上海外语教育出版社，1998.

后　记

本书是为东北师范大学网络学院编写的课件基础上加以丰富而成的。本书是美国文学入门教材，基本覆盖了美国文学发展的整个历史以及各阶段的重要作家与作品，力图使学习者对美国文学有一个概括性的认识。在教材编写中，我们力争遵循五个原则：首先要体现科学性，即科学准确地展现课程内容；其次要注意完整性，即完整包括各重要流派及作家；第三是前沿性，力争反映美国文学发展及研究中的最新成果；第四是生动性，做到内容的展现形式生动易懂；第五是可行性，充分考虑学习者自学的需要，在选材、语言表述等方面力争难易适宜，使学习者在读了教材内容之后，真正掌握所学内容。

本书文史结合，各章节按美国文学的发展顺序排列，同时，加入了一些重要作家的作品选读。在每一节前都有中文的“每节导读”，试图为学习者提供本节学习重点。选读的编写原则是尽量选择既有代表性又相对易懂的选段，选读后提出讨论题供学习者思考。

在本教材的编写过程中，我们参考了国内许多知名学者编撰的专著或教材，在这里我们向这些作者表示感谢。

曾经参加网络课件编写与制作的还有（按姓氏笔画）王林、王海燕、许波、宋世彤和单建国。

因编写者水平有限，时间紧张，本教材不足之处在所难免，敬请各位专家及使用者原谅并提出宝贵意见。

编　者